Irish Twist of Fate: Book One

Bailey's Revenge

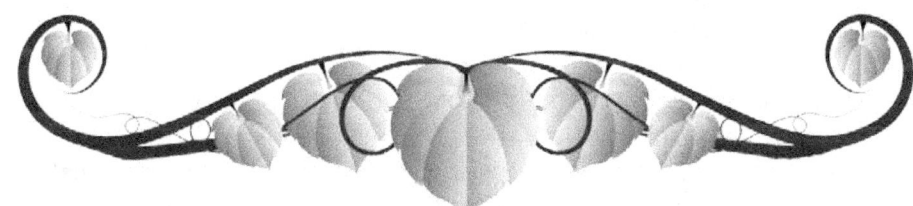

Allison Bruning

MOUNTAIN SPRINGS HOUSE
INDIANAPOLIS

ISBN-10:1940022541
ISBN-13:978-1940022543

Dedication

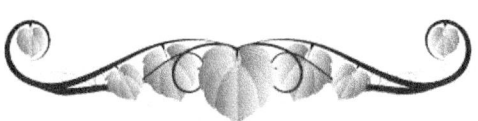

To my Irish friend, Lorna Irwin: Thank you for being a wonderful friend and for helping me with this book.

To my Appalachian Irish family, the McCanns and McCardles: Thank you for giving me a wonderful heritage and keeping our Irish ways alive in America.

To Highland Reign: Thank you for making the music that helped inspire me while writing this book. You are an amazing Scottish American band. I have enjoyed writing your music videos and helping to direct them with FilmSmith Productions. Keep the Irish and Scottish traditions alive, my friends.

To my fans: You are amazing!

Chapter 1

July 26, 1738 – Collinsworth, Wexford County, Ireland

The rolling hills and lush forest surrounded the large crystal lake. Kathleen drew her clothes out of the water, wrung them out, and hung them up to dry on the thick branches of the old oak tree. Her mind lingered to the fate of her brothers and the Catholic Irish rebels that were loyal to her family. Since the ancient days, this land had belonged to the native Irish. Invaders had come and gone, leaving their mark on the land and its inhabitants. Legends spoke of the first people of Ireland, the Fomorians, as giants with black hair and black skin who were eventually destroyed by a mysterious plague begun by the Partholanians, who had invaded Ireland three hundred years after Noah's Flood. Her own family legends spoke of different invasions. First there were the Norse, the Romans, and others; now came the English. The Anglicans from across the sea had been controlling the native Irish since the times of her great grandparents. They forced the Irish to abandon their Catholic faith or lose everything.

Her father, Alexander McGillpatrick, had once been a prominent member of society, a lawyer, landowner, and member of the Irish Parliament. Her family's estate had once held 300 acres until the day Earl James Turner had stolen everything from her father, thus beginning the feud between her family and the Turners. Then four years ago her brothers recaptured their ancestral castle and moved her entire family into the large estate. Their father once again sat upon the seat of power over the Kilmore estate. Kilmore was beautiful. For the first fourteen years of her life, all Kathleen and her younger sister, Calico, had ever known was poverty and farming. Never before could she have even imagined the wonders their new life held for them. Alexander and her older brothers, Bailey and Sherlock, transformed Kilmore into a Catholic stronghold. Their wealth, power, and prestige increased over the next four years. Soon her family had become a threat to the Irish Parliament. Alexander was educating and defending his Catholic tenants. Then fate had crashed down upon them. Three days ago, the Irish army, combined with a unit from the English army, attacked Kilmore Castle. Her brothers had stayed behind while Alexander had taken her and the rest of their family into the forest during the battle. After the battle, the remaining rebels who had escaped from the English informed them Isaac Turner was holding her brothers in the castle dungeon. It didn't take a fool to know what fate Bailey and Sherlock were to face. Death. That night, Earl Tomas Connelly and her father planned a rescue mission. For two days they looked for a way to break into the castle, yet all the entrances her father had known about were sealed. But last night they were able to break into the castle and rescue her brothers. A tear ran down her cheek as she thought of her older brothers, Bailey and Sherlock. She had never seen Earl Isaac Turner before but she hated him. She hated him for breaking her brothers' bodies. How could one man be so cruel?

Kathleen removed her corset, stockings, and shift. She walked into the waters and began to clean them. Her only gown, saved because she was wearing it when her family had to escape from the castle, hung on the branch beside her three petticoats and stomacher. An oval hoop lay beside the tree truck. She peered into the water at her reflection. A long row of smallpox scars laced the right side of her face. She had once been the most beautiful daughter until the smallpox had come to her village nine years ago as famine had stretched throughout the Irish countryside. She was grateful she had survived yet she knew her marital prospects were slim. Who would want a nineteen-year-old, scrawny, smallpox-marked woman?

Kathleen pushed back her long red hair, grabbed her clothes out of the lake, and walked to the shore. She wrung them dry then placed them on the branch. She peered through the trees to make certain no one was watching her. Secluded in the remote part of Tomas' woodlands with the nearest road in the distance, she was safe. She dove her long, slender body into the lake and relaxed. The cool water felt good around her body. She couldn't remember the last time she had taken a bath. Normally her family bathed once a week but with everything going on there wasn't time to bother with hygiene. She swam to the deepest part, taking in every sensation. She had always loved the water. It was her paradise. Beneath the waves she wasn't the younger sister of a rebel leader or the daughter of a deposed Irish Earl. Here she was one with the spirits. The water spirits were her friends. They granted her peace, taking away her chaotic thoughts. She twisted and turned in the water, playing with the fish and plants. This indeed was paradise.

Kathleen rose to the surface, leaning her head back so her long hair flowed down her back. She paused at hearing something draw close to the shoreline. The spirit world around her grew silent. She felt a sense of danger, as if the spirits were warning her. Frightened, she swam towards the clothes. As she drew near, she realized her clothes and hoop were missing. Only the wooden bucket she was supposed to fill and the bar of soap she had used to wash her clothes remained. She withdrew from the water and frantically checked the tree. Who would have taken her clothes? The rebels? No, Bailey was the leader of the rebels in this area. Everyone knew he protected his sisters. She heard the sound of footsteps.

"Are you looking for these?" a man asked, throwing all the clothes to the ground.

Kathleen grabbed her shift and put it on. She scanned her surroundings while she dressed. Who was this man? She wanted to scream, but if she did who would save her? It was at least a fifteen-minute walk back to the great house. "Who are you?" she demanded, adjusting her stomacher into place. Silence filled the forest around her. She crouched next to the bucket and slowly reached for the knife she had hidden underneath. It was gone. She patted her hand around the ground looking for it.

"Don't bother, I took it," the man said from behind her.

Kathleen turned and fell on her bottom as the tall, slender, handsome Englishman stood over her with a pistol aimed at her head. "Who are you?" he demanded. Kathleen stared into the man's beautiful blue eyes. They captivated her. "I believe I asked you a question," he snarled, moving closer to her.

"Kathleen," she answered, glancing at his gun.

"Very well, Kathleen. Why are you washing clothes in this lake?"

"And why, sir, did you take my clothes? Are you so desperate to be with a woman that you would treat me as if I am some common whore?"

"Well you do have a mouth on you, young lady. Get up!"

Kathleen slowly rose from the ground. She held her hands up and stared down her opponent. "Where's your rebel base of operations?" he demanded, grabbing her by the front of her gown.

"Rebel? What makes you think I am a rebel?"

He leaned close to her ear and snarled, "You must be a Catholic. I don't know you and I know every Anglican woman in these parts. I won't ask you again, Kathleen."

Kathleen swallowed hard as they glared into each other's eyes for a long moment. "Kathleen," a familiar tenor voice came from down the road. The man holding her glanced over his shoulder. He loosened his tight grip on her. Kathleen swung her right fist and slammed it into her captor's face. He stumbled backwards and dropped his gun. Blood flowed from his nose. She grabbed the gun and held it over him. "Kathleen," the other man's voice said from behind her as he placed his hand on her arm. "Don't." Kathleen turned her gaze towards the medium-height Irish Earl Tomas Connelly.

"Tomas," her attacker greeted him.

"Isaac," Tomas replied.

Kathleen peered at Tomas with confusion. "Who is he?" she asked.

"A friend. Lower your gun, Kathleen."

"That's my gun, Tomas," Isaac answered while rising from the ground and extending his hand out to her.

"Give Lord Turner his gun, Kathleen," Tomas ordered.

"Lord Turner. As in Earl Isaac Turner!"

"Ah, the lady has heard of me," Isaac answered.

Kathleen pushed Tomas aside and aimed the gun at Isaac's head. "I should shoot you right now for what you did," she threatened.

Isaac raised his hands and cocked his head, scanning her body with his eyes. "So was it your mother or your sister I slept with?" he asked. "You know you Irish converts are such a delight."

Kathleen growled and began to pull the trigger. How dare this English Earl insult the Irish? Those converts only did so in order to save their families. Some of the rebels had called them cowards for not sticking to their beliefs and heritage. Yet there were some converts, like Tomas, who had converted to keep their lands, wealth, and status, and were secretly aiding the rebels and the Catholic Church. It was those converts who deserved to be honored. They risked their lives to practice their faith and help restore Ireland.

Tomas grabbed Kathleen around her waist and thrust her backwards against the tree. He pressed his body against her with his arm bent over her chest. Pain seared through her body. She dropped the gun. "Enough," he whispered to her.

"Why? Why would you call him your friend when you know what he has done to my brothers?"

"He's not my friend, Kathleen. I have to pretend to be his friend to help our people."

"But he…"

Tomas put his finger over her thin, red lips. "Stop. He's already suspected you are with the rebels. If you continue to act uncivilized you'll only confirm his suspicions about you. And that, Kathleen, can't happen! Understood?"

Kathleen huffed, glaring across Tomas' shoulders. Isaac crouched next to the lake, washing the blood from his face. How much she wanted to kill him. It would have been so easy, too. His back was turned to them. All she had to do was... "Understood?" Tomas asked her again. She lowered her eyes to him.

"How long have you been friends with him?" she growled back at her sister's fiancée.

"It doesn't matter."

"Tom, someone had to have told the English my father has taken over the estate. You never fought alongside my family when the English attacked Kilmore."

"You shouldn't be speaking about things you don't know anything about, Kathleen. I'm not a traitor to our ancestors. I did not tell Isaac your family had taken over the estate. Quite the opposite. I tried to keep him as far away from Ireland as I could." Tomas released his strong grip on her. "Go home. Calico needs your help with her wedding dress."

Kathleen picked up her belongings and walked towards the road.

Chapter 2

Tomas watched Kathleen walk quickly up the long road until she disappeared from his view. His heart fell for his future sister-in-law. He knew the pain Kathleen bore deep in her heart. He had felt that pain too. She had every right to want Isaac's destruction. Like so many Irish Catholics, she was living a life where you had to keep your friends close and your enemies even closer. Tomas turned towards the large lake and stared at the reflection of his friend's face in the water. Ancient legends passed down from generation to generation claimed the forest they were standing in was haunted by fairies and spirits. According to legend, the lake contained a snake-like creature that would capture men who swam into the deep end, eat them, and leave only their liver behind. Too bad Isaac couldn't swim.

"How's your nose?" Tomas asked, walking towards his friend.

Isaac rose, holding a handkerchief over his nose as he replied, "It's not broken."

"Please accept my apology on her behalf."

"Who is she?" Isaac asked, stepping towards him and lowering his bloody handkerchief.

"My fiancée's older sister."

"I did not realize Calico had family."

"She had a family. Kathleen arrived this morning with the news rebels had attacked their village. They killed her parents and most of the villagers. Kathleen escaped in the chaos to find refuge with Calico."

"And where was this?"

"Nowhere close."

"Hmm."

"Have you ever met Calico's family?"

"Yes. Why do you ask?"

"I found Kathleen bathing in the lake. It looked as if she decided to bathe after she had done some laundry. If she is your guest then why do you allow her to do servants' work?"

Tomas glanced at the lake then back to his friend. Kathleen knew the ancient folklore and ways. Why would she ever swim in a lake that supposedly had a monster in it? It didn't make any sense. He shook his head, answering his friend's question. "Kathleen took the deaths of her parents very hard. She has not been herself since she arrived. My physicians suggested she be allowed to care for herself until she is able to trust anyone again."

"I found your future sister-in-law quite…interesting and appealing. How old is she?"

"Nineteen going on twenty."

Isaac grinned, casting his eyes towards the hill separating him from Kathleen. "She is quite…"

"Mentally distraught."

Isaac turned back to his friend. "It is permanent?"

"No, but I do not think it would be wise for you to pursue a courtship with her at this time."

"She will be attending church with you and Calico?"

"I do not know as of yet. It depends on how she is feeling. Calico tells me Kathleen is thinner than she was the last time she saw her. We believe she has foregone a proper meal for sometime since the attack. She requires her rest and stability before I can present her to the public."

"I understand. You will inform me when she is well?"

"Of course," Tomas bowed his head. "What brings you to Collinsworth?" Tomas asked, clasping Isaac on the shoulder.

"You."

"Me?" Tomas asked, lowering his hand.

"We have matters to discuss."

Tomas extended his arm towards the forest road. He nervously peered towards the hill then back at his English friend. "Something wrong?" Isaac asked.

"No. Please, shall we?"

Isaac glared at his friend with suspicion. What wasn't Tomas telling him? Tomas had been his faithful friend for almost eight years. Tomas' father had once held the estate of Collinsworth. A devout Catholic, his father had refused to convert. The last son of seven children, Tomas would have never inherited the entire estate. Penal Law dictated that upon the death of a Catholic landowner his estate would be broken into equal parcels of land amongst all his sons. It would continue to be so down the line until the Catholic family had nothing left to inherit. Tomas had done the unthinkable to his family. Ten years ago, Tomas denounced his Catholic faith and became Anglican. The after-effects of that fateful decision had disrupted his entire family. A few days after his conversion, all of his father's estate was totally in his possession. The Penal Law had dictated that if the eldest son converted from Catholic to Anglican he would gain all of his father's possessions and lord over his father. Although Tomas had been the last son, Isaac had persuaded parliament to grant Tomas the privileges as if he had been the eldest son. Thus, his father had been banished from the estate with his family. His parents, brothers, and sisters were doomed to become his tenant farmers on the land they had once owned.

"Isaac?" Tomas asked.

"We shall." Isaac and Tomas began to walk towards the great house on the lonely stone road.

"What brings you to my estate?" Tomas asked.

"I have heard rumors Bailey McGillpatrick has been seen in the vicinity. I thought perhaps you had information concerning his whereabouts."

Tomas swallowed hard. How could word have reached his friend of Bailey's presence in Collinsworth? Hadn't he been cautious enough to ensure the safety of Bailey and his family? "I have no knowledge of his location. Perhaps he has travelled north towards Dublin."

"I had thought the same yet one of your tenant farmers has come forth with information claiming he saw a band of rebels carrying Bailey and Sherlock's bodies in the back of a wagon towards your great house."

Tomas chuckled, "And you believed him? No Catholic tenant farmer on my estate is loyal to me. I betrayed my family."

"This person was not Catholic."

Tomas stopped in the middle of the road at the base of the hill. Every Anglican family he lorded over or was friends with had believed his lies. Who could have possibly betrayed him? Isaac stared at him with a serious look. "Are you insinuating that I had something to do with the rebels?" Tomas asked.

"Did you?"

"I am insulted, Isaac. If I had knowledge of the rebels' location you would be the first I would divulge that information to. How could you believe I would betray you?"

A moment of tension and silence passed between the two men. Tomas held his gaze on Isaac as his friend studied his reaction. Every minute mannerism had to be controlled. Isaac was not only a master manipulator but was also an excellent human lie detector. The English Earl could never learn the truth. Tomas was harboring rebels, helping Catholic priests, and allowing the priests to hold mass in his home for the entire Catholic population of Collinsworth. As if those activities weren't enough to endanger his livelihood, Tomas was also one of Bailey's closest advisors. Should Isaac ever learn of Tomas' treason he could steal the estate from him. He had to convince Isaac he was on the wrong path. He took a step towards the barrel-chested man. "Isaac, I think you have become paranoid."

"Paranoid?"

"You captured Bailey and Sherlock McGillpatrick, tortured them, and then went to England to report you had two of the most wanted Irish rebel leaders in custody. When you returned they had escaped. I know, my dear friend, that must have hurt not only your pride but also your standing at court. You're looking to lay blame with someone when it was your own ignorance that allowed the transgression to come to pass."

Isaac clenched his jaw. "Forgive me," he snarled.

Tomas nodded then began to walk down the road. Isaac silently kept his pace. Tomas had been right. His pride had been wounded. How could he have allowed the most dangerous rebel leaders to escape from his own dungeon, and how could he believe his best friend had betrayed him? But then Tomas had been a Catholic before his conversion. Tomas and he could have been closer friends if Tomas had been born Anglican. How can you trust someone who betrays his own family in order to appease God?

"Have you questioned your guards?" Tomas asked.

"What?" Isaac asked, not hearing Tomas' question.

"I asked have you questioned your guards?"

"Of course. They told me nothing helpful. Bailey and Sherlock were too injured to escape on their own. I made certain they were too weak with injuries to try anything while I was in England. I told my guards to deny them food except for bread and water over the weekend. While I enjoy a challenge in killing my enemies, I did not trust Bailey's strength. Had he been at full strength when I was to escort him to England for execution he might have overtaken me."

Tomas laughed

"You find that, amusing?"

"No, what I find amusing is how you are trying to convince me that you do not have the strength to overtake a simpleton like Bailey McGillpatrick. You are one of the most deadly and conniving people I know, Isaac Turner.

Chapter 3

Collins Great House, Collinsworth, Wexford County, Ireland

A soft midsummer evening breeze blew gently through Bailey's window as he lay on his bed. Pain resonated throughout his body. Three broken ribs, a broken wrist, dislocated shoulder, sprains, strains, and bruises. He couldn't sleep without discomfort. His broken right leg and left arm didn't help matters. Although his bruised eyes were closed he could hear his stepmother and sister talking. He loved his family dearly.

Twenty-two years ago, Bailey and Sherlock had married Irish Catholic sisters, Anne and Mary. They had never met their wives before. As the sons of a traditional Irish upper-class family, Bailey and Sherlock's marriages had been arranged through a matchmaker. At first Earl Alexander McGillpatrick had been wary of the match between his sons and the sisters. Alexander had never heard of their family and had every right to be suspicious of people he didn't know. After the death of Alexander's father at the Battle of Boyne, Alexander had inherited Kilmore estate. Two years later, Alexander had been dismissed from the Irish Parliament because he would not take an oath promising not to grant his allegiance to the Pope. Parliament had declared he could keep his lands but he could never vote in Parliament again. Alexander had returned to his newly wedded wife and continued to practice law. They had lived a life of peace and bliss for a few years then the Irish Parliament began to pass the Penal Laws, making it hard for any Irish Catholic to live and illegal for Alexander to practice law. Catholics could never be legally represented. In 1698, while Bailey's mother was pregnant with Sherlock, the Irish army mixed with English soldiers came to the estate and seized 200 acres of his family's land, leaving only 150 acres for Alexander. A few days later, the land went to auction and Catholics were not allowed to bid. It was bought by James Turner, Isaac's father. The shrewd English Earl had convinced Parliament that Alexander couldn't be trusted. Over the years, more laws against the Catholics were passed and there was nothing Alexander could do to stop them.

Then in 1702, Alexander's heart had been crushed once again. His wife delivered a stillborn son and she died three days later. He was devastated. Bailey was seven years old. He could vaguely recall his mother, which was good because Sherlock had no recollection of her at all. He was only three years old when their mother died. Alexander raised the boys on his own. When it came time for his sons to marry he sought out the matchmaker and when the matchmaker had approached him with the prospect of Anne and Mary, Alexander wasn't convinced it was the safest thing to do. What if the women were English spies working for Earl Turner? The matchmaker had told him the sisters' father had been a rebel in Omagh. He had been killed raiding an English farm. She urged him to verify the facts and his father did. Three weeks later, Bailey and Sherlock both married. It was the happiest day of his life. But never could the brothers have imagined that their father would fall in love with their wives' mother, Jane! A year and a half after his own wedding, his father married his mother-in-law. Kathleen was born the following year. He had never seen his father so happy. Life had changed for the better until they lost their home in 1726 after Earl James Turner had convinced Parliament it would be better if Kilmore was in his control and not in the hands of an Irish Catholic. Parliament agreed. Bailey and his family were forced from their homes to become tenant farmers for James Turner. A few years later, he and Sherlock lead rebel attacks throughout the area. Then the unthinkable had happened. James killed Bailey's wife and children. The following year, James had captured Sherlock's wife and murdered his children. Bailey rescued his brother's wife and killed James in the process. But that wasn't enough for him. He wanted Isaac dead, too. Oh, how he hated the Turners! All he wanted was revenge. Revenge so sweet he could taste it with every thought of it. James had killed his children and he was going to kill James' son. Earl Isaac Turner had to pay.

"Mother," Calico's voice lifted as the door to his bedchambers opened.

He moaned as every sound agitated his throbbing headache. "Shh, Calico, your brother needs his rest."

"I'm sorry but Kathleen has something she has to tell you."

"No. I don't," Kathleen argued, trying to pull away from her younger sister's grasp.

"Yes, you do!"

"No, I don't," she growled.

"Girls, stop arguing and come to me. Close the door behind you, Kathleen."

Kathleen sighed as Calico released her grip. She pushed her petite sister inward with a sneer, clenched her jaw, and closed the door behind her. The girls stared each other down. Tension filled the room. Bailey broke the long moment of silence with a deep groan of pain. Whatever his sisters were arguing about didn't help. It wasn't like Kathleen and Calico to treat each other with such contempt. They were not only sisters but also best friends. Something terrible must have happened to them. He wanted to know more but he didn't know how much longer he could listen in on their conversation. The herbal tea Jane had given him for the pain was starting to make him drowsy.

The room grew darker as Mary closed the window and curtains. "We should leave so he can sleep," Mary urged.

"Hmm, stay, please, stay," Bailey muttered, grabbing Jane's wrist.

"Alright, son. We'll stay until you fall asleep," Jane replied.

Bailey loosened his grip and Mary walked around his bed. She turned to them, saying, "The physician should be done re-examining my husband. I should go."

"Of course. If you two require anything…"

"I promise, Mother, I will let you know." She turned to her younger sisters.

"Kathleen. Calico." Kathleen and Calico bid their older sister farewell as they watched her leave. Bailey groaned at the sound of the door closing behind her.

Calico grabbed her sister by the arm and pulled her towards their mother. "Tell her," she urged her older sister.

"No, this is stupid. Nothing will come of it. I want to visit Sherlock," Kathleen said as she tried to pull away.

"If it is something important then tell me," Jane urged from the other side of the bed.

"It's not…" Kathleen started.

"It is. Tell her," Calico pushed her sister towards the bed.

"Ugh, you're making a little insignificant matter into something grander than it ought to be."

"Tell her!"

"Calico, have more respect. Your brother is trying to rest," Jane disciplined.

"If Bailey was conscious, mother, he would want to know what happened to Kathleen."

Jane glanced sharply in the direction of her daughter. Kathleen sighed under the pressure of her mother's disciplined glare.

"Very well, I met Earl Isaac Turner."

Bailey pushed past the pain and listened closer to his younger sister. Had he heard right? *How in the world could his baby sister have been anywhere near that dangerous English Earl?* He moaned, arching his head back.

Jane placed her hand on the side of her stepson's cheek. She rubbed her thumb along his cheekbone. "Shh, sleep, Bailey," she coaxed.

Sleep. How could he sleep when Kathleen had had an encounter with Isaac? Yet he knew his stepmother would never rest until she knew he was at peace. He pretended to fall asleep while listening in on their conversation.

"Tell me how this happened," Jane said, turning her attention towards Kathleen.

"I went to the lake to bathe and wash clothes. I did everything father had told me to do in order to evade the Anglicans."

"But you were spotted? Kathleen, how many times do your father, brother, and I have to tell you to be more careful when you leave the Great House? You know there is a price on your brothers' heads and your father is wanted for leading the rebels."

"But he's not their leader. Bailey, Sherlock, and Tomas lead them."

"The truth doesn't matter when it comes to the Anglicans. They make up their own truths in order to eliminate all the Catholics in Ireland."

"Her story gets better, mother," Calico proclaimed. "He saw her naked."

Jane rose from the bed. "He what?"

Bailey clenched his fist. It was one thing to murder his wife, children, and Sherlock's children, but to violate his little sister! If only he could get out of this bed and rip that man's throat out!

"It was nothing, mother. My fault, really," Kathleen tried to avert her mother's inquiry.

"Did he touch you?" she asked sharply.

"No! Ugh, oh, God, no, mother!"

"Then what happened?"

"While I was bathing he came upon my clothes, took them, and when I emerged I couldn't find them. I had no idea he was there, honest."

"And then?"

"He returned my clothes, I dressed…"

"Then she tried to shoot him," Calico volunteered.

Jane glanced between her daughters.

"It was nothing," Kathleen whispered.

"Nothing? She tried to kill him and accused my fiancée of being a traitor," Calico rebuked.

Kathleen snarled as she tried to pull her hand away from her sister, "Calico!"

"Kathleen," Jane called to her in her motherly tone.

"Mother," Kathleen responded.

"Don't lie to me. I know when my daughters are lying to me. There might be decades between Alexander McGillpatrick's daughters and Timothy O Shay's daughters, but I know my children well enough to know when they are lying to me."

"I'm not lying to you."

"No? Then what are you not telling me, young lady?"

Kathleen glanced at her brother. *What was she keeping from her mother? Oh, if it could only be so simple.* On the outside she had countered Isaac out of revenge for his family's actions upon her own, but on the inside she had felt something more personal. Something she couldn't describe. That first glance at Isaac had made her feel something wonderful. How quickly that sensation had turned to rage when she had learned of his identity.

"Kathleen," Jane urged more sharply. Kathleen looked back at her mother. "It mattered to you, Kathleen. Why?"

Kathleen bit her lower lip, looked at Bailey and then back at her mother.

"She accused my Tomas of betraying our family. Shouldn't the question be why she believes the one man who is risking everything for our cause could be the one who has betrayed us?" Calico yelled.

"Calico, enough," Jane disciplined.

"Of all the men in Ireland she chose him as the traitor!" Calico yelled.

"I said enough, young lady!" Calico crossed her arms with a huff as her mother continued. "We may not have the status of landowners but you will act like a civilized young woman. You are about to marry into wealth. Act like it, Calico."

"Yes, mum," she answered. Jane turned her gaze to her daughter just as the door burst open. She lifted her eyes. Tomas closed the door behind him and quickly approached the women. "Mother," he politely greeted then glared at Kathleen.

"What were you thinking?" he yelled at Kathleen.

Kathleen shook her head. Why was everyone upset with her? Hadn't she tried to kill Isaac? Wasn't that what Bailey would have wanted from her?

"I would like to know the same thing, dear," Calico said from behind him while he stared his soon to be sister-in-law down.

"I tried to kill him and you stopped me. What were *you* thinking, Tomas?" Kathleen countered.

Tomas held his anger as he stepped towards her. "If you were anyone other than your father's daughter…"

"Tomas," Jane said, placing her hand on his chest. Tomas glanced in her direction. "I'm certain my daughter meant you no harm. We know you are not the traitor."

Tomas stepped back from his future mother-in-law in confusion. He had forgotten Kathleen had accused him of betraying her family and the cause. There were more urgent matters to be concerned with than those accusations. "That is not what bothers me."

"But she accused you," Calico questioned.

"Perhaps, but I know Bailey, Sherlock, and your father know that accusation does not lie in truth. Your sister has done something even more dangerous than accuse me of that!"

"I don't understand. Does Isaac know you are working with the rebels?"

"He suspected but I have quieted those thoughts. Our traitor is an Anglican who lives on my lands."

Jane sighed, "If an Anglican knows the truth he could claim your estate."

"Yes, mother, but I will stop that from happening. In the meantime, we have a new dilemma that must be solved and is more pressing than my tenant farmer traitor."

"What could be more pressing than that?" Kathleen asked.

"Isaac Turner has fallen in love with you."

Kathleen gasped. She shook her head in shock and backed away. "No."

Bailey grinned on the inside. This was perfect. Who better to enact the revenge on his enemy than the woman Isaac loves. He hated the thought of Isaac seeing his sister naked before marriage but he could live with that. He could use this new information. Yet he knew his best friend, Tomas Connelly, would want to quickly dismiss Isaac from Kathleen's marital prospects. "Ugh, Tom," Bailey muttered. He continued to call out his name.

Tomas glanced over Jane's shoulder. "Excuse me, ladies," he said, walking towards the bed. Bailey motioned for his friend to lean down. Tomas put his ear next to Bailey's busted lips.

"Does my father know about this?" Bailey whispered.

"Not yet. He is still meeting with the priests and rebels in town."

Bailey took a deep breath and cringed. "Hmm, do not dismiss the attractions Isaac has towards Kathleen."

"Bailey?"

"I have a plan. Send for my father."

Tomas nodded then raised his gaze towards the women. "Tomas?" Jane asked.

"He needs his rest," Tomas said, rising from the bed then walking towards the door. He opened it then looked towards them. "Ladies, please," he said motioning for the women to leave.

Mother and daughters exchanged glances then left the room. Tomas peered towards Bailey, closed the door, then ran down the hall. He grabbed Calico and pulled her aside from Kathleen and Jane. They watched as her mother and sister disappeared down the hall. Tomas kissed his beloved in a long passionate kiss. She smiled as he pulled his lips away from her. "I love you," he told her.

"And I you."

He traced his finger along her cheekbone. "I know it must be hard for you to pretend to be something you're not."

"I do it to be with you."

"Yes. Calico, don't be upset with Kathleen. She will need you more than you know."

"But she—"

He placed his finger on her ruby red lips. "She is not a threat to us. Bailey is planning something that I think... No, I know...will involve something she may not feel comfortable doing. She will need you. Please, Calico, you are her best friend. Make amends with her. Promise?"

"What is he planning?" she asked as he lowered his finger.

"I don't know. He told me not to dismiss the attraction Isaac feels for Kathleen."

"You think he's going to use that against Isaac?"

"Perhaps, but not a word to your sister. Let Bailey tell her the plan. Make amends with your sister. That is all I ask from you."

"I will."

"Good." He kissed her on the lips. "I have to go. I love you," he said then disappeared down the hallway.

"I love you, too," she whispered.

Chapter 4

Grey-haired, slightly overweight, Alexander McGillpatrick sat in a chair next to his son's bed, contemplating what Bailey had just told him. "It would work, father," Bailey said, cringing in pain.

"You are placing your sister in a dangerous position with your proposal."

"Calico can help her," Tomas offered.

Alexander glanced at the wall across from him. Tomas stood confidently, leaning against the wall with his arms crossed over his chest. Two priests sat on either side of him while a physician continued to examine Bailey. Catholic men of all ages had gathered around their leaders listening to them. For years, these men had followed his sons and Tomas, causing havoc upon the Anglicans. Tomas had been an excellent spy. While upper classes believed he was a faithful Anglican who was dedicated enough to their faith, proven by how he had betrayed his family, little did they realize his conversion had been a ploy devised by the rebels. Tomas had been leading his own revolution four years before they had joined his army. "I only agreed to the union between my daughter and you because she always idolized you, Tomas. You've always been good to my girls since the day they were born."

"Alexander, you lived a hard, miserable life after Bailey and Sherlock's mother died. Every family here witnessed the hardships placed upon you by the Anglicans. The day you married Jane we saw a man we had all long forgotten, our leader. Kathleen and Calico brought joy to your household that continues to grow daily. There's not a man alive here tonight who would not stand to defend you and you family. We will protect Kathleen. I promise you, no harm will come to your daughter."

Alexander shook his head. "You and Bailey ask too much."

Tomas straightened his posture. "You have known me since I was a boy. Bailey can easily manipulate someone to do his bidding—"

"Ugh, thanks…" Bailey retorted.

Tomas grinned back at his friend. "It's true and you know it. That's why I agreed to share my leadership with you and Sherlock." He turned back to Alexander. "If Bailey had an idea I did not support I would not have agreed to what he just proposed. It takes three votes before we present it to the group. Sherlock's asleep with a head wound and the doctor doesn't know when he will wake. Bailey needs the third vote. I laid the rules out simply enough when you decided to join my cause. If one of your sons is killed or incapable of making an intelligent vote, you would vote on their behalf, just as my father would for me if the situation was reversed."

Alexander rose from his chair. "You are asking me to place Kathleen's life in danger. Tomas, you know my daughter. When she is under great distress, such as she is now, she acts without thought."

"Kathleen is very intelligent and I know she can keep a secret. I will make certain Calico is with her every step of the way."

Alexander held his wooden cane with both hands, lowered his head, and tapped the cane on the floor while he thought. It was one thing to allow Calico to court Tomas and for them to pretend to be Anglican, but it was another to ask Kathleen to court their enemy, Earl Isaac Turner. Isaac was ruthless, conniving, and just down right rotten to the core. If Isaac had already begun to question Tomas about his allegiance, then who was to say he wouldn't question Kathleen due to the association she had with Tomas? Kathleen had tried to kill Isaac already and he was certain Isaac wouldn't forget that. "Padric, what do you think of our sons' idea?" he asked Tomas' father, stopping the cane.

"It be dangerous, Alexander, but ya know they won't let Isaac harm her. If ya daughter were able to get inside the estate she could provide us with vital information and supplies. Ya family would regain part of the estate. She could aide the Catholic families who had to remain behind when you lost Kilmore. I be thinkin' the good outweigh the danger we be placing upon her shoulders. But she be your daughter, not mine. I haven't had another son ta marry her off to. I be thinkin ya make fine daughters."

"That he does. Ain't ever known any woman as beautiful and witty as Calico Jane McGillpatrick. Our wedding day can't come soon enough, I tell ya boys." Tomas grinned.

The group chuckled. Alexander cast his gaze up to him. He arched his eyebrow. Tomas swallowed hard. "We ain't done something we ought naught be doin."

"Good."

"Can't tell ya we ain't been tempted though."

The men chuckled. Alexander sighed, rising from his chair. He limped around the room, leaning on his cane. Tomas and the men continued to tease about Calico. He couldn't blame Tomas for his comments about his daughter. Twenty years older than his seventeen-year-old bride to be, Tomas had waited a long time to marry due to the penal laws. It was forbidden for any Catholic to marry an Anglican unless the Catholic converted. If an Anglican woman married a Catholic man she would lose her entire estate. Tomas had never planned to marry because if he had and the Church of Ireland ever learned the truth of his fraudulent conversion, he would have placed more harm on his wife and any of their children than he would have cared to. At first he attempted to remain a bachelor and Tomas had never been challenged, yet the older he grew the more Isaac and his friends tried their best to persuade him to take a wife. There were certain expectations the British King George II had for all noblemen. Alexander knew it would only be a matter of time before Tomas was forced to marry. As hard as he tried, Tomas couldn't escape the inevitable. He would have to take a noble woman as his wife so she could give him an heir and a spare. Isaac had introduced him to many beautiful noble women throughout the years and he had courted them all. Some had even come close to stealing his heart and making him forget the promise he had made to himself. Each time Tomas had found his emotions getting the best of him he would confide in Bailey. Last year, Alexander's son came up with a plan. If Tomas' heart was so eager to fall in love then who better to do it with but one of his sisters. Together, Bailey and Tomas had approached Alexander with their plan with a very persuasive argument. At first, Alexander had been reserved about the union between them. Not because Tomas wasn't a good man. By no means, he had known Tomas since the day he was born and considered him like another son. What had bothered him were the differences in ages. Calico was only sixteen when Tomas had approached him with the proposal to court her. He had tried to push Kathleen towards the man but Tomas had been adamant. Calico would be a better match for him because she was naïve enough to believe whatever he told her and loyal enough to do whatever he asked of her. Alexander couldn't argue with his logic. Alexander ordered Calico to court Tomas.

It had been Bailey who had supported Tomas' proposal and now he was talking about proposing another fate for his other sister. Alexander wasn't certain if Tomas was supporting Bailey out of gratitude for helping persuade Alexander into allowing the union between Tomas and Calico, or if Tomas truly believed it was in the best interest for Kathleen to court Isaac. Either way, what the men proposed placed Kathleen in greater danger than Calico would ever face with her courtship. Kathleen would have to learn how to be an Anglican. He would never ask her to convert. No, that would go against God and the Pope. Kathleen would have to be convincing. If Isaac ever learned she was Catholic it wouldn't take him long to make the connection Tomas and Calico were as well. Once Kathleen married Isaac, she would own half his estate.

He wasn't certain Kathleen could be a good Earl's wife. He had begun his daughters' educations when Kathleen was seven. A year later, he lost the power and resources required to continue their studies when James Turner evicted the family from their home and stole the estate. They were given an acre of land to tenant farm on. James had made certain it had been located on the farthest and worst plot of land in Kilmore. No longer considered daughters of a noble man, Kathleen and Calico had to learn to survive in destitution, especially since their mother was with child. With so much pain and destruction, Kathleen had never learned the lessons she required to be a nobleman's daughter and it had become illegal for any Catholic to receive an education. By the time he had regained control of Kilmore, Kathleen was fifteen and old enough to be introduced to society. Yet she and Calico were not ready for that, not at all. He had worked to teach his daughters everything they should have spent years learning. Kathleen had developed a talent for painting while Calico enjoyed submerging herself in the library. The four years he had given his daughters at the estate had been the best of times. Now he was grateful he had kept his daughters sheltered away instead of out in public where any Anglican might have seen them. Calico had done well in convincing them she was from a family in the Northern parts of Ireland. Isaac had never seen his daughters before and Bailey had killed James, so no one would have any reason to suspect Kathleen wasn't who she claimed to be. But still, in order for the courtship to work, Kathleen would have to be convincing.

Alexander pivoted on his heel, leaning for support on his cane. "We ask her."

The room grew quiet. "Alex?" Padric asked.

Alexander walked towards the group. "I propose before we send this matter to the rest of the group for a vote we ask Kathleen."

"She tried to kill him," Bailey yelled, trying to rise. He groaned, heaving his chest as the physician tried to lay him down.

"Lie down, son," Alexander ordered.

Bailey reluctantly complied. His father looked up at the physician. "How is he?"

"I see no signs of infection. He will need to stay in bed for at least two months for the wounds to heal properly. Your son disagrees."

"Of course he does. He's a McGillpatrick. Stubborn and prideful, just like my father was."

"He is in a tremendous amount of pain. I have something for it but he refuses to take it."

"Why?"

"He says he wants to be of sound mind to aide Tomas. To be honest, sir, your son is strong but I do not doubt that his strength will waiver as he continues to fight the pain. The more strength he uses to fight, the weaker his body will become. The weaker the body the longer it takes to heal and it is more susceptible to ailment. He requires rest not rebellion."

Alexander stared at his son. "I will not give up my vote," Bailey argued.

"Bailey," Tomas said while walking towards him. "You heard the doctor. You should rest."

"No, you need my vote."

"I have your vote. It was yes, was it not?"

"Yes, but we still have my father's vote to hear then we present it to the men."

"My vote," Alexander started. He peered around the room then back to his son. "I give my vote to Kathleen."

"Father!"

Alexander slammed the end of the cane on the hardwood floor. Silence fell. All eyes fell on him. "We all know Irish women have the strength and determination that could win many battles between them and their husbands. When we have a mission for a man we take into consideration his own needs and weigh them against the needs of the many before we command him to conduct himself in whatever way we desire. While I know my son and Tomas have thought about the needs of the group, I very much doubt they have considered Kathleen's own needs and desires. The mission we are planning for Kathleen is as dangerous for her as placing her on the frontlines of any battlefield. She would have to be fully committed to her assignment in order to fool Isaac Turner and the

Church of Ireland. I do not believe if we make this decision without her input on the matter she will be able to complete what we ask of her. My daughter is not afraid to stand up and fight when there is injustice. While that is an asset it can also be her downfall. She is bold, brave, and quick to loosen her tongue when she is provoked by inhumanity and injustice. We cannot play her for the fool; she is not one."

Bailey and Tomas exchanged glances. "What if she doesn't agree?" Bailey muttered as the doctor pulled the blanket over his patient.

"Then you will accept her decision and we think of another way to regain control of Kilmore."

"Father, please. We can—"

"No! It will not work if your sister doesn't commit to the plan." Alexander lifted his head to the doctor. "Give him the laudanum after Kathleen gives her decision."

"I don't want it," Bailey yelled.

"You will take it and you will rest after your sister has granted her answer. You have nothing to prove to us, Bailey. Everyone here knows you are a strong, intelligent man. Take the laudanum, let your body heal, and we will keep you informed while you heal from your wounds."

"Your father's right, Bailey," Tomas said. Bailey looked at his best friend. "You are no use to the resistance if you're dead, crippled, or ill."

Bailey glanced at the physician then back to his father. "Very well. I will comply with your wishes, father."

"Good. Tomas bring Kathleen."

"Yes, sir," he replied then left the room. Bailey closed his eyes, groaning softly. He arched his head, breathing quick, shallow breaths. Alexander sat on his son's bed, took his hand, and comforted his son while they waited for his daughter.

Chapter 5

Kathleen quickly walked down the long hallway leading from her room to her brother's room. "Do you know why my father has sent for me?" she asked Tomas, trying to keep up with his quick stride.

"Yes."

Silence fell between them as they turned the corner. Frustrated and confused, she wanted answers. After encountering Isaac at the lake, everything had been upside down. At least she could be certain of one thing—Calico was no longer upset with her. They had spent the last hour making amends. It felt good to be able to talk to Calico. She had feared Calico would never want to speak to her again after she accused Tomas of treason. She never meant to harm anyone. On the contrary, Kathleen had only acted to protect her family. Everything had happened so quickly ever since the English-Irish army had attacked her home. Bailey's body lay broken and she wasn't certain if Sherlock was ever going to regain consciousness. No one was. Of her two brothers, she had always admired Sherlock. He was nothing like Bailey. Bailey was demanding, straightforward, and aggressive. Some days she even wondered if her older brother regarded her as his sister or just her mother's daughters. But it was opposite with Sherlock. Sherlock was the quieter, more sensitive brother. Some people said Sherlock was a lot like his mother while Bailey favored their father.

"Are you upset with me?" Kathleen asked as they came closer to her brother's bedchamber.

"No."

"Then why are you acting like you are?"

Tomas paused with his hand on the door and turned in her direction. "Kathleen, I understand why you think I have wronged your family. I honestly do, child. But I am not upset with you for it."

"I'm sorry. It's just…"

"You spoke before thinking?" He sighed, let go of the doorknob, then took a step towards her. "Kathleen, you have to think about more than your family and yourself when you are presented with any decision you have to make. I do not act without thinking about everyone's welfare and how my decision will affect another. Everything is connected. From the enemy to the poor farmer three counties away, we are all connected. The decision you made today about me…" He exhaled a deep breath then continued. "Was a foolish assumption. I forgive you. Come, we have matters to discuss." He opened the door and held it open for Kathleen.

Kathleen stared across the crowded room. So many men surrounded her brother's bed. She swallowed hard then stepped towards Bailey's bed. Her heart jumped at the sound of the door closing behind her. She turned at hearing Tomas locking the door. "Kathleen," Alexander called to his daughter.

Kathleen turned towards her father. Alexander sat in his chair, leaning on his hand-carved, wooden cane. "Father," she answered.

"Come here."

"Yes, sir," she replied then walked to her brother's bed. Bailey clung to his blanket, clenching his jaw. He slowly turned his eyes in her direction. Droplets of sweat poured down his face. He breathed quick, shallow breaths as a man in tremendous pain. "Bailey," she greeted him.

"Hmm, Kat." He turned his gaze to Alexander. Kathleen followed his gaze.

Alexander tapped his cane. "Very well. I do not wish my son to last any more time with the pain he feels so we shall commence with the decision. Tell her, Bailey."

Bailey nodded his head. He released his death grip on the blanket and motioned for his sister to lean over.

"What do you want?" Kathleen asked her brother.

"Sit," he pushed out of his mouth. Kathleen smoothed her long skirt and sat on the edge of his bed. Brother and sister stared at each other. "You remember when Tomas told you Isaac Turner had asked to court you?"

"Yes."

"I think you should."

"Should?"

"Court him."

"Have you gone mad from the pain?" she yelled, rising from beside him.

Alexander lowered and shook his head. "Kathleen, listen to your brother. I assure you he is speaking with intelligence."

Kathleen slowly returned to her place beside Bailey. Bailey continued, "We need someone inside his estate to feed us information."

"Then use one of the servants."

"He's too smart to talk about important things around servants, "Tomas added, joining them.

Kathleen turned her attention towards him. "And you believe by courting him I can grant you the information you seek?"

"That and more," Alexander said.

"You would have to marry him first," Bailey added.

"Marry…him," Kathleen gasped. "You want me to break the law?"

"No."

"I won't convert," she yelled, starting to rise.

"I'm not asking you to, Kathleen. Sit down and listen to me. Do not speak until you have heard everything I am going to say. Promise," Bailey pleaded, grasping her wrist.

Kathleen stared at her brother. He was speaking nonsense. Worst yet, Tomas and her father seemed to be in on the ploy he was about to tell her. She shifted her eyes to her father. Alexander sat motionless in his chair with both hands on the hilt of his cane. His head hung low so she couldn't see his face but she recognized his mannerism. Her father was deep in thought. She wondered if he was thinking about her. A highly educated man, her father had been known throughout Ireland as a fair, intelligent, and impartial lawyer. Yet people had only seen what her father had wanted them to see. To her he wasn't that lawyer or the ruler of an estate. No, Alexander McGillpatrick was her daddy. She knew her father better than any of these men and she knew he was hurting. He had been hurting ever since the English had attacked their estate three days ago, captured his sons, tortured them, and even when he had aided in their rescue his heart had broken even more. One son close to death and another in constant pain. Hadn't her father been through enough already? Yet, here he sat in Sherlock's place contemplating her courtship with the man who had beaten his children. What sort of father gives his enemy his daughter?

"Father," she whispered, stepping towards him, jerking her wrist away from Bailey's loose grip.

"Sit down and listen to Bailey, Kathleen. Then we shall discuss the matter at hand," he answered, avoiding her inquisitive gaze.

"Yes, father," she answered softly, then complied. She stared at Bailey's bruised and swollen face. She hated to see her brother like this. "You want me to court Isaac and marry him when he seeks my hand," she whispered, averting her eyes away from his.

"There is more to that plan, Kathleen."

"Tell me. I'm listening."

"According to the penal law," Tomas answered from his place along the wall. Kathleen turned her eyes towards him. "...a Catholic woman may not marry an Anglican man without converting to Anglican. Now, Isaac can be convinced you are not a Catholic woman because I told him you are Calico's sister. He believes I am an upstanding Anglican who found an upstanding Anglican from the North to marry. If you are her sister—"

"Then I'm Anglican too."

"Yes. After you marry Isaac, you will inherit half of his estate. That will allow you the power to hand off small parcels of land to us without

Isaac suspecting anything. We will insert rebels disguised as poor Catholic families on Kilmore lands."

"It will take time to do so in order not to cause suspicions," Alexander said.

Thomas nodded and continued, "Once all the families are inserted you will provide them with guns and ammunition."

"But you will have to be careful. It is against the law for a Catholic to own a gun. If you are caught supplying weapons to the Catholics you will be tried and punished," Bailey added.

"Punished how?" Kathleen asked, worried she might be physically harmed.

"I do not know, Kathleen. It would depend upon the judge who oversees your trial. Just make certain you are not caught," Alexander stressed, looking at his daughter.

Kathleen nodded then looked at Thomas. "How long until Isaac asks for my hand?"

"That depends on you."

"Me?"

"Isaac is not known for courting a woman very long. You would have to win his heart and keep it. He has taken many women to his bed after stealing their hearts. Once he's slept with them he discards them from his life as if they were trash."

"That's why he wasn't shocked I held a gun to him and he asked me if it was my sister he had slept with?"

"Yes, women throw themselves at him hoping they can break that pattern. No one has ever come close enough to him to get him thinking about marriage, and even if you do marry him there is no guarantee he will remain faithful to you."

"You'll have to use your womanly charms to please him, without holding anything back," Bailey suggested.

Kathleen gasped at her brother. "You want me to…"

"No, Kathleen. I want you to make him desire you so much it hurts. You heard Tomas. If you allow Isaac to bed you, you have given Isaac all the power you hold over him. Seduce without fornication."

"You will have to be careful, though," Tomas continued. "He is a very paranoid man. He would have to believe you are seducing him because you love him."

"But I don't."

"Kathleen, he spots a liar a mile away. You have to make him believe the truth we want him to believe."

Alexander raised his hand to silence Tomas. All eyes turned in his direction. "I will not lie to you, Kathleen," he said, lowering his hand. "We are asking you to risk everything to aide the resistance, even your very life. Should Isaac learn you are deceiving him, I hate to think what fate might befall you. You have seen the works of his hands on your brothers. And he will not stop at you. He will come for your sister, Tomas, your mother, and brothers. If he ever gained control of this estate it would not only double the size of his property but would also increase his power over the area. What we ask from you tonight is not asked lightly. We have discussed this matter much amongst us but I do not believe we should make a decision for you."

"There is more, "Tomas said. Kathleen lifted her eyes to him. "Isaac is a very dangerous man. That is true. But he is also very intelligent and ruthless. He has secrets that we would like you to learn from him."

"Secrets? Such as?"

Tomas look at Bailey. She followed his gaze. Bailey grunted then spoke. "When Sherlock and I were in our cell we heard voices."

"Voices?"

"Children. We did not know where they were being kept. There were moments of much commotion. Groups of soldiers would pass us. We would hear noises that no child should be making. When Tomas and father rescued us from the estate they did not find anyone in the cells but

Sherlock and me, but we know there are children down there. Kathleen, I know what I heard."

Tomas continued, "There are rumors that Isaac provides prostitutes secretly to the upper classes. He kidnaps young girls from the poor, transports them to his estate, and breaks them in personally. We cannot find proof of his actions. Sources also tell us he has been selling Irish Catholic families into slavery to the colonies and the West Indies, among other places. We have tried to infiltrate the estate before and were unable to do so. It was only by the grace of God we were able to rescue your brothers yesterday. We have found bodies thrown into a deep pit in a field close to the estate. They look to be beaten. Had we not rescued your brothers I know they would have joined them."

Kathleen sat in silence, taking in everything they had told her. Isaac was more of a threat than she had ever imagined. Fear crept slowly throughout her body as images of beaten children and families sold into slavery beckoned her. She couldn't do what they were asking of her. She had never been good at keeping secrets or lying. What if Isaac learned the truth about her? If Isaac was as ruthless as they were telling her, who was to stop him from killing her then throwing her body in the deep pit with the rest of the bodies? She wanted to help her father and brothers. She wanted her family to regain control of Kilmore. She wanted her father to be happy again. But she didn't want to die and she especially didn't want to ruin everything her family had built up through the resistance. She glanced at Bailey. Every bruise, every broken bone and strained muscle was caused by the man they wanted her to court! She didn't want to end like her brother.

Kathleen rose abruptly from the bed and stared towards the door. "Kat?" Bailey asked, watching her run.

"Kathleen," Alexander demanded, rising out of his chair.

She turned swiftly, tears running down her cheeks. "I'm sorry. I'm so, so, so very sorry. Find another, father. Please! I...I...I can't do what you want." She opened the door and ran out of the room, slamming the door behind her.

Alexander glanced at Tomas then to Bailey. "Take your medicine, son. You have your answer."

"Make her court him," Bailey said as the physician began to pour the dosage.

"No, we said we would ask her and we did." He turned towards the crowd. "Go home."

The men grumbled as they filtered out of the room one by one until no one except the four of them remained.

"She's scared, Bailey," Tomas said, sitting beside him.

"My sister is nothing but a coward. We knew this when we asked her."

"Your sister is not a coward, Bailey," Alexander disciplined. "She's young, inexperienced, and terrified. You have to remember her life has not been a stable one. You and Sherlock had a better life than I could ever have afforded to Kathleen and Calico. She is also marked. Kathleen's not a fool. She knows no man would call her beautiful because of the scars on her face. Her marriage prospects are limited because of that. We will leave her alone and perhaps with the time we have granted her she will change her mind."

"Perhaps," Bailey answered. He turned his eyes to the physician holding a spoon full of the brown medicine. Bailey lifted his head, opened his mouth, and allowed the spoon to enter his mouth. He swallowed the medicine and rested his head on the pillow.

"You have about five to ten minutes before he is sedated," the physician informed Alexander and Tomas.

"Thank you, doctor. You will not speak of what you have seen here," Tomas commanded, handing the middle-aged man a large bag of coins.

"No, sir. I attended to your sick fiancée."

"Good man. You may leave us."

"Yes, sir." The physician bowed then quickly walked out of the room.

Chapter 6

July 27, 1738

Shadows danced on the walls of Sherlock McGillpatrick's bedroom. Mary sat next to her husband, holding his hand. Tears fell from her eyes. "Sherlock, husband, please I beg you, please wake," she whispered, clutching her rosary in her right hand. How many hours had she sat beside her husband waiting for him to regain consciousness? The physician had said the longer Sherlock remained asleep the closer he drew to death. She couldn't fathom a life away from her husband. Their children were dead and now Sherlock's life was threatened as well. She leaned her head on his chest, closed her eyes, and listened to his heart. The steady beats provided little comfort to her weary mind. Mary stroked her hand on his firm chest and peered upward. She fixed her eyes on the blood-stained rag over his head. The blow to the head he had received from Isaac had fractured his skull. The physician had little hope for her husband's survival but she dismissed his claims. She needed Sherlock alive. He was her strength.

The door to the bedchamber slowly began to open. Mary turned her head to see who had entered. They had received countless visitors from the priests, rebels, family members, friends, and the physician since early this morning. She was tired of them. All she wanted was time alone with her husband.

Kathleen knocked on the door, slightly opening it. "May I enter?" she asked in a hushed tone.

Mary rose from her position, wiping away her tears. She silently motioned for her younger sister to enter the room. Kathleen closed the door behind her then joined Mary. "Any changes?"

"No."

Kathleen stared at her brother then sat in the chair beside the bed. "You didn't come to dinner."

"I wanted to be with him in case he should wake up. I don't want him to wake up and not see me."

Kathleen turned her head towards Mary. She took her sister's hand and gently patted it. "Mother wants you to eat something. She sent me to watch Sherlock while you eat in the kitchen."

Mary clasped Kathleen's hand with both her hands. She pressed the rosary into her hand. "Please, I can't leave him. Tell mother, I won't leave my husband."

"Mary, Sherlock would want you to take care of yourself. I promise if he wakes up I will send for you."

Mary turned her heard towards her husband and locked her eyes on her husband's face. He slept peacefully without a care in the world. At least he wasn't feeling any pain. She would hate to think of him in the state Bailey was in. Kathleen tapped her sister's hand. She pulled the rosary away from Mary's grip. Mary turned her head towards her. "I will pray the rosary over him. I promise. Please, Mary, you know mother will fret about you."

Mary exhaled a deep breath with a nod. "You're a good sister, Kathleen. There is no one other than you I'd rather Sherlock see first when he wakes if he can't see me. He loves you dearly, you know that, right?" Mary whispered the last part, softly squeezing Kathleen's hand. Kathleen smiled.

"I know, Mary."

Mary kissed her on the forehead, leaned over her husband, and gently kissed him on the lips. She moved her mouth to her husband's ear and whispered, "Don't give up on me, Sherlock McGillpatrick. Don't. Just don't, my love. I love you." Mary rose from over her husband with tears falling down her cheeks. She sniffed her nose, wiped the tears from her eyes, and silently walked out of the room, closing the door behind her.

Kathleen wrapped the stone thread of rosary beads around her right hand and began to caress them individually, muttering the rosary prayers. She gently took Sherlock's hand in her own, carefully watching her brother as she continued to pray over him. Over and over again the beads twirled around her hand. Her soft voice lifted for what seemed an eternity as she tried to hide her tears. The more she prayed the more the pain tore at her heart until she could no longer stand the pain. Sobbing profusely, Kathleen laid her head on Sherlock's chest. She clung to his shirt, letting her tears cascade onto his chest. "Oh, Sherlock, I…" She continued to cry; unable to speak the deepest of feelings she had wanted to articulate. Kathleen gathered herself, turned her head, and looked up at him. "When I was little, you used to hold me and let me cry on your chest. You were there for me, Sherlock." She peered down and played with the collar of his shirt. "You were always a better father than Bailey was to his children. You treated Calico and me like we were your own children, even though you had children close to our age who needed you more than we did. It didn't matter. We weren't just the children of father's second wife to you. We were family. You taught me that no matter what, family sticks together. Sherlock, I need you. Last night, Bailey and father asked me to do something. Something to help our family. They wanted me to court Isaac Turner, marry him, then spy against him. I was so scared for my own life I told them no. But Bailey and father are upset with me. Bailey keeps reminding me that if Calico can spy against the English then why can't I. He says I'm weak and useless. Weak and useless, Sherlock! All day long, I dread visiting him but father has insisted on it. I'm subjected to Bailey ridiculing me because I chose my life over the rebels. But look what Isaac did to you and him. And that's not even all that Isaac has done to others. Father has barely spoken to me. He can't keep eye contact with me, either. I know he's disappointed in me but I think Bailey pressures him and that pressure has added more stress to our father. Tomas was there too last night. He refuses to be in my company or speak to me. I don't know what to do. If I continue to deny my family's desires then it will cause the rift between us to grow, but if I choose to comply with their desires then I place my own life within the hands of a killer. Oh, Sherlock, I wish you were awake to guide me." She laid her head down, closed her eyes, and gently cried.

The door to the room slowly opened. "Kathleen," Calico called into the room.

Kathleen turned her head. "In here," she answered, sitting upright.

Calico entered the room and closed the door behind her. She carried a plate full of cookies and a glass of milk to a small table and laid them down. "You left the table before mother brought out desert. She wanted me to give you some cookies and milk."

Kathleen smiled, "Thank you."

"You're welcome." Her graceful younger sister slowly walked towards her and sat in the chair beside her. "I want to apologize on behalf of Tomas. He shouldn't be treating you like he is."

"It's alright."

"No, no it's not. I told Tomas I was appalled at the lack of respect he is showing you. It is one thing for Bailey and father to act in the manner they are towards you. We're family, after all, but Tomas isn't family. We're not married yet."

"He was family long before you and I were born. You know how father feels about him."

Calico lifted her hand and gently pushed a strand of Kathleen's red hair behind her ear. "Kat, I understand why you decided not to help the rebels. I think if I were in your position I would have answered the same as you did," she said, lowering her hand.

"No. No, you wouldn't. You're the strong sister. I'm weak and useless. You heard father. All I'm good for is painting my pretty pictures." She sniffed and cried. "I cause problems whenever I open my mouth. I...I...I'm so ugly from this," she pointed to the smallpox scars on the right side of her face, "that no man would ever want me." Kathleen lowered her hand. "I'll die penniless, barren, and utterly useless! You're the good sister.

You're smart enough to spy against the English, you have a good man who wants plenty of babies from you, and you make father happy with how you've become a useful woman."

"Oh, Kathleen, father loves us. He's just upset."

"More like disappointed in me."

"Did you know that Bailey and Tomas asked father to force you into the courtship?"

Kathleen stared at her sister in confusion. "What?" she whispered in shock.

"Tomas said they tried to force the vote out of father but father felt you should make the decision, not him. I don't think our father wanted to put you into that situation because he knew what harm you would face if Isaac ever learned the truth."

"Then why won't he speak to me?!"

"I don't know, Kathleen. Why don't you ask him? He has never denied our attentions when we have sought them from him."

Kathleen took a deep breath and swallowed hard. Seek her father's attention. A part of her wanted her daddy to hold her in his arms but the other part of her was loath to even approach him. If anyone had the right to be upset it was she. "If father didn't want me to be placed in harm's way then he should have stopped Bailey from ever approaching the idea to begin with!"

"Kat, our brothers are grown men. There's nothing he can do to stop them from leading the lives they have chosen for themselves. Besides, Bailey would never ask one of his siblings to do something he thought would place them in harm's way."

"Huh! Look," Kathleen yelled extending her arm out to Sherlock. "Bailey did this to his own brother."

"You can't blame Bailey for that. He's not the one who hit him."

Kathleen lowered her arm. "Calico, it was Bailey's idea for him and Sherlock to fight while father escorted all of us to safety. They should have stayed with us. If they had they wouldn't have been injured. But no, our arrogant, self-centered—"

"Mm," Sherlock moaned repeatedly, moving his hand towards Kathleen as she continued to speak. Calico thrust her hand over Kathleen's mouth.

Confused, Kathleen mumbled under her sister's hand, "Calico?"

Calico glanced quickly to her sister, "Listen."

The sisters grew silent. "M…ar…y," Sherlock continued to mutter under his breath. His fingers touched Kathleen's. She jumped up quickly, pushing her younger sister aside. Sherlock moved his hand around the bed, searching for his wife's hand.

"Go, get Mary. I'll stay with him," Kathleen ordered Calico. Calico ran out of the room, leaving the door ajar.

Kathleen sat beside her brother and took his hand. "Mary," he moaned, turning his head to the side. Sherlock gasped, lifting his left leg. She gently placed her hand on the right side of her brother's long face and turned his head towards her. His light brown eyes, stared back at her. "Hmm, Kathleen," he pushed out of his chapped lips.

"Yes, it's me," she grinned. "I'm so grateful to see you awake."

"Is it true?" Sherlock placed his hands on the bed and raised his body to a sitting position. He grabbed his forehead and leaned his body over, breathing deeply.

"Sherlock?" she asked in concern, grabbing him by the arms.

"I'm dizzy."

"You should lie down."

"How long have I been sleeping?"

"Three and half days. What do you recall?"

"The cell Bailey and I were in. The guards were beating him. I had escaped from our cell and tried to stop Isaac then everything went dark."

"Bailey said Isaac hit you over the head with a brick. You never woke."

Sherlock nodded. He took a deep breath then glared at her. "I heard everything. Where are we?"

"Tomas' home."

Sherlock nodded. "I take it we are in the servant's quarters?"

"No, we're in the empty wing on the bottom floor next to the servant's quarters. Tomas said we deserved more than servant's quarters because of who our family is."

"Help me up," he asked, grabbing the sleeve of her dress.

"You should lie down."

Sherlock glared at his sister, "I heard and I don't approve."

"Approve or not, you should rest."

"No, Kathleen, you were right not to trust Bailey's plan."

Kathleen gasped. She didn't think Sherlock had heard a single word she had spoken. It was a miracle he was awake at all but even more so that he had heard her words. She wondered if he understood the complexities of the decision she had to make or if the injury to his head had affected his intelligence. She had heard of sound people who had been hit on the head becoming idiots. How she hoped Sherlock would have his senses returned to him. "You asked for my counsel, did you not?" he asked, drawing her attention back from her thoughts.

"Yes, but...how did you know I asked for your help? You were asleep."

"Kathleen, help me up. I want to see my wife and I want to help my sister."

Kathleen complied, throwing the blankets aside. She helped her brother rise from the bed. He stumbled around the room, holding on to the furniture. "Are you hungry?" she asked, catching him staring at the cookies.

"Famished."

"You can have those. Mother made them for me."

He turned on his heel, addressing her. "Thank you."

"You're welcome," she said, sitting in the middle of the bed with her legs crossed. She watched her older brother quickly eat the cookies and gulp down the milk. He wiped his mouth with his sleeve and asked, "Why do Bailey and father think you should court Isaac?"

"I met him yesterday."

"How?" Kathleen told her brother every detail from her encounter with Isaac at the lake, the lies Tomas gave of her identity, the offer of courtship, and the meeting she had with the rebels. "You did the right thing."

Kathleen shrugged her shoulders, lowering her head. She played with his quilt as she responded, "I don't think I did. Everyone is upset with me."

"Kathleen, look at me." Kathleen raised her head. "Bailey is an arrogant, prideful fool. It's his pride that caused us to be captured by Isaac. The day the English attacked our home we had enough time to escape and rejoin the family after everyone had left."

"Then why didn't you?"

"Bailey wanted something from the cellar. I told him we should leave but he didn't listen to me. He said we needed to secure it before we left."

"What was it?"

"I don't know. Father and Bailey have a lot of secrets they have kept from me over the years. They used to meet in the cellar with other rebels. I was never allowed to join in their private meetings."

"If you're one of the rebel leaders then how is it you don't know what was down there?"

"Because it's not part of Tomas' group. I don't know who or what is down there, Kathleen, but I know Isaac suspected something of value is down there."

"Why?"

"We never made it to the cellar. We were captured before that and thrown in the dungeon. Bailey had a key around his neck that I had never seen before. Isaac took it and asked what it went to. Bailey refused to answer. Isaac isn't stupid, Kathleen. He knew Bailey was hiding something from him and he suspected we were in the lower levels for a reason."

"The old castle portion of the house?"

"Yes."

"Those catacombs are numerous. Calico and I used to play down there. It was like a maze—"

"And you two always got in trouble when Bailey or father learned what you were doing."

"Yes. I thought it was just because they were concerned for our safety."

"They were more concerned for their secrets than your safety. Kathleen," Sherlock began as he took a step towards her. "Bailey was beaten for the information Isaac could not determine for himself. He never gave it. If you are to court Isaac and he learns your true identity, then I have no doubts he will beat you for the information he seeks, or use your broken body to force Bailey and father's hands. But the thing is, I don't believe for a second Bailey would ever trade the information Isaac seeks for your life."

"Father would."

"Yes, he would. He loves you, Calico, and mother very much. I don't remember what life was like with my mother. Bailey used to tell me father changed for the worst after the death of our mother. I would not want our father to become the man he was when I was growing up."

"Why not? Father is a wonderful man."

"Kathleen, he changed into the man you know after he married your mother. You don't want to know the man he was before he married Jane."

"He can't be that bad, Sherlock."

"Where do you think Bailey learned to be the man he is today? His wife and children are dead, Kathleen. That changed him into a very bitter, shrewd, dangerous man. The man Bailey is today is the same as the father we grew up with. No, you don't want father to be placed in that position again. I know if you, Calico, or mother were to die he would become that man again. I saw it almost happen when you and your little brother died with smallpox."

"I came back from the dead, he didn't," she whispered with her eyes lowered.

Sherlock nodded in silence. Kathleen instinctively traced her finger along the scar on her face. "Your children died too."

Sherlock exhaled a deep breath. "I took their deaths better than Bailey took the loss of his wife and children."

"They were murdered. Your children were not."

"Kathleen, the day James Turner murdered Bailey's wife and children was the day our brother changed for the worst. When James kidnapped Mary, Bailey didn't want to rescue my wife. James had sent a ransom letter saying he would trade a life for a life. If Bailey surrendered into his custody he would release Mary. There was a large ransom on our brother's head and James wanted to collect it. I urged Bailey to rescue my wife but he refused. He said if he rescued Mary then he would risk his own life, that it was better that she should die than face endangering his own life."

"But...I...I thought you two had planned the rescue together."

"Ha! I only wish we had. No, he went to meet with James. James had Bailey bound by two soldiers but was unaware of the knife Bailey was hiding. Once James released Mary, Bailey told Mary to run. He attacked, killing the soldiers and James. He's been upset with me ever since because now the bounty on his head is larger and Isaac wants to collect in revenge for his father. Bailey wants Isaac eliminated. He'll stop at nothing to see that happen, even if it means using his little sister as bait."

Kathleen thought about her brother's words. She had no doubts Sherlock's advice was in her own best interest. He had always been honest with her. But the facts still loomed over her. As long as she denied Bailey, her father would be so upset with her he'd refused to speak to or see her. It was a side of Alexander she wasn't accustomed to. "Sherlock, what do you suggest I do?"

"Stay strong, my little Kitty Kat. Whatever you do, don't give in to Bailey."

"What if—?"

"No, Kathleen, don't start doubting. I don't want Bailey to ruin your life. Anyone who is associated with him loses something for their loyalty. Don't let him ruin your life! Promise me."

"I promise."

"Sherlock," Mary's screams lifted from the door as she ran into Sherlock's arms. He grabbed his wife's face and kissed her in a long, deep, passionate kiss. Their arms wrapped around each other, lost in a world of their own. Kathleen smiled as the couple's kiss grew with intensity. The couple breathed heavily as they drew their lips away from each other.

Sherlock scanned his wife's face. "You're safe?" he asked her.

"Yes."

"Good."

"Oh, Sherlock, I thought... The doctor...you were dying."

"Shh, Mary, I won't leave you."

"Oh, I missed you."

He kissed her fully on her thick ruby lips.

Kathleen smiled as she rose from the bed. "I'll leave you two alone. Goodnight." Sherlock waved his hand downward, motioning for her to leave. She walked to the door, held it, and looked back. Her brother was working his way to the bed, pushing Mary backwards. She closed the door behind her, allowing the couple their privacy. Someday, she wanted a man just like Sherlock to be her husband. She lingered on the thought of her dream husband touching the long scar on her face. She wanted a husband who would love her with the kind of passion and kindness Sherlock had for Mary. Love. It was such a rarity for any married couple to love each other. A majority of married couples she knew rarely fell in love with their partners. The matchmaker arranged marriages. It was the matchmaker who made certain the groom could support his future wife. The matchmaker also took the negotiated bride's dowry to the groom. Kathleen and Calico once had large dowries, ensuring they would have the best suitors possible. All of her hopes and dreams of a proper marriage ended when Isaac Turner had stolen her father's estate. At least Calico had been able to give her dowry to Tomas. Without a dowry, Kathleen had little to no hope of a marriage. Her best action would be to fall in love with a man who loved her, let him kidnap her, then they could go off and secretly marry. Their parents couldn't do anything to stop them. She doubted that would ever happen. England had outlawed kidnapping the bride before a wedding, but there were still some who kept the Irish tradition.

Kathleen sighed, lowering her hand from her cheek. It was useless to think she would ever marry a man she had fallen in love with. The sound of her brother's bed moving and low moans came from Sherlock's bedroom. She placed her hand on his door, listening to them, hoping Mary would give her brother another child. Sherlock needed a child. Kathleen gazed across the thick hall into Bailey's room. Brother and sister glared at each other until Tomas closed the door between them. She could hear the best friends speaking behind the door but couldn't understand their words. What secrets could Bailey be keeping from the family and why? Kathleen lowered her hand and walked towards the kitchen.

Chapter 7

September 14, 1738 – Kilmore Cathedral, Wexford County, Ireland

The sanctuary in the old country cathedral was full of people from throughout Ireland. Lords and ladies gawked at the couple before them. Kathleen stood beside the alter staring into the groom's side of the sanctuary. Isaac Turner sat in the front row, watching Tomas and Calico stand before the pastor. He turned his gaze towards her. Kathleen swallowed hard, gripping the hilt of her bouquet. How long had she been staring at him? He nodded his head gently in her direction. His light brown eyes gazed into her deep, emerald green eyes. The sunlight seemed to twinkle off of his brilliant eyes. She slowly lowered her gaze up and down his body. When did he become so radiant? Her heart fluttered. He smiled with a light chuckle.

"Kathleen," Calico whispered to her sister.

Kathleen never moved. His long white wig, held back in a ponytail with a black ribbon, highlighted his high cheekbones. "Kat," Calico growled.

"What?" she whispered, turning in her sister's direction. Isaac chuckled, lowering his gaze back to the couple.

"I need the ring," Calico said, extending her long slender hand toward her sister.

"Oh, sorry," Kathleen whispered, pulling the golden band out from inside her bouquet.

"Are you alright?"

"Yes, here," she replied, handing her sister the ring. Calico stared at the Claddagh ring in Kathleen's hand with a look of disappointment. She lowered her eyes to it then lifted them swiftly to meet Kathleen's. Kathleen shook her head slightly. Calico clenched her jaw, glancing at the ring then back up at Kathleen.

"Please tell me, you have his ring," she snarled, trying not to make a scene. Kathleen looked at her brunette sister with a confused look on her face. What was she talking about? She lowered her eyes to the ring and inhaled a deep breath. Her Claddagh! How could she have mistaken Tomas' ring for her ring? She must have slipped it into the bouquet when she left the house. Oh, how could she have been so stupid? The Claddagh was worn by Irish Catholic women, not Anglicans, as a way of keeping the old ways. Her father had given her the ring on her fifteenth birthday, announcing she was ready for marriage. The two hands holding an emerald heart in the center of the ring signified her Catholic faith. The emerald heart, love, and the crown over the heart, honor. Every Catholic Irish knew the ring's motto by heart "Let love and friendship reign." It was that motto that scared the Anglicans in Wexford County because to them it meant the native Irish were claiming let love and friendship reign under a true Irish noble. Yet the ring had a social meaning as well. Any Irish man looking for a potential wife knew to look on the woman's left finger. If the heart faced outward, the woman was single and if it faced inward it meant the woman was engaged. Tomas had turned Calico's ring inward in front of all the rebels after their secret handfasting ceremony almost a year ago. Calico had taken great pride in wearing her ring inward. Yet when she pretended to be Anglican she couldn't wear it. If any Anglican knew either she or Kathleen had a Claddagh, they would know instantly they were Catholic.

"I'm so sorry," Kathleen whispered.

"No, no, no, Kathleen, please no," a tear fell from Calico's terrified round face. Kathleen placed her ring back into the bouquet and searched. "It has to be in here. I remember hiding it, just like you said."

Calico sighed deeply, rolling her eyes and tapping her feet. The crowd began to talk among themselves. Nervously, Kathleen searched harder for Tomas' ring. It had to be in there, somewhere, it had to be! Tomas stepped to the sisters, placed his hand on Calico's lower back and whispered to them, "Ladies, everyone's waiting."

Calico leaned into his chest, looked up, and whispered, "She lost your ring and tried to give me her Claddagh."

"You what?" he growled in a low tone at Kathleen. Kathleen's heart jumped out of her chest. She breathed hard and fast with fright. "Why do you even have it? You should have left it back at the house. If anyone should suspect—"

"Lord Collins," Isaac Turner rose from the front row, lifting something in the air. Sunlight danced off the small object in his hand. Kathleen stared at the object between his fingers, trying to figure out what he was holding. She squinted her eyes, focusing more on his hand. A sliver of gold caught her attention. Could it be? How did he? Isaac stepped through the crowd. Men and women scooted out of the way so he could pass between them. He worked his way down the aisle, and walked towards them as he lowered his hand. Isaac bowed towards the sisters. "Ladies," he greeted them.

"Isaac," Tomas replied, stepping closer to him. Isaac lifted his eyes to Kathleen, extending his hand to her, "My lady, you seem to have dropped this. I did not realize it had escaped from your lovely bouquet. I have been so captivated by your beauty I seem to have forgotten time and place."

Kathleen exhaled a deep breath, glaring at Tomas. Isaac must have stolen the ring. There could be no other explanation. She had tied the ring to the ribbon in the middle of her bouquet and she had made certain it was tightly bound. When had he been so close to her that he could have taken it? Worse yet, if he took the ring then he knew she had a Claddagh! If he knew it was there, then he knew the truth. Her worst fears had come true. She had endangered her family by her own ignorance! Kathleen's heart

beat faster. She gasped for air, her lungs tightening. Her vision began to grow dark. She clutched her chest, gasping, leaning over.

"Kat," Calico said, embracing her sister around the waist.

"I...oh....," she glanced up at Calico, closed her eyes, and fell limp in her sister's arms.

"Kathleen," Calico yelled, lowering her sister to the floor. Isaac rose, clutching the ring, and yelled for the doctor. Tomas grabbed Kathleen's bouquet, took her ring, and put it inside his vest pocket. He glanced up at his wife while the crowd grew restless. "Kathleen, please, wake up," Calico cried, tapping her sister on the cheek.

Chapter 8

Kilmore Great House, Kilmore, Ireland

Warmth filled the room as Isaac sat next to the fireplace in his guest bedroom, studying Kathleen's still figure. He played with her bouquet, thinking how foolish he felt about her. He knew nothing about Kathleen other than she was the older sister of his friend's wife, a woman who wanted to kill him, barely spoke, and had the tendency to faint at weddings. He sighed, playing with the long lavender ribbon in her bouquet. He barely knew her yet he was more attracted to her than any other woman he had ever chased.

Kathleen moaned. He rose from the chair, put the bouquet down, and walked to her bed. Laughter and music drifted into the room through the half-opened door separating the bedroom from the hallway. He had preferred to keep the door closed for Kathleen's sake but didn't want to give anyone the impression he was less than a gentleman to her, so he ordered the door to remain partially opened. Isaac sat on the edge of the bed and watched her rouse from her sleep. She yawned, wiped her face with her hands, then slowly began to open her eyes.

Isaac's blurry image began to form in her mind as Kathleen opened her eyes. She closed them quickly then reopened them. This wasn't a dream. Her enemy was sitting on her bed in…where was she? She leaned up on her elbows, recognizing the tapestry on the wall across from the bed. "My room. I'm in my room," she whispered.

"Lady Kathleen?" Isaac questioned, thinking she was still in a daze. He reached for her hand. Kathleen pulled her hand away and sat upright. How dare this man try to touch her? "I will not hurt you."

Kathleen glared at him sharply. If looks could kill he would be dead all right. What spirit she had in her! He had loved that about her when she had tried to kill him. For years, he had been searching for a woman who was equal to him in intelligence and spirit. Perhaps in her he had found his match. "You are safe."

"Safe, huh," she retorted.

"Lady Kathleen, I assure you, no harm has come to you since you fainted."

"Where am I?" she asked, wanting him to think she was disoriented in her location.

"Kilmore Estate. It is my home. You are in one of my guest rooms. It used to belong to the eldest daughter of Chief McGillpatrick. The locals say she was very beautiful and quite charming. She was a master painter with a heart for her people."

"Was? What happened to her?"

"I do not know. She disappeared when my army evicted her family months ago. She, her sister, mother, and the rest of her family have not been seen since."

"Have you ever seen her?"

"Oh, no, Lady Kathleen, never. I didn't even know she existed. Alexander McGillpatrick kept his daughters secluded. Very few have ever laid eyes upon her or her sister."

"What were their names?"

"I do not know."

Kathleen nodded. She pushed the blanket aside and sat upright. Isaac gently slid his hand on top of hers. Her delicate, slender hand showed years of hardship. Most upper class women's hands were smooth and tender but Kathleen's hands were thick and hard. She had worked with her hands. He wondered if that was due to the lack of servants her parents had been able to acquire. If he were to wed her, she would have all the servants she ever needed. Kathleen deserved only the best.

She pulled her hand away from his and stood. "I thank you for your hospitality, sir. Yet I would like to know why you are in my room, and where is my sister?" she asked in a cold tone.

Isaac sighed. When was this woman ever going to allow him in her heart? "After you fainted, the physician and I escorted you here. I have the closest house to the church. Tomas and Calico finished the ceremony then came here with their guests to partake in the dinner feast I am hosting for them. Calico has been periodically leaving the feast to check on your condition. She will be most grateful to see her sister has fully recovered." He extended his arm to the door. "If you wish to attend the festivities you may. Head out the door and go straight until the hallway forks. Take a right; walk three doors down then the first door on your left will be the hall where the festivities are occurring. I can escort you, if you would like."

"No!"

Isaac cocked his head.

"I mean, no, thank you. You have been a gracious host for taking care of me. Thank you." She curtseyed then began walking towards the door.

What was it about this woman that made her loathe him so much? It wasn't like him to have to work so hard to get a woman he liked in bed with him. Ever since he had met Kathleen, he had tried to win her over. He would send her gowns, flowers, jewelry, and expensive perfumes. Never did she keep them. Tomas would always return them to him with a note from her saying while she appreciated the gifts she would not accept any tokens of his devotions to her. After a few weeks of her constant refusals, he persuaded Tomas to allow Kathleen to dine with him at lunch. Tomas had agreed. But at the meal, Kathleen was cold, silent, and indifferent towards him. He was about at his wits end with this woman. What normally worked didn't with her! He didn't know how to get her attention. If words wouldn't work then perhaps he would have to show her. He rose from the bed, ran to the door, and placed himself between her and the door. "Sir," she protested.

Isaac grabbed her head with both his hands and kissed her fully on the lips. Oh, those delicate lips tasted sweeter than honey. She was stiff and cold yet her lips told another story. There was warmth in her. Small as it may be, he would take what he could get from her. Kathleen pressed closer to him. She kissed him back, wrapping her arms around him. Her long, slender arms around his body felt so wonderful. Isaac moved his hands down her back. She was perfection, elegant perfection. His lips made their way down her long neck. He turned her and pushed her back against the door. Yes, she was finally responding! He was going to have what he wanted from her and there was nothing Tomas could do to stop them. He kissed her strong jawline and whispered in her ear, "I love you."

Kathleen opened her eyes and pushed him off of her. What was she doing? How could she deny him when he knew by her reaction she wanted to be with him? "Lady Kathleen, how have I offended you?" Isaac asked, straightening his clothes.

"How? Huh…how have you…huh…if you don't know the answer to that, sir, then perhaps you should pray upon it," Kathleen yelled, opened the door, and slammed it closed behind her.

Pray about? Was that the best insult she had for him? Kathleen had more self-control and discipline than he had believed was inside her. She wasn't some weak, shy woman. She was a goddess. His goddess. There was no other man in this world who deserved her more than he did. Isaac tugged on his coat then walked out the door. He walked down the hall, turned to the right, and then left into the hall. Musicians played loudly as the floor was crowded with dancers. People laughed and enjoyed the conversations with their friends and family. It was a crowded, joyous affair. He watched his guests amuse themselves, scanning for any sign of Kathleen. He paused, glancing across the hall as Calico hugged her sister. Tomas ordered a plate of food and whiskey for his sister-in-law. Isaac grinned. Maybe if Kathleen was drunk he could bed her. But what was the fun in that? It would be like sleeping with one of the many whores he owned. Kathleen was not a whore. He couldn't treat her like that. Maybe a dance. Yes, dancing. Now there was an excellent idea. He would woo her with dancing.

Isaac walked through the crowd to the bridal table. "Ah, Isaac," Tomas grinned, holding up a glass of Irish whiskey.

"Congratulations," Isaac bowed to Tomas and Calico then rose, glaring at Kathleen. "I was wondering if I might have your permission to dance with Lady Kathleen."

Kathleen bore her eyes upon Tomas and Calico, shaking her head.

"But of course."

"Tomas," Kathleen protested.

Tomas turned his attention to her. "It would do you some good to move around a bit. If it would help, Calico and I can join you two on the dance floor."

"N…"

"That would be lovely," Calico interrupted.

Kathleen leaned over and whispered in Calico's ear, "I hate you. I really hate you at this moment."

Her sister learned over and whispered out of view of Isaac. "Remember what Tomas told you. In public we are cordial to him so he does not grow suspicious."

"Suspicious? He kissed me and had his hand on my bottom while we were in the bedroom. Tomas trusted him to care for me and he tried to take advantage of me."

Calico exchanged glances with her. "He did what?"

"I know you heard me. If Sherlock were here he would have punched Isaac for his actions against me. Yet you and Tomas want me to dance with him?"

"Lady Kathleen," Isaac offered his hand in her direction. Kathleen looked at it, unsure of what she was going to do. To accept his offer was only proper. She hoped Tomas would put an end to this little charade. Yet she couldn't deny that she had felt something for Isaac. There was something about this man that made her feel as if she was the only woman in the world. Calico leaned over and whispered into her husband's ear. Tomas glanced several times in Kathleen's direction. He held his wife's hand and squeezed. Kathleen could tell Calico was telling her husband everything. Tomas' death grip was a sign he had wanted to protect her but couldn't. There were too many people around and if he reacted he would place everyone in danger. Tomas rose from his chair, lowered his glass, and addressed Isaac. Here it was. It was coming. Kathleen smiled to herself, waiting for her older brother-in-law to defend her honor.

"Lord Isaac Turner, my wife and I thank you for your hospitality. You have been a most kind and gracious host. Yet due to the circumstances surrounding Kathleen's health I think it is for the best if my wife and I accompany her back to our estate."

Kathleen couldn't believe her ears. Tomas didn't yell at him or do something to defend her honor? At least bring the matter to Isaac's attention. If Isaac knew Tomas had learned of what transpired in the bedroom then perhaps that would stop him from pursuing her.

"Of course, good night," Isaac replied, bowing. He turned and left them.

Tomas led Calico beside her and whispered in her direction, "Are you alright?"

"Yes. I...I just want to go home, Tomas."

He extended his hand. Kathleen placed her tender hand into his larger one. She rose from the chair, asking, "Are you upset with me?"

"No, why."

"We're leaving the party early."

"Kathleen, this ceremony means nothing to Calico and me. We won't even share a bed until we are truly married in the old ways. This is all just pretend to appease the Anglicans. The real wedding takes place on Wednesday."

"The best day of all to marry?"

"Yes. Now let's go home. I'll ask my mother to make you something for dinner."

Kathleen smiled, "I would like that. Thank you."

"You're welcome."

They walked through the crowd and into the hallway. The long hallway seemed to go on forever. Kathleen studied the familiar tapestries and paintings that hung on what was once her family's estate as they walked to the front door. They exited the large house and walked down the stone path towards the stable. "You know what the scariest moment was at your wedding?"

The couple stopped and turned to her. "No, what?" Calico asked.

Kathleen shook her head with a nervous laugh. "When I woke up and saw Isaac over me the first thought that came to my mind was that he had kidnapped me so I would become his wife. Just like the old tales when two lovers want to marry but the parents won't allow it so the groom kidnaps his beloved in the middle of the night. They run off together and marry."

Tomas asked with a serious tone, "Do you have feelings for him?"

"No! Oh, God no."

Calico smiled, "You're lying."

She turned her head to her sister. "I am not!"

"You always get defensive when you don't want to admit the truth, especially one that you know father would disapprove of."

Kathleen opened her mouth to speak then closed it. She couldn't refute that. Calico spoke with truth. "Kat," Tomas said. She looked at him. "If you have feelings for Isaac, you could use those feelings to draw close to him. Just because you refused the proposal Bailey, your father, and I asked of you doesn't mean the matter has been forgotten."

"Sherlock…"

"Can be naive and idealistic." He grabbed her by the shoulders. "Look, I know why you said no that day."

"You do?"

"Yes, you were scared. I saw it in your eyes, as did your father. You let that fear dictate what actions you would take. When Sherlock woke and you told him what happened, which I have no doubt you did because of the way he is reacting towards his brother, he wanted to protect you. So he told you a lie."

"He said Bailey is dangerous."

"This war is dangerous, not Bailey. Bailey is trying to protect all of us. Do I agree with everything he has done? No. Does that mean I will abandon him? Never. If you don't want to marry Isaac because you are scared of what he might do to you if he learns the truth, then that is okay."

"Do you approve?"

"No. I think you are being stubborn and self-centered. You are only thinking about what could happen to you instead of the many people you will be able to save by developing a relationship with him and turning his information against him. All in all it's your life and your decision. I don't have to agree with you but I will always honor your decisions and protect you." Tomas kissed her on the forehead, turned, and walked towards the stables with Calico. Kathleen watched them disappear down the road towards the outer stone gate.

She turned to face the Great House. Somewhere in there, Isaac had stolen the key to her heart and she hated him for it. Kathleen walked down the road to the wagon that awaited her outside the stable. She climbed on the bench next to Calico. Tomas slapped the reigns. The wagon rolled out of the gate. Kathleen leaned into Calico's side. Calico shared her cloak with her and embraced her older sister. "I love you," Calico whispered. Kathleen closed her eyes and snuggled closer.

"Hmm, I owe you."

"Yes, yes you do."

Kathleen looked up at her sister. Calico laughed and gently pushed her. "Not funny," Kathleen smiled.

Chapter 9

Collins Great House, Collinsworth, Ireland.

Sherlock sat at the kitchen table with a pounding headache, staring at his dinner plate. He picked at the roasted duck with his fork and leaned his head on his left hand. His stomach turned at the smell of the food. He peered towards the back door. The moon had begun to rise as the sun descended over the horizon. Kathleen, Calico, and Tomas had been gone almost an entire day. He lowered his fork, rose from the wooden table, and walked to the door. The top half stood open while the bottom half was closed. He watched the house servants gather the laundry from the line while others began to feed the horses. Sherlock leaned over the door and peered towards the stone road. What time had Tomas said they would return? The longer Kathleen was away from him, the more he grew concerned for her safety.

Despite his warning, Kathleen had been placed in a rough situation. A few days after he arose from his sleep, Kathleen had begun to receive gifts from Isaac. Alexander, Tomas, and Bailey had been overjoyed. Isaac still had eyes on her. But Sherlock had warned her that to accept the gifts would be a mistake. She would do better to claim she was in mourning and return them. His wonderful little sister took his advice. She returned the first gift but Isaac was relentless. The gifts kept coming and grew larger each time she denied him. Then a month passed and Isaac didn't send her anything, not even a correspondence. They had been able to relax, thinking Isaac had forgotten her. Then the unimaginable happened. Last week, Isaac had come to the estate asking Tomas if he would grant him lunch with Kathleen. All Tomas had to do was tell his friend that Kathleen was still in mourning, but no, he did the opposite. He granted Isaac permission and forced Kathleen to dine with the English Earl. No matter what he could say or do to try to convince Tomas it was a fool's errand to allow it; Tomas wouldn't listen.

Sherlock turned at hearing the sound of a woman's heel. Mary clutched her stomach, approaching him. "Mary?" Sherlock asked walking towards her.

She cringed, holding her stomach harder. Sherlock guided his wife onto the bench and sat beside her. She looked at his plate of food then back to him. "You still have not eaten," she said.

"My mind's too preoccupied to worry about food. What are you doing up?"

"I was hungry again."

Sherlock passed his plate towards her. "You can have it."

"Are you certain? You should eat something."

"I'm certain."

"Thank you." Mary said then began to eat his roasted duck, potatoes, and vegetables. Sherlock watched his wife in bewilderment as she ate. The seven weeks since he had awakened from his sleep had been the most wonderful time he had in marriage for years. It was almost as if they were newlyweds all over again. The two of them had rarely left their bed except to eat, relieve themselves, or if they were feeling ill. Sherlock glanced at his wife's chest. Mary's clothes had begun to become tighter in the last week. His poor wife had been suffering from exhaustion, nausea, and headaches for weeks, along with an increase in appetite. This morning she had begun to complain of heartburn and indigestion. He had wanted to call the physician but Mary wouldn't have it.

"Sherlock," Mary said, wiping her mouth with her sleeve.

Sherlock rubbed her back and nodded to her.

"I think…I mean…Well, I haven't told anyone because I'm not certain. It's too soon to tell but the signs are all there."

"Mary, what is it?"

Mary pushed the plate away and turned to her husband. "I don't know if I should tell you yet."

"Why? We don't keep secrets from each other."

"Because it changes everything for us."

"Mary, I don't understand."

"Are you happy with your life in the rebellion?"

Sherlock took his wife's hand. "Why are you asking that?" he asked defensively.

"Are you?"

Silence fell between husband and wife as Sherlock thought about her question. Was he content with the life he had chosen for himself? To be honest, he would have never chosen to be a rebel leader. He had followed Bailey's desire for him to join the rebellion six years ago as a broken man. While Bailey harbored a deep resentment and bitterness from the loss of his own family, Sherlock harbored defeat and hopelessness from his own struggles. His life since the death of his six children had been a vicious cycle of heartache he couldn't always control. Was he happy without his children? No. Was he happy with the dashed hope at the death of their unborn child four years ago? No. Was he happy that his wife was miserable and couldn't conceive? No.

"It's the only thing that takes my mind off the pain," Sherlock admitted.

"Bailey uses that pain against you. You know he does. When James Turner captured me four years ago, you said Bailey hadn't wanted to rescue me because you had a wife and I was four months pregnant. Our lives were turning for the better and he wanted you to feel the pain he bears in his heart."

"I did feel that pain, Mary. I almost lost you and you lost the child because James Turner threw you down the stairs into your cell. When I finally got you back you had sunk into a great depression again. I was full of anger and said things to him that should have never come out of my mouth. He didn't care, Mary. It took me a year to break you out of that depression."

"Sherlock, why are you still leading this rebellion alongside Bailey and Tomas when you know what kind of men they are?"

"I don't do it for us anymore."

"Then why?"

"I don't want our sisters involved with Bailey. They shouldn't have to live a life of heartache and disappointments."

"Calico sides with Bailey. She won't listen to you."

"She never has. Calico takes after my father but Kathleen is much like your mother. In a way she reminds me of you, before the famine. Young, naïve, and intelligent."

Mary smiled. She removed her hand from Sherlock's, rose from the bench, and ran to the chamber pot by the door. Mary knelt in front of it and vomited. Sherlock sighed. When was Mary's illness going to end? Hadn't his poor wife been through too much already? He began to rise from the table and stumbled as a wave of dizziness overcame him. His head throbbed. Sherlock fell back onto the bench. He closed his eyes, trying to regain his control. The intensity of his headache grew with each sound and smell. Oh, he was so tired of these annoying headaches. He jumped at feeling a hand on his back.

"Shh, it's just me," Mary said, rubbing her hand along her husband's spine. "Lay your head on the table." Sherlock complied. He relaxed as she began to massage his shoulders. She pushed aside his shoulder-length brown hair and rubbed the back of his neck. "I'm worried about you."

"Don't be. It's just a headache."

"These are not just headaches, Sherlock. You barely eat and sleep—"

"We've been a bit too preoccupied for me to eat and sleep as much as I should."

Mary grinned. "Well I can't argue with you on that point." She leaned over and whispered in his ear. "You are an amazing lover and husband, Sherlock."

"Hmm, glad you have enjoyed it." Mary kissed him then leaned back and silently massaged her husband's shoulders. "What are you keeping from me?" he asked after a long moment.

"Keeping from you?" she tried to deflect his inquiry.

"You said you hadn't told anyone what you wanted to tell me and weren't certain if you wanted to tell me at all. Does it have to do with the rebellion?"

"It might."

Sherlock sat up and turned to face her. He scrunched his eyes, trying to focus on the blurry image of his wife. "Hmm," he groaned, leaning over his lap.

Mary knelt before him, grabbed his hands, and studied him. "Perhaps we should continue this discussion at another time. You require rest."

"No. I'm tired of resting. I'm just nauseated and have a headache. It will pass."

"Don't lie to me. I saw you stumble, and don't pretend your eyes aren't bothering you. You're dizzy too, aren't you?"

Sherlock rubbed his hands over his face then sat upright. "It will pass."

"Huh, are all you McGillpatrick men stubborn and foolish?"

Sherlock grinned, grabbed her by the waist, and pulled her onto his lap. "Why Mary McGillpatrick, I thought you liked that about me." She wrapped her arms around his neck and stared into his deep brownish-green eyes. The feel of his hand on her bottom tickled her insides. She caressed the side of his short beard and leaned her lips towards his mouth. They shared a long, deep kiss. Oh, this man. All he had to do was look at her and he stirred her heart. She had been more fortunate than her sister when it came to their marriages to the McGillpatrick brothers. Her older sister, Anne, had never fallen in love with Bailey. Quite the opposite. She had hated her husband, and the more Bailey had beaten her into submission the more Anne hated him. But there was nothing Anne could do. They were devout Catholics. Divorce was a sin so Anne had to remain married to Bailey. Mary, on the other hand, had fallen in love with Sherlock the moment she had met him on their wedding day. Sherlock had been smitten as well. Lust had turned into love quickly between them.

Sherlock lowered Mary to the bench and lowered his pants. "What if someone sees us?" she asked, lifting the skirt of her gown, petticoat, and shift.

"You're my wife. Who can object to that?" he said, crawling on top of her. Mary opened her legs, embraced him, and kissed him deeply as he pushed into her. Her hand slid down his lower back to his round, well-formed bottom. God, how she loved his body! The rebellion had transformed her farmer into a well-toned soldier. At least something good came out of his six years of leading raids against the English. Mary moaned as he pushed deeper inside her. Sweat lubricated their bodies as the bench scraped against the floor beneath them. Sweet pain rolled through her body as he suckled on her sensitive breasts. She groaned, clawing at his back. The waves of delight made her want more despite the protest of her breasts.

"Ooh," she groaned, pushing him upright. Sherlock rotated his leg to the front and leaned against the table as Mary straddled her husband. "Oh, God, yes, Mary," Sherlock cried out, arching his head back and pulling her body closer to his. She pressed his face into the crevice of her breasts, rocking her hips as he played with her bottom.

Mary closed her eyes, allowing their passion to overtake her. Sherlock moved his hand along her back and caressed her lower stomach with his other one. She bit her lower lip as his fingers moved down to her clit. The sharp wave of familiar delight erupted through her. She thrust harder, moaning louder with each flick of his finger. She cried out his name several times as the waves grew stronger within her until she could no longer control herself. "Ah, Sherlock," she yelled. Sherlock pushed his wife to the floor and thrust deeper inside her. They screamed as they erupted together.

Sherlock rolled off Mary's body exhausted. He closed his eyes as she stared up at the ceiling, holding his hand. Mary turned to her left side and snuggled next to him. She rubbed her hand on top of his bare chest. When had she removed his shirt? "You alright?" she asked, playing with the hairs on his chest.

"I am. Mary?"

"Hm?"

He turned his head towards her and opened his eyes. "I like this."

Mary chuckled. "You have never complained when laying your seed in me before. Why wouldn't you like it?"

"No, not that. This."

"Sherlock, I don't understand."

"It's been four years since you have carried my child. I know since you lost our baby that life has been hard on you."

"Life was hard on me before that. All of our children died in famine. The oldest was only ten and the youngest not three months yet. Six children, Sherlock. Six!"

"I know. It tore at me too."

"Then when we do conceive again I lose the child when I was thrown down the stairs. I don't blame James Turner for that. I blame your brother! You were on patrol that day, not Bailey! Bailey promised to protect me but where was he? Nowhere, Sherlock. He let James Turner kidnap me. He let the child I carried die within in me. He let me have those injuries, and he would have let me be sold into slavery had your father not done something about it. God forbid I let him touch this child!"

"This child?" Sherlock asked, lowering his hand. He stared at Mary's stomach then back to his wife. "Mary?"

"You said before you were captured you wanted to rebuild your family. I was ready for it too."

Sherlock rose on his elbow. "Are you?"

Mary nodded. "I think I am."

"You think?"

"Well I can't be certain, yet. I did not bleed this month and I am too young to stop my bleeding. My mother is fifty-five years old and she stopped bleeding last year. The change comes late to women in my family. I'm thirty-six years old, much too young for the change to happen. Besides, mother was my age when she had Kathleen. I won't be certain until I start showing. I'm a small woman so it won't be long before I do."

Sherlock leaned back on his elbows, stunned by the news. "We had been trying for months before I was captured. You never conceived."

"I was never easy to conceive. It took three years after our wedding night for me to carry our first child, while Bailey and Anne already had two."

"I should have known something was going on with you. You were always more receptive to my advances when you were with child than naught. How long until the baby comes?"

"I don't know, Sherlock. Eight maybe seven months?" She moved her hand down his chest and bore her gaze into his eyes. "You said that when the time came you would protect our unborn child and me someplace where we would not be in danger. You had a plan. What is it?"

"I was going to buy land close to New Orleans."

"French Louisiana?"

"I met a Frenchman in Dublin whose family owned land in New France. His parents had died and he had inherited twenty acres of mostly unusable land, a few servants, and some tenant farmers. He told me although he had grown up in New France he didn't want to live his entire life there. He had spent most of his life on the seas and was looking to start his own trading company. We talked for quite a while and formed a friendship. He was intrigued with my story and then the idea formed in his head."

"He offered you his estate?" she asked quietly, not certain she believed her own words.

"Yes. He said since I was an Irish noble and the eldest son I would have the education and expertise to lord over his estate. He had some slaves and asked if that would bother me, seeing as the Irish were being sold into servitude. I told him it wouldn't. The offer would grant us the freedom and lifestyle we were accustomed to."

"At what cost? We don't have the funds required to operate an estate let alone a small farm."

"I told him such. He told me the only expense I would incur was the transportation of my family to his home. If I could afford the journey then he would give me everything upon my arrival."

"Then let's do that. Let's leave this place and start our lives over in the New World."

"I can't."

"Is it too expensive?"

"No, I have the funds for the trip."

"Then why don't you want to take him up on his offer? Sherlock, I don't want to bury another child. Do you?"

"No, Mary. But now we have Kathleen to think about. Bailey is trying to use her and we promised we would try to protect her from Bailey."

"We'll take her with us."

"It's not that simple. Our situation has become more complex now that Kathleen has won Isaac's attentions."

"Or has become more complex because Tomas wouldn't support you when it came to that very situation?"

Sherlock huffed, rising from the floor. He grabbed his shirt and put it over his naked body then walked to his pants. "Leave it alone, Mary," he said as she began to speak.

"No, I will not leave it alone," she protested, rising from the floor and straightening her clothes. "You don't trust Tomas, do you?"

Sherlock turned in her direction, picking up his coat from the floor. "He is my friend."

"Liar. He's Bailey's best friend, which makes him a threat to you and your family."

"I am trying the best that I can to protect you!"

"You're trying the best you can not to stir the pot because you're so scared of Bailey you won't do anything to turn against him. Sherlock, you're the elder brother! That's why you carry your grandfather's name, not Bailey. You have always acted like the youngest. When are you going to stop being so scared of Bailey and act like the man you really are, the heir of Kilmore!"

"I'm the heir of nothing. Haven't you heard, Mary, it's illegal to be Irish in Ireland?" He huffed, walking to the table. A sharp stabbing pain erupted from his forehead. He paused in step, stared at his wife, and fell forward. Mary grabbed her husband by the arms and lowered him gently into a wooden chair by the fireplace. "Hmm," he moaned, grabbing his head and leaning over his legs.

"Sherlock," she said, kneeling in front of him.

"It's nothing."

"Will you please stop lying to me tonight?"

"Alright it's something."

"Thank you. How bad is it?"

"Ugh, it feels like my brain wants to come out of my skull. Hmm, Mary, it hurts more than I think I can bear."

"I'll get the doctor," she said, rising. Sherlock grabbed her by the wrist and pulled her towards him.

"No, I cannot appear to be a weakling. Bailey will kill me. He'll do it in a way father won't suspect he is the culprit. Besides, I want to make certain Kathleen is safe. You were right, Mary, I don't trust Tomas. Sit with me until the pain passes." Mary knelt beside her husband. He smiled in her direction and leaned back in the chair with his eyes closed. "You don't trust Tomas either, do you?"

"Kathleen isn't the only one who is questioning Tomas' role in the attack on Kilmore. I suspect you have wondered if his friendship with Isaac is more important than his loyalty to your family."

"I have. Nothing makes sense. Kilmore isn't a large estate and for years the Irish Parliament did nothing to relinquish my father's control. We had been secretly importing supplies for the rebellion from other European Catholics. Our men had been in position under Tomas' leadership to attack Isaac Turner's estate at Grange, but somehow Isaac learned of our attack and brought an army to our door instead."

"You think Tomas informed Isaac of our plans? Why would he do that, Sherlock? His family has been close friends with yours since before the English came to our shores."

"I don't know, Mary. Tomas is Bailey's best friend. That is the only reason I haven't brought up my suspicions to father."

"If Tomas has betrayed your family then why wouldn't he slip the information to Isaac that you and your brother are here? When Isaac grew suspicious of Tomas, Tomas denied all allegations."

"To save his own life? It's hard to go from riches to living in destitution as a tenant farmer. Kathleen was fortunate. She spent more of her life as the daughter of a farmer than as a girl from the upper class. Mary, you and I weren't so fortunate. We know what it is like to have servants, abundance of food, shelter, and the finer things of life. Don't you recall how hard it was for us to adjust?"

"But we did."

"Yes, but I don't believe Tomas would ever be able to do that. I don't think he converted to aide the rebellion. I think his motivation was more selfish than that. He converted so he wouldn't lose the life he grew up with. How many times have you seen him help his parents on the farm?"

"He has an image to maintain as the lord of a great house."

"Tomas won't even collect the taxes himself when it comes time. He sends a tax collector so he won't have to face the poverty he placed his own family in."

"Aren't all of his servants his family members?"

"A majority of them are. Mary, what makes Tomas and Bailey best friends is that they are so alike. I hate that Calico is going to marry him in three days. She already became involved with his and Bailey's ploys. Father allows it. But now he, Bailey, and father are trying to get Kathleen involved and there's nothing I can do to stop it." He groaned, holding his hand to his forehead. Sherlock leaned over, rubbing his forehead. A stabbing, nauseating pain spread from the side of his head to his forehead. Mary gently rubbed his back.

"Let's go to bed," she coaxed him.

"No, I have to know she's safe."

"Sherlock, please. I can ask mother to inform us when they arrive."

The sound of a wagon approaching the house startled them. Mary and Sherlock sat up. He rose from the chair, ran to the door, and watched Tomas halt the horses. He opened the lower portion of the door and motioned for Mary to join him. Mary grabbed her husband's hand. The couple walked outside as Calico and Kathleen descended from the wagon. A wave of relief swept through him. He walked quickly to his sisters, greeted them, then approached Tomas as he handed the reins to a servant.

"I take it everything went well?" Sherlock asked while Mary conversed with Kathleen and Calico.

"Everything is fine," Tomas answered while walking around the wagon. "Kathleen fainted at the wedding. Isaac offered for her rest in his guest bedroom and he watched over her as Calico and I finished the wedding. She slept through most of the feast. When she awoke, Isaac was by her side and he kissed her," Tomas grinned, glancing at Kathleen.

Confused and frustrated, Sherlock grabbed his friend by his coat and jerked him towards him. "I'm a little confused here, Tom. Are you saying you allowed that God-forsaken, English abomination to touch my wife's and my sister?"

"On the contrary, Kathleen refused his advances. He kissed her. She said he touched her bottom."

"He what?!"

"She ran away and ended up at the feast. Isaac chased after her and sought her hand for a dance. I thought it was a wonderful idea but I didn't know what had transpired between them at the time. Calico whispered to me what had happened. I could tell Kathleen was upset so we came home."

Sherlock glared at the shorter, more slender man. He knew something like this would happen under Tomas' care. Tomas, despite all his charm and wit, cared nothing for his family. Worst of all, Alexander was allowing everything to happen to Kathleen. His father claimed to love his daughters, yet where was he while Tomas played with Kathleen's life? Seemed to him, he was the only man who cared about Kathleen. Sherlock heaved, as his headache grew worse. The world around him began to blur. He moaned, taking a step back, loosening his grip on Tomas. He could hear voices but couldn't understand what they were saying. Sherlock grabbed both sides of his head and leaned over. Lightheaded and dizzy, he began to fall backward. He could hear the women yell his name. Someone lowered him to the ground. He lifted his eyes. Tomas stood over him, saying something. He scrunched his eyes, trying to make out Tomas' words. But it was no use. The pain grew so strong he wanted to vomit. He screamed, thrashing his body. Oh, God, the pain. Never had he felt so much pain.

"Kathleen, get your father," Tomas ordered.

Mary ran to her husband's side as Kathleen disappeared into the house.

"Sherlock," she cried, kneeling beside him. Sherlock rolled back and forth in agonizing pain, pleading for help. Tomas knelt on the other side of his friend.

He pulled a sack of money from inside his coat and handed it Calico, ordering her as he tried to hold Sherlock still. "You remember the priest who agreed to marry us?"

"Yes."

"His brother is the physician who is helping Bailey. They live in the next town over in the same house next to the stables. Bring the doctor, Hurry!"

"I'll be noticed. I'm still in my wedding dress."

"I'll go," Mary answered, sobbing, taking the bag of coins.

"Mary?" Calico asked her.

"I can't... I can't bear to see my husband in that much pain. The longer we wait for the doctor the more he suffers. Please, I will go."

"You will need this," Tomas said, removing a simple wooden crucifix from beneath his shirt. He handed it to Mary. "The priest will not recognize you. You will need to give him this. He will know I sent you."

Mary kissed Sherlock, ran to the stable, grabbed a horse, and took off towards the west.

Chapter 10

September 24, 1738

The music from the bagpipes floated over the congregation inside the Great Hall. Sherlock stood at the front of the long aisle with Mary beside him, staring at the crowded hall. Family and friends from both Calico and Tomas' families sat on the wooden pews waiting for the ceremony to begin. It was rare to see all his parents' kinsmen in one place. His aunts, uncles, cousins, and distant relatives had secretly been pouring into Collinsworth since last week. The first to arrive was his mother's eldest sister soon after the physician had arrived to treat him. He had been grateful his aunt had been there. Calico had told him Mary had been an emotional wreck while he slept in his bed for four days. His aunt had noticed his wife was ill and distraught. Between Jane and his aunt they had been able to convince Mary to rest. He only wished he could have convinced his wife to have stayed in bed today. Mary's condition had grown worse since last week. Instead of nausea and headaches alone being her ailments, she had also begun to complain of bouts of dizziness and she was more exhausted than usual. She had slowly slipped into a wild range of emotions. One moment she was happy and the next she was angry or crying. He never knew what state he would find her in and had begun to insist Mary stay in their bedroom. Yet Mary hadn't wanted to miss Tomas and Calico's wedding out of the loyalty they had to their family, and because they didn't want the family to know she was with child. It was best to keep that little secret between the two of them.

Mary clutched the inside of Sherlock's arm. He glanced to his right. "Mary?" he asked.

Mary held her hand to her stomach. "My stomach. Your child is making it very difficult not to cause a scene. Must be the McGillpatrick in him," she whispered to him.

"How do you know it's a boy?"

"Because none of our daughters ever gave me this much trouble. I remember when I carried our son. He was worse on me than our five daughters ever were." He lowered his arm, grabbed her hand, and began to walk towards the back of the room. "Where are we going?"

"You are going back to bed."

"Sherlock, please, I don't want to miss our sister's wedding."

He stepped in front of her with a serious look. "Mary, you were present at their handfasting ceremony a year and a week ago."

"So?"

"You were already at their wedding. This is just a formality. They have to approach the priest and when the priest asks if they object to the union, which you know they will not, then he will officially marry them. They've been living together for a year and a week. There's nothing more for them to do than make themselves husband and wife before God tonight after taking their vows."

"I want to see them take their vows."

Sherlock grabbed her by the shoulders. "Mary, I can see it in your eyes that all you want to do is sleep. You shouldn't place too much pressure on your body. We promised each other we would not allow the family to know about your delicate condition so Bailey won't learn the truth."

"This ruse will only last a few more weeks at the most. I'm already gaining weight and my breasts are getting larger. My mother has already begun to notice the changes. She confronted me this morning about them."

"What did you tell her?"

"I was eating more because of the stress of my husband's condition."

"Did she believe you?"

"She said I need to go on a diet."

"You don't think she told my father about it, do you?"

"As if your father would listen to a woman's ramblings about weight. You men never pay attention to the things of a woman unless you are trying to lay your seed in us."

Sherlock smiled. "Yes, well, there is that."

Mary returned his smile. She dropped her smile and placed her hand on her stomach. "Ugh, Sherlock, I don't feel well but if we leave people will take notice."

"It won't matter. My family knows you have been ill. We'll just say it was too early for you to leave your room."

Mary embraced her husband and closed her eyes as she listened to his strong heartbeat. "Carry me," she whispered, holding onto his coat. Sherlock scooped his wife up in his arms as she wrapped her arms around his thick neck. He walked past the rest of the wedding party to the back door. Calico stood outside in the hallway in a beautiful light blue wedding gown that highlighted the curves of her body. Jane closed the door behind them. He stopped before the women. "I must apologize to you, Calico. Mary and I had hoped to participate in your wedding but she is still frail with ailment."

"I understand. Will you be returning to see the ceremony?"

"No, I want to stay with her."

"I can do that, Sherlock," silver-haired Jane said, walking towards the couple. Jane stroked the side of her daughter's cheek.

She lowered her hand as Sherlock answered his mother-in-law, "No, I'm certain you would want to see your daughter married. You were there when Bailey and I married your daughters. You should be there when Calico marries."

"Of course I want to be with her but if my daughter is ill…"

"Mother, have you ever been disappointed in the care I have provided for your daughter?"

"No, you are a better husband to her than Bailey ever was to my other daughter. Go," Jane ordered. Sherlock nodded then walked quickly towards their bedroom.

Chapter 11

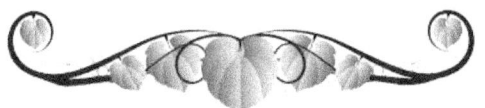

Bailey leaned on his crutches as he stood upon the raised platform watching Calico and Tomas partake of their first Holy Communion together as a couple. It was bittersweet to be watching his best friend marry his little sister, let alone participate in the wedding. Unlike Kathleen, Calico was an obedient sister. She had fooled all the Anglicans into thinking she was one of them. They loved her almost as much as her own people did. He had been preparing himself for a little over a year for this momentous occasion. It was hard to be happy for the joyous union when your own heart missed the woman you loved. Every act from the handfasting to today's ceremony brought back vivid memories of his own wedding on April 7, 1716. It had been a dual wedding within the Catholic Church during a time when his people could freely worship without the threat of the Anglicans destroying their very lives for doing so. The Anglicans had killed his wife and children four years ago. Each day without them was harder than the last. Alexander had told him it would get easier with time. Bailey had trusted his father's wisdom. His father had found happiness after years of mourning. Yet Bailey knew he wouldn't ever remarry as long as Isaac Turner was alive. No, he wasn't going to allow the threat of that egotistical, self-centered Anglican to ever lay a hand on a woman he loved. If he was ever going to find happiness again, he was going to destroy the Turner line and he was going to use his family to help him whether they liked it or not. They owed him that much.

"Amen," Calico and Tomas said in unison then rose.

Bailey shifted weight on his crutches. His broken lower leg throbbed. All of Bailey's broken bones, sprains, and bruises had healed completely over the past eight weeks except for his leg. The doctor had reassured him his leg would heal soon enough if he took it easy, but Bailey was too impatient. As soon as he was able to withstand the pain he began to direct the rebel activity from his bed. He couldn't sit around while Anglicans still controlled his ancestral home. Tomas glanced at his friend, asking, "Do you need to sit down?"

"No, finish the ceremony then I will sit."

Tomas nodded and returned his attention to the priest. This was no time for delay. Tomas was a popular man among the Anglicans. He was not only a landowner but was also one of the county judges. Alexander had been a county judge and eventually worked his way up into Parliament. Bailey was hoping Tomas would do the same. If he served in Parliament then they would have a Catholic in disguise at the very seat of Irish power. They couldn't risk the Anglicans learning of Tomas' ruse. Of course there were other landowners who had converted from Catholic to Anglican and still secretly held Catholic mass in their homes, but Bailey didn't like that Tomas had joined them. Kilmore was too close and Isaac valued Tomas' friendship. Who was to say Isaac wouldn't show up someday while they were in mass and learn the truth?

The priest raised a shawl over their hands and proclaimed, "Let it be known Earl Tomas Patrick Collins and Lady Calico Jane McGillpatrick faithfully bound their lives in unison one year and one week ago. Whereupon Calico and her parents, in accordance with our traditions, relocated to Collinsworth, whereupon Tomas and Calico have shared their lives and not their bodies. I ask them today," he looked down at the couple, "Do you Earl Tomas Patrick Collins find Lady Calico Jane McGillpatrick a good and suitable woman to be your mate?"

Tomas looked into Calico's eyes and replied, grinning. "I do and I want it to be official."

Calico smiled. She kept her gaze on Tomas' eyes as the priest asked, "And do you Lady Calico Jane McGillpatrick find this man a strong provider and suitable husband?"

"I do and I want it to be official."

The priest peered over the couple, "Does anyone here have reason these two should not commit to the fulfillment of their union?"

A long moment of tension and silence filled the small hall. Bailey peered across the couple into the mixed crowd of family, friends, and rebels. He knew both of them had been faithful to each other. The love between the two was almost too disgustingly cute. He suspected it wouldn't be too long before Calico carried Tomas' child. He turned his eyes towards his left. Kathleen fidgeted with her bouquet of white roses. "Kat," he whispered to her. Kathleen turned her head to face her older brother. "Have something to say and I'll make sure you'll regret it," he threatened under his breath.

Kathleen opened her mouth to speak. He glared at her with a low growl. Although Kathleen had welcomed her sister's happiness, she still had her doubts whether Calico was marrying Tomas out of love or because Bailey had ordered Tomas to marry her. His little sister wasn't shy about expressing her feelings to Calico or Sherlock, yet little did she know Calico told him everything. He knew the sister by his side was against his ploys. She had been spending a lot of time with Sherlock and Mary since Sherlock woke from his slumber, and he greatly disapproved of it. Sherlock and he had once been the closest of friends. All of that changed when Sherlock's wife had been captured by James Turner and Bailey had refused to rescue his sister-in-law. Why should he rescue his brother's wife? If Sherlock had wanted to rescue Mary then he should have gathered an army to barge into Kilmore and do so. But his brother had other plans. His brother had wanted him to risk his own life for her. It was his head the Turners wanted after all, not Sherlock's.

Bailey glared at Kathleen with stronger determination. What was it with his brother and sister not complying with his desires?! Kathleen closed her mouth and turned forward. "Good girl," he smirked then looked forward.

The priest opened the bible and began by delivering a sermon about love. He reminded the young couple the vows they were to take today were meant until death. There was no divorce. He explained the biblical role of husband and wife. Tomas and Calico publically announced they would comply with the scriptures. The hour and a half wedding ceremony seemed to move quickly. Thankfully. The more time that passed the more nervous he had become. Even before the wedding had commenced, Bailey had made certain uninvited guests would not disturb them. He had ordered guards to be posted on all sides of the estate for security. His rebels had been causing trouble for many Anglican tenants and landowners alike. He had even staged trouble for Tomas by setting his barn on fire so his "friends" would not grow suspicious about him.

Calico and Tomas turned to face the crowd. "Ladies and Gentlemen, I introduce Earl and Countess Tomas Patrick Collins," the priest proclaimed to the crowd. The crowd cheered loudly. Bailey stepped down from the platform. "Now don't all you women who wanted Tomas for yourselves be thinking of ruining their luck by kissing the bride before a man does. I am taking care of that!" Bailey proclaimed beside Calico. The crowd laughed. Bailey kissed Calico on the side of the cheek. "Congratulations," he mumbled.

"Thank you, Bailey," she replied.

The back door suddenly opened. The crowd grew silent, turning their heads to the intruder. A teenaged brunette boy entered the hall with his rifle. He ran up the aisle quickly, bowed to Bailey, then proclaimed, "Sir, a rider's coming up the road. Looks to be Earl Isaac Turner. He has a few men with him."

Alexander rose from the front pew. "How many is a few?" he asked.

"It's a posse of ten, Lord McGillpatrick."

"Armed?"

"Yes. He will be quickly upon us."

The crowd began to panic. Alexander raised his hands to calm them. "Stay quiet. He's not here yet. The louder we are the more attention we will draw upon ourselves. Someone extinguish the candles. This house isn't as large as Kilmore and sound does travel well between its walls."

Alexander turned to his son. "We have at least 100 people in here. We're too large to move quickly. We need a distraction. Any ideas you two?"

"I can't meet him in these clothes. He'll suspect something. This is the same attire I wore at our wedding," Tomas answered.

"Kathleen," Bailey offered.

They all turned their eyes in her direction. Kathleen clutched her bouquet even tighter. "He's smitten by her and she is very beautiful in that lavender gown. If she can seduce him..."

"He will be so distracted by her beauty it would buy us time to hide," Alexander finished his son's sentence. He extended his hand to her, helping his daughter down.

"Father, I...I...don't like him," she answered.

"Liar," Calico replied. They turned towards her. "She's been infatuated with Isaac Turner since the first day she set eyes on him."

"Calico! I told you that in secret," Kathleen protested.

Calico released her bound hand, grabbed the side of her train, and stepped towards her. "Kathleen, our lives are at stake. You may not think Bailey and father are trying to protect you but they are. Like it or not, there's a war outside my house!" She grabbed Kathleen by the arms. "I know Sherlock has told you not to trust us and I admire him for trying to keep you safe. I love you, dearly. If you won't seduce Isaac for Bailey, will you do it for me?"

"Calico, he's dangerous."

"Oh, I think he's more dangerous to your heart than to your life. What matters more, your family or you?"

Kathleen glared at the men before her. Alexander crossed his arms and looked at her with authority. "Is it true?" he asked.

"Father," Kathleen answered.

"You have fallen in love with our enemy?"

Calico stepped away from her sister. Kathleen exchanged glances with her then looked to her father. She couldn't deny him the truth any longer. "Fallen in love is a bit drastic and dramatic, don't you agree?"

"Answer me!"

Kathleen took a step back with a nod. She lowered her head. "I'm sorry. I shouldn't have these feeling about him but I do."

"Is that why you don't want to commit to our plans?" Bailey asked. "You've chosen to protect him because you love him?"

Kathleen lifted her gaze to him. "No." She threw down her bouquet and stepped towards him. "I hate what you have done to our family! You bribed the matchmaker so when father questioned the match between Calico and Tomas the matchmaker would agree to the union! Tomas never loved Calico. Calico loved him first. You saw that and used it to your advantage because you knew Tomas would never marry an Anglican and he requires an heir!"

"That's enough, Kat," Calico yelled, pushing her sister down the stair.

Kathleen rose from the floor. "You know it's true."

"That was the past and we all know I love your sister. You have no respect, Kathleen Anne McGillpatrick," Tomas snarled.

"I might not, but as least I have more common sense than to listen to Bailey. It's Bailey's own fault his family is dead, just as it's his fault Mary almost died at James Turner's hands. Why should I trust a murdering, lying thief?!"

Bailey had enough of his sister's outrage. "How dare you accuse me of killing my family!"

"Why are you so upset, Bailey?" she questioned while approaching him. "It's true."

Bailey grabbed her by the front of her dress and pulled her towards him. "You have the mouth of a McGillpatrick but the common sense of a sheep. Stupid girl! If you don't seduce Isaac then the deaths and destruction he brings upon everyone here won't be on my hands but yours!

Do you want more of that or do you think for one second you can be smart enough to act upon those feelings you have and seduce the God damn Englishman!"

Tears fell down Kathleen's cheeks. She turned to her father then peered out at the crowd. Another guard ran into the hall. "Lord Alexander, Isaac Turner and his men are close to the house."

Kathleen turned her gaze back to her brother. She sniffed her nose with a nod and mumbled. "What was that?" Bailey asked.

"I said I would do it this one time. Only this time. You hear me, Bailey, only this one time."

"Good girl," he pushed her to the floor. Kathleen rose from the floor, collected herself, and walked out of the hall.

Bailey turned to the guards. "Make certain she distracts him. If you believe she is protecting him then you know what you need to do."

"Yes, sir," the guards replied.

"Dismissed."

The guards ran out of the hall. Alexander turned to his son. "What did you just order them to do to her?"

"Nothing important, father."

"Bailey?"

"They won't kill her. Just scare her into thinking they will. I'm hoping Isaac will protect her and give chase."

"They better, Bailey, or so help me, son…"

"Let's get these people to safety," Tomas interrupted.

The men nodded and began to evacuate the people into the lower quarters.

Chapter 12

A light breeze blew softly in the air as Isaac and ten Irish soldiers rode up the hilly stone road towards Collinsworth. Isaac Turner gazed towards the medium-sized Irish great house. Usually by the time he approached the crest of the hill Tomas had taken notice of his arrival and was standing outside waiting for him. Yet the area outside was void of servants and masters alike. How odd. There should at least be a servant around. It took a staff of at least 20 servants to man the great house, yet no one was about. Where was everyone?

Isaac slowed his steed, carefully studying the house and its surroundings. Every ounce in his being told him something was wrong. Perhaps the McGillpatrick brothers had killed Tomas, Calico, and Kathleen. It would surprise him they would do so to the sisters, but not to Tomas. It was common knowledge the brothers loathed Tomas for turning against his people. They hated all Catholics who had turned Anglican just to keep their lands. The large, double, wooden doors burst open. Kathleen ran out of the house in a beautiful lavender evening gown. Sunlight sparkled off the sequins on her bodice. He wondered why she was so elegantly dressed. It was barely three in the afternoon, too soon for a dinner. Was she going somewhere with a suitor? Perhaps in Dublin or Cork? Oh, he hoped not.

The light-colored gown looked stunning. It highlighted her pale skin tone, while her fire-red hair—loosely gathered in a bun atop her head—captivated his attention. He had never laid eyes on someone with such beautiful natural red hair before. Most of the Irish peasants wore red-colored wigs and whenever he would visit them they would take their wigs off, use them to dust off a chair for him, and place the wigs back on their heads. He had even heard the peasants sing "Heigh for the apple, and ho for the pear; But give me the pretty girl with the red hair." To the Irish peasants, Kathleen's most beautiful attribute was her red hair. Isaac loved everything about her. She was his eternal sunshine.

Isaac stopped his chestnut horse in the middle of the stone road. His small army of ten Irish soldiers halted their horses behind his. His eyes bore on the image of Kathleen as she ran down the road from the front of the house. Why was Kathleen sobbing? Where was Tomas or Calico? Isaac jumped off his horse and handed the reigns to the unit's commander. "Stay here," he ordered.

"Yes, sir. Who is she?" the heavyset man asked.

"Tomas' sister-in-law."

Isaac turned and walked swiftly up the hilly road. A slight breeze blew through the air. The hem of Kathleen's lavender dress danced under her feet as she ran as if she was barely touching the earth. His heart skipped a beat. She was even more beautiful in sorrow. Why had God created such a magnificent creature who wouldn't accept his attentions? He had never felt so strongly for a woman before, let alone a native Irish woman. It was almost unbearable to think her name. Kathleen. The sound of her name on his lips was sweeter than all the nectar of God's heaven. It was dangerous to even have feelings for her. He had promised himself years ago, when he had come of age to marry, he would never court an Irish woman. You just never knew if they were lying about their conversion or not. He didn't even know if she had converted or if she had been born Anglican. Tomas had only told him his wife's family had a great house in Northern Ireland. He knew nothing else about Kathleen, yet, surprisingly, he didn't care. "Kathleen," he yelled, running closer to her.

"Stay back," she yelled at the top of the hill, extending her arms. He stopped mid-stride in curiosity. He was used to her defiance. Isaac nodded. He would give her the control but not for long. He needed her to trust him so he could make his move. This woman wasn't going to deny him much longer. He was growing tired of her games.

The couple stared at each other in a long moment of silence. She was a mess. Her puffy eyes and the streaks of tears on her cheeks gave away her true feelings. His heart hurt to see her in so much pain. When was she going to end her mourning and begin her new life with happiness? He could make that happen for her.

She sniffed her runny nose. Isaac pulled a white handkerchief from the inside of his coat and presented it her. "Thank you. Lay it on the ground, please, Earl Turner." He complied with curiosity. "Step back." Isaac bowed, took a step backwards and waited as a hunter waits for his prey. Kathleen stepped forward and picked up the handkerchief. Now was the time to get the answers he so desperately needed her to answer. He sprung towards her and grabbed her small wrist. She tried to fidget her hand loose from his strong, tight grip. "Let go," she pleaded.

"No." Isaac knelt to the ground, grabbed her face and forced her to look at him. Eye to eye she wouldn't be able to lie to him. The eyes were the windows into someone's soul. Whatever she was hiding he was going to draw out of her. He pulled her towards him. "Kathleen, what's happened?"

"Sick. They're all sick. You have to leave."

"Are you ill as well?"

Kathleen shook her head. "No, but I could be. You don't know. Feel those lumps under your right hand? Those are the scars I carry from the smallpox. I will never forget. I brought the smallpox to my family and…and…my family died."

"I thought your parents were killed by rebels?"

"They were. The smallpox killed my younger siblings. There were four of us. My father's heir died from that dreadful disease."

"I'm sorry. I did not realize."

"I was to marry so that our wealth would pass onto me but the rebels killed my fiancée."

"Who is in charge of the estate now that your parents are dead?"

"We lost everything to my father's distant cousin. All I have left is my dowry. Tomas has been kind enough to allow me to stay with him and Calico."

"Kathleen, surely if I speak to this cousin of yours…"

"No!"

"No?"

Kathleen swallowed hard. She shook her head. "I mean. I'm grateful for the offer, Earl Turner, but I cannot ask you to interfere in a private matter. Tomas is a good man. I am content with my life at Collinsworth. Now please, you have to leave. Leave and…and don't return. Please," she pleaded, rising to her feet. Isaac let go of her. Hadn't he had lunch with Tomas and Calico at his home after services last Sunday, and hadn't he hunted with him yesterday? How could Tomas and Calico be ill?

"What is it?" Isaac asked, rising from the grass.

"We don't know. Calico came down with a fever last night. Tomas had it this morning. It does not break no matter how much we try to lower their temperatures. I've been caring for them since Calico first grew ill."

"Perhaps I should send for my personal physician?"

"There is no need, Earl Turner. I thank you. We have our own physician. Now please, go. Go and pray to God for our deliverance. We shall send word to you once the illness has passed or we have died of it."

"Kathleen, if you are not ill then perhaps I may offer you a stay at Kilmore?"

"I can't. I would be a burden to you."

"You, my dear, are more of a burden to my heart if I am to think of the great illness that will surely threaten your life should you remain with your sister and her husband."

"Perhaps I am already infected."

"And perhaps not."

Isaac walked towards her and took her hand in his own. "Kathleen, my lady, you deserve better than to be subjected to illness. Please, if I cannot protect you at Tomas' estate then allow me to do so at my own."

Kathleen looked downhill towards the Anglican men waiting on their horses. "What business do you have at Collinsworth?" she asked, changing the subject while still glaring at the men.

Isaac glared at her with a perplexed look. Obviously he would have to try harder to win her affections. This stubborn Irish red-haired woman was going to make his life miserable until he figured out a way to win her affections. There must be many men who were interested in making her their mate, yet he was determined to make certain she never had a chance to be with any other suitors. He would be the only man for her. Perhaps the mourning she had for the deaths of her parents at the hands of the rebels had made her less sensible. No woman had ever denied him before, yet this stubborn woman did so on almost a daily basis. What would it take!

He turned towards the men then back to Kathleen. "There has been a report that Sherlock McGillpatrick has been spotted in the area."

Kathleen turned her attention back to him with shock. "Wha…what?"

"Oh, my lady, you have nothing to fear. Tomas and I will ensure no harm will come to you or your sister."

"When did you hear of this?"

"This morning. Have you not heard of the same rumors?"

"No, my lord. Is he still in the area?"

"That I do not know. I have come to Collinsworth to aide Tomas in the matter. I thought perhaps we and our men could join forces to inspect all the tenant farmers we have on our lands and make certain Sherlock is not among them."

"All the tenant farmers?"

"Yes, the report came from an Anglican tenant farmer who lived close to where the boundary of Collinsworth and Kilmore meet. He stated some of the Catholic farmers are aiding Sherlock and his brother."

"Would this be the same Anglican family who had informed you months ago concerning the location of the McGillpatrick brothers?"

"Yes, my lady."

"And yet you found that information unreliable?"

"So it seems."

Kathleen nodded her head and stepped back. He studied her pale face. He walked slowly towards her.

"Might I ask, my lady, why she is so elegantly dressed in the afternoon? Do you have a suitor, madam?"

Kathleen curtseyed. "Farewell, Earl Turner. Be safe and healthy." He bowed silently. He watched her turn from him and walk away. Something wasn't right with that woman.

Chapter 13

Kathleen walked down the hallway towards Sherlock and Mary's bedchambers. After her encounter with Isaac, Bailey had told her she had done a good job. She should have felt gratitude for his complement but the only thing that she felt was a very gnawing sense of disgust with her brother. When was all this going to end? Sherlock had been right. Bailey was nothing but a self-centered, prideful man bent on the destruction of his own family, yet Bailey never saw that.

She paused at her brother's door and knocked. "Sherlock," she called to him.

Kathleen heard movement in the room. She lowered her hand and waited. Sherlock opened the door and greeted his younger sister. "Kathleen?"

"I need to talk," she cried, embracing the one man who understood her the best. Sherlock closed the door and embraced her. He pressed her head against his firm chest, kissed her on top of her head, then lifted her face with the crook of his finger beneath her chin. "What happened?"

"Calico hates me."

"She's your best friend. I doubt she hates you."

"I made a mess of her wedding. The entire family is upset with me."

"Where are they?"

"At the wedding feast in the Great Hall."

"You are her maid of honor. Why aren't you celebrating with her?"

Kathleen wiped the tears from her eyes and heaved. She took a deep breath then bore her soul to him, recalling the events that had transpired at the wedding when Isaac was approaching the estate. She told him of her encounter with Isaac and how when she had returned Bailey had congratulated her. "I feel as if I endangered our family even more."

"It wasn't you who did, Kathleen. It was Bailey."

Mary moaned. Sherlock released her then walked to his bed. He pulled the blanket over his wife's body, sat beside her, and stroked her hair as he whispered something to her. Kathleen watched her brother tenderly care for his ill wife. How she wished she had someone like him. Mary had the perfect life, yet her life had been filled with hardships as well. She had a wonderful husband who cherished her, a mother she could confide in, and two younger sisters she could spend time with. Yet on the flip side, she had six dead children, a dead older sister, a father she had lost only a year before she had married Sherlock, and had almost lost her husband. Despite all the tragedies and hardships, Mary was a strong woman with an even stronger Catholic faith. She was the perfect rebel leader's wife. Sherlock kissed his wife and then rose from beside her.

"How is she?" Kathleen whispered as he approached her.

"Her stomach is still giving her problems but she doesn't have a fever. I don't know what it is. She's been like this for a week, Kathleen. She says it's worse in the morning and I shouldn't concern myself with her ailment. But to be honest, I cannot comply with her request. I love her too much."

"You're a good husband to her."

Sherlock grabbed his coat from behind the door and put it on. "Is there anyone down here other than us?"

"No, the servants are at the wedding."

"Good, let's walk," he said, opening the door. Kathleen looked at Mary then turned her attention to Sherlock. She walked out the door and waited. Sherlock closed the door behind him, took her arm underneath his, and began to guide her through the passageways.

"You're upset?" Kathleen asked him.

"Yes. Bailey has no right to endanger your life like that."

"I couldn't refuse him. I'm an unmarried woman living in father's household. Father supports Bailey."

"And yet you found the need to accuse Bailey of sabotaging the matchmaker in order for Calico and Tomas to be together?"

"It just came out of my mouth, Sherlock. Calico is so mad at me she refuses to be near me."

"You expected anything but that reaction from her? You basically claimed her marriage was a fraud."

"I never meant for her to get hurt. She's as much of Bailey's victim as I am."

"No, that's where you are wrong," he said, stopping in front of her.

Kathleen shook her head. "I don't understand. Bailey has set her up and she is playing into his hand. I've been set up as well. Bailey wants me to court Isaac."

"And you want that too."

"Good God, no!"

"Don't lie to me, Kathleen. You're not against helping Bailey because you are against him. You are against helping Bailey because you have fallen in love with Isaac. You're afraid that love will betray you and your family. What separates your motives from Calico's is that Calico didn't love Tomas at first."

"She didn't?"

"No."

"But...I...I don't understand. When she had spoken about him to me she couldn't stop talking about him as if she was infatuated with him."

"She was practicing on you so that when she was in public it would come across as if she truly loved him."

Kathleen gasped. She wiped her hands down her face. How long had Calico been lying to her? Never in her life would she have imagined Calico would have deceived her. All those precious moments she had shared with her sister were just lies. "I was just a pawn in her game,"

Kathleen muttered with a broken heart. "What else has she been lying about?"

"I don't know. Mary has caught her in several lies. You would need to speak to her about them. I can tell you this: at first Calico and Tomas played the game well and eventually they convinced themselves that they had fallen in love."

"You don't believe they have fallen for each other?"

"Why should I? They are in bed with Bailey. Calico is only in bed with Tomas because Tomas needed a wife. The Anglicans were growing suspicious. He is after all almost in his forties. He needs an heir. The only woman he could trust to be his wife was another rebel. Who better to marry than one of the McGillpatrick sisters?"

"But I'm the eldest. He never asked for me."

"You are also the most honest and weakest sister. You are prone to speak before you think; that's a dangerous attribute for any rebel to have. Think about it, Kathleen." He turned and began to walk down the hallway towards the kitchen. Kathleen thought about Sherlock's advice. As much as she hated to admit it, he was right. She was the weaker sister. She had always been the type of person who hated injustice and dishonesty. Her greatest habit was how she reacted to things that troubled her. Whenever something or someone bothered her she would just bottle up her emotions until her internal vessel was so full she had to burst. It didn't take much to make her burst and often times an insignificant thing would cause her to pour her wrath upon anyone who stood in her way. Thankfully, she didn't have many outbursts. She had often found painting soothed her torrid emotions. But Calico, on the other hand, had always been strong and stable. She knew her sister was capable of hiding her true feelings but never could she imagine her sister would lie to her and for so long. Why would her best friend do such a thing? Hadn't they shared their entire lives with each other?

Kathleen walked towards the end of the hallway and entered the kitchen. Sherlock sat at the simple kitchen table, eating an apple as the servants moved throughout the large room. The cook noticed her entrance and rang a tiny bell. The servants stopped what they were doing and bowed to her. "My lady," the cook greeted her.

Kathleen looked to the chef then back to Sherlock. He arched his eyebrow, bit from the apple, and leaned back in the chair. Kathleen turned back to the cook. "Has the wedding feast started?" she asked.

"Yes, mi lady. All the dishes have been served. They have finished their meal and are dancing."

"Good and have the dishes been cleared from the table?"

"Yes. We were washing them."

"You should eat, Kathleen. They are fixing a meal for my wife and me," Sherlock said then took another bite of the apple. He cringed in pain and heaved, spitting the piece of apple out of his mouth. Dropping his apple to the floor, he held his hand to his forehead and leaned over.

"Sherlock," Kathleen gasped, walking around the servant to her brother.

"Hmm, get something to eat," he shooed her away then rose from the table. Sherlock stumbled through the kitchen, bumping into several servants as he headed towards the door. He clutched the doorpost and fell to the floor. Kathleen ran to his side. "Sherlock," she said, shaking her hand on his chest. He never moved. His eyes were open and he never moved. She leaned her ear over his chest. Oh, god, he wasn't breathing and she couldn't hear a heartbeat. "Sherlock," she yelled, grabbing his face. His glassy eyes, devoid of life, stared into her own. "No, no, no, no," she whispered, trying to coax him. She turned to the servants. "Help! Somebody help!" The cook ordered the other servants. Kathleen turned her head towards her brother's dead body as a servant ran past her. She sobbed, lowering her head to his chest. Her beloved older brother couldn't be dead. She couldn't lose him. Oh, God she couldn't lose him. He was everything she had in this world. She lifted her gaze to his face, sobbing. How could this be? She was just talking to him and now he was dead. No, he had to be asleep. Yes, that was it. He was just fooling her by pretending to be asleep.

She traced her finger along the top of his forehead and paused where the skull fracture had been. Who was she fooling? The blow to the head he had received should have killed him when he was unconscious. Yet, he had survived. The doctor had said there might be aftereffects of the head trauma. Sherlock had defied those warnings until now. He was dead. He was dead not because of Isaac but because of Bailey. What was it Sherlock had told her? Bailey ruined every life he touched. Anger burned deep within her. She was done. She wasn't about to allow Bailey to ruin any more lives. She had a plan. She lifted her eyes at hearing movement.

Alexander knelt beside Sherlock as Bailey stood over them. "What happened?" Alexander asked her.

Kathleen bore her eyes at Bailey. "We were talking. He was sitting at the table eating an apple when he moaned with pain. He dropped the apple, stumbled around the kitchen, then fell." Alexander checked for vital signs then noticed the blood pouring out of Sherlock's ears. He placed his finger in his son's ear then lifted the bloody finger to Bailey.

"Must be from the brain," Bailey said coldly.

Alexander nodded with sorrow. "The headaches. I should have known something was wrong when he started to have the debilitating headaches."

Kathleen tuned out the conversation between her brother and father. She prepared herself mentally. Bailey needed to come down from his place of power over her family and her people. She couldn't do it alone and she knew the perfect person who could help her with her new-found calling. There was honestly only one man who could help her. One man Bailey had no control over and would never be able to control. One man who was determined to protect her. She rose from the floor. "I'll do it."

"Do what?" Bailey asked her.

"You want me to seduce Isaac Turner into marrying me. I'll do it."

"Kathleen, I don't think this is the proper time to be discussing this," Alexander protested.

"No, father, I think it is the proper time for her to do so," Bailey countered. He turned back to Kathleen. "You have a plan, I take it?"

"Isaac is looking for Sherlock. I told Isaac that Tomas, Calico, and I were ill. What if it was just a ruse to get him away from the estate because Sherlock had taken us captive? I was too scared to tell him anything. We were able to escape because we had overpowered Sherlock. Sherlock had told us you were incapable of leading the raids that have been happening for months due to your injuries."

Bailey peered over at his father. Alexander stared at his son's body with tremendous grief. "No, you don't endanger her too," he mumbled.

"Father, I want this," Kathleen rebuked.

Alexander lifted his distraught face. "What you want is foolishness, girl! What makes you think Isaac will believe you?"

"Because he loves me, father. I can see it in his eyes and I'll have Sherlock's body as proof."

"He should be buried and not paraded around as some trophy for the Anglicans."

"She's right, father. You just can't see it through your grief," Bailey said.

Alexander turned to face Bailey. "Do you not grieve for your brother?! He never even had his last rites. His soul has gone on to purgatory without protection. There's no intercession for him now. Your brother is dead!"

"Better dead than to live the horrors of this life. We're treated worse than animals all because of our faith! Besides, he had his last rites when you thought he was dying after Tomas rescued us."

"Bailey, have you lost all respect for your family?"

"No, father. Sherlock was a good man. He has done more good works than naught. I am not concerned for his soul. What I am concerned about is this family and our people. Kathleen's plan will work. Once we have Tomas in Parliament and Kathleen in Kilmore we will not only have greater access to the law but to our lands as well. I have faith in my little sister. She was able to deter Isaac from intruding on the ceremony. I believe she will be able to fool him into thinking the rebels have gone north to join the rebellion in Ulster." He turned to Kathleen with a mischievous grin.

"I can do it," she replied, staring at her brother's body.

"Good, we will have to shoot him in the head to make your story plausible."

Kathleen stared at Sherlock's body. She swallowed hard, thinking about the destruction Bailey wanted to do. She could understand why he wanted to do it but every ounce of her being was against it. She hated the thought of desecrating her brother's body. It was a sin to do so. She clenched her jaw and pushed down her feelings. "Will you do it or shall I?" she asked.

Bailey smiled. He pulled a pistol from inside his coat, started to hand it to her, then pulled back. He looked towards two male servants. "Take my brother's body into the stable and place him in an empty stall. Make certain no one sees you."

"Yes, sir," the two men answered. Kathleen watched as the men carried her brother's body out the back door. Alexander rose from the floor. "Your plan?" he asked his eldest son.

"Sherlock had…" He slammed his fist hard in Kathleen's face then hit her with the brunt end of the gun as she leaned over.

"Bailey!" Alexander yelled, grabbing his daughter. Kathleen cried out in pain as her father held her.

"The plan will never work if she arrives at Isaac's home without believable wounds. I didn't hit her hard enough to break her head. I'll be back. Have her ready."

"She's about to pass out, Bailey."

"Don't let her. She needs to be woozy but not unconscious. Hit her again if you need to, father," he said as he walked out the door with his crutches.

Kathleen clung to her father's shirt. The pain turned her stomach. She would never have imagined that Bailey would ever hit her. Her mind

was foggy; she didn't know if she could remember what she was supposed to do. But she had to press on. Bailey had to be eliminated. He was a scourge upon her family and people. Yes, that was what she was supposed to do. She was supposed to give Bailey over to Isaac without endangering herself, Tomas, or her family. Oh, but it sounded harder than it should. "Walk," Alexander guided her towards the door. Blood trickled down her forehead into her eye, making her world blurry. More so than it was already. She wiped the sticky substance from her face. The bright sun hurt her head. She turned her face into her father's chest. He clutched her harder as they walked towards the stable. Kathleen jumped at the sound of a gun. Chaos reigned inside the stables from the scared horses. Every sound bothered her headache even more. Alexander stopped before the stone-walled stables while the servants hitched two horses to a wagon. Bailey exited the stables, putting his gun back into his coat. He approached her, allowing the servants to gather Sherlock's body. "You will tell Isaac everything I am about to tell you and you must make it believable. Do you understand, Kathleen?"

Kathleen nodded.

"Good."

Chapter 14

Isaac sat at his father's desk in front of a tall window in his large library. He looked out the window towards his mother's garden. Kilmore was the largest great house in Wexford County. Built upon the remains of a 16th century castle, it sprawled across the top of Kingston hill and was visible for miles. His father, Earl James Turner, had gained control of Kilmore in October of 1726 when Isaac was sixteen years old. Isaac had fallen in love with the magnificent large house. He'd been born and raised in a country cottage, so for him Kilmore was as if heaven had come to grace the Irish lands. As an eager young man, he dove into the history and architecture of Kilmore. Despite the discontent he felt towards the McGillpatricks, he had admired Alexander McGillpatrick for the wonders of Kilmore. Alexander had taken his family's castle and incorporated it into the design of Kilmore so that the antiquity of the place was not demolished. His plan had been masterfully executed. Each room of the four-level house had its own unique features. Parts of the castle, such as the four towers and the tall flagpole on the highest part of the house, were still in use. With over 100 bedchambers, there were still areas of the house he had yet to explore. He had never had much time to explore the house. When his father had taken over Kilmore, he had been overseas in boarding school. He had planned to return to Ireland after his graduation in 1728 but his father had told him to stay in London with his sister. Ireland was in the grips of a famine. Disease and hunger were everywhere. James didn't want to risk losing his only son. Isaac had enjoyed his time in London and stayed on until he learned of his father's murder in 1733. He was coroneted in London as the new Earl of Kilmore, returned to Ireland, and vowed to avenge his father's death. He was going to take care of the rebel leaders once and for all. Irish law required political prisoners to be sold to English families in the American colonies and in the West Indies as slaves. He had the perfect buyer for Alexander McGillpatrick and his sons.

"Isaac," a young woman's voice lifted from behind him.

Isaac turned his attention to the right. His younger sister, Sarah, stood in the doorway. "Are you busy?" she asked, holding something in her hands.

"I was going over the slave trade reports from our sea captains."

"Oh, I didn't mean to bother you," Sarah replied then began to turn away.

"Wait," Isaac called out, rising from his chair. She turned as he started to walk towards her. "What's in your hand?"

Sarah peered down at the letter then back at her brother with a sweet smile. "It's from Dublin," she answered, handing it to him. "Seems I have a possible suitor," she whispered in tears as he pulled out the letter and began to read it.

Isaac smiled. His sweet, eighteen-year-old sister was all he had left of his siblings. The famine of 1727-1730 had been hard on all classes of society. Influenza had hit his family in the winter of 1729, killing his three brothers and two sisters. Sarah, the youngest of them all, had been fortunate enough to survive but the knowledge of that had turned her into a soft-spoken, insecure young woman. She feared death, disease, and hunger to the point she refused to ever leave the house. It was hard to get her out of the house this summer for her coming out this season. Against her will, Sarah was forced to attend all the functions that a debutante was supposed to employ. Isaac smiled at her.

"Mother said I had to have your permission to accept the offer since you are the Earl."

"Is this something you want?" he asked, putting it back in the envelope.

Sarah shrugged her shoulders. "I don't want to leave Kilmore."

"Sarah, it's an offer of courtship, not a proposal. Besides, I would rather the duke present himself to me with the question of courtship than in some letter."

"It says he will do so if I consent to his asking."

"You should accept. It would be good for you to keep his affections. He would raise your standing through your marriage to him. Write him back and invite him to Kilmore."

"Thank you," she beamed then began to walk out the door. "Oh, mother," she replied, bumping into the Dowager Countess Charlotte Turner.

Charlotte looked into her son's eyes with a grave look on her face.

"Mother?" Isaac asked.

"Lady Kathleen has been injured."

"Is it serious?" Sarah asked.

"I've sent my maid for the doctor."

"She's here?" Isaac asked.

"Yes."

Isaac's heart skipped a beat. What was Lady Kathleen doing at Kilmore? "Mother, how serious? Where is she?"

"She's unconscious."

"I knew something was wrong this morning! I should have followed her and burst through Tomas' estate. Where is she?" he demanded.

"In one of the front parlors."

Isaac pushed his mother and sister aside, running down the hall. His mother's voice echoed behind him. "Isaac wait," she yelled, running down the mahogany-paneled hallway. Isaac turned to his right. He didn't have time to wait. If Kathleen was unconscious he needed to be there when she woke up. She would be distraught, just as she had been when she awoke in his home after she had fainted at the wedding.

"Isaac, she isn't alone!"

Isaac slid to a halt. He turned on his heel to face to his mother. "What do you mean she isn't alone? Who is here with her?" he asked, perplexed at the new information.

"She had a dead body with her."

"What? Mother I don't understand. You are saying Lady Kathleen is at our home unconscious with a dead body?"

"One of the kitchen maids found her wagon overturned at the base of the hill leading to the house. She was unconscious. I suspect she fell unconscious while driving and the horse took off without her."

"Where was her driver?"

"She had none."

"No driver, a dead body, and Lady Kathleen unconscious? Who died in the accident?"

"No one, my son. The man was shot in the head."

Isaac sat on a bench against the wall next to a statue of a knight in armor. "I'm confused, mother. Nothing you are saying makes sense to me. Why was Lady Kathleen driving a wagon for herself when she has a servant to do that for her? And whose body was she carrying. It almost sounds to me like you are telling me Lady Kathleen shot a man and stole his wagon."

"I do not believe she did."

"Then who...?" he paused as his mother pulled out a warrant for Alexander, Sherlock, and Bailey McGillpatrick's arrest. He looked at the sketches of the men's faces then peered up at his mother. "Which one?"

"Sherlock. He was killed with a bullet to his head. His body is in the barn."

Isaac took the warrant from his mother's hands. "Did she shoot him?" he asked, still staring at the men's faces.

"She did not have a gun on her. She's been beaten, Isaac."

Isaac growled, crumbling the paper in his fist. He threw it, proclaiming, "I knew it! This is all my fault!"

"I do not see how you can blame yourself for her situation."

Isaac turned towards her, red with anger. He spilled his true feelings to the one woman who understood him best of all. "I was there, mother. She had run from the house in tears. She told me there was a sickness in her home and to leave Collinsworth, never to return. I knew something was wrong by the way she spoke to me."

"How could you? She has always defied you."

"I think she defies me because she has feelings for me."

"Oh, Isaac, every young woman has feelings for you. You bed them as soon as they proclaim their love then throw them away as if they were rubbish. You have to stop seducing the ladies of society and marry one of them. They are proper women, not the whores you sell to the upper-class men."

"I know, mother."

"It's one thing to build upon the slave trade business your father had established by kidnapping and selling the Irish to the colonists in the New World and in the West Indies, but it's another to exploit upper-class women as if they were your personal whores."

"Are you saying you do not approve of the business transactions that have brought more wealth to our estate? This house is large, mother, with that comes large expense. Our wealth has greatly increased since I took father's place."

"Yes, my son, but it has done so at a greater cost. Someday, someone is going to learn of your secrets and expose you."

"I have nothing to fear about that. His majesty knows of my business transactions and greatly supports them. I have spies throughout the kingdom who report back to me and I give him the information they have gathered. He is most pleased at my network of spies. I am making a name for this family!"

"If you plan to continue in these transactions then you need to be more careful, my son. Trust no one, not even Lady Kathleen."

"You don't trust her? We barely know her."

"That's my point, Isaac. Who is she? Where does she come from?"

"She's Countess Calico Collins' sister. They had a cottage in Northern Ireland. Their father was a lawyer."

"What else do you know about her?"

Isaac thought long and hard. Kathleen. Beautiful, red-haired Kathleen with the spirit to match the flames of her hair. Bright emerald-green eyes that drew him in every time he looked at her face. "She's beautiful," he said softly with a large smile. The countess smacked her son hard. Isaac jerked his attention back to his mother, rubbing his cheek. "What was that for?"

"You can't tell me anything about her because you're in love with her."

Isaac lowered his hand. "She is just another conquest, mother."

"I doubt that. Isaac if you plan to marry this woman then you must know where she comes from, who her parents are, and how much her dowry is worth."

"Yes, mother. Can you tell me one thing?"

"Yes?"

"What do you have against her?"

"Nothing."

"Don't lie to me mother. You may fool others with your ploys but I inherited that from you."

His mother grinned. "Seems you have. Do you recall the stories your father wrote to you concerning the McGillpatrick family who lived here?"

"Yes, Alexander had two sons who had already established their households in the cottages on the back of the estate. He had two daughters and his wife living with him. When father evicted Sherlock and Bailey from their homes they ran to their father's aid, dragging their families behind them. Their wives led the daughters, their mother, and the children out of Kilmore while Alexander and his sons tried to fight my father. Kilmore was still under construction. Father backed Alexander and his sons into a corner. Alexander knew the law. He told father he would rather die than be sent overseas as a slave. My father compromised with Alexander, since Alexander had been a gentleman. He gave them a fate worse than death—poverty."

"What became of the daughters?"

"No one knows. Alexander had rarely allowed them out of the house and when he did there were large walls around the perimeter of the castle and no one could ever see them."

"What were their names?"

Isaac though for a long moment then shook his head, "I don't know, mother."

"No one knows, Isaac."

"Then how do we know they ever existed?"

"Because the locals still speak of them. The locals know their names, what they look like, and where they are today. It was only the Anglicans he kept the girls away from and he continues to do so to this very day. All you ever hear about are his sons. But I wonder, where are the daughters?"

"And you think the daughters are among us?"

"I don't know, Isaac. But it's common knowledge you love your women. Who is to say the McGillpatrick's won't try to use that against you?"

"And you suspect Kathleen might be one of the daughters?"

"I do."

"I don't."

"What makes you think she hasn't been playing you, Isaac? You said when you went to Tomas' house she had tried to persuade you away from the house as soon as you were at the bottom of the hill. Sounds to me like she was watching you."

"Mother, I know what I saw. I could see the fear in her eyes. It wasn't an illness that she feared. It was Sherlock! He must have beaten her after we spoke."

"Are you certain?"

"Yes, because if she is a McGillpatrick daughter then that means Calico is as well. Which would mean Tomas had married a McGillpatrick woman and lied to everyone about whom he married. Why would Tomas do such a thing?"

"You had suspected him of helping the rebels."

"Suspicions that have no proof. I need proof to expose him! Besides, he's one of my closest friends."

"And therein lies the problem. He's too close to you."

"I've had enough of this talk, mother."

Isaac quickly walked past his mother. As much as he loved and respected his mother, her allegations bothered him. Kathleen couldn't be the woman his mother had claimed her to be. Sure, Kathleen had a fiery spirit. What woman didn't? Let alone a red-haired woman. Kathleen had been through so much. The deaths of her parents at the hands of rebels, the loss of her father's estate to a cousin, a wedding, and now this! It was no wonder she was reacting like an obnoxious little girl. Women were the weaker sex. She needed a man to protect her and he was going to be that man.

Isaac turned and ran down the long hallway separating his private quarters from the main household. With each step, worse thoughts came to his head about the woman he had fallen in love with. No matter how much he had tried to deny his feelings, Kathleen was more than a woman he had to conquer. She was someone he cherished. No one hurts the people he cherished without repercussions.

He turned to the right and entered the hall. A pair of housekeepers ran up the stairs with fresh linens while another stood on a wooden ladder, cleaning the chandelier. They stood at attention as he entered. "My lord," a housekeeper greeted him from the stairway on the left mirroring the one on the right.

"In which parlor did my mother instruct Lady Kathleen be placed?" he barked.

"The Grand Parlor," the housekeeper answered.

He nodded then ran straight down another hall across from him. He turned left and burst through the room. Isaac straightened his clothes as his butler and head housekeeper greeted him. "She is starting to wake up, my lord," the head housekeeper informed him, wiping the side of Kathleen's head with a clean cloth.

"Leave us," he ordered, walking to the couch where Kathleen lay. The housekeeper handed the cloth to Isaac then walked out of the room with the butler. Isaac sat on the edge of his red sofa and placed the cloth on the side of Kathleen's head. He examined her black eye, broken nose, and busted lip. Whatever had happened to her she was lucky to be alive. The size of the bruises on her face told him a man with a large hand had beaten her. He lifted the cloth. There wasn't a large amount of blood. It looked to be a minor wound but with head wounds looks could be deceiving. He peered at her body. She was still in her evening gown but there were tears in her dress that he hadn't noticed before. Those could be from the accident, or had she been mistreated by whoever had beaten her?

Kathleen moaned, slowly opening her eyes. The blurry vision of Isaac entered her sight. "Isaac," she groaned, trying to rise.

Isaac lowered her back to the coach. "Lie back down. My mother has sent for the doctor."

Kathleen nodded. She cringed as she began to feel the pain in her head. She lifted her hand to her nose and slowly pulled her hand away, feeling something sticky. Blood. She sighed, lowering her hand. "Is it broken?" she asked.

"Yes, looks like my butler reset it. He had blood on his clothes. Try not to move. Your head has stopped bleeding." He rose from beside her, lowered the cloth, and pulled on a long cord next to the fireplace. A few moments later his butler entered the room. "My lord," he greeted.

"Have a basin of water and fresh clothes sent to me for Lady Kathleen."

"Yes, my lord."

"When you have finished with that change into a clean uniform."

"Anything else, my lord?"

"No. Go."

The butler nodded and closed the door behind him. Kathleen searched her confused mind as he walked towards her. What was the story again? She had to make certain she told him everything Bailey had ordered her to say. If only her brother hadn't hit her so hard! She pushed through the muddy waters of her mind searching for answers. A sharp pain erupted in her chest, arm, and stomach. Why hadn't she felt the pain before?! She screamed out in agony. What had happened to her? Isaac ran to her side and held her hand.

"Shh, Lady Kathleen," he coaxed, placing his hand on the side of her head and turning it towards him.

"Wh..what happened to me?" she cried. "It hurts. Oh, Isaac it hurts."

"Where?"

"My arm, side, and stomach."

"My mother said some of the kitchen maids found you in an overturned wagon. Do you remember the accident?"

Accident? What accident? She had left Tomas' house dazed and confused, driving the wagon towards Isaac's house. Bailey had said he would follow her to ensure she made it to Kilmore safely. She must have passed out and Bailey. Bailey! Bailey must have caused the wagon to overturn. Instead of helping her he made her injuries worse. Oh, the gall of that man! He hadn't caused her injuries so that Isaac would believe her story. He had done so to spite her. It was her punishment for defying him.

"Kathleen," Isaac called to her softly.

Kathleen turned her eyes towards him. She had learned her lesson. Bailey had suspected she was a problem to his cause but he couldn't kill her. She was still of use to his plans. If only she could turn those plans against him without harming her family. Bailey had made her plans more attainable with her punishment. She became the wounded damsel in distress that she needed to be so Isaac would have pity on her.

"Kathleen," he called to her again.

"Hmm, I'm sorry. It hurts."

"I know. Kathleen, do you know whose body was in the back of the wagon?"

"Sherlock McGillpatrick."

"Were you coming to Kilmore with his body so I could help you?"

Kathleen nodded. "He...he..." she swallowed hard, not believing she was about to say what she was going to tell him.

"It's alright, my dear, you are safe. Who shot him?"

"Tomas."

"What happened?"

"We were enjoying our dinner last night when Sherlock attacked Collinsworth with a band of rebels. Tomas and some of the servants tried to defend us but they were quickly overpowered. They beat us and then dragged us into the parlor. Tomas was beaten then they threw his body into the parlor with Calico and me."

"Is he alive?"

"Yes, but badly wounded. Oh, Isaac it was the worst night of my life. The Irish rebels did the most unthinkable things to us."

"Did he touch you?"

"No, he was saving that for this morning."

"For this morning?"

"All of the rebels were gathering by the stables when you arrived at our house. Sherlock was going to allow the rebels to have their way with Calico and me after they hung Tomas for treason. You saved Tomas' life. Sherlock sent me to tell you to go away. I wanted to tell you what was happening to my family but was too scared to do so."

"I thought something was wrong. I should have acted on my instincts."

"You would have made matters worse for us if you had. Sherlock said Tomas and all the Irish nobles who turned Anglican in order to keep their lands and titles deserved to be hung for treason. They would have hung you too. Sherlock was furious with you for what you did to him and his brother."

"Did he say where his brother is?"

"No, only that Bailey is severely wounded and is unable to walk without crutches."

"Good. That will make it easier to find him. How did you end up in a wagon with Sherlock's dead body?

"When I returned Sherlock had taken his eyes off of Tomas long enough for Tomas to kill to him. Sherlock fell onto the back of the wagon that had brought them to the house. Tomas told me to take the wagon to you and plead for your aide. When I left, Tomas, Calico and the servants were fighting the rebels. Uhmm," she groaned, turning her head.

"Well, it would be unsafe for you to return to Collinsworth. You must stay at Kilmore."

"I agree. What about my sister and Tomas?"

"I will personally lead a unit of soldiers to Collinsworth in order to rescue them."

"Where will the soldiers come from?"

"Here"

"Here?"

"A few months ago, I contracted with his majesty, allowing his army to use parts of Kilmore as a garrison. They have taken residence in the cottages where Sherlock and Bailey used to live. How ironic, huh? The English army residing in the same residences built by the very hands they hunt for. They even use the stables the brothers had shared."

"Ironic indeed."

Isaac rose from beside her. "You require rest, Lady Kathleen. I will make certain one of the maids prepares a room for your stay."

"If it's not too much of a bother I would like to request the room I was in when I fainted at my sister's wedding."

"It's not a bother at all. I shall see to it, then. Rest well, Lady Kathleen." Isaac bowed. Kathleen watched him begin to walk out of the room. Finally, she was in his home. Oh, but she could do without the pain she felt. She relished the thought of helping Isaac destroy Bailey and being able to live in her old room, but…

"My lord," she called to him.

Isaac turned to face her. "Yes."

"What is to be done with Sherlock's body?"

"I was going to dispose of it in a manner not befitting a woman's ears."

"How?"

Isaac closed the door behind him and stepped towards her. "Kathleen, why does it matter? He invaded your home, beat and tried to kill Tomas, and then was going to hand you over to the rebels so they could rape you. I would think you wouldn't have any concern for his body."

"I don't but even Jesus taught his disciples to love their enemy."

Isaac clenched his jaw, "Bah, these rebel rats have no love for us, why should we have love for them?"

"Isaac, it takes two to have a war. If we keep retaliating then they will too. If we show love and compassion to their beloved leader then perhaps the fighting will end."

"And how do you suppose I show them this love and compassion you speak of?"

"Kilmore is ancient, is it not?"

"Yes, it was built in the 16th century by an Irish duke. Local legend says before that it was a castle built with wood dating to the 13th century. The Irish duke ordered the castle be built in stone. Duke Alexander McGillpatrick converted the castle into a great house. He began the work and my father finished a few years after he had displaced Alexander from title and estate. My father was granted the title earl because his majesty felt the title of duke was too high of a station for my father."

"Surely a noble family as old as the McGillpatrick family was buried beneath the floor of the Kilmore Cathedral. It was a Catholic place of worship until the Catholics were removed from their places of worship in 1704. There must be a graveyard near the church for those less fortunate."

"It's illegal to bury a Catholic in a church's graveyard."

"Do you not think Alexander McGillpatrick would know this as well?"

"Kathleen, you are not thinking with a rational mind. If I bury Sherlock McGillpatrick, a Catholic, in Kilmore Cathedral's graveyard, I would be fined and ridiculed by our society for doing so. Is that what you want? You want me to lose my standing with the other nobles? My father worked hard to establish this estate and the title I inherited from him. I risk losing everything I have by conducting myself in the manner you desire."

"No one has to know, Isaac."

"Everyone will know! The rebels will proclaim what I had done to everyone they can get to listen."

"But not everyone listens to them, do they?"

Isaac exhaled a deep breath. "Kathleen."

"Alright, let's say you don't bury him in the graveyard. Surely there is somewhere else on Kilmore they cherish."

"There's an ancient cemetery close to a burial mound about an hour's ride from the house. The locals claim the mound holds the ancient ancestors of the McGillpatrick family. I could bury him in the cemetery then slip it to one of the locals I have done so. I'm certain word would travel fast to Alexander and Bailey."

"Would you disturb the mound?"

"No, I'll bury him beneath the mound. There are several large, flat boulders sticking out of the ground. I am told those are the markers where his ancestors are buried. I've been wanting to explore the area myself for sometime."

"Promise me, you will show me where you bury him when I am well enough to travel."

"Of course. Why the interest? Do you not trust I will do this?"

"I trust you, Isaac. I have an interest in the history of this place too. My sister and I were raised Anglican by our Anglican parents. It was their parents who had converted. I know so very little about my Irish heritage. The stories intrigue me."

"That I can understand. I shall leave you so you can rest, Lady Kathleen."

"What if I am in need of something?"

"I shall not be far. I need to inform the general of your story then I will return to you. I will never leave you, Kathleen. Never."

Kathleen smiled. "Thank you," she whispered.

Isaac walked next to her, knelt beside her, and kissed her on her smallpox-scarred cheek. "I promise I will never allow any harm to come to you again." Kathleen turned her face, as his lips delicately traced her skin. Eye to eye they stared lovingly at each other. He lowered his lips to her swollen ones and gently kissed her. "I...I lo...," he rose suddenly and pulled down his vest. "Lady Kathleen," he bowed then left her room. Isaac leaned against the wall in the Great Hall, closed his eyes, and heaved. How dare he try to kiss her! Kathleen wasn't some woman he was trying to bed with. At first she had been that to him but the more she had tried to dissuade him the more he had fallen in love with her. He wasn't going to treat her like the other women. No. Kathleen deserved respect and he was going to give it to her. He was going to win her love. He was going to treat her like the precious jewel she really was and he was going to start by burying Sherlock with his ancestors.

Chapter 15

Calico stared up at her bedroom ceiling in complete amazement. So many thoughts had gone through her mind about her wedding night. Fears of how painful sex would be or how Tomas might be ugly underneath his clothes. What if his penis didn't work right or he found her body to be less than desirable? All those silly little fears no longer existed for her. The sex she had shared with Tomas was magnificent. He was magnificent. She never wanted him to leave her bed, yet she knew he must at some time. It was improper for husbands and wives to share the same bedroom. Tomas had given her the entire right wing of the great house while he controlled the left side. Their master bedrooms lie next to each other on the second floor but were separated from each other by a personal dressing room and a personal parlor for each. They would have to walk down the hallway, enter the parlor, then work their way to their beloved's bedroom. Of course there was a secret passageway where Tomas could sneak into her bedroom and vice versa so that no one would be the wiser if they wanted to keep their marital encounters a secret.

Calico pulled the white sheet over her large breasts and rolled next to her new husband. She laid her head on Tomas' sweaty body. "You are the most wonderful creature God has ever placed on this earth," Tomas said, cupping her cheek with his hand. Calico's long raven-black hair fell over her shoulder. She grinned as he leaned in to kiss her. Her lips gently touched his. Tomas pushed Calico underneath him, kissing her with more passion. Then he pulled away from her, gasping, "I want more from you. You intoxicate me," he whispered as his lips trailed down her long neck.

Calico gasped, "I take it you're not sleeping in your bedchambers tonight."

"Sleep, who said anything about sleep? This is our wedding night. I wasn't planning to do anything but create my heir."

"So soon?"

"This night wasn't soon enough for me, Calico. I have wanted you to carry my son for some time now."

They rolled around several times until she sat on top of his erect penis. She rocked her body as he held onto her hips, their sensual groans lifting in the air. He pulled her over him and suckled her breasts. Suddenly a knock on the door beckoned to interrupt their passion.

"Go away," Tomas growled, grabbing Calico and rolling her underneath him.

"I wish I could, Tomas, but I can't. Bailey and I need you," Alexander's deep voice called from behind the door.

"I'm a bit preoccupied with my wife at the moment and I suspect we will be asleep throughout the day tomorrow. I plan to make love to your daughter well into the night. Whatever it is, wait until tomorrow night!" Tomas said, thrusting hard into Calico.

Tomas and Calico rolled several more times in the bed, grabbing and kissing each other.

"Tomas, I understand you and my daughter have waited a long time for this night."

"Ugh, you have no idea," he yelled, arching his back while underneath Calico and grabbing her firm bottom. Calico's groans grew louder with each thrust. She arched her back and pushed faster as he played with her clit.

"Tomas," she screamed, grabbing his legs as he moaned.

Alexander yelled behind the door, "It has been three hours since you entered my daughter's bedchamber."

"Go away, father," Calico yelled.

"I have tried to give you two plenty of time to join together under God."

"Leave us alone," Calico and Tomas yelled together.

"Tomas, have you spilled your seed inside her?"

Tomas moaned sexually, ignoring Alexander's question.

"Tomas, I need you to open this door. Sherlock is dead and Isaac has Kathleen! It will only be a matter of time before Isaac comes for you."

Tomas and Calico paused and stared into each other's eyes. "He…did he just say…?" Calico started to speak, leaning over her husband with her hands on his broad chest. Tomas placed his finger over her lips.

"Get off me," he ordered her softly. Calico rolled off her husband and got out of bed with the sheet wrapped around her body. She watched Tomas rise from the bed. He picked up her shift and threw it towards her. "Put it on," he ordered, grabbing his shirt and pants. Calico dropped the sheet, grabbed her shift, and complied with her husband's orders. She picked up her red robe from the chair and wrapped it around her body, tying it in the front with the string hanging on both ends. Her long hair hung down her back.

"Tomas," she muttered as he put his coat on. Tomas turned in her direction with his boots. "Do you think she's hurt?"

"I don't know. Open the door and let your father in," he said, fully dressed and putting his boots on.

Calico nodded, fearfully walking towards the door. *How could Sherlock be dead and Kathleen be with Isaac? Sherlock had taken Mary back to her room. What about Kathleen? Kathleen had been at the dinner feasts, hadn't she?* She searched her mind for answers but couldn't come up with a single one. The last time she had seen Kathleen was at the wedding when she had accused Tomas of marrying her out of convenience. She had been livid with Kathleen for suggesting Tomas didn't love her. Of course, Kathleen hadn't been far from the truth. When she and Tomas had begun their courtship she didn't have any feelings for him whatsoever. Love was a luxury for any couple. If they fell in love then it was an added blessing. What mattered most in marriage was the benefits one derived by the union. She had risen in Anglican society with her union to Tomas and was able to become the perfect spy for the resistance. Tomas could have had any Catholic woman he had wanted but he chose her instead, his best friend's little sister. Calico opened the door and stared at her father and brother.

Bailey gazed his eyes up and down his sister's body with a grin. "Tomas?" he asked. Tomas looked up at his friend. "How well did she do in your bed?"

"That is the most inappropriate question…," Calico objected.

Bailey grabbed her by the jaw. "Your satisfaction doesn't matter to me, Calico. Have you or have you not satisfied your husband more than this one encounter is all I'm concerned about," Bailey demanded.

"She has, Bailey," Tomas answered. "She makes me very happy. I've spilled my seed in her three times already. I can't get enough of her body."

"Good," Bailey snarled then pushed his sister back. "He needs an heir," he ordered, pointing to Tomas.

"I will give him more than one, Bailey. I promise. I know my marital duties," Calico answered.

"May we come inside?" Alexander asked, changing the subject.

Calico nodded and opened the door wider. Alexander and Bailey stepped into her large bedroom. "I'll go to Mary," Calico said to the group of men.

"No, Jane has gone to your sister to tell her of your brother's death. I need you here," Alexander ordered.

Calico glared at her father. Why would they need her? She closed the door and locked it in place. Calico joined Tomas on the side of the bed, holding his hand. Alexander and Bailey sat in front of the couple in Calico's chairs. "What happened?" Tomas asked.

"We don't know much about Sherlock, only that he was in the kitchen with Kathleen. The cook says he was talking to her. When he rose from the table it looked as if he was in pain. He stumbled then fell dead," Bailey said.

"What does Kathleen say," Calico asked.

"Not much. I have not seen her since we found her over Sherlock's body."

"Do you think she killed him?"

"No, we know she didn't kill him." Alexander answered. "I think Sherlock's brain was damaged by the blow to the head he received from Isaac. It was only a matter of time before he died. There was blood coming from his ears when we examined his body."

"What does this have to do with Isaac and Kathleen?" Tomas asked in confusion.

"My sister has agreed to woo Isaac into marrying her and then spy on him for the resistance," Bailey answered.

"She has?" Tomas and Calico asked together.

"Why would she? She hates everything we have done for the resistance," Calico replied.

"I don't know why she has agreed to it, only that she has. We have given her a cover story but we need you and Tomas to play your parts," Alexander said.

"Alright, what do you need from us?" Tomas said.

"The story Kathleen has given Isaac is that Sherlock attacked your home last night while you, Kathleen, and Calico were at dinner. You tried to fight him off but he beat you until you fell unconscious."

"You would need...," Tomas glanced at Bailey, "You want to beat me up!"

"Yes, but not enough to kill you. There's more," Bailey answered.

Calico clutched Tomas' hand tight. She couldn't believe her ears. Never could she imagine Bailey would want to lay a hand on her husband. They were best friends! "How...?," she swallowed hard, not wanting to think what Bailey could have done to Kathleen. "How did Kathleen escape and where is Sherlock's body?"

Alexander continued, "Sherlock locked you, Kathleen, and Isaac in this room. The three of you were bound and gagged. Thus no one heard your screams. He had locked the servants in the pantry. They stayed there all night. The next morning he led you, your sister, and Tomas to the back yard. I led a small group of rebels close to the stables. Sherlock had handed you ladies over to several rebels who were being less than gentlemen with you,"

"Father! If I become pregnant then someone could suspect the child doesn't belong to Tomas," Calico cried.

Alexander waved his hand to her. "Don't fret, Calico, the men never raped you or Kathleen. There wasn't enough time. Sherlock had just placed the rope around Tomas' neck and I had slapped the horse underneath him when Kathleen broke loose from the rebels. She ran towards Sherlock. Sherlock beat her face in. She still didn't submit so he hit her over the head with a gun. The gun slipped out of his hand. Somehow the servants had been set free, you were gone and the servants began to attack the rebels. You reappeared in the chaos and were able to release Tomas from his noose just in time for Tomas to find the gun and shoot Sherlock in the head. Kathleen escaped with Sherlock's body in the back of a wagon and went running to Isaac for aide. You have not seen her since. The servants were able to drive the rebels away but Tomas needs time to recuperate from his wounds."

"Isaac will come to my aide once he learns of this. He'll expect to see my wounds," Tomas said.

"Yes," Bailey said, pulling out a large rope from inside his coat.

"No," Calico panicked, grabbing Tomas's shirt.

Tomas pulled Calico away. "You shot Sherlock in the head after he died?" he asked Bailey.

"Yes. I beat Kathleen too. She wasn't very willing. I followed her when she was taking the wagon to Kilmore. She was disoriented enough for me to cause her wagon to overturn. Now she has believable wounds for being in a fight with rebels. I suspect she may have more than one broken bone."

"Bailey," Calico rose to her feet.

"I don't see why you are objecting, Calico. You have always been stronger than Kathleen," Bailey said.

"Desecrating Sherlock's body is one thing, but now you're attacking your own siblings and best friend? Where does it end?"

"It ends when father is the Earl of Kilmore once again!"

Calico and Tomas exchanged glances. She had given her life so that her father would control Kilmore. Everything, her marriage and infiltrating the Anglicans, was all for her father. She was used to Bailey using people for the resistance, but never would she have imagined he would hurt his own family for the cause. Tomas rose from the bed and stood before her, holding her hand. "Calico," he said to her.

"I was so angry with her at the wedding. But she's more than a sister to me. She's my best friend."

"I know it must hurt to hear what Bailey has done to Kathleen. I know I would be upset if something had happened to my best friend."

Calico huffed, "Bailey is the best fighter we have on the resistance. I doubt anyone can harm him."

"I beg to differ," Bailey said, casting his eyes on his broken leg. "If I was so unbreakable I would not have suffered as I did and Sherlock would be alive. I failed Sherlock, Calico." Calico turned to Bailey. "Do you not think it hurt me to know the state he was in?" Bailey said.

"I know it did," Calico answered. "There must have been another way to deter Isaac from interfering with the wedding. Kathleen is unstable. One moment she is supporting our decisions and the next she's not. How can you be certain she will commit to the plan we have set forth?"

"Because she's angry at me," Bailey answered.

"She's angry with me as well but Kathleen is quick to forgive. It's one of the traits she gained from mother."

"Your mother has another trait that Kathleen possesses as well," Alexander said.

"What is that, father?"

"Loyalty. Kathleen is a hopeless romantic who has fallen in love with our enemy. If she wins his affections she will be loyal to him."

"The problem with that is what she will do with the loyalty," Tomas said.

"What do you mean?" Bailey asked him.

"First of all she's a woman. Women are the weaker sex because they are incapable of thinking with logic. If Kathleen has fallen in love with Isaac, which we all know she has, then the question that remains to be answered is whom does she love more, her family or Isaac?"

"Her family," Calico interjected.

"Are you certain?" Tomas asked her.

"She told me so."

"She also told you she hated Bailey and it's no secret her loyalties had lain with Sherlock. Sherlock is dead. If I was Kathleen and harbored that much resistance towards my brother I would do anything in my power to punish him. That is if I wasn't listening to my logic. My logic would tell me it would be a dangerous move to place myself against Bailey and throw myself into Anglican hands."

"And you think that is what she has done?"

"I know that is what my daughter has done," Alexander said. Everyone turned their attention to the grey-haired, slightly heavy man. "Calico, Bailey and I aren't ignorant to her motives. What remains now is to ensure she does not turn against this family. We need Isaac to believe the attack on Collinsworth happened. You will be Kathleen's contact and you must, I cannot stress this enough, *must* ensure she remains loyal to our cause."

"Do you think you can do that?" Bailey asked.

"Of course, but she's angry with me," Calico said.

"You two have never stayed angry at each other for longer than a day. Make amends with her. You are the best choice for ensuring she remains true to the cause. With you by Kathleen's side, she will feel more comfortable with her situation once the shock of what has happened has passed from her mind."

"And what do you want to do with me? Am I to be beaten as well?"

"No, Calico. Father made the story up so you wouldn't be harmed. But I do need to hurt your husband."

Tomas grabbed Calico's hand and squeezed. She looked back at her husband. "I know you can do it," he encouraged her.

"That is not what bothers me. We have had so few times to be alone and tonight was supposed to be our night to create your heir."

"We've tried many times tonight, Calico. Bailey's ensured if we have conceived then no harm will come to you or our child. Isaac won't believe our story unless he sees the wounds on me. I need my strong, Irish wife."

"You have her. But what if they kill you?"

"They won't. Bailey knows how hard to pull the noose to make someone pass out and not die. We've done it plenty of times when kidnapping people." She grabbed the sides of his face with her hands and kissed him fully on the lips. He pushed her lips away from his. "You always said you wanted Kathleen to join us."

"Not like this!"

Tomas lifted his eyes to hers. "It seems to be the only way."

"No!"

He pressed his finger to her lips. "Calico, it has to be done. I don't want you here when your father and brother attack me. Go to the servants and order them to tell the story your father and brother just told us. Do you think you can remember it?"

"Yes," Calico cried.

"Good. A majority of the servants are in the resistance. You tell my brothers if anyone doesn't believe you then they have it on my orders to make them do so. Understood?"

"Tomas," she pleaded.

"Understood, my wife?" he stressed the last two words.

"Understood," she replied, knowing he wasn't going to back down.

"Good. Tell the servants they must spread the news to the tenant farmers. Word would have spread quickly about the incident by now. Isaac isn't a fool. He'll talk to the tenant farmers that border our property and Kilmore. Make certain they all lie, even that Anglican farmer who's been feeding him information. You tell my brothers to lead raiding parties to ensure the story spreads. Do you understand everything I have asked you to do, Calico?"

"Yes."

"Good, go," he nodded towards the door.

Calico grabbed his head and kissed him again. "I love you, Tomas Patrick Collins," she whispered, released her grip, and walked out of the room. Calico leaned her back on the door, closed her eyes, and listened to the scuffle inside. She closed her eyes and prayed to her saint for Tomas' safety as the sound of her father and brother beating her husband echoed in her ears.

Chapter 16

Jane quietly closed the door of Sherlock's bedroom with her eyes on the bed. Mary slept quietly with her hand on Sherlock's side of the bed. She hated to bring the news to her ailing daughter of Sherlock's death. Mary had been through so much in her life. Mary had married Sherlock when she was seventeen years old, twenty-two years ago. Sherlock had instantly been smitten with Mary when he met her on their wedding day. Bailey, on the other hand, never loved Mary's older sister. Their marriage had been a marriage of convience. Jane's daughters had come from a long line of Irish nobles. Mary and her older sister had added to the Kilmore estate with money, jewels, and land. When Jane married Alexander the following year, she brought with her thirteen acres and three cottages close to the border of Kilmore and Kilmore Village. The times were plentiful yet through her twenty-one years of marriage to Alexander she had seen that prosperity turn into heartache and poverty. Her poor daughters had gone through it with her. It was heartache enough to know her youngest daughters, Kathleen and Calico, had to live through it, but Mary and her dead sister—that was another matter. Mary had been strong for all of them. She had lost her father, children, sister, and now her husband was dead and Kathleen was missing. Oh, if this pain would ever go away. Jane didn't know how her daughter was able to cope with it all. Her own heart ached knowing Kathleen was in danger. Her motherly instincts had kicked into overdrive when Alexander told her Bailey had beaten their daughter and sent her into their enemy's hands. She wanted to run straight to Isaac's house and snatch her daughter from his grip. But she couldn't. If she did that she would place her family in further danger. Her only hope lay in Calico's hands.

"Hmm, Sherlock," Mary moaned, rolling onto her back and opening her eyes.

"Mary, it's mother," Jane answered, walking around the bed. She sat beside her daughter and stroked her long black hair. "How do you feel?"

"My stomach is still upset. Where's my husband?" Jane averted her daughter's gaze, trying to find the best way to deliver the blow. Mary leaned up on her elbows. "Mother, what's happened?"

Jane turned her eyes back to her daughter. "Mary, he's…"

"Where's Sherlock?"

"I'm so sorry, my colleen. He left with Kathleen while you were sleeping. They went to the kitchen, conversed, and he had a headache."

"I told him to rest when he has those."

"He is at peace now, Mary."

"I'm glad but why isn't he in here with me?"

"You misunderstand me, daughter. Sherlock cannot come to your bed any longer."

Mary's face fell with comprehension. She knew that look on her mother's face. She had seen it the day Jane had told Bailey that her sister was dead. "Wha...what?"

"He rose from the table, stumbled around, and fell dead in front of your sister. There was blood coming from his ears. Alexander said his brain must have been damaged."

"No," Mary yelled, rising from the bed. "I want to see him," she cried, grabbing her robe and throwing it over her body.

Jane stepped in front of her shorter daughter. She grabbed her by the arms, stopping her in mid-stride. "You cannot."

"Mother, please, he was my husband!"

"I know, Mary, but his body isn't here."

"Then take me to him. Please."

"I cannot. Mary, Bailey shot his brother in the head then sent Sherlock's body with Kathleen to Kilmore."

Mary gasped and fell limp in her mother's arms. Jane grabbed her daughter and led her to a chair by the window. She knelt before her, caressing her daughter's face. The shock of the news had been more than Mary could bear but Jane knew Mary needed to hear it from her first. If anyone should bear the news to her daughter, it needed to be her. "Mary," she called softly to her.

"Wh…why? Was Bailey certain my husband was dead?"

"Alexander examined him before he allowed it."

"But mother, Alexander was a judge and lawyer not a doctor. How would he know?"

"There was a trail of blood coming out of your husband's ears. Mary, Alexander and his sons have been in enough battles to know when a person is dead or not. Do you not trust what I am telling you to be the truth?"

"But his last rites?"

"They were given when he laid upon your bed and Alexander had feared his son would die. Sherlock's soul will have a quicker journey through purgatory." Mary put her hands on her face, leaned over, and began to sob. Jane held her daughter. She knew the sting of that pain all too well. She had been married to Mary's father nineteen years when her husband had died unexpectedly from a heart attack. The shock hits you so hard you don't know how you will ever cope. She had no warning and the shock had hit her so hard Mary and her sister had to care for her during the first year after their father's death. Mary, on the other hand, had it worse than she ever did. Death had taunted her and hope had seduced her into believing Sherlock had overcome death's grip. It wasn't right. How can a woman prepare for her husband's demise when she believes he had overcome death? Mary had every right to be more distraught than usual for a grieving widow.

"This is his fault," Mary cried, lifting her head.

"How can Sherlock be at fault?"

"No, mother. Bailey! Bailey McGillpatrick," she yelled, rising in her chair. Her face grew red with anger. Mary clutched her stomach and vomited in the chamber pot beside her bed. Jane knelt beside her and held back her daughter's long hair. "That man abused my sister…"

"You have no proof of that."

Mary turned her eyes towards her mother. "How can you say that when you saw the bruises and her spirit broken by that man? She's dead because of him. Him and his stupid rebellion!"

"Mary, he's fighting for the old ways. There's something noble in that."

"Noble. Ha! All he… Ugh…" She groaned then vomited again. Jane rubbed her daughter's back. Mary glared at the pot, saying sternly, "My sister, my children, my nieces and nephews, and now my husband are dead because of that man. I swear by God, mother, he will not lay a hand on Kathleen, me, or my child!"

"Child!" Jane gasped. Mary wiped her mouth with her sleeve and faced her mother with a stern look. "I had suspected as much but wasn't certain."

"Does anyone else suspect?'

"No, the women have thought you were overcome with grief concerning your husband's ailment. I let them believe that, but Mary, I knew. I just knew you were with child."

"How?"

Jane laughed, "Because you are acting like you did with your last seven pregnancies. Why didn't you say something?"

"Sherlock and I didn't want Bailey to learn of my condition. We felt with the way things went the last time I was with child it was best if we disappeared so Bailey would not continue to ruin our lives."

"Disappear? Where would you go?"

"I can't go anywhere now. Not without seeing my husband's body."

"Mary, I don't understand. What does Sherlock's body have to do with your disappearance?"

"He kept a letter inside his vest from a French contact in New Orleans who had made a deal with my husband. He would give Sherlock his entire estate if he could make the journey to the New World. Sherlock was planning, when things got too rough or if I ever conceived, whichever came first, to buy three tickets on a ship in Dublin bound for New Orleans."

"Three?"

"Kathleen."

"Oh, that explains Sherlock's added interest in your sister of late." Jane rose from the floor and paced the room as Mary rose to her feet. "Why didn't you ever tell me?"

"Sherlock was afraid you would tell his father and Alexander would tell Bailey."

"Was Sherlock able to save money for your expenses?"

"Yes."

"You know this contact?"

"No, but I know how to find him. Sherlock showed me a map he kept with the contract."

Jane pivoted towards her daughter's direction "Well then, there is only one thing left for you to do then."

"What?"

"Have Kathleen steal the letter from Sherlock's body, give it to you, and then the two of you leave for New Orleans. But it may prove more difficult than it sounds."

"Why?"

"Bailey beat her then ordered her to take Sherlock's body to Isaac."

Mary wiped her mouth with her sleeve and turned to her mother. "You let him do that to your own daughter? Mother!"

"I was not there when it happened. Alexander was."

"Alexander's worse than the devil himself."

Jane slapped her daughter hard. "How dare you speak about your step-father like that!" She lowered her hand, catching the glimpse of pain and shock on her daughter's pale face. She had never struck any of her daughters before. Jane couldn't believe her actions. Mary was with child and grieving for her husband. Jane had struck her mentally and physically distraught daughter. "Mary, I'm so sorry," she whispered.

"How could you?"

"I don't know what came over me."

"Alexander," she growled and walked to the window.

Jane wiped her hands down her face, lifting her eyes to the ceiling. How was she ever going to reach her daughter? She couldn't bear to allow Mary's bitterness to turn her daughter against her. She was all Jane had left from her life before she had married Alexander.

Jane walked to her daughter and rubbed her arms from behind. "Mary, I am so sorry. I know the pain you bare. You loved him. I think some days the women who never fall in love with their husbands have it easier than the ones who do when their husbands die. They don't feel death's sting. Oh, Mary. My dear, sweet, Mary, don't let your pain ruin your life."

"The only thing that has ruined my life is the day the matchmaker arranged for my sister and me to marry into the McGillpatrick family!"

Jane turned her daughter towards her. She wiped the tears from Mary's eyes. "You cannot believe that. If the matchmaker had never made the arrangement then you wouldn't have ever met Sherlock let alone bare his children. You can't deny those were the best years of your life. You were a wonderful wife and mother. And look at you now. You're with his child again. Sherlock has given you the opportunity to start a new life for yourself far away from Bailey."

"I don't doubt my marriage to Sherlock was the best of my years, but something has to be done about Bailey. He killed my husband! He wanted James Turner to kill me a few years ago. I know Bailey didn't want to rescue me. Sherlock told me the truth."

"It doesn't matter. What matters is that you are safe." The door burst open. Mary and Jane turned in the direction of the noise. Calico stood in the doorway, watching her mother and older sister.

"Go away," Mary yelled, pushing their mother behind her in rage.

"This is my house, not yours. I will go where I see fit to go and I see fit to be in this room," Calico said, closing the door behind her.

"Get out," Mary yelled, pushing her sister against the door. Calico glanced at their mother then back to her distraught sister.

"Why are you angry with me? I didn't kill my brother."

"No, you aided in it. I know you did, Calico. You're a traitor to our mother. You, a countess of Ireland. Bah! You're nothing but Bailey's servant."

"I was born into my title. You're just the daughter of a middle-class lawyer who happened to own his own farm! Tell me, Mary, did your father steal that too?"

Mary lunged towards Calico. "Liar, my father was an earl!"

"Oh, excuse me. I forgot my father was richer than yours," Calico pushed her sister back.

"That's all you McGillpatrick's do. Lie, cheat, and steal. I despise that we share the same mother!"

"The feeling is mutual. You and Sherlock have been poisoning Kathleen with thoughts against Bailey ever since you lost your children from the smallpox. I won't have you interfere with Kathleen's mission. I know you will. I know what kind of woman you are, Mary. I really wish Sherlock had never convinced Bailey to free you when James Turner captured you."

"Calico," Jane gasped. "She's your sister."

"Yes, mother, and Sherlock was my brother! So what?! Mary is going to do what Mary always does. Cause trouble for the resistance. I won't stand for it. Kathleen knows her assignment." Calico stepped closer to Mary. She grabbed her sister by her robe and pulled her towards her. "Let me make myself crystal clear, sister. You do anything to convince

Kathleen not to proceed with Bailey's plans and I will have you arrested as Sherlock's wife, tried as a political prisoner, and sold into slavery so fast you won't see it coming. Do we understand each other?"

"Look at you, Calico. Bailey has his claws deep inside you. Why are you allowing him to destroy you? Sherlock was more of a brother to him than you are a sister to me. You know what he did to him. You're married to his best friend. What makes you think Tomas won't turn on you if Bailey gives the order? Bailey cares about no one except himself."

"I didn't come here to fight with you, Mary, but if it's a fight you want then so be it!"

Mary and Calico grabbed each other's hair and fell to the floor, wresting each other. They rolled several times, clawing at each other. Jane ran to her daughters. She pulled Calico off Mary. "Enough, both of you," Jane yelled to them, glancing from one to the other. Mary wiped the blood from her busted lip. "You all right?" Jane asked, holding Calico back.

"Yes, mother," Mary answered while rising from the floor.

Jane turned her attention to her younger daughter. "What, other than to torment your sister, do you want?"

Calico snarled at Mary, pushing against her mother. "You're not the only one whose husband is being hurt by Bailey! It's your fault. You know that? Your fault!"

"I don't understand," Mary answered.

Jane grabbed her daughter by the jaw and forced Calico to look at her. "I asked you a question, Calico. What do you want?"

Calico looked at her mother with tears in her eyes. "I did everything Tomas asked of me. His brothers have gathered the rebels. Six patrols have left this house and are raiding Collinsworth in all directions. Father has told me to inform you and Mary that you are not to leave the ground floor. He says he doubts Isaac will come to the servant's level."

"Have you seen your husband?"

Calico sniffed her nose, shook her head, embraced Jane, and buried her head in her mother's chest. "Oh, dear child, come," Jane said, guiding her to the bed. The women sat down. Jane kissed the top of Calico's head and rocked her. Mary walked closer to them.

"I don't understand, mother," Mary said, sitting on the other side. Jane wrapped her arm around Mary's back.

"Bailey has beaten her husband to make it look like he was attacked by rebels. She is Kathleen's best friend. You lost a husband today. Calico's husband and sister were beaten. Kathleen is in the lion's den, so to speak, and Tomas, well, Tomas was not only beaten but also almost suffocated to death. She has been asked to stand by her brother's story while her husband and sister are risking their lives for the resistance more so than they have done before. Mary, she has a right to be as distressed as you are."

Mary took Calico's hand. Calico lifted her eyes to her sister. "We cry together, little sister, in mother's arms?" Mary coaxed.

Calico sniffed her nose and nodded. "I still don't like you," Calico protested, pulling her hand away.

"I know," Mary, acknowledged, as Jane held both her daughters close.

"You may not like each other but I love both of you dearly," Jane said softly, kissing both their foreheads.

Chapter 17

Isaac rode hard in the pouring rain towards Tomas' great house. He leaned over his horse, clutching his coat as his chestnut mare splashed through the puddles. His mother had urged him not to ride in such treacherous conditions but he had to see Tomas. He had to make certain his friend was all right and that he knew Kathleen was at his home. Isaac could have sent a servant to deliver a message to Tomas concerning Kathleen but he didn't trust servants. Not with this kind of information. If Tomas killed Sherlock, and Kathleen had attacked Sherlock, then it wouldn't be long before the rebels would attack them again in retribution. Kathleen and Tomas had placed their lives in danger. He was going to make certain no harm came to them.

"Earl Turner," the stableman said to him as he stopped his horse next to Tomas' stable.

Isaac dismounted quickly, handing the young man the reins. "Where is your master?" Isaac demanded.

"In his bedroom."

Isaac nodded then ran around the house to the front door. The thunder rolled behind him as the sharp wind moved the rain sideways. He looked up at the dark sky. Even the heavens mourned for the tragedy that had befallen them. Isaac lowered his eyes back to the door and knocked loudly. He hoped the butler would hear his knocks in these horrible weather conditions. Isaac waited, impatiently tapping his foot. The cold rain soaked down to his bones. He knocked harder. A few unbearable moments later Tomas' butler opened the door. "About time, Gerald," Isaac scowled, entering the main hallways.

Gerald closed the door behind Isaac then quickly turned his attention to him. "I'm sorry, Earl Turner. I did not hear you with the rain. May I offer you something warm to drink or a blanket?"

"No, take me to your master. I must speak to him at once," he barked, handing Gerald his hat and outer coat.

"I'm afraid he has been injured," Gerald answered, placing the hat and coat in the other room.

"Yes, yes, yes. I know all about that. Lady Kathleen has told me. Take me to him!"

"Very well, sir. This way," Gerald answered without hesitation, walking swiftly out of the side room.

Isaac followed the tall Irishman up the stairs on his right. The long second floor hallway was much larger than the ones at Kilmore. Beautiful paintings of the Irish landscape adorned the hallway between various tapestries. Tomas loved his country dearly and the hallway showed it. They continued to walk down the long hallway until they were in the middle of the house. The butler paused as a door at the end of the hallway opened. Calico exited Tomas' parlor and closed the door behind her.

"Countess Calico," the butler said, bowing his head. "Earl Isaac Turner," he introduced, moving out of the way so Calico could see her guest.

"Oh, dear," she gasped, taking notice of Isaac's state. "Gerald, find a blanket and warm clothes for him. He'll catch his death in his miserable state."

"Yes, ma'am," the butler said then disappeared.

Isaac stepped towards Calico, studying her very closely. She didn't seem to have been injured yet strands of her hair had fallen out of its bun as if she hadn't been able to maintain her composure. Her cheeks showed the signs of crying. Everything about her showed a woman who was trying to hide her distress. Calico wasn't the kind of woman to bear her emotions in public. "I came as soon as I heard," Isaac said, stepping towards the slender woman.

"My sister is missing. There was so much chaos we have no idea where she went. All we know is Sherlock's body is missing and so is she."

"She is at Kilmore."

"Oh, thank the heavens," Calico exhaled as if a huge weight had been lifted from her shoulders.

Isaac stepped towards her. "Kathleen lost control of the wagon and it overturned just outside the outer gates of Kilmore."

"Is she...?"

"No. My physician says she has a concussion, broken ribs, black eye, broken nose, and a bruised abdomen. She is quite fortunate that is all. I gave her one of the guest rooms so she could recuperate safely under my care."

"Thank you. Tomas and I appreciate your kindness."

"You're welcome. May I visit with your husband?"

Calico silently turned to the door. She opened the parlor door and stepped aside. Isaac moved towards the fireplace and warmed his body next to the fire while Calico closed the door behind him. He watched her walk towards the back of the parlor to the two doors on his left hand side. "Wait here. I'll see if my husband is awake," she said.

"Of course," he answered.

Calico stepped through the door on the right and closed it behind her. Isaac turned his attention back to the fire. He crouched, rubbing his hands together. What little of the house he had seen looked to be in order. That didn't surprise him, though. It was evening already. The attack had happened last night and Tomas had killed Sherlock this morning. It would make sense for Calico to want to have the house in order so soon after the attack. She wouldn't want the servants to stop working, nor would she want a reminder of what had happened. Everything so far had confirmed Kathleen's story. His mother was a fool to think Kathleen wasn't telling him the truth. Of course, Kathleen would tell him the truth. She may have a spirit of fire but underneath all her unladylike manners was a heart of innocence.

"Lord Turner," Calico said from beside him.

Isaac rose, gathered himself, and walked towards the door. "Countess?" he asked as she held the doorknob.

"My husband said he would grant you a visitation. I must warn you sir, he can barely speak."

"I understand."

Calico opened the door to Tomas' bedroom wider. Isaac walked into the bedroom with his eyes on Tomas' still body. His heart sank for his friend. Tomas' face was barely recognizable and his neck was raw from where the rope had clung tight around his neck. That was going to leave a scar for his entire life. Isaac sat on the edge of the bed and peered into his friend's swollen eyes. "Dear God, Tomas," Isaac gasped.

"Not…that…bad," Tomas pushed out of his mouth then coughed.

Isaac grinned. Typical Tomas. It was like him to not place that much emphasis on his own health. Tomas had always had a sense of humility about him. Tomas' servant heart had been something not all of the lords had admired in him. Tomas was known to be kinder to his servants than most lords, including Isaac. In some sense, Isaac could understand why Tomas would be kinder to his servants than he was to his own. Most of the servants were kin to him. Even the butler was Tomas' uncle.

"Tomas, the doctor said for you not to talk," Calico chided her husband as she closed the door and returned to her chair beside his bed.

Isaac lifted his eyes to Calico, "How much damage did they do to him other than what I am seeing?"

"He's fortunate to be alive. The doctor said he would need to be confined to the bed for at least a month, maybe more, depending on how fast his wounds heal. After they beat him last night, he slept so hard until morning Kathleen and I feared he died. He had only awakened a few moments before they placed him on the horse, led him to a tree, and put the noose around his neck. He didn't realize what was happening until it was too late. By then he was dangling."

"You were brave to get the servants when you did."

"It wasn't bravery, Isaac. My husband and sister's lives were in danger. I had to protect my family."

Tomas coughed and moaned in pain. Calico grabbed her husband's hand. He tightened his grip while he coughed uncontrollably and loosened it as his cough began to subside. "Has he been given anything for the pain?" Isaac asked.

"Yes. I was about to give it to him but he wanted to hear your words. I told him my sister is at Kilmore. He is greatly relieved to know she is in good hands."

Isaac cast his eyes to Tomas. "I promise you, Tomas, I will continue to take care of her and protect her."

Tomas nodded. He opened his mouth to speak then closed it. Isaac leaned his ear to his friend's mouth. Tomas whispered, softly pushing out each word with much effort. "Thank you for your visit. Thank you for taking care of Kathleen. You are a true friend, Isaac. But you are also a man who once thought I had betrayed you. What do you want?"

Isaac leaned back, boring his gaze into Tomas' eyes with a slight grin. "I don't know if I should be insulted or not."

Tomas shook his head. "Not. What do you want?"

"Very well. I have buried Sherlock's body where no one will find him."

"The rebels will want his body returned," Calico objected.

"I know, Lady Collins, and they will blame your family for his death. I'm afraid this most likely won't be the last time the rebels attack Collinsworth. Alexander and Bailey McGillpatrick are still on the loose. I'm certain by now they have heard of Sherlock's death at the hands of your husband. They will blame Kathleen for the uprising and you for getting the servants to aid them. Kathleen is safe at Kilmore but as long as you two remain here I cannot guarantee your safety."

"What do you propose? Abandon Collinsworth?"

"That is exactly what I propose. Tell your servants you are taking Tomas to your home in Dublin where he is closer to medical treatment.

Instead of going there, you bring him to Kilmore. The servants can take care of Collinsworth while you are away. If the rebels should attack, you and your husband will not be in danger. Tomas will be able to sleep peacefully knowing he does not have to defend his home and his wife."

Tomas and Calico exchanged glances. Isaac watched the two stare at each other as if there was some sort of unspoken communication between them. He had always been envious of their relationship. Ever since Tomas had started courting Calico two years ago, Tomas had held a deeper bond with Calico than with him. The lovers shared a special unbreakable bond between them. A bond Isaac hoped one day he would share with the woman he would eventually marry. He was getting to that point in his life where he needed to take a wife. There were many women in the English courts who had wanted to be his wife. Yet how could he find a wife who would understand his need to be with other women? Where would he find a woman who would turn her back on his prostitution and slave trade business? He not only sold black slaves but white Irish ones as well.

"We will come," Calico said, turning her gaze to Isaac.

"What?" Isaac asked, dismissing his thoughts.

Tomas motioned for Isaac. Isaac leaned his ear to his friend's mouth. "My wife is concerned for her sister."

"Understandable. If my sister was injured and had taken refuge with another family I would feel the same."

"I do not dismiss your claims that the rebels may attack my home again. I know they will. I cannot defend my wife and home in this state."

"Most certainty not. Kilmore is a half a day's ride from Collinsworth. I can't guarantee my men and I would arrive to give you support in time to persuade them away from Collinsworth should they attack once more."

"I realize that. Hmm, Isaac," Tomas arched his head, shimmying his weight with a low moan. He fell still and continued, "I will not survive if they come again. You must stay the night. In the morning, we can leave for

Kilmore in my carriage together. Calico will tell the servants you are accompanying us so that you can protect us on the journey."

"Agreed."

Tomas turned to his wife. "Tell Gerald to have your sister's bedroom prepared for Isaac." Calico rose from the chair and left the room. Tomas turned back to Isaac once the door closed behind her. He could tell his friend had wanted to say something more away from his wife's ear. "She likes you."

"Who, Calico?"

Tomas grinned. "No, Isaac. Kathleen. I want to make certain you don't abuse her affections towards you. I know what you do to any woman who has affections for you. You woo them, bed them, then throw them away."

Isaac pulled down his vest. "Well, you are still bluntly honest despite your infirmities."

"Why have you allowed Kathleen to stay at Kilmore?"

"Out of the kindness of my heart, I assure you."

"Do you still want to court her?"

"I do."

"You have my permission to do so as long as you do not take advantage of her. Promise me she will not become one of your many conquests."

Isaac grinned a sly grin. "Tomas, surely you know me better than that."

"Don't play me for a fool, Isaac. I do know you better. What's the real reason behind the kindness you are showing Kathleen?"

"You wouldn't believe me if I told you."

Tomas silently stared at Isaac. Deep behind his swollen face laid the face Isaac knew so well. That stubborn look Tomas gave when he wasn't going to back down from an argument. It was a look that had served him well as a county judge. The kind of look that told you he wasn't buying your story and you had better get to the truth before he grew tired of your nonsense. God, how much Isaac hated that look.

"You're not going to back down are you?"

"No."

"Very well. Kathleen has done something to me. I can't think, eat, drink, or sleep without thoughts of her. I've never felt this way about any woman I've courted. There's just something intoxicating about her."

"Intoxicating as in you want to bed her?"

"Yes and no."

"You can't have both, Isaac. Which is it, yes or no?"

"I want…," Isaac closed his mouth. He couldn't believe he was about to tell his friend the very words that had almost spilled out of his mouth. He thought about them. How could he tell Tomas this when he wasn't certain he believed it himself? Where had the words come from?

"You want," Tomas muttered.

Isaac shook his head. "It's nothing."

"No, it's something. You stopped your words, which tells me you didn't think before you spoke. That's not like you. You are very cautious about what words you use to convey what you want. It seems to me what you want is something you can't believe you want at all." Isaac huffed with a grin. "What is it, Isaac?"

"I want to be with the Lady Kathleen but not until we marry. She is the only woman I ever want to be with."

Tomas laughed then coughed.

"Tomas," Isaac said in concern.

Tomas calmed down and looked at his friend. "You're in love."

"Certainty not. To be in love with a woman is to give them power over you. No one holds power over me!"

"Kathleen does."

"That's absurd." Isaac paused then smiled. "You said she holds affections for me."

"What woman doesn't? Even Calico held affections for you at the start of our courtship."

"Really," he grinned. "Now how did I not bed her before she became your wife?"

"Oh, I told her the truth about you. She was quite livid when she learned of it and then the truth came out that I knew she had feelings for you. I can quite assure you those feelings are no longer there. She's cried out my name several times since our wedding night and is well satisfied with me. Be that as it may, she is very concerned over her sister's welfare in your estate."

"She has nothing to concern herself with. I promise you, Tomas, I have no plans to bed her until we are married. You will inform Kathleen of our courtship once you arrive at Kilmore?"

"I will. She is yours, Isaac. If you find her suitable after the period of courtship has expired then return to me for permission to marry her."

"I understand she has lost her inheritance. What of her dowry?"

"It is small but I may be able to add to it when the time comes. Isaac, we shall discuss the dowry when the time comes to do so. For now, court her and see if your feelings hold true. I'm so tired," Tomas said, turning his head to the right. He closed his eyes and fell asleep. Isaac rose from the side of his friend's bed, pulled the covers up Tomas' body, and sat in the chair beside the bed. He silently watched his friend sleep. Courtship with Kathleen. It was more than he could have dreamed of. What was he doing? Who was this man he was becoming?

Chapter 18

The rain beat against the window under the dark night sky. Bailey hobbled down the hallway towards his father's bedroom. The thought of Isaac Turner remaining in this house overnight bothered him. How could Kathleen work her charm on him when he wasn't even at home? A part of him wanted to take the servant passages to Kathleen's room and kill Isaac himself. Yet that would be a fool's errand. If Isaac were killed in Tomas' house then that would only bring suspicion to Tomas, his servants, and his household. He couldn't do that to his old friend.

Bailey stumbled as someone bumped into him. "Oh, Bailey," Jane said, helping Bailey stabilize himself.

"Mother." He glanced down at the sack in her hand then back up at her. "What do you have there?"

"Oh, this? It's for Mary. What are you doing up so late?"

"I need to speak to my father. Has he turned in yet?"

"He has not. Goodnight, Bailey."

"Goodnight mother."

Jane ran down the hallway, turned left, and disappeared. She had been acting odd since dinner. Bailey wondered why his stepmother was in such a hurry with a bag for Mary. Now that Mary was a widow she had nothing to her name except Sherlock's farm and their belongings. She could work the small one-acre farm on her own but it would be tough on her. She was in even greater danger should anyone learn she is Sherlock's widow. Bailey was certain the Anglicans would want to arrest her as a political prisoner just for being Sherlock's wife. Mary couldn't leave his family. He couldn't trust her. Mary was a thorn in his side and he knew she would continue to fester in his affairs with Kathleen. His sister-in-law and Sherlock had not hidden the fact they didn't approve of his ways. What Mary needed was to be controlled and he knew just how to control her.

Bailey hobbled down the hallway until it dead-ended with another. He peered to his left. Candlelight poured into the hallway from Mary's slightly open doorway. He hobbled towards her room with determination. Mary would have no choice but to accept his offer if she knew what was good for her. Bailey paused outside Mary's doorway, watching the mother and daughter interact.

"Oh, I'm so hungry," Mary proclaimed as Jane opened the bag in front of her.

"You need to keep your strength for the baby. Eat it all and if you're still hungry I can get you more," Jane answered, taking the bag away.

Baby? Bailey clenched his jaw and leaned against the hallway wall. So that was Sherlock and Mary's secret. Mary was pregnant. He tightened his fist with anger. How dare Sherlock keep that from him! They had agreed not to have children until their family controlled Kilmore again. Yet Sherlock had gone behind his back and had relations with his wife. Now his wife carried his heir. But it wasn't a house or property the child would inherit. No. Sherlock's child would inherit his father's reputation as a rebel leader, a small farm, and no money. Why would Sherlock ever allow it to happen? Sherlock's body wasn't even cold a day and once again the man had infuriated him. When had his brother lost all sense of reason?

Bailey exhaled a deep breath. Fine, if Sherlock wanted to rebuild his family then so be it. He would just take that from him too. Hadn't Alexander been pestering him about finding a new wife, anyway? Bailey turned to Mary's door and knocked on it. A few moments later, Jane answered the door.

"Bailey, is something wrong with your father?" Jane asked him.

"How long did you think it would be before I learned about Mary's condition?

Mother and daughter exchanged glances.

Mary swallowed her food, bearing her eyes on Bailey. "You have some nerve coming to my door, Bailey McGillpatrick," she yelled from her bed.

"Lower your voice, Mary. We have an unwelcomed visitor staying in the room above yours. Invite me in or I'll have one of the servants drag you to Calico with an order to hand you over to Earl Isaac Turner."

"Bailey, she's my daughter," Jane protested.

"I don't care," he snarled with his eyes on Mary. "Let me in."

Jane reluctantly opened the door wider "Thank you, mother," he replied with charm as he hobbled into the bedroom. Jane closed the door behind him. He glanced at the fruit, bread, cheese, and meats scattered on a tray beside Mary.

"How far along are you?" he asked, sitting in a chair beside the bed, laying his crutches to the side.

"What do you care?"

"Mary," Jane scolded.

Bailey huffed with a grin. "You're as charming as ever, Mary."

"And you're as obnoxious as ever, Bailey."

"Watch your tongue! If you weren't with my brother's child I would have you punished for those words. I am the leader of this family."

"Did you kill your father, too?"

"Mary," Jane scolded her.

"You will show me respect," Bailey demanded.

"You are nothing bur a liar, thief, and murderer. You stole your position in this family from my husband. Sherlock was born first, not you. My husband was an intelligent and loving man full of great wisdom. He would have made a wonderful Earl but you stole his inheritance. You cast him into a position of servitude all because you wanted the glory and honor that was his birthright. The only reason your father has let you treat Sherlock the way you have is because he fears you, Bailey. They all do! But not me. I don't fear you. I can see right through you. I see the monster you truly are. So did Sherlock."

"Mary," Jane corrected her.

Bailey clenched his jaw and stared at Mary with a stern look of disapproval. There was no turning back from his decision now. No, if Mary had done one thing with her words it was reaffirm his decision. She was dangerous. Too dangerous to be out of his control. "I will take your words as the ramblings of an expectant mother," he said to Mary.

"Take them however you want, Bailey. They are the truth." She placed her hand on her stomach. "This child will know you killed its father."

"And where do you plan to raise this child?"

"Bailey?" Jane asked sitting next to Mary. She took her daughter's hand. Bailey lifted his eyes to Jane.

"Your love and devotion to her blinds you from the truth, mother. Mary cannot stay with the rebels if she defies my authority over her, nor can I allow her to freely leave."

"I'm to be a prisoner of the rebellion?" Mary asked, clutching her mother's hand.

"If that's what you want."

"Bailey, you kill your prisoners."

"I would wait until after the child is born."

"That's why you wanted to know how long she has until she gives birth?" Jane asked as Mary sobbed on her mother's chest.

"Yes."

"You killed my eldest daughter…"

"James Turner killed my wife and children!"

"You beat my middle daughter and sent her into enemy hands."

"Kathleen volunteered, as has Calico."

"Now you want this one too? Bailey, you can't have her!"

"She poses more of a threat to me than Kathleen does. I won't have it. Either she submits to my authority or the rebellion will make an example of her."

"If you want to make an example of her then order Tomas to hand her over to Isaac. My heart would not break as much knowing she was a slave and not executed."

"I can't risk her giving up our location or Tomas, Calico, and Kathleen's identities."

"Have you spoken to your father concerning this?"

"No, but I don't need his permission. She either submits to my authority or is hung for treason."

"What of the child?"

"Tomas and Calico will raise the baby as their own. It will never know Sherlock and Mary were its true parents. My brother's line ends if she refuses my authority."

Jane and Mary glanced at one another as Bailey watched them closely. He couldn't care less about Mary. Mary should have been dead years ago when James Turner captured her. The only reason Mary had survived the ordeal was because Alexander had convinced him he could use Mary's rescue to his advantage. And he did. He had exchanged himself for Mary and then murdered James Turner. But now his loose end was causing him too much grief.

"I...," Mary began, wiping away her tears. She sniffed her nose as she turned to face him. "I take it I would have to do something to publically show my allegiance to you?"

"Yes."

"What would that be?"

"Marry me."

Mary gasped, "My husband hasn't been dead a full day and you want me to marry you?"

"Yes," he answered matter of factly, leaning back in his chair. He crossed his arms, adding, "You will marry me or face the gallows the day after your child is born to you. Choose, Mary. What do you want more, your life and Sherlock's child or death? It is an easy question. To be perfectly honest I don't care what you choose as long as you choose."

"You beat her sister. What is to convince her that you won't beat her too?" Jane asked.

"I only beat my wife when she disobeyed me. I beat my children for that too. As long as you and our children obey me then I will not beat you."

"Your children?" Mary asked.

"That baby will not know Sherlock was his or her father. It will be my child. I will expect you to act in all areas of wifely duties whenever I require them of you."

"I have trouble conceiving. What makes you think I will bear you more children?"

"Oh, I have faith you will, Mary. I take it you are not showing yet."

"No."

"Good, then we will need to marry soon. What is your decision? Death or life?"

Mary took a deep breath, swallowed hard, and looked at her mother. Mother and daughter spoke in a low whisper. He tried to read their lips but couldn't make out a single word. "As my wife you will still have the same standing in the rebellion as you did with Sherlock," Bailey said, trying to persuade her.

Mary nodded to her mother then turned to face him. "I have one request if I am to marry you."

Bailey laughed, "You are in no position to be bartering with me. I hold your life in my hands. What could you possibly give me that I want? I don't even think bedding you would be pleasurable."

"Tomas and Calico are leaving tomorrow morning for Isaac's house. Gather the rebels and get the priest to marry us tonight. Then bed me. I'll make your night so pleasurable the rebels will never suspect I am not carrying your child. In the morning you allow me to accompany Calico as her maid. I can get close to Kathleen and make certain she does everything you want her to do."

"What makes you so certain I would agree to that?"

"Because you know I'm the only one Kathleen will listen to."

Like it or not Mary had been right, but he had to test her to make certain she was telling him the truth. He couldn't allow Mary to trick him. He grabbed her by the shoulder and pulled himself on top of the bed. Mary heaved. Bailey held her head in his hands then kissed her. Mary's tense body gave way to his suspicions. She was playing him; but then Mary kissed him with more passion. Her body relaxed under his firm grip. Why wasn't she fighting him? Bailey leaned back, gasping for a breath. "I may not love you but I can serve you. Know this, Bailey, every time you kiss, touch, or are inside me it will not be you that I see but your brother. You want passion like that then accept it on my terms. I am and always will be Sherlock's wife," Mary spat in his face.

Bailey pushed her away from him with a loud grunt. "Worthless piece of trash."

"Not so much. You can't kill me because you won't be able to control Kathleen if you do. What makes you think my death won't cause her to turn against you?"

"I'll force her to submit to me."

"How, Bailey? You can't bed her. Mary and Kathleen are my daughters but you and Kathleen share the same father. Admit it, you need Mary," Jane answered.

Mary nodded in Bailey's direction. "Give me what I want and I'll submit to your desires. I'll even make it easy on you tonight. I know how to make a man happy while he's injured. Had plenty of experience with Sherlock on that."

Bailey grabbed his crutches and stood with them before her bed. "Very well. Prepare yourself. We marry in the hour. I will expect you to conduct yourself in a manner becoming of your station as a rebel leader's wife."

"I've been a rebel leader's wife long enough to know what that entails. Get out of my room, Bailey. Let me mourn Sherlock's passing until our wedding."

"You have one hour, Mary. Nothing more than that. Goodnight," he ordered then left Mary's room. Bailey closed the door behind him. That hadn't worked out the way he had planned but it was at least something. Bailey hobbled down the hallway then paused at seeing Calico head his way.

"Calico?" he asked, moving faster to her. She stopped in front of him. "What are you doing down here? I thought you had a guest."

"I do. But mother sent me this," she said, showing him a note.

"May I?"

"Yes," she answered, handing the note to Bailey. Bailey opened it, read it, then crumbled the paper in his hand. He clenched his jaw. "Bailey?"

"She played me for a fool."

"Who?"

"Mary."

"Mary wants to ruin you. She can't be trusted."

"I know that quite well, Calico. That's why I am going to marry her tonight. I can control her better as her husband. What concerns me is this note. Your mother said in it that she had a request of you that is of the utmost urgency and one only you can fulfill. I know what that request would be and I just granted it to Mary."

"Mary?"

"She desires to serve as your maid when you and Tomas travel to Kilmore tomorrow."

"Why? She hates me."

"She told me she wanted to draw closer to Kathleen in order to reassure her about the plans I have for her. I thought she had wanted to do so to prove I can trust her. But now that you have showed me this note I very much doubt her request was something she had not thought of before I made my proposal to her."

"Bailey, it isn't like you to not know when someone is lying to you."

"Hmm, Tomas is better at that than I am." Bailey looked at the note then back to Calico. "Calico, take Mary with you to Kilmore. I want you to do something for me while you are there."

"What?"

"Convince Isaac Turner to eliminate our problem."

Calico grinned. "It would be my pleasure."

Chapter 19

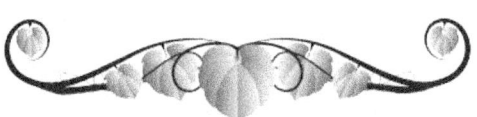

September 25, 1738

Kathleen pulled the warm blanket over her body, snuggled in its warmth, and rolled to her left side. Peace enveloped her. This was her bed. She had been born at Kilmore nineteen years ago and lived in this very room until she was seven years old. She couldn't remember much about her early life at Kilmore, except that her family was prosperous and she had enjoyed a happy childhood with her sister, nephews, and nieces. All of that had changed when her father had refused to take the oath before Parliament denouncing the Catholic Church and giving his allegiance to the Church of Ireland. He had lost everything. Money, power, status, and their beloved castle. Kilmore Castle and the surrounding lands were transferred to James Turner. Her family had been subjected to living on a one-acre farm. Bailey and Sherlock had been given their own farms as well. All three of their farms had been located on the worst lands in Kilmore and her family had struggled to provide a suitable crop, especially when the famine had come over Ireland a year later. Kathleen had never experienced hunger and hardship before. It had been the hardest thing she had ever had to face, especially when the smallpox had come to her family. Five years after the famine had left them her father had regained control of Kilmore. She and Calico had become young women. Alexander had been diligent in getting their house in order so she and Calico would have dowries. She had only faint memories of Kilmore Castle. When the family had moved back to Kilmore it was larger than she could recall. Alexander had told her James Turner had converted parts of the ancient castle into a Great House. The outer wings and living quarters were still part of the castle but the center had been converted. To Kathleen it was beautiful but to her brothers and father it was a sacrilege. The Turners had tried to turn something Irish into something English. It was as if the Turners wanted to forget that the land they were standing on was Ireland.

The warmth and comfort of her bed hid the reality of her situation. It was almost as if the tragedy that had befallen her family had never occurred. But the reality was, although this was her bed, this was no longer her home. She moaned, rolling to her back. She couldn't stay in that perfect place of peace and comfort for much longer, no matter how much she wanted it to be real. The reality was Sherlock was dead, her family no longer controlled Kilmore, and she needed to win Isaac to the idea of saving her from her own family. A family he had vowed to eliminate. If Isaac knew the truth about her, would he eliminate her as well?

"Good morning," Isaac's voice rang in her ear.

Kathleen opened her eyes and sat upright. A wave of dizziness overcame her. She leaned over her lap, grabbing her cloth-bound head. Isaac sat on the edge of the bed and embraced her. "You must lie down, Lady Kathleen," he said, guiding her downward.

"Wh…what are you doing in my room," she asked as her head hit the pillow.

"I think this is my room. You are a guest in my home."

"Right. I'm sorry."

"Apology accepted. My butler told me you have been asleep for sixteen hours."

"Oh, I'm sorry. I should really return to Collinsworth. My sister will be worried about me," Kathleen said, pushing aside the blanket and rising.

Isaac grabbed her by the arm. She turned in his direction. "Tomas and your sister know of your location."

"They do?"

"I went to Tomas' house yesterday. There was a great storm so I slept there last night."

"You what?" Kathleen panicked, thinking about how close Isaac must have come to discovering her family was living in the bottom portion of the house. She pulled her arm out of his grasp, rose from the bed, and stumbled. Kathleen braced herself on the back of a chair. She pressed her hand to her head, trying to compose herself. She looked down at her body. Someone had removed all of her garments except for her shift. Her anxious heart skipped a beat. Why was she undressed? Had Isaac done something to her while she was unconscious? No man would dare be caught with an unmarried, undressed woman. Yet Isaac wasn't your typical man. Hadn't he stolen her clothes at the lake and seen her naked?

"Lady Kathleen, you are suffering from a concussion. Please return to the bed," Isaac instructed, interrupting her paranoid thoughts.

Kathleen raised her eyes towards the handsome man. "Why?"

"Because I care about you. Now please, return to the bed."

"No, why did you go to my home?"

Isaac rose from the bed and studied her. He addressed her as he walked towards her "I was concerned about Tomas. We have been good friends since he denounced Catholism. I also wanted your sister to know you are safe and well. I am grateful you told me of the situation. Tomas was badly wounded in the attack and if the rebels decide to attack Collinsworth again then there is no doubt in my mind he would not be able to defend it." He placed his hands on her arms and asked, staring deep into her eyes, "Why have I offended you by going to Collinsworth? Is there something I should know?"

Kathleen bit her lower lip. His captivating baby blue eyes and thin lips mesmerized her. How could she lie to him when all she wanted to do was kiss him? What was it about this man that made her weak in her knees when she should be upset that he had once again stolen her clothes? "Kathleen?" Isaac asked.

"What if the rebels had decided to attack while you were there?"

"Then I would have defended your family and your home."

"Why?"

"Why not?"

Kathleen shook her head. "Why are you being so kind to me when you don't know anything about me?"

Isaac traced her cheek with the crook of his finger. "I would like to get to know you better."

"You have a strange way of proving how much you admire me, Earl Turner."

"I have done nothing but shown you kindness, Lady Kathleen. I do not understand why you would think I would want to harm you."

Kathleen lifted an eyebrow and extended her arms to the side, motioning for him to look at her attire.

"Right, clothes," he whispered in understanding. "I didn't remove them from you."

"This coming from the man who stole my clothes, saw me naked, and has had every intention of courting me even when I plainly show him I am not interested in his advances."

"Kathleen, I have a younger sister."

"So do I."

Isaac smiled and shook his head. "You misunderstand me," he explained, stepping towards her. She nervously stepped backwards and stumbled, fighting the wave of dizziness that threatened to overcome her. He grabbed her by the elbow to stabilize her but she resisted.

"Let go of me," she snarled, pulled her elbow loose, and walked away.

"My sister, Sarah, is about your age. Do you remember her? You met her at Tomas' wedding."

"No."

"Understandable. Sarah is quite shy and doesn't like crowds." He stepped towards her. "Sarah has been caring for you since you arrived. She must have removed your clothes so you could rest better."

Kathleen glared at him with suspicion while she stabilized herself with a hand on the armoire. He slowly approached her, placed his hand on the side of her face, and turned her face towards him. "You can't deny what I know you desire most."

"What is that?"

"I can see it in your eyes. You're a stubborn, prideful woman, Kathleen. Most Irish women are. You don't want to admit that you are interested in a…shall we say…more intimate relationship with me?"

Kathleen pushed Isaac away from her and walked towards the window. Her heart pounded and butterflies stirred in her stomach. She couldn't allow her feelings to get the best of her. She was here on a mission. Bailey wanted her to use Isaac for the rebellion and she wanted to use Isaac to kill Bailey. Her job was simple enough. Let the two men battle between them and she would move right in to control the estate. If she let her feelings get in the way she couldn't act with logic. But oh, Isaac was so tempting.

"I have brought Tomas and Calico to Kilmore this morning with their maid and valet."

"They are here?" she asked, turning in his direction.

"Yes. My physician is attending to Tomas as we speak."

"And my sister?"

"She went for a ride with my mother and Sarah this morning. They should return in time for supper."

"You said Sarah is close to my age? How old is she?"

"Yes. She just turned sixteen. After my father died, the king coroneted me as Earl of Kilmore and then I returned home to care for her and my mother."

"That's very noble of you."

"They mean everything to me."

"I feel the same about Calico," she said then walked to the bed. Kathleen sat on the edge while Isaac walked to the chair in front of her. He sat down, took her hands, and looked into her eyes. "Forgive me for being too forward with you a moment ago."

Kathleen smiled. This man was just too much. Where was the evil Turner man she had been raised to believe he was? This man showered her with compassion. She needed to loathe him not love him. She took his hands, turned them over, and studied them. "You must write a lot."

"I do."

"What do you write?" she asked, looking up at him.

"Essays on Irish and English politics mainly."

"Hmm, and those Irish political essays are in support of the Penal Laws?"

"Some are. I have some about the history of Kilmore."

"Oh?"

"This place fascinates me. Did you know that this castle stands upon the ruins of an older one?"

"No," Kathleen lied.

"The castle was built in the 12th century after the Normans invaded Ireland under the reign of King Henry II. It was placed far enough from the coast to protect the inland route from invaders, but not so far that it couldn't send aide to the outpost in Kilmore Village should the docks on St. George's Channel be breached."

"Was there ever a confrontation?"

"That I do not know. Local legends claim the first McGillpatrick to live at Kilmore Castle was given control of it soon after it was built. From the 12th to the 15th century the family continued to add onto the castle but it wasn't until the late 15th century when the castle transformed into a work of art. Painters, sculptures, carpenters, and other artisans were called in to create masterpieces. Oh, did they ever create a work of art! There are rooms in this castle that just beckon for you to stare and wonder at the beauty created in those places."

"I thought all of the old castles had been demolished in the 15th century."

"Most of them were. Kilmore was one of the few castles remaining that were still in use by the military as a defensive fortification. The castle was known far and wide for jousting competitions. Some say the McGillpatricks are descended from one of the oldest Irish noble families and that's why King Henry honored them with the castle, village, and land."

"Do you believe that?"

"I do."

"Then do you believe that Kilmore should rightfully be in their hands and not under English control?"

"I believe Alexander McGillpatrick should have been able to keep his estate. My father should have never forced Parliament to evict him. Parliament made a mistake by allowing my father to do so. The law clearly states any land that a Catholic man owns is divided equally among his sons when he dies. Parliament should have allowed Alexander's sons to inherit Kilmore."

"Kilmore would have been divided in half. And the lands would keep being divided through the generations until there was nothing left. The only way to save Kilmore is for Bailey or Sherlock to convert, then they would have the complete estate. Tomas did that."

"Sherlock and Bailey would never convert. They were given the opportunity to take the oath and they refused. My father valued Kilmore land and the history that surrounded it. He wanted the estate to remain in tact. That is why he forced Parliament's hand. But to be honest with you, I don't see how he could keep up with the expenses. Our lands are large and this house is monstrous. I have even closed off portions of it to lower our expenses."

Isaac leaned back and changed the subject. "Calico tells me you share a maid with her?"

"I...uhm....what?" she asked, distracted by the thought that her brothers had had the opportunity to denounce their Catholic faith but had never done so. She never knew Sherlock and Bailey had been given the chance to take their place as lord of Kilmore. Why hadn't either Sherlock or Bailey done what Tomas had and lied about the conversion? If they had wanted to keep the estate in the family that seemed like the most logical decision.

"Your maid. You share a maid with your sister. Her name is Mary," Isaac explained.

"Oh, yes, we do. Mary, right. I'm sorry, Isaac, my head hurts so bad it's hard to think."

"It's alright. I completely understand. You have been through a traumatic experience. Why don't you lie down?"

Kathleen nodded. Isaac pulled the blankets back as she crawled back into bed. He pulled them up over her and sat beside her. "You have been too kind to me," she said.

"I would do anything for you."

"Anything?"

"Yes, is there something you want? Name it and it is yours."

Kathleen studied his face. Anything she wanted. Anything at all! Now was her chance. What was it that she wanted from Isaac? Freedom from Bailey and the chance to rule Kilmore on behalf of her father. She couldn't allow Isaac to learn the truth. She was Kathleen McGillpatrick, daughter of his enemy. Somehow she didn't think that would sit too well with Isaac. "Did you bury Sherlock McGillpatrick?"

"I have."

"In the ancient graveyard you spoke about?"

"Yes, and I marked it in the same manner his ancestors would have."

"Do you suppose you might take me there once I feel better?"

"Why?"

"Your family is English. You wouldn't understand."

"Kathleen?"

"When I was little my parents used to tell me stories about the old families. The McGillpatricks were one of those families they told me stories about. I would like to honor Sherlock."

"He tried to kill you."

"I know but I think had he been Anglican we might have been friends."

"Do you support the rebels, Kathleen?"

"No, but you must understand—Catholic or Anglican, we are still Irish. I don't understand why it's illegal to be Irish in Ireland. It is who I am."

"Very well. When you are feeling better I will take you to where I buried him." A knock on the door broke their attentions. "Who is it?" Isaac demanded.

"Mary, my lord. I have brought lunch for the Lady Kathleen," Mary announced from behind the thick wooden door.

"Come in," he answered then turned back to Kathleen as Mary entered the room. "I sent Mary to bring you lunch. I hope you don't mind if I asked her to do so. Calico said it would be alright."

Kathleen nodded. "It is." Kathleen and Isaac stared into each other's eyes for a long moment. Isaac leaned his slender lips towards hers and gently kissed them. She opened her mouth, letting him slide his tongue inside. How could her enemy make her feel so weak? She grabbed the back of his head and kissed him deeper. Her mind was telling her this was her enemy. It was just a ruse to make him do her bidding, but her heart melted with every kiss. This wasn't her enemy. This was the man of her dreams! Isaac pulled away from her. "I'm sorry," he apologized.

"Don't be."

"Don't be? Just a moment ago you were offended by my touch and now you aren't offended by my kiss?"

"Isaac, I'm confused and scared."

"Scared? Scared of what?"

"You."

"Me?"

"I hear the rumors. Don't trust Earl Isaac Turner. He'll woo you, bed you, and then lose you. It is common for a man and woman to share a bed during their engagement but not before. I made a promise to my father before he died that I would remain a virgin until my wedding night. I intend to keep that promise."

"I wouldn't want to dishonor you. You mean too much to me."

"You barely know me!"

"It doesn't matter, Kathleen. I will get to know you. I asked Tomas to grant me permission to court you and he has consented."

Kathleen smiled. "And have you done so because you want me to marry you or because you want to conquer me?"

"Marriage is not about love."

"Neither is courtship."

"Kathleen, it's not like that."

"Then please explain it to me, Earl Turner."

Isaac exhaled a deep breath. "I have tried to get you out of my head but I can't. You consume me. I want to be with you all the time. I have never felt like that with any other woman before."

"How many times have you said that to another woman?"

"Never!" He rose from the bed. "Perhaps, Lady Kathleen, we should have this conversation when you are feeling better. I do not need your consent to court you, but I would rather hope that you would accept the courtship. The more willing you are with the arrangement between Tomas and me, the more pleasurable the experience will be for us all. I have shown you my hospitality and have revealed my true feelings to you. In return, you act most unbecoming and reject me? Who are you to reject me!?"

"I…I didn't mean to reject you, Isaac. I want you to court me."

"You have a very odd way of showing that." He walked over to Mary, stared down at the food, then walked out the door, slamming it behind him. Mary jumped at the sound.

Kathleen's heart broke. She rolled onto her stomach and sobbed in her hands. What had she just done? How could she have treated him so horribly? She had feelings for this man and obviously he had them too. Life was too complicated. If she chose to honor her family she had to deny her feelings for Isaac, yet if she betrayed Bailey, Tomas, and Calico then she would be able to accept her feelings but endanger not only herself but also her family. How could she choose between family loyalty and love?

"Kathleen," Mary whispered from beside her, rubbing her little sister's back.

"It's not supposed to be this hard," Kathleen cried.

"You love him."

Kathleen turned onto her back to face Mary. "What?" she whispered, sniffing her nose.

Mary held her lower stomach as she gently wiped away Kathleen's tears. "I know why you came here."

"I'm so sorry about Sherlock."

Mary shrugged her shoulders. "It was my greatest fear he would die soon. I had prayed the head wound he had received wasn't that dangerous to him, but I knew, Kathleen, I just knew."

"That's why you tried to keep him in bed. He argued with you about that a lot."

"You know Sherlock. He was always more concerned about me than himself." Mary rubbed her stomach, rose from the bed asking, "Chamber pot?"

"Under the bed."

Mary nodded, she grabbed the pot from underneath the bed, and vomited. Kathleen rolled onto her side and peered at her. "Why are you here if you are ill?"

"Ugh, I'm not contagious. I'm with child."

"Really? When did this happen?"

"The day Sherlock awoke from his deep sleep he craved my body and I granted it to him. I have missed my monthly cycle twice."

"Have you told Bailey about this?"

"No but he learned of it and confronted me about it. He said if I didn't marry him then he would have me arrested until I gave birth to my child. Then he would hang me until dead and give my child to be raised by

Calico. I had no choice in the matter. I married Bailey last night and gave my body to him."

"Oh, Mary. I'm so sorry."

"He was rough with me but not so much that he endangered the child. He wants to claim Sherlock's child as his own, and demands I keep bearing him children."

"You're not that fertile."

"I know and that concerns me. Kathleen," she wiped her mouth with her sleeve then sat on the side of the bed. Kathleen sat up and tapped her side of the bed. Mary sat next to her, wrapped her arm around Kathleen, and allowed her sister to lean on her. "I have a plan but I need your help. Bailey thinks you are here to spy on Isaac but I think you might have come here for another reason. Am I right?'

"Maybe."

Mary smiled. "If Sherlock was alive he would tell you whatever you have planned it is a fool's errand."

"I think he would be surprised." Kathleen grabbed the tray of food from her nightstand then placed it on her lap. She noticed the double helpings then began to pass the extra food to Mary. The sisters ate as they talked. "I was so mad at Bailey for what he did to Sherlock that I decided I would end this once and for all," Kathleen admitted.

"How?"

"Isaac has feelings for me."

"And you for him."

Kathleen dropped a roll and looked at Mary.

"You can't hide it, Kathleen. I saw how you kissed him. You love him. That love you have for Isaac could be your best weapon."

"Or my own undoing. Sherlock always said it's wiser to act out of logic than out of emotion."

"Yes. Oh, I miss him," Mary cried.

Kathleen placed her hand on Mary's stomach. "You will always have a piece of him in your heart and in this child. Bailey may claim the child belongs to him but you will always know the truth."

Mary smiled. "You are too much like your brother."

"Sherlock I hope."

"Of course Sherlock, silly girl."

The women laughed then ate in silence for a few moments. Kathleen swallowed, picked a piece of bread off her roll, then said, "I plan to use Isaac against Bailey, Tomas, and Calico."

"How can you do that without exposing the truth?"

Kathleen shrugged. "I haven't thought about that yet."

"You need to because he knows Calico is your sister. To accuse her is to accuse you as well. You don't want to become a slave do you?"

"No, but I don't think Isaac would ever harm me. He said he would do anything for me."

"Anything?"

"Hmumm. I asked him to bury Sherlock's body with our ancestors in the ancient graveyard that lies close to the old chapel. He did."

"Do you know where?" Mary asked, laying her food down with a serious look.

"No, I asked him to take me there. He said when I am feeling better he will do so."

"I need your help when he does."

"What for? You want to say goodbye to Sherlock?"

"Yes and no. You can't tell anyone what I am about to tell you, especially Calico."

"I promise."

"Good." Mary laid the tray aside, took Kathleen by the arms, and sat across from her. "Sherlock had been planning to escape to New Orleans with you and me."

"When? I never knew about it."

"He had been planning it for some time. He said he had been waiting until either things got too rough with our lives in the rebellion or if I conceived again. After I told him about the baby he told me about his plans. He had been carrying the deed in his vest pocket along with three tickets to be used anytime, and money for our provisions. We were supposed to travel to Dublin, board the vessel with our provisions, and never look back."

"Did he have that on him when he died?"

"Kathleen, you know Sherlock didn't trust to leave his prize possessions anywhere except on his body."

"True, he didn't trust anyone. Do you know where he kept them?"

"I do. I need to get to my husband's body so I can escape from Bailey. You can come with me. Will you help me?"

"I will. We can leave this evening while everyone is at dinner and be back by morning. It shouldn't be that hard to tell where he buried Sherlock. I know that graveyard well and it will be easy to find a newly dug grave. Calico and I used to play in there all time. I have every marker memorized."

Chapter 20

A slight evening breeze blew gently through the curtains of Tomas' bedroom. Exhausted, he was grateful Isaac had brought him to Kilmore. His family had doted on him so much he didn't think he would be able to rest while he was at Collinsworth. While he valued his friendship with Isaac he was loyal to Bailey and his people. It didn't bother him that Bailey and Alexander had beaten him up. He would do anything for the rebellion. What bothered him was Calico. He had hoped the rebellion wouldn't interfere with his wedding night, but he knew that was more of a dream than reality. Reality was the rebellion was always going to interfere with his marriage. If not the rebellion then his duties as an earl of Ireland. At first his courtship with Calico had been a matter of convenience, but over time he had fallen in love with her. His feelings for the younger woman had shocked him. He could recall the day she had been born and had watched her grow up. Calico had become a beautiful, intelligent, and strong Irish woman. At eighteen years of age, Calico surpassed all of his greatest expectations.

The sound of his bedroom door slamming closed aggravated his pounding headache. He groaned, rolling onto his back. He fidgeted as the pulsating pain spread through his face. His father, Padric, sat beside him and held his hand with a wooden rosary between them. "Shh, Tomas. Relax my son."

Tomas clutched the rosary. "Be careful with that," he pushed out in a whisper.

"You don't have to worry about me. I won't allow anyone to know you have kept the faith and are deceiving England."

"I think had I been younger this wouldn't have hurt so much."

Padric chuckled. "You did well, Tom. God will bless you for your persecution because you have chosen to defend the true faith. You are not alone in this fight. Get some rest. "

"Yes, sir."

Padric rose without the rosary. Tomas lowered his hand underneath the blanket and began to press the rosary beads one at a time. He closed his eyes, taking comfort in his faith, muttering beneath his breath a prayer to his saint. He needed strength. The sounds of the room disappeared as his spirit entered into communication with his saint. The pain dissolved. Peace and bliss surrounded him. He released his grip on the rosary when he heard his name. Why did it sound so much like Calico? Tomas ignored the calling and focused deeper on the void in his mind. Yet again Calico's voice called his name, this time with more urgency. He tried to push deeper but each time her voice would grow louder. Tomas groaned, leaving the peace behind him, and opened his eyes. The pain shot through his body once again. He gasped, grabbing his wife's hand.

"Tom?" Calico asked beside him.

"Hmm, I'm alright," he coughed. He tapped her hand and looked into her light green eyes. "What's wrong?" he asked.

"Have you seen Mary?"

"I thought she was with you."

"She never ate with the servants," Padric answered from behind Tomas.

"Nor was Kathleen at dinner. Isaac thought she might have decided to remain in her room and recuperate. Bailey did hit her in the head."

"He did but not hard enough to cause her any brain damage. She should be able to walk around by now," Tomas said. "I'm the one with a broken nose, swollen and bruised face, my throat damaged, two broken ribs, and several sprains, not her. Have you seen her since we arrived?"

"No, Isaac said the doctor told him she had broken ribs and a concussion from the accident. He told her to stay in bed."

"And you don't think she has?"

"Tomas, this is my sister we are talking about. Have you ever known Kathleen to do anything someone has told her to do, especially if Mary tells her to do the opposite?"

Tomas peered up at Padric. "Have you seen Mary today?"

"Not since she went to visit Kathleen."

Tomas grunted, rising in the bed. He pressed his hand on the bed to aide him.

"What are you doing?" Calico asked, guiding him back to bed.

"Deterring Isaac so you two can find them," he said, placing his feet on the floor. He leaned over, closed his eyes, and tried to regain his balance. "Ugh, when I get my hands on that sister of yours, I swear, Calico, it will only be because she is Bailey's wife that I won't kill her."

"Well, that is another matter we must speak about," Calico said, kneeling before her husband.

He lifted his eyes to her. "What, Bailey wants her dead?"

Calico stared into his eyes with a stern look of approval.

"Calico, no. I will not kill Mary! We've been friends too long for that," he yelled, rising to his feet. He stumbled in a wave of dizziness. Padric grabbed his son while Calico rose quickly.

"Bailey doesn't want you to kill her. He's charged me to convince Isaac to eliminate her."

"Eliminate," Tomas yelled at her. He pushed off his father and approached his wife. "Why didn't he tell me this?"

"He said you would believe me, and if you didn't I was to give you this," she said, pulling out a note from her pocket. Tomas took it from her hand, opened it, then tried to read it but his swollen eyes made it difficult. He handed it to his father.

Padric took the note and began to read it. "Tomas, Our war with the English has become complicated with the threat of a traitor. I fear with Sherlock's death Mary is more of a threat to our cause than naught. Kathleen has agreed to do our bidding but I do not trust her either. If Mary should come into contact with Kathleen I fear she will persuade her to turn against us. We cannot allow this to happen. I have agreed to allow Mary to accompany you so that Isaac may arrest her. I never want to see Mary again, nor the child she carries. Find just cause to have Isaac grow suspicious of her then let it be revealed in some way that she is my wife. Do so in away that does not turn his suspicions toward you, Calico, Padric, and Kathleen, Make Isaac believe Mary was Sherlock's wife before we married and she will not let her husband's death go in vain. After he has arrested her, kill her before he is able to place her on the slave ship. Your friend and confidant. Bailey."

"Thank you, father," Tomas said, taking the note from his hand. He glanced at the note then lifted his eyes to Calico. "I swore to protect your family and yet Bailey wants me to kill your sister and her unborn child?"

"In God's name," Calico answered. "Mary goes against God by sabotaging our efforts to regain Catholic control over Kilmore."

"Still Calico, this is your sister. Your mother's daughter. Don't you care about that?"

"I care more for God and his church than her. She's a threat."

"And if Bailey ever ordered me to kill Kathleen, what then? Would you support that as well?"

Calico held her husband's forearms. "Tomas, the order cannot be given without my father's consent. You know the rules. Three votes."

"I also know with Sherlock's passing it should be Mary who is consulted, not your father."

"She's a traitor and must be dealt with. The only reason she married my brother last night was to save her life. Bailey told me this morning she sobbed while he bedded her. She cried out for Sherlock and for God to have mercy on her. Each time Bailey would slap her but it didn't matter how hard he hit her she would still cry out for God's forgiveness."

"She's a grieving widow."

"A grieving widow without respect for God's church. She must be dealt with before all is lost. Kathleen would do anything for Sherlock and Mary. You know that."

"Yes." Tomas exhaled a deep breath with sorrow. He hated to have to kill Mary, but Calico was right. They couldn't risk Mary upsetting Bailey's plans. The more Mary resisted Bailey and the greater access she had to Kathleen, the greater risk there was that Isaac would learn of their plans. He had to protect Calico, her family, and himself from the threat of slavery. He wasn't about to be enslaved in the New World. Tomas crumbled the note and handed it to his father. "Burn this," he ordered. Padric took the note and walked to the fireplace on the other side of the bedroom. "Go and see if Mary is in your sister's bedroom then let me know what you learn," he told Calico.

"Where are you going?" she asked as Tomas grabbed his shirt from the back of the chair. He grunted while putting it on.

"I'm going to create the diversion you need. I gave Isaac permission to court Kathleen. If I know him he'll be on his way to her bedroom, wondering why she was not at dinner."

"Do you think he knows she is missing already?"

"We don't know if your sister has disappeared or not. If she has then you will need to stay in her bed and pretend to be her."

"How can I? My hair is black and hers is red. He'll notice the difference."

"Not if you hide under the blankets. Go, Calico. You know this castle better then he does. Use the secret passages."

Calico kissed Tomas. "How do I let you know if she is there or not?"

"I'll bring Isaac to Kathleen's room. If I don't see you there then I will know you are under the covers and Kathleen is gone. I'll make certain he doesn't disturb you. Now go."

Calico ran to the back of the room and pulled a book from the bookcase. The wall behind the lower shelf of the bookcase swung open to reveal a small crawlspace. Calico disappeared inside. Tomas walked to it,

crouched down, and watched her disappear down the tunnel that lead from Bailey's bedroom to Alexander's bedroom. From there she would have to walk through the corridors to her mother's chambers, where she would have to take the secret passage into Kathleen's room. Tomas closed the shelf, grabbed his coat from the armoire, and put it on. He turned to his father. "Hide my rosary," he asked.

"Of course. Go, do what you must for the glory of God and his church."

Tomas nodded then left his bedroom in search of Isaac.

Chapter 21

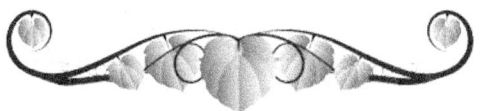

The long hallway twisted and turned every few feet through the large castle. Tomas slowly walked the dark hallways, bracing himself with his right hand along the wall. His head pounded with each move he made. What little light shone through the windows didn't help with his blurry vision. He wasn't certain where he was, just that he was going in the right direction. How many times had he roamed these ancient hallways with Bailey and Sherlock when they were just boys? He could almost hear the echoes of their laughter and the pitter of their childhood feet. There were too many fond memories of their families together in this castle. He was deep within the center of the castle where the grandest of rooms sprawled throughout the hallway. In true 16th century style, the earl's apartment was the largest of them all. The master bedroom was hidden away with an outer chamber bordering it that contained a living area for the master's most trusted servants. Off to the corner was a small room used for dressing, bathing, and other bodily functions. Outside the chamber was another larger one that was used as a parlor, and from there an even larger chamber where the master of the house held his business transactions. It was a well-designed maze ensuring the master of the house his privacy when he wanted it. Only a select few were ever granted permission into the inner chambers. Tomas had no doubt Isaac would leave his apartment tonight and make the long walk to the other side of the castle where Kathleen was supposed to be sleeping in her bed. It would be easier for him to gain access to Kathleen's chamber. The children's bedrooms were only separated by a large common parlor area. Kathleen had been given her old room. Although the five bedrooms in the children's wing were easy to get to, it was almost impossible for anyone to gain access to them. Tomas didn't feel like walking down the long hallway from Bailey's chambers to the children's wings. There were too many corridors to go through.

A door on his left opened. He paused next to the statue of a knight dressed in full armor and leaned on it for support. "Tomas," Isaac's voice came from his left. Tomas turned in his direction and stepped towards his close friend.

"Hmm, Isaac. I'm glad I found you," Tomas pushed out of his swollen lips then stumbled towards him.

Isaac grabbed Tomas before he fell to the ground. "Thank you," Tomas said, holding onto one of Isaac's well-toned, muscular arms for support.

"What are you doing out of bed?" Isaac asked, helping him to stand.

"I needed to talk to you."

"Whatever it is I'm certain it could have waited until you are stronger."

"It could not. It is of a most urgent matter."

"So urgent you could not speak of it when we were alone earlier?"

"I did not know then what I know now. Please, Isaac, I did not rise from my bed and walk halfway through your house on a whim. What I have to speak to you about is as much of an interest to you as it is to me."

Isaac peered down his hallway. The thought of being with Kathleen beckoned him to leave Tomas for his red-haired, green-eyed Irish goddess. His heart skipped a beat just thinking about her. He would give everything he had just to be her husband. She was the only woman he had ever known that made him feel that way, yet Kathleen was stubborn. He knew she had feelings for him but didn't want to admit it. What woman tries so hard to persuade a man to leave her alone then kisses him like she had? She was playing games with him but he didn't care. He wasn't playing to win her into his bed. No, more like into his life. She already held his heart in the palm of her hand.

"Isaac," Tomas said.

Isaac turned back to the square-jawed, round-headed Irishman. "What?"

"I never thought I'd see the day a woman would control Lord Isaac Turner's heart and mind."

"Kathleen doesn't control me! I think and act of my own accord."

Tomas tapped Isaac on the chest, opened the door behind him, and peered inward. "Looking for something, Tomas?" Isaac asked.

"The whore you're sleeping with while you're courting Kathleen."

Isaac grabbed the door handle and closed the door. "I assure you I have and will not bed another woman while I am with Calico's sister."

Tomas glared at Isaac, studying him carefully. Isaac was a master at manipulation and deceit, yet Tomas knew his one downfall. His left eye always twitched when he was lying. He concentrated to push through his blurry vision. He couldn't be certain, but he thought Isaac was telling the truth. "You're serious," Tomas gasped.

"I consider you one of my closest friends. I don't lie to those who are close to me."

Tomas nodded. "Isaac, I still must speak to you."

"I was on my way to visit with Kathleen. Will you join me?"

"Oh, I would like that but my head is pounding, my body is weak, and it hurts to breathe. Perhaps we could sit in the parlor for awhile then leave to visit Kathleen?"

"Of course," Isaac said then opened the door to his apartment. Tomas scanned the hallway as Isaac entered the room. He had moved quickly through the castle so that he could deter Isaac from reaching Kathleen's bedchamber, but now he needed to keep Isaac preoccupied a bit longer in case Kathleen wasn't in her room. Isaac could never learn Calico was in Kathleen's bed. It would jeopardize everything they had worked hard for. Fifteen minutes. Yes that should do it. He would give his wife fifteen more minutes before he brought Isaac to the room. Tomas stepped through the door, closed it, then walked to the round table where he sometimes played poker with Isaac. Isaac sat down at the other end as

Tomas sat as well. Tomas pulled Calico's silver-beaded rosary with rubies and emeralds from his innermost coat pocket and slid it across the table. Isaac stared at the beautiful strand then cast his gaze up at Tomas.

"Where did you find that?" Isaac asked, picking it up and examining it.

"It was on my wife's maid."

"I take it you knew Mary was Catholic?"

"It doesn't bother me that Mary is Catholic. What bothers me is who I think she is. Turn the cross around and read what's inscribed on the back."

Isaac peered at him with curiosity, lowered his eyes, and turned the cross over. "McGillpatrick," he read aloud. He raised his gaze. "Are you certain this is hers?"

"I am."

"How could you not know who she is? Didn't she give you a last name when she came to your estate?"

"She said her name was Standish and that she had family in the village."

"Have you ever met her husband or family?"

"Never. Mary keeps to herself. I do allow my servants to return to the village at night if they have family there. I never thought Mary was somehow involved with the rebellion. She's a good woman."

"And do you think her real name is Mary?"

"That I do not know. I don't know if she has married into the family or is one of the daughters who disappeared during the attack. Alexander McGillpatrick did keep his daughters secluded."

"Yes, but they have to be somewhere."

A moment of silence fell between the two men as Isaac contemplated everything Tomas had told him. A McGillpatrick in his house. It was almost too hard to believe. He had been expecting one of Tomas' servants to be working with the McGillpatrick family. How else would they have known the perfect time to attack Tomas and his family?

Tomas had always trusted his servants to be loyal to him. Most of his servants had known him since he was born or were kin to him in some way. But Tomas had betrayed his family. Although Tomas had never wanted to believe his family would betray him to the rebellion, it wasn't something Isaac hadn't thought would happen to Tomas someday. In fact, he was quite surprised it had taken this long for the McGillpatrick family to attack Collinsworth, seeing as how there were rumors Tomas' father and Alexander had once been close friends.

"Your father is your valet?" Isaac asked.

"Yes, why?"

Isaac tapped the end of the cross on the table. "How long has Mary worked for your wife?"

"Only a few months."

"Would you say since I attacked Kilmore?"

"She arrived a few days after."

"And how did you learn about her?"

"Calico's maid had died a week before. She was very old and had been with Calico since the she was a child. She needed a maid. I wrote an advertisement and sent my father to deliver it in the village."

"I want to speak to your father."

"Why, Isaac? Mary and my father have nothing to do with each other," Tomas protested, leaning on his forearms.

"Do you not see the connection?"

"I see you are trying to make this into something it's not. I may have betrayed my family but I will not turn my father over to you for questioning. I have my boundaries."

"Those boundaries are what placed you in the condition in which you find yourself."

"Bah," Tomas huffed then leaned back in his chair.

Isaac turned his eyes to the rosary. He watched it for a while as he tapped it over and over again on the wooden table. Tomas wasn't a fool but he did have a compassionate heart towards his people. A compassion that often stopped him from taking advantage of the Catholics. It was a quality Isaac found detestable. Family was family but the church was more important than where you came from. The Catholics were a menace to society. A menace that had to be dealt with, using swift and harsh judgments cast against them. Why couldn't Tomas see that? Isaac slammed the rosary on the table with the inside of his hand. "Tomas, what makes you think your father wouldn't conspire against you to regain control of Collinsworth?"

"Because if he was he wouldn't still be in my room."

Isaac leaned back in his chair and crossed his arms over his chest. "I'm listening."

Tomas leaned on the table. "Mary has stolen my wife's jewels and a purse full of coins. She only discovered them missing a few moments before I came to you. Mary had disappeared. When Calico asked my father about Mary's location he told her Mary had not come down to eat with the servants. That is most unusual for Mary. She loves to eat with the other servants. My wife is searching for her as we speak."

Isaac rose from the table. "She was with Kathleen earlier. Perhaps Kathleen knows something."

"Are you trying to insinuate Kathleen helped her?"

"Never. You said Kathleen and Calico share a maid."

"Yes, I couldn't afford to buy Kathleen her own maid. Calico said they had always shared one until they parted ways."

"Sometimes when two people share a servant, the servant takes more to one than the other. I wonder if the same can be said of Mary. And if Mary has stolen from your wife, has she done the same to Kathleen? You did bring Kathleen's belongings with her."

Tomas rose. "I'll go with you."

"Are you able to keep up? Only moments ago you were stumbling."

"I will do what I must to stay by your side. I want to know the truth as much as you do."

"Very well."

Chapter 22

Kathleen sat on her knees on the cold hallow ground of the ancient graveyard of her ancestors, staring into the shallow grave of her older brother. Sherlock's face poked out of the ground as if he was just peacefully sleeping underneath the earth. But he wasn't sleeping. Sherlock was dead. Kathleen was surprised how much seeing his cold, grey, solemn face affected her. She had seen him die. She barely recalled the sound of Bailey's gun and her brother lifting Sherlock's body into the back of the wagon. A part of her had hoped it was all just a bad dream, but it wasn't. Sherlock was dead and God had cast his judgment on Sherlock's soul. She hoped God would find favor with Sherlock. Of her two brothers she had her doubts that God would ever forgive Bailey for all the crimes he had committed. But certainly God would forgive Sherlock even if that meant Sherlock had to spend time in purgatory before going to heaven. Purgatory was for those souls who had found God's favor and friendship but were still affected by the sins they had committed. Sherlock had killed, lied, and stolen for the Catholic Church.

"You think he's in purgatory?" she asked Mary across from her.

"I don't know, Kathleen. If he is I don't want to think about it. Purgatory isn't hell but it's close enough to it. People who go there are tortured in the fires until they are refined enough to be in God's presence. My husband has sinned but I pray those sins haven't affected his soul."

"He was a good man, Mary. We can pray for him in case he is there. Father taught me that if we pray for the dead it will decrease the time they spend in purgatory."

"I have been praying for him since I learned of his death. Haven't you?"

"No," Kathleen sighed, lowering her eyes to Sherlock's face. "I should have. But…"

"I understand, Kathleen. You've been through much since his death and your injuries don't help in that matter."

Kathleen smiled towards her. Mary grabbed her hand, leaned over her husband's body, and encouraged her. "Have faith, my dear sister. God knows your sufferings." Mary squeezed her hand then released it, looking at her husband's face. She wiped away the dirt from her husband's face. Soft light danced on Sherlock's grey face, illuminating the hole in his forehead. Her long fingers gently traced down his cheek to his full lips. Mary sniffed her nose. Tears gently rolled down her cheeks. "I keep thinking he is going to rise out of this grave and tell me it's another of his practical jokes," she cried, caressing her husband's face.

"I wanted to believe none of this ever happened."

Mary lifted her face to the early night sky. She closed her eyes, allowing herself to mourn under the soft moonlight. Kathleen glanced around the ancient graveyard. How many times had her ancestors repeated the same scene time and time again? What was it Sherlock had always told her? You can't escape the grave but you sure can try. Someday, some way, it will find you. Be it would be a shame if a man had to die alone. Die alone. Sherlock hadn't died alone. She had been with him. But Kathleen was certain it wasn't her he had wanted by his side when the angel of death came for him. No. He had wanted Mary.

Mary wiped the tears from her eyes and gathered herself. She turned to Kathleen. "Was he dead when Bailey shot him?" Mary asked.

"What?" she asked, shocked that her mourning sister would ask her that. Hadn't she just been consumed with grief?

"I have to know, Kathleen. You are the only one who will tell me the truth. Mother said he collapsed in front of you."

"He did. He was sitting down at the table, eating, then rose with a headache. I asked him about it. He dismissed my concerns then fell unconscious. I tried to revive him but I couldn't feel a pulse. He was dead, Mary. Father confirmed it. Besides, there was blood coming out of his ears."

"You saw that?"

"Yes. He never felt the shot. He was already dead. If Bailey hadn't done it, I would have."

Mary grabbed the front of Kathleen's blouse. "Don't turn into them, Kathleen. Never! Sherlock wouldn't want that for you."

"I won't. Mary?"

"Those words are not from you. You would never harm Sherlock nor desecrate his body."

"I only said it because…"

"I don't care why you said it. Just don't. You must comply with the teachings. Don't let this family take your faith or your morals from you. Please, Kathleen. I don't care how much you think you can stop Bailey by becoming the woman he wants you to become, it will never work. Promise me! Promise me you won't follow Calico's path!"

"I…I…I promise."

"Bailey will turn you if you let him."

"I won't."

"Good." Mary released her grip and turned back to her husband. "Help me," she asked, starting to dig the dirt away from his chest.

"Aren't we desecrating his body by disturbing it?" Kathleen asked with her hands on to the dirt.

"God will forgive us. We are doing this for Sherlock's child. I don't want Bailey to raise Sherlock's child. My baby needs to know its real father. The only way I will be able to escape from Bailey is to leave Ireland and I don't want to do that in slavery. Sherlock would want this. I know God will forgive us. Dig, please. I need to remove his coat.

Kathleen joined her sister. Together they dug into the cold dirt with their bare hands, throwing clumps to the side. The farther they dug the more pungent the smell of Sherlock's decaying body became. Several times Mary had to leave to vomit. The mixed smells of vomit and decay made Kathleen want to join her sister but she couldn't. They had to hurry. Kilmore castle was two hours away and they needed to be back before the sun rose so no one would suspect they had gone missing.

"Mary?" Kathleen asked as Mary vomited next to the large tree beside Sherlock's grave.

"Ugh, what."

"When did you know you were in love with Sherlock?"

"I had feelings for Sherlock the first time I laid eyes on him at our handfasting ceremony."

"And he had feelings for you?"

"Yes. We were blessed to have found love. Bailey loved our sister but she never loved him."

"I didn't think Bailey ever loved anyone but himself."

"Why do you think he was so upset when our sister died? That wasn't a man who had just had his prize toy taken away. That was a man who had lost the love of his life."

"I guess." Kathleen sighed as she continued to work. Mary wiped her mouth and rejoined her. The women dug in silence. After a long moment, Mary clutched her sister's hand. Kathleen peered up at her. "Mary?"

"Why are you asking me about when I fell in love with Sherlock? Do you finally see...? I see it...you're in love with Isaac."

"Ridiculous. I told you I am only here to seduce Isaac into helping me get rid of Bailey. He has feelings for me and said he would do anything for me," Kathleen protested, pushing more dirt aside and trying to hide her true feelings.

"That plan will never work unless you make Isaac believe the attractions he has for you are the same you have for him." Kathleen stared at her sister with a serious look. "Kat, this is a very dangerous game you are playing," Mary whispered.

"I'll win this game and let them destroy each other. When Isaac's dead I'll inherit Kilmore. A McGillpatrick will be in control of Kilmore. Isn't that what we have always wanted?"

"Not like this."

"You said it yourself plenty of times. The times are always changing and we must adapt to those changes or face the destruction of our very lives. I'm adapting and changing the situation."

"You're being a fool. Either one of those men will kill you if they learn you are deceiving them."

"They'll never learn the truth."

Mary snarled, "Sherlock would not have wanted this for you! He wanted you to get away from this island. That's why he bought the tickets for you, me, and him. You can escape with me."

"There is no escape for me, Mary."

"We can start a new life in New Orleans. You, me, and the baby."

Kathleen huffed, "You say my deed is a fool's errand but think about what you are asking me. We'd be two women with a baby and no man to protect us. We wouldn't survive alone on a ship to the colonies let alone in the wilderness."

"We're Irish, Kathleen McGillpatrick! We've been through worse times than that and survived them. I'm certain there will be someone who will see your beauty and want to help us."

"Hmphf," she grunted, pushing her hair back from the side of her face, revealing her smallpox-scarred cheeks. "I'm the ugliest girl in Ireland."

"No, Kathleen, you're far from that. You have won Earl Isaac Turner's affections and he is known to court only the most beautiful of women."

Kathleen lowered her attention back to the dirt. Tension fell between them. She could understand why Mary would be concerned for her welfare. She had every right to be. Yet Mary had struck her last nerve. She was in love with Isaac. As much as she tried to convince herself that she was only using Isaac to get back at Bailey, there was a larger part of her that wanted Isaac as her husband. It was that part that scared her the most. Who falls in love with their enemy? If she knew what was best for her she would find a way to escape. Just like Mary had. Kathleen stopped as the lapel of Sherlock's coat lifted out of the dirt. "Mary," she called.

Mary smiled, taking notice of the cloth. The two women glanced at each other then began to dig faster. Dirt flew out the grave as their digging intensified. One, two, three buttons appeared. The women dug harder until Sherlock's barrel-chested figure came into view. "Ha," Mary smiled with tears strolling down her cheeks. The women stared at his firm chest. Mary rubbed her hands up and down his dirt-covered coat then laid her head on his chest. "I used to love to lie in our bed with my head over his chest. I could listen to his heartbeat all day long," she said, with her eyes on Kathleen.

"He was so strong. He used to carry me when I was little and I would play with his buttons."

Mary chuckled. "I remember that. I would always have to fix them. He gave you, Calico, and our children piggy back rides. There were so many times he had one of you on his chest and the other on his back."

"Sometimes all five of us at once."

Mary sniffed her nose, rose from over his chest, and wiped the tears from her eyes. She ran her hands over his chest and looked into his face as she unbuttoned his coat. "The last night I took his coat off was…" Mary shook her head.

"Was?"

"We had sex in the kitchen while waiting for you and Calico to return from Isaac's house."

"You did? I would have never suspected."

"There are many things you would not have suspected Sherlock and I had done. Things kept only between a husband and wife. Things that only a couple in love with each other would ever consent to doing." She opened Sherlock's coat then shoved her hand underneath his vest to his pocket. Mary paused then turned sharply to Kathleen. She moved her hand all over beneath Sherlock's vest. "No," she whispered, frantically removing his vest.

"What's wrong?" Kathleen asked again as Mary examined the vest then moved to the coat, checking every pocket. Kathleen grabbed Mary's arm and jerked. "What's wrong?"

"It's gone. I know he had it."

"Are you sure he had it on him when he died?"

"I know he did! He never took it off of him. He always kept it in his vest and he made certain he was always wearing his vest. Ugh!" She yelled then leaned over sobbing. "Oh, God. That was supposed to be my way out of Ireland. He did that to protect our child. Now what am I suppose to do?"

"There are only two people I can think of who would have taken it from Sherlock's body."

Mary nodded in understanding. "Bailey or Isaac." Mary sniffed then turned to her. "Bailey caused your wagon to overturn. He could have taken it then."

"Or in the barn after he shot him. I don't remember much about the incident but I know he was alone with Sherlock's body. As for Isaac, I asked him to bury Sherlock here. He could have searched Sherlock's body before he buried him."

"There is only one thing we can do then," Mary said, rising.

"Play my game until the culprit is revealed, take back the title, money, and boarding passes, then leave Ireland to follow your plan."

"And you would accompany me to New Orleans?"

Kathleen shrugged. "Do I even have a choice? After I steal what you need my ploy will be discovered. Either Bailey or Isaac will want me dead. You know as well as I do when those men have their eyes fixed on something they won't give up until they have it. Tomas and Calico will help them to destroy me. The way I see it, Mary, I have to go with you to save my life."

Chapter 23

Tomas lay on the edge of his bed as the late night moonlight trickled into this bedchamber. Weak with pain and exhaustion, all he wanted to do was sleep. But he couldn't. Hours ago, he had accompanied Isaac to Kathleen's room, where they found the room empty except for a woman underneath the covers. Tomas knew it was Calico. Anger and frustration had rolled in his body but he had kept his composure. Mary was playing Kathleen against him and Calico. He just knew it. Whatever scheme Mary had concocted had to end before Isaac ever learned the truth. Bailey had been right. They couldn't trust Mary. He was glad Bailey had wanted Isaac to kill Mary. He didn't think he had it in him to kill her. Not Mary. He had been friends with Sherlock and Mary for too long to ever cause her any harm. Isaac had walked halfway into Kathleen's room before Tomas ever realized just how close his friend had come to learning Calico was in Kathleen's bed and not her older sister. Tomas had acted quickly to deter his friend from drawing closer. He released what little strength he had gathered, letting the pain overcome his body, then collapsed in Kathleen's room. Isaac had gone to his side immediately. Twenty minutes later, Tomas awoke in his own bed to find Isaac sitting beside him and Isaac's personal physician examining him. The physician had told Isaac that Tomas should have never been out of bed and he was to ensure Tomas did not rise again until he had released him from his care. Isaac had agreed then Tomas had fallen back asleep. Thirty minutes later, he awoke to find that Isaac and the physician were gone. Panic set in. What if the physician had returned to Kathleen's bedroom to check on her as well? Isaac would know he was being played a fool. He had tried to rise out of bed but his father had stopped him. Padric had told him not to concern himself about the situation. He had taken care of everything.

"Ugh," Tomas groaned, grabbing his head and fidgeting. Pain coursed throughout his body. Just how late was it? He knew he shouldn't have ever left his bed earlier. It had taken every ounce of strength he possessed to walk to Isaac's chambers and speak to him. Now he was paying the consequences. Bittersweet as it was, his actions had been in the best interests of Calico, Kathleen, and himself. "Calico," he muttered through his dry, swollen lips. He turned his head expecting his wife to be by his side. With his eyes still closed he moved his right hand towards the edge of the bed. She wasn't there. "Hmm, Calico," he called to her again a little bit louder, tapping his hand. Still nothing. The dull pain of his sleep began to intensify as he became fully awake. "Ugh, Calico," he screamed as his body protested. He rocked back and forth, each breath causing more pain than before. Tomas breathed shallow, quick breaths. He felt someone sit on the edge of the bed. A woman's voice spoke to him.

"Tom, it's alright. Calm down" The female's familiar voice echoed in his mind. Did he dare open his eyes? He pushed the blankets down with his legs. The woman helped him to lower them. "Bring me the tea I made, Padric," she called to his father. He could hear his father move then the sound of someone walking towards his bed. Who was here with him? Where was Calico?

"Jane," a man called to her.

Jane? There was only one Jane he knew of. His mother-in-law. But what was Jane McGillpatrick doing at Kilmore Castle? If that Jane was the woman beside him then the man speaking to her had to be Alexander McGillpatrick. Tomas found Jane's hand and squeezed. She was real. This was real. The McGillpatricks were here! Did that mean the rebel army was close to Kilmore Castle? It was too soon for them to attack; besides they needed to attack his estate, not Kilmore. Tomas released his grip and kept still, listening in on their conversation.

"He needs to remain still for his wounds to heal," Jane answered.

"I don't understand, Jane. When Bailey and I injured Tomas we made certain his wounds looked worse than they really are. He should not be in this much pain."

"Bailey did this to him, Alexander."

"How? My son has a broken leg. We punched Tomas several times, tried to strangle him, and bound his hands so that the rope marks would be there, but I know he was not this wounded when I left the room."

"Was my son still bound when you left?" Padric asked, bringing the tea to the nightstand.

"Yes, Bailey said he was going to untie him."

"I see. Your son tried to kill him."

"Padric, our sons have been best friends for years. I know Bailey would never kill Tomas. If he had beaten Tomas…"

"There are no ifs about whether Bailey did it or not, Alexander," Jane interrupted, dipping her finger into the tea and pulling out a droplet. She cupped her hand, leaned over the bed, and placed the droplet on Tomas' lips. Tomas pressed his lips together, taking in the medicinal brew. "Good Tomas. A few more droplets." She picked up the cup and continued to place the tea on his lips. She spoke to Alexander as she did so. "Truth be told, Alex, the rebellion has changed since Bailey joined. We all know Tomas had the right idea to infiltrate the English and strike them from the inside. Calico has done well to aide him with that but Calico pays too much attention to Bailey."

"He's her brother and my heir."

Padric interrupted, "Sherlock was firstborn, not Bailey. I don't know why you ever let those boys exchange birthrights. Seems to me if you hadn't then perhaps things would have been a lot different. Trouble is, now Bailey's power over the rebels has grown so much he has no need for Tomas or you anymore."

"My son still needs me," Alexander countered.

"So do your daughters," Jane protested, laying the cup on the end table. "I don't understand why you haven't done anything to stop this, Alexander.

"Oh and what do you want me to do, Jane? I can't just appear to Parliament and plead for mercy. I'm no longer a judge or an Irish Earl who can make demands of others. I will not have my family torn apart and sold into slavery."

"Your family is already being torn apart. Sherlock and my daughter are dead! Bailey almost killed Kathleen. You see what he has done to Tomas. And you have seen the letter Tomas received from Bailey ordering him to have Isaac arrest Mary. If that isn't enough, Alexander, Bailey forced her to marry him then raped her several times last night, knowing that she carries our grandchild. All the while Calico is spying for him and Kathleen is in love with your enemy. What part of all this doesn't qualify as your family falling apart?"

"Shooting Sherlock in the head after he was dead is one thing, but to endanger the lives of his family, that is not my son."

"Your son has become a monster, Alexander McGillpatrick! A monster that is bent on the destruction of my daughters! I don't see how you can be so shocked. He didn't want to save Mary when she was captured…"

"But he did, eventually."

"Only after you forced him too. You think you can control him but you can't. He tells you one thing to appease your sense of justice, but once you turn your back on him he does things like this," Jane argued, pointing to Tomas.

The sound of their voices increased the pain Tomas felt in his face.

Tomas moaned, reaching for his mother-in-law. "Mother," he pushed out between his labored breaths.

Jane took his hand. Tomas turned his head towards his three parents and slowly opened his eyes. He cringed with pain as the light hurt his eyes. "Ugh, what time…hmm…what time is it?"

"A quarter after one," Padric answered.

Tomas nodded. "Mary?"

"She and Kathleen are asleep in their own beds."

"Where were they?"

"I do not know. Kathleen returned to her room around ten o'clock. Calico asked where she had been but Kathleen only told her that she had gone for a walk in the castle and got lost."

"Lost, humpf, I doubt that."

"She does have a concussion."

"What of Mary?"

"Calico found her in her room around nine thirty. She demanded of Mary to know where she had been but Mary only said she had been in the servants' area the entire time. Calico must have missed her."

"You said Mary never came to dinner."

"She didn't but that doesn't mean she could not have gotten something to eat and ate by herself in her room. She is with child. Perhaps she was embarrassed with the amount of food she is eating."

"Per…" Tomas inhaled a deep breath, arching his head back, then cringed. He grabbed his belly and rolled onto his stomach.

"Tom?" his father asked, sitting next to Jane and rubbing his son's bare back.

"Good God, what is in that tea?" he demanded, grabbing the pillow.

"It's been passed down in my family from the old days. Give it some time. It'll relieve the pain," Jane answered.

Tomas peered over at his mother-in-law. "If a few drops do that to my stomach, I hate to see what the entire cup does."

"I have to make certain your stomach can handle it first. Once it does you will need to take more of it. I've given your father the recipe."

"Where's Calico?"

Padric answered, "I told her to sleep in her own room. You need your rest."

"Why?"

"I do not want my children to know their mother and I are here," Alexander answered. "Tomas, I need to know your intentions with Mary."

"My…huh…my what?"

"Are you going to accept Bailey's demands?"

"I thought you had agreed to them."

"I most certainly did not! Mary is Jane's daughter. I care about her as much I care about Calico and Kathleen."

"Why would Bailey send me that letter if you didn't approve. It takes three votes."

"Why do you think?" Jane rebuked.

Alexander gazed sharply at his slender, beautiful wife with a look of disapproval. She crossed her arms and glared right back at him as if to say she wasn't going to back down from her argument. Tension filled the room. Both were stubborn and proud, and Tomas knew neither of them would relent. Tomas leaned on his side, grabbed his pillow, and rested his head on it with his arm underneath. "We…," he moaned, closed his eyes, and gathered his strength. "Ugh, Alexander," he pushed out of his mouth.

Alexander turned his attention to Tomas. "Tom?"

"She's right." He opened his eyes and lifted them to Alexander. "After you left, Bailey came at me from behind. I thought he was going to untie me but he didn't. He pulled the rope around my neck tighter until I could almost feel my very soul leave my body. I fell unconscious. When I awoke, I was laying on the floor next to my fireplace. On the floor were items that had been sitting on the mantle. I can only assume he had thrown my body against the wall then beat me harder."

"How? He has a broken leg."

"He also has servants in my household that are more loyal to him than to me!" Tomas coughed.

Alexander turned to Padric as Padric explained, "There are some in our family who do not agree with Tomas' conversion. They would rather see him deposed than rule over Collinsworth Manor. Tomas has suspected for quite sometime that they may rise against him. If they were looking for a leader I would not put it past them to choose your son."

"Are his brothers among them?"

"I believe so. His eldest brothers were more upset with him than his younger one."

"Because he's not your heir."

"Yes."

Alexander nodded. Tomas grabbed his pillow, closed his eyes, and turned his head towards the door. All he wanted to do was sleep but he couldn't sleep, not while Alexander and Jane were in his room. His bare back rose and fell as he tried to breath through the pain. Alexander stared at the deep bruises on his back. They were without a doubt markings made from someone being thrown hard against a wall. "Tomas, roll over."

Tomas opened his eyes and slowly rolled onto his back. He fidgeted as the movement aggravated his body. Deep bruises lay on his chest. He turned his head towards his father and closed his eyes. "You see, Alex," Padric began. "These are not the wounds of battle but of torture."

"Internal bleeding?"

"No, and he's quite fortunate Bailey didn't go that far. He has broken ribs, bruises, several cuts and sprains, broken cheek bone, broken nose, damage to his face, and some of his organs are bruised, as far as Isaac's physician can tell. They want him to rest but he couldn't do that tonight. Not with Mary and Kathleen missing."

"No, certainty not," Jane said. The men looked at her then continued.

"How long until he can move?" Alexander asked.

"They want him to stay in bed for a month at least. They will be checking on him periodically. They told him not to speak since they suspect his larynx may be injured from the attempted hanging. But my son hasn't listened to them." Padric lowered his eyes to Tomas.

"Hard to not speak when people expect me to answer," Tomas said then swallowed. He arched his head back, rubbing his throat.

"Can you see?" Alexander asked. Tomas opened his mouth to speak. "Don't talk. Just nod or shake your head."

Tomas looked to his father. Padric answered, "He can't see too well. His eyes are almost swollen closed. I have to read for him."

Alexander looked to Jane and began to walk away. "Alexander," Jane protested, chasing after him.

"He is useless to Mary in the condition he is in," Alexander yelled, turning to face her.

"No, no he's not. He will recover. Alex, there are things you do not know about your son. I understand why you would be upset but you have to act. You have to do something. Mary's my daughter. Please," she grabbed him by the lapel of his coat. "I beg of you have mercy on my daughter!"

"I have always been merciful to Mary." He put his hands over Jane's and looked down to her. Jane looked up to the tall, robust man with tears in her eyes. "Everything I have seen and heard would be enough proof to convict my son of attempted murder, murder, assault and battery. I just can't believe that he would do such deeds to his own family."

"But he has," she sobbed.

Alexander held her close and pressed her head to his firm chest. He glanced at Tomas, rubbing his wife's back as she cried. How could his son be so cruel? He just couldn't understand why he hadn't seen all the warning signs. Bailey had been upset after the loss of his wife and children. What man wouldn't be? He knew that sting of pain well. Hadn't he lost his wife when Bailey and Sherlock were small? Hadn't his own young son died of the smallpox? Now Sherlock was dead. It wasn't supposed to be like this. But he always knew the reality of life. You have large families because death often took your children before it came for you. It was one thing for death to come but it was another for family to strike against one of their own. Bailey had done just that. The more time passed from when Bailey had lost his family, the more bitter Bailey had become. Everything was starting to make sense. He couldn't see it before. The truth had been cold and hard. Hard enough to make him see life not through a father's eyes but through the eyes of a judge. He couldn't protect his son anymore. Bailey was on a path of destruction. He just wondered if that path would lead to more devastation, not only for his family but for their people as well. Those who had decided to leave Tomas and follow Bailey were like sheep being led to the slaughter.

Alexander kissed his wife's forehead. She lifted her eyes to his. "I won't let Bailey hurt Mary. I promise, Jane, I won't let it happen."

"Thank you," Jane whispered. He released her then walked to Tomas' bedside. Alexander watched Tomas sleep then turned to Padric. "How much do you know, Padric?"

"Bailey's been slowly building up his resources, power, and reputation so that the rebels only listen to him. Tomas had believed Bailey was going to cause a war within our organization."

"That wouldn't do anyone good except the English. They won't stop him. They'd let the rebels destroy themselves."

"You aren't the only one who believes this."

"Bailey's too smart not to have thought of that himself. What does he hope to accomplish with that?"

"What do you think, Alexander?" Jane protested. "He's been angry with you for marrying me. You know full well Bailey resents our marriage because he feels you have betrayed his mother."

"I married you after he started his own family. I never wanted to remarry until my sons each had a household of their own."

"And when I gave you children that made his bitterness against me even stronger. He can't fathom why you would allow it. It's no wonder he treats Calico and Kathleen with contempt."

"Jane I needed to be with a woman. I was miserable without my wife for so long. Just ask Padric. He had been pleading with me to take a wife for years before your daughters married my sons."

Padric answered, "He was a mess, Jane. Only thing that kept him going was those boys."

"I remember how bad he was when we met. I saw what no one else saw. A warm, loving man hidden deep inside a hard shell, afraid to love again. It took some time but he learned to love me," Jane said.

Alexander took a deep breath. "Jane, Bailey never showed bitterness towards you."

"No, he refused to talk to me. Alexander, you can't see the truth that's right before your eyes because you think all your children are equal. They're not. With or without Tomas' aide, Calico is going to follow through with Bailey's scheme. She will act on Bailey's order. She and Mary have never gotten along," Jane said, wiping away her tears as she rejoined them. "What did Tomas do when he read the letter from Bailey?" she asked Padric.

"He said he was going to plant evidence against her so Earl Isaac Turner would arrest her and then asked me to burn the letter. I pretended to do so, hid it in my coat, then brought it to you after he left his room," Padric answered.

"Does Kathleen know about the order?" Alexander asked.

"Not that I am aware of unless Calico told of it."

Jane sighed, "Calico would never tell Kathleen of Bailey's intention to eliminate Mary. She knows her sisters are close."

Alexander turned to his wife. "And you are certain Sherlock had the money and contract on him when he died?"

Jane answered, "Why would Mary lie to me?"

"Money, contract?" Padric asked.

Jane shook her head. "We can't speak of it in front of Tomas. Calico must never know the truth."

Padric nodded. "If Mary was alone with Kathleen and they both disappeared, then it is Kathleen we should be talking to," Alexander said, looking at his wife.

"Agreed."

Alexander turned back to Padric. "Where is my daughter sleeping?"

"In her own room."

Chapter 24

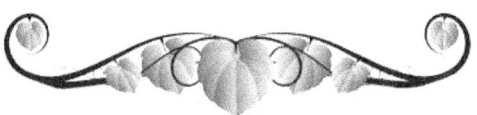

Sweet blissful slumber. Her old bed was as comfortable as she could recall before her family had been evicted from their home. Kathleen lay still on her bed, allowing her sweet dreams to carry her away into an ancient world. She could stay here forever. Her headache had grown numb and the pain from her fractured ribs wasn't as bad as it had been yesterday.

"Kat," her mother's voice beckoned for her to wake. She turned her head, ignoring the call. Her mother couldn't be here. She was in Collinsworth. "Kathleen," her mother's voice grew more persistent. "Sweetheart, wake up."

"Mummy," Kathleen muttered, turning her head towards them. She took a deep breath then fell silent.

"Kathleen, wake up," her father's deep voice ordered her, shaking her forearm.

Kathleen slowly opened her weary eyes. Soft moonlight poured into her room from the window on the left side wall, illuminating her parents' faces. She rubbed her eyes. This has to be a dream. How could her parents be in her room when Isaac was at Kilmore? Kilmore wasn't just Isaac's home but a military outpost for the English also. Wouldn't one of the English guards notice her parents? Maybe she was having one of her confused moments. She had been exhausted, dizzy, nauseated, and confused sometimes since she had awakened after the accident. Isaac's physician had told her she had a concussion and it could take days, weeks, even months for her to heal. They had further warned that she could experience confusion, memory loss, become easily upset, lose track of time, have mild headaches, and be less tolerant of noise while she recovered.

Isaac had made certain she maintained her privacy in order to heal. She lowered her hands and stared at her parents.

"Are you real?" she asked.

Jane exchanged glances with Alexander, sat on the side of the bed, and took her daughter's hand. "We are, my little one," Jane whispered, moving strands of Kathleen's hair from her eyes.

Kathleen smiled then cringed from her throbbing head. "Papa," she whispered.

"Tomas' father told us you have a concussion, broken ribs, black eye, broken nose, and a bruised abdomen?"

"Yes, sir."

Alexander looked at his wife. Jane lifted her eyebrow, nodded, then turned back to Kathleen. "Sweetheart," Jane said. Kathleen turned her eyes towards her mother. "What do you recall?"

Kathleen shook her head. "Bailey hit me in the head. Papa caught me. I woke with reins in my hand. Rain. I drove a wagon down a road." She shook her head, trying to recall more, but her muddy mind could barely recall anything. She turned to her mother. "I woke up in Isaac's parlor. He took care of me. We're courting. That's all. I'm so sorry, mother."

Jane wiped her hand down the side of Kathleen's check "Shh, it's alright, little one. It's alright. Your father and I know what has happened to you."

"Kathleen," Alexander called to her as he sat on the foot of the bed. "Have you spoken to your sister?"

Kathleen shook her head, "I only saw Calico when I returned to my bed."

"I mean your other sister, Mary. Have you spoken to her?"

"Yes, sir. She comes to feed and care for me."

"What has she told you?" Jane asked.

Kathleen thought long and hard. Told her? Mary had told her something? She pushed through her thoughts, trying to recall what had transpired from when Isaac had brought her to this room to now.

Fragments of images of her with Mary, the graveyard, and Sherlock's body scattered her thoughts. They were all connected somehow, some way they had to be connected. What was reality? Tears strolled down her cheeks. If Mary had told her something or she had done something important with her sister, it had faded from her memory. Why couldn't she recall it?¡

"I…mummy," she cried, sitting up and reaching for her mother. Jane embraced her, pulling her into her chest, pressing her head into her breasts, rocking her. "I'm so scared." Safety and comfort filled her. There was no other person in the world who could comfort her like her mother.

"Kathleen?" Alexander asked, moving closer to his wife and daughter. Kathleen lifted her eyes to her loving father. "What do you recall? You don't have to tell me everything, only what you remember. Think you can do that?"

Kathleen nodded sniffing her nose. "Mary was here."

"In your bedroom?"

"Yes, sir."

"Good. Can you tell me if she said anything to you?"

Kathleen scrunched her face. Why was it so difficult to remember? Why was her mind so filled with mud as if she was— She gasped. "We were in the mud."

"Where?"

Kathleen bit her lower lip, trying harder. Flashes of large erect stones in every direction filled her mind. It looked familiar but where could it be?

"Tell me what you see," Jane said gently.

"Mud, lots of mud. Big flat stones growing in the dirt like trees. Hands digging. Mary crying in a hole." She shook her head. "I'm so sorry. That's all I can remember. I feel like I did something important but I can't remember what I did."

"Shh, it's alright," Jane coaxed as Alexander rose from the bed. Jane held her daughter close. Kathleen's pain seemed to slip away with each stroke of her mother's hand. Safe in her mother's arms, Kathleen closed her eyes and fell asleep.

"Alexander," Jane whispered. Alexander turned in their direction. "She fell asleep. Do you want me to wake her?"

"Let her rest. She's needs that more than I need her."

Jane slowly lowered their daughter to the bed. Kathleen moaned, turned her head to the side, and then fell silent. Jane kissed her gently on the side of the cheek, pulled the blanket over her daughter, then rose from the bed. She walked over to her husband. "I felt like I did something important but can't remember what I did."

"Hmm, I caught that too," Alexander said, glancing towards Kathleen. He turned back to Jane. "Erect stones growing out of the ground like trees. You remember when the girls were little? We would take them into the country to picnic near…"

"Ha, the ancient graveyard. You would take them in there and tell them stories about the old days. The girls liked to play around the—"

"Big stones that grow out of the ground like trees. That's what Calico used to call them."

"Hands. Mary crying in a pit. You don't think she and Mary dug up Sherlock's body, do you?"

"It sounds like it."

"Why would Isaac bury Sherlock in the ancient graveyard?"

"I don't know. What bothers me is our daughter's head. Her head injury was not that severe after Bailey hit her in the head."

"Alexander, obviously Bailey did more damage to her head after she left you, just as he had done more harm to Tomas after you left the room," Jane countered. "She can't accomplish helping Mary if she can't recall anything."

"Bailey knows that. I'm sure that's why he made certain her injuries were more severe than I realized."

"We need to get to Mary to let her know."

"Mary will figure that out on her own. We need to get back to Collinsworth before dawn. I don't think now is the time to help Mary."

"But what about Calico? Surely she is already plotting against Mary."

"I know she is, but Tomas and Kathleen are useless until they heal. Isaac will be too bothered with Kathleen to bother with Mary. Mary is safe for now, my love. We'll come back in a few days to check on Kathleen and Tomas. Come, we must hurry home." He took his wife by the arm and led her to the fireplace. Alexander crawled into the hearth and pulled a brick towards him. A small door opened before him. He pushed it open, crawled inside the hidden compartment, and turned around. Jane stood staring at Kathleen's bed. "Jane," he called to her with an urgent tone. Jane knelt before the hearth.

"Our baby."

"She will be fine. Isaac is in love with her. A man in love protects the woman who has captured his affections, just as I am trying to protect you. Come on, Jane."

She took his larger hand, turned to take one last glance at Kathleen, then disappeared into the secret passage. The door slammed closed behind her.

Stillness and darkness filled Kathleen's bedroom as if nothing had occurred. She turned her head, returning to her place of bliss and serenity, lost in the comforts of her bed.

Chapter 25

September 26, 1738

Light entered from the tall windows of the long formal dining hall. A rectangular mahogany dining room table sat in the middle of the room. Food sprawled before Isaac, his mother, sister, and Calico. The women ate and conversed while Isaac peered at the empty plate beside Calico. Once again Kathleen had missed a meal. It had been three days since her injuries. Calico had told him Kathleen was sleeping more than usual. He couldn't blame Kathleen. A concussion could last for days, weeks, or months. He hoped her condition didn't last too long. His greatest fear for her was that she would never recover from her head injury. His heart ached to be by her side but he didn't know if he could take Kathleen's mood swings for much longer. He had visited her several times but the woman he found wasn't the Kathleen he was used too. His vivacious, strong, caring Irish love had become an irritable woman. Every sight and sound had bothered her. Sometimes she would even forget the conversations they had or that he was even there. Isaac knew it was just a sign of her head healing from the trauma. He should at least be grateful that her injuries had not been worse.

"Isaac," his mother called his name. Isaac lowered his wine glass from his lips and turned his attention to his grey-haired, slender mother.

"Mother?" he asked placing his glass on the table.

She nodded over her shoulder. Isaac lifted his gaze over his mother's right shoulder. Kathleen stood in the hall, bracing herself against one of the pillars holding up the vaulted ceiling. A row of pointed arches lined the right side, hiding the stairs that lead to a balcony overlooking the medieval hall. "Kathleen," Isaac said, rising from his red-cushioned chair. He walked around his mother and sister, quickly approaching her. She stared at the floor with a slight headache, trying to steady her feet.

She had been of sound mind as Mary had dressed her for the day, but had quickly overexerted herself through the long walk to the front of the estate. Why did this house have to be so huge? It was like a city inside a building with its tight hallways running throughout the castle as if they were village streets. At one time she might have enjoyed living in the closed up city, but not today. Oh, not today. Kathleen felt Isaac's hands on her jawline. She raised her gaze to meet his. "Hi," she greeted him softly.

"Hello." He replied.

Kathleen swallowed hard. She removed her hand from the pillar and stumbled forward. Isaac caught her. With his hand around her waist he gently led her to the table as they conversed. "Why are you out of your bed?" he asked.

"I was hungry."

"You should have sent for Mary."

"I wanted to be with you." Isaac stopped with a grin and stared into her beautiful emerald eyes. Forgetting where he was and the company he kept he leaned in and gently kissed Kathleen on her thin, ruby-red lips. Kathleen opened her mouth, allowing him to slip his tongue into her mouth. The touch of his lush lips on her own was so delicious. How much she wanted to be with him! This she remembered. Yes, she was in his arms, the man of her dreams. The enemy of her family. There was a plan. The plan. She had to stick with her plan and not let this man seduce her. Wasn't she supposed to be seducing him?

He pulled away, swallowed, smiled then bowed. "Forgive me."

"What for? We are courting, aren't we? I mean you told me we were."

"Yes, we are. You remember?"

Kathleen nodded. "It's coming back to me."

"Good." Isaac placed his hand on her lower back, gently guiding her to sit in her place beside him and Calico. Calico rose from her place and embraced her older sister.

"It is good to see you out of bed," Calico greeted her.

"It feels good to be out of bed."

Isaac, Calico, and Kathleen sat down. Kathleen turned to face Isaac with a slight grin and took his hand. She leaned over the table towards him as the servants brought out the first course. "I'm sorry if I have been rude."

Isaac squeezed her hand. "Apology accepted. I'm just grateful you are recuperating. May I introduce you to my mother and sister?" he said, turning his gaze to the women across from her. "The Dowager Countess Charlotte Turner," Isaac said, indicating the woman across from Calico.

"It is a pleasure to meet the woman who raised such a fine gentleman," Kathleen said.

"The pleasure is mine, Lady Kathleen. You have an effect on my son I have yet to see any woman have on him. When Isaac asked Earl Connelly permission to court you, I was not amused. We know nothing about you other than you are Calico's sister. You are her sister, are you not?"

"Mother," Isaac snarled in a low tone toward her.

"I only ask her an honest question to ensure the woman you desire to marry isn't one that should not birth your son. We know nothing about her other than Tomas claims she is Calico's sister. To be honest, we know nothing about Calico either. How can we trust someone we don't know?" she glared towards Calico.

Kathleen heaved, trying to remain calm despite her anxiety. What if Isaac knew the truth? She could recall only brief conversations with her father and Tomas about how dangerous it would be if Isaac ever learned the truth. It would ruin everything. Worse yet, Isaac could just make her disappear. The image of her dead body flung into the deep pit came to her mind. She gasped, trying to rise from the table. Calico grabbed her hand and pulled her down.

"Dowager Countess, while I know you do not approve of my sister and me, let me ease your concerns. Kathleen and I come from a small estate in the north. Our father never served in Parliament, nor did he serve as a judge. We had more land, little money, and very few servants. I have enjoyed my time with your daughter and you when we have been able to converse. I have never kept anything from you, nor has Tomas concerning my own family. What would make you suspect that my sister and I are not whom we appear to be?"

"It is interesting you should ask that, Lady Calico," the older woman replied. She then put her hand under the table, pulled out a silver-beaded rosary with rubies and emeralds, and slid it in front of the sisters. Kathleen swallowed hard. "Look familiar?" the countess asked her.

"No," Kathleen lied then turned her eyes towards Isaac.

"Mother, this is the most inappropriate time to be discussing this matter with them," Isaac countered.

"I beg to differ, my son. Look at her face. The Lady Kathleen recognizes it," the countess answered with a stern look of disapproval.

She turned to her daughter. "Sarah, leave us."

"But mother. I haven't…"

"Leave," she commanded sharply, turning to the younger woman.

Sarah glanced at her older brother. Isaac nodded then muttered as he gripped Kathleen's hand. "I'll bring you something to eat later," he told his sister.

Sarah curtseyed then walked swiftly out of the room. All eyes turned towards the older woman. "Well, now that my daughter has left us, shall we return to this conversation?"

"There is nothing to discuss," Calico proclaimed, pushing the rosary towards the older woman.

"Oh, I beg to differ, Lady Calico," the stern woman objected, pushing the cross towards her. The woman leaned over the table and whispered. "Why is it that the stories you have been telling cannot be verified?"

"Mother," Isaac objected.

His mother turned her face to him. "It's true, Isaac. You've grown soft with the affections you feel for the Lady Kathleen." She rose from the table and walked closer to her son. "I was intrigued with Lady Calico when she first appeared by Tomas' side, but did not question her story until recently."

"Why?" Calico asked as Kathleen leaned into Isaac's chest. He wrapped his arm around her back and pulled her closer.

"Might we do this another time, mother? You're upsetting Kathleen," Isaac interrupted.

"No." She turned towards the sisters. "Your husband, Lady Calico, has always been a good friend to my son."

"Tomas is loyal to the English crown and appreciates the friendship Isaac has shared with him. We would never betray him."

"Then how is it he already has?"

Kathleen's stomach turned. It was all over. If Isaac believed his mother's accusation it would bring only the worst fate upon her entire family. She had to do something to stop this woman from corrupting her son's mind with the truth. But what could she do? Perhaps she could convince Isaac to be alone with her. It wouldn't be so far-fetched for him to think she was so unwell she needed to leave the room. She rubbed her hand on Isaac's chest with a low moan. Isaac lowered his eyes, grabbed her hand, and kissed it.

"Kathleen," he whispered.

She shook her head. "My head hurts," she whispered.

He placed his hand around her waist and helped her to stand. "We shall discuss this later, mother. Lady Kathleen requires rest," he said as he helped Kathleen walk out of the room.

Calico and the countess stared at each other in a long moment of silence. Calico stared at her rosary. How typical for Kathleen to have left the room when the going got tough. She had been scared of the repercussions of their actions against the Turner family, and now that all their scheming might have been caught Kathleen didn't know what to say out of fear. Calico exhaled a deep breath as the grey-haired woman silently sat across from her. All she had to do was treat this woman like Bailey. Don't give too much information away or it would ruin everything, but give just enough not to raise her suspicions. She lifted the rosary and examined it as if she had never seen it before, then laid it back on the table.

"I don't see what this little trinket has to do with my sister and me," she proclaimed as she pushed it back to the countess.

"Oh, you don't? Well that surprises me since it was your husband who gave it to my son." Calico swallowed hard. "Tell me Countess, who names their daughter after fabric? Your older sister has a very elegant name yet your name speaks of poverty. No upper-class family would ever degrade their child with a name like yours."

"My parents' estate had much land but most of it was not suitable for farming. They had established a textile trade that had supplemented the income we gleaned from our farms, but it was just enough to keep the estate running. I was named after the calico fabrics we made and traded so that neither Kathleen nor I would ever forget our heritage."

"It is very interesting to me that you speak of your heritage."

"Oh, how so?"

"I still have contacts at Parliament who owed my husband a favor or two. While Isaac has been so concerned with winning your sister's heart, I, being the overly cautious mother that I am, asked one of my contacts, whose estate lies close to where you claim yours to be, to verify your story. And do you know what he found?"

"No," Calico pushed out of her lips.

"The people speak of the event you have told us but yet the location of your estate does not actually belong to your family."

"Of course it doesn't. It belongs to my cousin."

"Ah, now therein lays the dilemma. According to my sources the land you described actually has always belonged to a different Irish Earl." She leaned closer to Calico.

"The noble who owns the land and contracted it out to my family is my kin."

"Don't lie to me. The Irish noble who owns the land is a close friend of mine and he assures me that your family has never resided on his lands.

"Now, as to this so-called trinket." She picked it up, admired it, and then stared at Calico. "Your husband claims he found this rosary in the possession of your maid."

"Mary?"

"Yes, and that he had no idea she is Catholic."

"That is true. She came to the estate shortly after your family regained Kilmore."

"Hmm, that I do not believe." The countess laid the rosary back on the table and leaned closer to Calico. Calico's heart skipped a beat. As long as Isaac denounced his mother's suspicions concerning her and Kathleen's true identities, everything would be alright, but how long would it be before the countess had her son's full attention. She had to do something to stop this woman from ruining it all. Calico reached to her side. Lucky for her, Bailey had armed her with one of his trade knives in case she ever needed to defend herself. She slowly reached into the side of her gown and felt for the leather sheath Tomas had made for her. She removed the five-inch, sharp knife and laid it on her lap. All she had to do was kill this woman and pin it on Mary. Bailey had shown her how to kill someone at close range. She replayed the lesson in her mind, ignoring the words of the countess. Incapacitate your victim with a thrust of the knife into the neck and then remove the head. It would be a horrible death but she had no choice in the matter. The countess had to die for the glory of God. The death of his mother would infuriate Isaac and would be the perfect excuse for Isaac to arrest Mary. With Mary gone Kathleen would have to listen to Bailey.

Calico leaned over the table, grabbed the back of the countess' neck, and thrust the knife deep in the woman's throat. The older woman gasped, reaching for the knife. Calico leaned closer and pushed the knife deeper. "Go to hell, Anglican. This is my family's estate, not yours," Calico snarled as she pulled the knife out and slit the woman's neck. She leaned back as the countess' head hit the table and her body landed on the floor. Calico heaved at the sight. She couldn't believe she had actually killed someone, let alone a noble. Her mind raced with anticipation. She peered at her bloody gown and hands. If she was going to pin this on Mary she would have to make certain no one would ever suspect she was the culprit. Calico dropped the knife next to the rosary and fled the room through one of the secret passages.

Chapter 26

Calico ran through the parlor and opened the door to her husband's bedroom. Her father-in-law stared at her dress with shock. "What have you done?" he demanded, grabbing her by the arm.

"I did what needed to be done. Go to my room and get me a new dress, please."

The older man snarled, "Who did you kill?"

"It doesn't matter! Get my dress! Hurry, Padric. I don't know how much longer I can remain hidden. Oh, and place this in Mary's belongings," she said then removed the knife sheath from her leg and handed it to Padric with her bloody hand.

"I will not," he huffed, crossing his arms over his chest.

Calico leaned closer to him. "You will do what I say, old man. I respect you because you are my elder and my husband's father, but this is something that has to be done now! For Ireland."

"She's your sister."

"She's our enemy. Bailey wants her gone and I have made certain this time Isaac pays attention to the accusations against her. Now go," she demanded.

Padric took the leather sheath in his hands. He glared at his daughter-in-law for a long moment then walked out of the room. Calico's heart sank as he closed the door. She had always respected Padric since she was a young child. He had been the grandfather she had never known and his opinions had always mattered to her. She could tell he was disappointed in her and for good reason. She had broken one of God's commandments. Wasn't she the good Catholic daughter?

Calico walked to the side of her husband's bed, scrubbed her hands, arms, and face clean, and dried off with a towel. She watched her husband sleep peacefully in their bed and wondered what he was dreaming about. Hopefully it was something good and not something tragic. Someone knocked on the door. "Who is it?" she asked, lowering the towel.

"Mary. I brought food for Tomas."

Calico looked at her dress. Mary couldn't see her like this. Yet it would be perfect if someone saw her emptying a basin of bloody water and have a bloody towel in her possession. That would only verify her story. She grabbed the chamber pot and ran behind the privacy screen with it. Calico placed the pot on the floor and pretended to sit on it. "Come in," she yelled from behind the screen.

Mary entered the room and closed the door behind her. "Calico?" she questioned.

"I'm using the chamber pot. Just lay his food on the table beside him and I'll feed him when I finish."

"Alright," Mary answered with her eyes on the bloody water and towel. "That's a lot of blood. Has something happened to Tomas?"

"I was cleaning his wounds. Oh, Mary, can you do me a favor?"

"What do you want, Calico?"

"Will you empty the basin and then switch it with Kathleen's."

"You want me to take a bloody basin to Kathleen's room? Why? What did you do?"

"I told you. I cleaned my husband's wounds."

"Right, and why do you want me to take that basin to Kathleen's room? You're not going to set her up for something are you?"

"She's my sister."

"So am I, and you have done nothing but treat me with the greatest of contempt."

"You better watch your words, Mary McGillpatrick. I don't care if you are Bailey's wife or that we share the same mother. I outrank you! You don't want me to tell Bailey that you have been less than accommodating with my requests, do you? You know what he will do to you if you disobey him. I could send word to Bailey and have him beat you into submission."

"I'm with child. Would you want me to lose Sherlock's child?"

"That child belongs to Bailey now, not Sherlock."

Mary huffed as she grabbed the basin and towel. "One of these days, Calico, you're going to regret the way you treat me."

"I doubt it. Do what I asked, Mary. Empty the basin then switch it with Kathleen's clean basin, please. Tell her you ran out of clean basins and you don't have time to clean this one."

"But I do."

"Just do it!"

Mary clenched her jaw and walked to the door. She paused as Padric entered the room with a fresh gown. "Padric, why are you getting a fresh gown for Calico? She just changed."

"I don't know, Mary. She said she needed a new one and couldn't find you."

"Sure she did," Mary glanced at the screen then back to Padric. She shook her head then entered the hallway. Padric closed the door and walked to the screen. He placed the gown on the edge and sat on the bed next to his son as she dressed.

"Who...?" Tomas asked with a moan.

Padric turned to his son as Tomas arched his head. "Shh, Tom," Padric coaxed, rubbing his son's chest.

Tomas turned his head to the right and stared at the screen as Calico dropped her dress to the floor.

"Padric, take my gown to Mary's room and then make certain Isaac finds it before she does."

Padric rose from the bed, took the gown, and walked out of the room as Calico grabbed her new gown.

"And what is the excuse for the new gown?" Tomas asked after the door closed.

Calico stepped in front of the screen in only her shift, corset, and hoop. "Tomas," she greeted him as she ran to his side of the bed. He swallowed hard and took her hand. Tomas lifted her fingers to his eyes. "Is that blood?" he asked, lifting his gaze to his wife's face.

She pulled her hand away from him and scrubbed underneath her fingernails with a knife. "Damn it, I thought I removed all of the blood."

"It's hard to remove blood under the fingernails. What happened?"

Calico exhaled a deep breath. Suddenly someone knocked on the door. "Who is it?" Calico asked.

"Isaac."

Tomas looked at his wife. Calico lowered her knife, removed her petticoat hoop, and climbed into bed with her husband. Tomas lifted the blankets over them as Calico snuggled close to his chest. "Come in," Tomas said.

Tomas kissed the top of her head as Isaac entered the room. "You okay?" he whispered to her.

"I will be."

"Good. We will talk about this after he leaves. Understood?"

"Yes."

"I'm sorry for the intrusion, Tomas. I thought Calico might be in your room. I never thought she would be in your bed," Isaac said, glancing at the couple.

"She's upset and needed me," Tomas answered.

"Yes, well that's what I wanted to talk to her about."

"Oh? What happened, Isaac? She came back to my room sobbing."

"I wanted to apologize for that."

"What did you do to her?!"

Isaac raised his hands. "Nothing. It wasn't me. I…"

"Isaac! Isaac," Sarah screamed from somewhere down the hallway.

"Will you excuse me, please?" Isaac asked in a disappointing release of a long breath.

"Of course," Tomas replied.

Isaac walked quickly to the door and peered into the hallway. "Sarah, over here," he called to his distraught younger sister. Sarah ran down the hallway sobbing. He grabbed her by the shoulders. She heaved with streams of tears cascading down her beautiful cheeks. Isaac took his sister's head in his hands and peered into her eyes. "What has happened?" She shook her head, unable to speak. Isaac lovingly pulled his sister into his chest, walked her into Tomas' room, and then closed the door.

He pulled her away from himself and looked into her eyes. "Breathe, Sarah. In and out. Like that." She glanced at Tomas and Calico then began to heave again. "No, no, no. Look at me, Sarah," Isaac coaxed, grabbing her head and directing her to face him. "What happened."

"D...de...dead."

"Who is dead?"

"Mur...mur...murder."

"Someone's been murdered?" Sarah nodded between her sobs. "Who Sarah?"

"Mother," she wailed louder and clutched Isaac. Isaac lifted his head with a clenched jaw as he wrapped his arms around her back. He glanced at Calico and Tomas then swallowed hard.

"How?" he asked, tightening his fists.

"Her head's on the table and her body's on the floor."

"Ugh," he exclaimed, pushing Sarah aside. Isaac paced the room with clenched fists. He turned towards the bed, walked to the footboard, and glared at the couple. "My mother said some harsh things about you and your sister, Calico."

"Now wait just one minute," Tomas exclaimed. "Why would Calico kill your mother? She's your friend."

"She was the last one who saw my mother alive!"

"I left right after you and Kathleen did. I came to cry on my husband's shoulder after those horrible accusations," Calico replied from under the sheets. "You have a traitor in this house and you know who she is."

Isaac nodded then stood upright. Of course he had a traitor! How could he have forgotten about Mary McGillpatrick? Hadn't Tomas given him the same rosary his mother had charged Calico and Kathleen with? "Are you certain the rosary you gave me belongs to Mary, Tomas?"

"I am," Tomas answered. "Why do you ask?"

"Because I came here this morning to apologize on behalf of my mother. She accused Calico and Kathleen of being the owners of that rosary and not Mary."

"Preposterous. My wife and her sister are devout Anglicans."

"I know. That is why I never believed my mother's accusations. She believed Calico and Kathleen are the daughters of Alexander McGillpatrick."

Calico clutched Tomas tighter. He rubbed his hand on her back. "And do you believe that as well?" Tomas asked.

"I do not. Did you confront Mary about her lineage?"

"How could I? I have been in too much pain to do much of anything. Calico was distraught with my wellbeing and has never confronted the woman either."

"Will you grant me permission to interrogate her and if I find her guilty punish her for the crimes she has committed?"

Tomas took a deep breath and nodded. "Yes. Do what you must with the woman, Isaac. I just ask you to inform Calico and me of your findings."

"Of course. I suspect if she is whom you believe her to be she is the one who murdered my mother."

"I understand."

"The repercussions?"

"I will stand by you on that. You have my word."

"Very well."

Isaac took his sister by the arm and went to the door. "Isaac," Tomas yelled towards him.

The younger man turned towards the bed. "Our most deep condolences."

"Thank you," Isaac said harshly, walked out the room, then closed the door behind them.

Tomas rolled on his side, grabbed Calico's jaw, and then glared into her eyes, whispering under the blankets. "Did you kill her?"

"Yes."

"What the hell were you thinking?"

"Bailey wants Mary eliminated. Your accusations against her with the rosary did nothing but add to the suspicions his mother had against us."

"I could have controlled that."

"But you didn't, Tomas. Isaac believes everything you say but his mother did not. She confronted Kathleen and me with the rosary at lunch. Kathleen was able to evade her interrogation because she coaxed Isaac into leading her back to her room. When I was alone with the dowager countess she told me she had investigated the story of Kathleen's and my heritage. She found out our ruse is based on lies. I couldn't have her words carry any weight with Isaac, and I knew Bailey needed Mary gone, so I killed her."

"Calico, you only aided Isaac's suspicions, not halted them with his mother's death."

Calico shook her head. "I don't understand. She can't proclaim them if she's dead."

"No, but if Isaac knows of her suspicions and the wife of the rebellion's leader killed his mother, it will only give him more cause to believe the words of his mother. He could believe Mary murdered his mother so she could remain silent in order to protect you and Kathleen."

Calico gasped with realization. She rolled onto her back, wiped her hands up her face, and exhaled a long, deep breath. "I...I...I never thought of that. I just thought it would be so much easier to do Bailey's will by pinning the murder on Mary. Tomas, I didn't...I...oh, god."

Tomas placed his finger on her mouth and leaned over her. "No more ploys without my permission first, understood?" Calico nodded. "I know why you did it, Calico, and I do appreciate that you are trying to help Bailey and me, but this has to end. I am your husband. Your only duty is to grant me an heir. While I want to share my entire life with you I will not do so if I believe you will endanger not only yourself but our families and the rebellion as well. Understood?"

"Yes, but can you fix this?"

"I believe I can. Ugh, I'm never going to heal properly if I have to keep fixing things. I'm not a young man, anymore. You have to remember that." He leaned down, kissed her on the lips, and rose from the bed. "Stay in my bed until I tell you otherwise," he said with his arm across his chest. He grimaced, putting on his coat. "Where's my father?" Tomas asked in pain.

"I sent him to place my bloody dress in Mary's room. I figured if Isaac found it during his investigations he would blame Mary."

"Calico, did Isaac see you in that dress?"

"Of course, I wore it to lunch."

Tomas shook his head with disappointment.

"What?" she asked.

"If Isaac has already seen you in that dress and finds it in Mary's room then he will think Mary helped you to kill his mother. You didn't blame Mary. You gave Isaac evidence against you!"

"But I could claim she had a duplicate made of my dress so she could pin the murder on me."

"And where was she to have gathered the funds to make such an expensive dress?"

Calico opened her mouth to speak as Tomas crossed his arms. She couldn't find the words. Tomas was right. She closed her mouth and shook her head. "Tomas," she whined.

Tomas shook his head. "I don't know if I can fix this, Calico."

"Please," she begged with tears cascading down her cheeks.

"How long ago did my father leave with the dress?"

"It's been a while. He should have been in Mary's room by now."

Tomas nodded then burst out of his room. Calico rolled over and traced her hand along her husband's side of the bed. She rolled onto her stomach and cried into her pillow. All she ever wanted to do was please her husband and Bailey, and restore her family to Kilmore. Now she had perhaps ruined it all.

Chapter 27

Kathleen slept peacefully in her bed as Mary entered the room with a clean basin. Chaos had erupted throughout the house with news of the dowager countess' murder. It hadn't taken long for some of the servants to treat her with indifference. She had heard their whispers. Many of the servants had believed she was in some way loyal to the rebellion but couldn't piece together where they had seen her before. Now with the countess brutally murdered they had begun to fear she would strike out against them if any of them reported their suspicions to Isaac or Sarah. Mary hated all the commotion and the added stress wasn't doing her pregnant body any good.

"Kathleen," Mary said, placing the clean basin on the table. Her little sister never moved. Mary sighed. Kathleen's head still wasn't quite right and she needed her rest. Under normal circumstances she would have let her little sister rest but these weren't normal circumstances. She walked swiftly to Kathleen's bedside, sat beside her, and rubbed her sister's back as she leaned over to whisper in her ear. "Kitty Kat, wake up," she coaxed the young woman just as she had done so many times before in Kathleen's childhood.

Kathleen moaned, turned her head to the side. "Hmm, Mary? You have medicine for my head?"

"No, sweetheart, you already took some. Isaac gave it to you before he left the room. It puts you to sleep, remember?" Kathleen nodded. "But I need you awake. Open your eyes. We don't have a minute to spare."

Kathleen rolled onto her back, rubbed her face, and opened her eyes. She waited as Mary's blurry image slowly came into focus. "How long have I been asleep?" she asked.

"An hour."

"No wonder I'm so tired."

Mary leaned over her sister, supporting her weight with her left hand on the other side of Kathleen. "Were you ever able to locate my husband's belongings?"

"I felt something inside Isaac's coat at lunch that could be Sherlock's documents."

"If they are on Isaac then there is certainly not a way you could retrieve them for me before it's too late."

"Too late? Too late for what?"

Mary rose from her sister's bed and grabbed Kathleen's empty basin. Kathleen sat upright then leaned over her lap as a sharp wave of dizziness overcame her. She clutched the blanket and lifted her eyes to Mary. "What has happened?"

"If anyone should ask, that basin is yours."

"I don't..."

"The less you know the better. Go back to sleep, Kathleen. I was never here," Mary said then walked out of Kathleen's room.

Kathleen lay on her back and wiped her hands down her face. Why was Mary acting so strange all of a sudden? Perhaps it was due to her being with child, yet Mary had never acted like that before when she was pregnant. Quite to the contrary, the entire family had spoken about how much Mary was able to maintain her sensibility while carrying a child. It was quite rare to see a woman keep her senses while with child. But if Mary was sensible then that could only mean she was protecting her. What in the world could Mary be protecting her from? Nothing made sense to her. Perhaps this was all a dream. Kathleen settled on her side, pulled the blankets over her body, and went back to sleep. She eased her mind, allowing the drug Isaac had given her to once again work on her body.

This was her room, her security, her sanctuary. Whatever had happened outside the walls of her room would have to wait until tomorrow. All she needed was respite from the chaos of her world.

Chapter 28

September 30, 1738

Kathleen walked down the long, dark hallway towards Isaac's quarters with confusion. She had awakened from her sleep with a clear mind but it seemed off that neither Mary nor Isaac had been by her bedside when she awoke. It wasn't like either of them to leave her alone while she rested. Despite how much she wanted to deny her true feelings for Isaac, she found herself wanting to be with him even more. Constantly she reminded herself she was only here to guide Isaac towards Bailey's location without harming herself or her family. Yet the more she tried to rationalize her situation the more it became clear to her she wasn't here for that alone. No, deep in her heart she wanted to be the Countess of Kilmore.

The sound of a crash came from Isaac's parlor. Kathleen paused at the half-opened door and peered inward. Isaac sat next to the fireplace on his knees and sobbed with papers and books sprawled on the floor around him. Kathleen's heart broke at the sight of the strong man broken into uncontrollable tears. She wondered what had happened to the Englishman. Isaac wasn't one who could easily be broken emotionally. She grabbed the side of the door and inhaled a deep breath. There hadn't been a servant to deny her entrance into this part of the castle. She wondered why his security had been so lax and would his anger be so great against her if he learned she had seen him so vulnerable. Kathleen swallowed hard. The entire house had echoed there was something wrong since she awoke from her deep sleep only a few hours ago. Servants were missing. Mary had disappeared. She had even tried to visit Tomas and Calico but guards had refused her entrance into their chambers. Where was everyone and why was Tomas against her?

Kathleen gathered her strength and knocked on the door. Isaac turned his tear-stricken face towards her and rose quickly. He wiped the tears from eyes, sniffed his nose, and pulled down his vest. "Lady Kathleen," he addressed her.

"I'm sorry to intrude. I awoke and wondered why you were not by my side."

Isaac shook his head with a long drawn out breath. "I have…been…preoccupied."

Kathleen stepped into the parlor, stared at the mess on the floor, and then turned her gaze in his direction. "What happened here?" she asked.

He quickly walked to the correspondences and gathered them. "It's nothing. How do you feel?"

"I have fully recuperated. Thank you for your hospitality."

"Hmm," he nodded as he placed the books and letters on his desk.

"Isaac?" she asked, stepping close to him and placing her hand on his back. He turned swiftly to face her. His charming face had become the face of a man lacking sleep and distressed. She placed her hands on his firm chest.

Isaac quickly grabbed her wrists and pushed her hands down. "Don't," he ordered.

"Don't?"

He leaned closer to her face. "How can I trust the woman whose servant murdered my mother?" he whispered, stepped to the side, and walked away from her.

Kathleen heaved with shock. Murder? How could Mary have murdered his mother? It wasn't like Mary to take the life of another. Besides it was a fool's errand for her to have done so. If Mary had killed Isaac's mother then she would have placed suspicion not only on herself but also on their entire family. Mary was much smarted than that. Perhaps

Isaac was trying to play her for a fool. He was a spy for King George after all. If this was a game to make her divulge information then she couldn't allow her emotions to get the better of her. Perhaps he had finally listened to his mother and decided to act on her suspicions. She couldn't allow him to get the better of her. She turned to face him. "Where is my servant?" she demanded with authority.

"In the dungeon. Tomas and Calico have been confined to their quarters with two guards posted outside their door. As for you, well I never expected you to wake so soon. While I was interrogating your servant she admitted to me that she had awakened you from your slumber. I ordered my doctor to administer a higher dose of your medicine. He did but obviously it was not enough. I had hoped you would have been asleep for at least one more day."

"How long have I been asleep?"

"Three days. We buried my mother yesterday."

Kathleen swallowed hard and stared deep into her beloved's eyes. She gently placed her hand on his arm. Isaac growled and pushed her aside. "Don't touch me. I want nothing to do with you or your family!"

"Isaac please. I would never harm you or your family. If my servant murdered your mother the order did not come from me or my sister."

"I will believe that when I have the proof."

"Isaac, ple…"

"That is Earl Turner to you, Lady Kathleen! I am an earl and I will no longer entertain such pleasantries with you!"

Kathleen gasped, unable to speak. She politely curtseyed, in shock and horror. Her heart broke at the thought of this man pushing her aside. "Please Earl Turner. Please, I beg of you. Listen to my words. You once found the sound of my voice pleasing and my words rational."

Isaac grabbed the collar of her bodice and pushed her against the wall. She cringed at the pain that resonated throughout her body. Isaac pulled a knife out from his coat and placed it against her neck. She peered at the long blade and into his angry eyes. Her beloved, charming man had become the very monster her brothers had spoken about. "Shut up, Kathleen. I care not to hear your voice, see your face, or be anywhere near you."

"Is…"

"Shut up," he growled, thrusting the knife closer to her neck. He glared at her slender throat and fidgeted with the knife close to her skin. "Your servant cut off the head of my mother and by God I swear I will do the same to the person responsible for it."

"Then kill my servant, not me." Kathleen couldn't believe the words had come out of her own mouth. Kill Mary? That was the last thing she would ever want to happen.

"I would but the woman is with child. I suspect she would not endanger the life of her unborn child without provocation. Just," he yelled, pushing his body against hers even more. She heaved as the pressure between the wall and his body aggravated her broken rib.

"Is…," she tried to push out despite her body's protest to breathing.

"Don't Isaac me," he yelled then slammed his fist into her face. Kathleen fell to the floor. A small drip of blood trickled from her neck. She placed her hand on the cut and peered at the blood as Isaac kicked her in the face. Kathleen rolled onto her back and fell unconscious. Isaac crouched beside her as he put his knife back into his coat. He grabbed her face by the jaw, leaned down, and kissed her. "Don't be the woman I think you are, Lady Kathleen." Isaac glanced down her body, picked her up in his arms, and walked into his bedroom with his prisoner. He placed her on his bed then grabbed two pair of shackles from inside one of his chests. How he hated to use these on her but he had no choice. He should have placed her in the dungeon with Mary but there was something about this woman that made him not want to let her out of his sight. He shackled her hands and feet to his bed, stepped back, and admired the beautiful creature that lay helpless in his bed. Oh, just the sight of her in his bed stirred something inside him. He could just take her as he had done with so many others of the Irish rebel women. He had broken in so many girls and young women

in the dungeon it was hard to keep count. When the prisoners came to him he would take the most beautiful ones, break them, and use them as prostitutes. The others, he would send off as slaves to the colonies. He couldn't fathom doing either of those things with Kathleen, which made her more of a threat to him than any other woman alive. What was it about this woman that made him question everything he knew? Isaac huffed and then stormed out of his room. He needed answers and there was only one way to learn the truth. Search Tomas' house.

Chapter 29

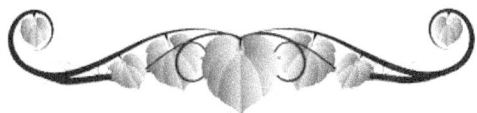

Alexander sat at the kitchen table next to Jane and across from Padric as Padric's wife, Margaret, fixed a plate of food for him. "How badly beaten is Mary?" Jane asked, clutching her husband's hand.

"I don't know, Jane. I couldn't gain access to the dungeon. There're too many guards."

"And Tomas?" Margaret asked, putting the plate in front of her husband.

Padric shook his head. "I don't know. Isaac had come into the room soon after Calico admitted to her husband what she had done. That arrogant English Earl blamed Calico for the murder."

"No," Jane gasped. Alexander pulled his wife closer to him.

"Did Tomas defend her and Kathleen?"

"Yes," Padric answered as Margaret sat beside him. "He handed Mary over to him and granted Isaac permission to interrogate her. Tomas has reassured Isaac that neither he nor the girls had any knowledge of Mary's true identity. So far Isaac has believed his words but I don't know how long that ruse will last, Alexander. He has placed Tomas and Calico under house arrest. They are not allowed to leave their chambers. Tomas' wounds are not healing fast enough. For now Isaac has granted him a doctor, medicine, and rest in his own bed, but I do not know how long that will last. As for Kathleen, Isaac ordered his doctor to keep her sedated in order for her wounds to heal." Padric looked at his food with a long, drawn out sigh.

Alexander clenched his jaw. "How much time does she have?" he asked after a brief moment of silence.

"I don't know." He lifted his head. "Bailey's won and there's nothing Tomas can do to stop it," he whispered.

"Alex?" Jane questioned, grabbing her husband's arm with tears still running down her cheeks.

"He'll wait until the baby is born. Does Isaac believe Tomas?"

"He'll want to verify Tomas' story," Padric said, rising from the table.

"Where are you going?" Margaret asked as her husband walked to the door.

"I have to return to the estate before Isaac notices I'm missing. Thank you for the food, Margaret. Be safe and well," Padric said as he walked to his wife then gave her a kiss. Alexander, Jane, and Margaret watched in silence as Padric left the house.

"He can't kill her, Alexander," Jane yelled, rising from her chair. "She's my daughter!"

"Mary knew the dangers."

"You said you would save her from Bailey's plan but all Bailey has done is endanger all of our children!"

"Shh, Jane. Bailey can never know my plans. He's been walking around the house all morning. Sit down and finish your breakfast," Alexander coaxed, grabbing her wrists and guiding her to her chair. She huffed and complied.

"Truth be told we just don't have the numbers to counter him as long as Tomas is Earl of this estate," Margaret said, picking at her bacon.

"You think when Isaac comes to investigate the house his brothers would endanger their own family just to have Isaac depose him?"

Margaret nodded. "That I do."

Alexander leaned back in his chair and wiped his hands down his face. "Ugh, I miss the simpler days when our children actually had some sort of common sense in their heads."

Margaret chuckled. "The question is how do we convince Bailey not to hand Tomas over to Isaac? If his life is threatened he will take down anyone who supported him. He cares not for anyone but himself," Jane said.

Alexander rose from his chair and paced. Jane was right. One of their children would have to be sacrificed for the wellbeing of his family and the rebellion. But who? He hated the thought of his children's lives in the hands of that English monster. It didn't matter which of his wives had born them. Bailey, Sherlock, Kathleen, and Calico, he loved them all the same. Just as he loved Jane's daughters, Mary and Anne. He tapped his cane on the floor and peered at the floorboard. There really was only one thing that could save all of his children. It was a sacrifice he was willing to make to save all their lives, but how was he to save Mary? He lifted his eyes to Jane and Margaret. "Padric said Kathleen told Mary she knew the location of Sherlock's documents."

"Yes," Margaret answered.

Alexander nodded his head and silently carried his plate to the counter.

"Alex?" Jane questioned.

He stared at the dish, playing with the leftover bacon. "You will board the ship with Mary and ensure her safety."

"And where will you be?"

Alexander shook his head.

"No! Absolutely not," she yelled with complete understanding as she rose from her chair.

"I have no choice in the matter," he yelled back, turning to face her.

"Gather the rebels and attack the dungeon. Rescue Mary instead of sacrificing your own life."

Alexander turned to Margaret. "Prepare the house as if I had accompanied Sherlock. Tell everyone I have forced my leadership upon Tomas' estate and brutally used Sherlock's wife to infiltrate Kilmore. Be certain to spread Mary's innocence. If Isaac believes she's innocent then perhaps I can convince him to let her go."

Margaret nodded and rose from the table. "It should be Bailey, not you, Alex."

"He's my son. You should understand that, Margaret."

"That I do." She patted Jane on the shoulder then hurried out of the room.

Jane ran to her husband and embraced him. He lovingly embraced her and kissed the top of her head. "Bailey cannot take your life," she repeated, pounding the palm of her hands into his chest as she sobbed.

"I offer it freely to save Kathleen, Calico, and Mary." He placed his hands on the sides of her face and lifted her face to meet his own. "We have to evacuate the estate. Isaac will search everywhere for evidence against Tomas. I need to make certain it all points to me and not Tomas."

"That won't save Mary. Isaac knows the truth of her identity."

"Isaac will expect the rebels to attack after I am arrested. He will be so busy planning his defense he'll never expect my escape. Who better to be in the dungeon than me? I know all the passages. Do you remember how to get into Kathleen's room?"

Jane nodded.

"Good, you will need to send word to Calico, Tomas, and Kathleen once I am arrested. They must work together to help Mary escape."

"And you?"

"Jane, I will not survive this. Please, my love, accept that."

"No," she sobbed. "Oh, God, Alexander. I can't live without you," she sobbed and buried her head on his chest. Alexander lowered his forehead to her head and closed his eyes. He hated to see her like this and deep in his heart he never wanted to leave her side either. Jane had been the perfect Catholic wife. After years of living with a broken heart from the loss of Sherlock and Bailey's mother, he never fathomed he would ever love again. Jane had mended his mind and heart with her beauty, grace, and kindest of hearts. She had been the blessing he had needed. He lifted his eyes at the sound of Bailey's crutches thumping down the hall towards them. Alexander watched his son enter the kitchen.

"Is it true?" Bailey questioned with a devious grin.

Alexander nodded.

"Good," he answered, making his way around the table. "How long do we have?"

Jane clutched Alexander's vest with a deathly grip. "He can't have you," she whispered. "You're his father."

Alexander pressed Jane's face closer to his chest. Bailey stared at his mother-in-law and then lifted his eyes to his father. "You had no right to order Calico to endanger Mary's life," Alexander snarled at his son.

"I have every right, father. She's a threat to the rebellion and would have convinced Kathleen not to follow my orders." He turned his attention to Jane. "Humpf, good riddance to bad rubbish and all that comes with it."

Alexander pushed his wife aside and grabbed Bailey by the shirt. "Those are my daughters!"

"You have no idea what you have done," Jane cried.

Bailey spit at her. Alexander pushed his son against the counter. Bailey dropped his crutches and tried to stabilize himself with the counter. "They are not my sisters. I only have one mother. Why did she have to die giving birth when this whore gave you three children and still lives?" Bailey countered.

Alexander gasped with realization. He turned to Jane. "Leave us," he ordered. Jane nodded, wiped her tears, and left the room, closing the kitchen door behind her. "It's been a little over forty years, Bailey, since I lost your mother. Why now?"

Bailey groaned as he reached for his crutches. He shook his head. "You wouldn't understand," he grunted, only inches away from his crutch.

Alexander walked to his son's crutches and put them in his son's hands. "I have always known you missed her. You were so young when she died and for years I didn't know how to console you, but now? Bailey, Jane will never replace your mother in here, son," he said, putting his hand on Bailey's heart. "But she loves you dearly as if she bore you herself. Neither she nor her daughters ever deserved to be treated in the manner you have treated them."

"They need to know their place! I am your heir, not them! Thank God the son she bore you died from smallpox or you would have forgotten who your true heir is."

"Sherlock was my heir, not you."

"He's dead. I'm all you have left, father. Never forget that," Bailey growled then walked away from his father towards the door.

"I need you to protect Jane when you leave the estate. I need to know I can trust my son!"

Bailey paused at the door for a moment then turned towards his father. "You are coming with us."

"I am not," Alexander replied, pulling down his vest.

"And where are you going?" Bailey asked, although he suspected he already knew the answer.

"Nowhere."

"Father, Isaac Turner will arrest you."

"I count on it."

"No! I will not be an orphan!"

"Bailey, there comes a time when a man must face the reality that his parents will not always walk the same earth as he does. That time has come for you. Jane will always be the mother you need."

"She is not my mother!"

"Is your priest still in the house?"

"Yes. Father don't do this!'

"I want my last rites given before Isaac comes."

"No!"

"Don't deny my request, Bailey. Get the priest."

"But you're not…"

"Get the priest!"

Bailey stumbled backwards at the sharp sound of his father's voice. "It was supposed to be Mary who died, not you," he muttered.

"Answer me this, my boy. If someone had threatened to kill one of your children, would you allow it?"

"No."

Alexander tilted his head. "Nor would I. Calico and Kathleen's lives are in as much danger as Mary's is. I do this in order to save all of them. If Isaac believes I am such a cruel man to have used Sherlock's wife against him then perhaps he will have mercy on her. She's much better off as a slave than killed for the deed Calico committed. Besides, whoever buys her gains double the slaves with her child. They could use her for breeding purposes."

"She would be out of my way and I could control Kathleen once again."

"Yes."

"I'll lead rebels to aide in your escape."

"Not wise, considering Isaac will be expecting that. It would be for the best to let me die."

"No!"

Alexander stepped towards Bailey and took him by the shoulders. "Bailey, it would be a fool's errand for the rebels to attack Kilmore. The rebels can never be associated with Tomas or his family. It would take days, maybe even weeks to gather the men. By then, Isaac would have plenty of time to fortify his defenses. It would be best to allow my death to occur and use Kathleen to rescue Mary while small bands of rebels cause commotion over my execution."

Bailey swallowed hard. "Father, no."

"It is the only way." Alexander kissed his son on the forehead then pulled away from him. "Get your priest so I may prepare for my death. Go." Bailey clenched his jaw. "You know I speak the truth in this matter, Bailey. Quit trying to deny it."

Bailey turned silently and hobbled out of the kitchen. Alexander exhaled a deep breath and sat down on one of the chairs. He pulled a locket from inside his coat, leaned over, and opened it. A small painting of a beautiful, raven-haired woman stared back at him. He wiped his finger over his deceased wife's face and smiled. "I miss you, Kathleen. It won't be long before we are reunited in heaven." He kissed her picture and stared longingly at it.

"I miss her, too," an older man's voice proclaimed from the doorway. Alexander turned to face the grey-haired priest.

"Father, come in," Alexander said, closing the locket.

"Do you know how strange it is to hear those words from you?"

Alexander chuckled, handing the locket over to the priest. The priest opened the locket and sat beside him. He shook his head. "I still can't believe it's been over forty years since my daughter died. Some days, it's as if it all happened only yesterday. The day you named your daughter after her was the greatest honor I have ever received, Alexander," he said, handing the locket back to Alexander.

"When are you ever going to tell Bailey the truth?" Alexander asked, placing the locket back in his coat.

The priest shook his head. "I can't, Alex. It's too hard. It's best for him to know me as a priest rather than as his grandfather. My wife committed suicide a few months after Kathleen died. The only absolution I ever found from my pain was when I became a priest. Please don't make me relive that to my grandson."

"He's the only family you have left."

"I know but it's for the best. Now what is this I hear about you wanting last rites?"

"Don't question it, father. Just give them. You won't like my answer."

Chapter 30

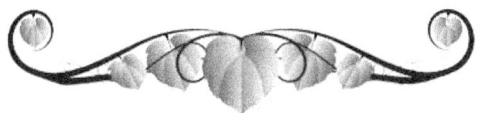

October 1, 1738

The smell of warm bread, scrambled eggs, and bacon filled Kathleen's nose as someone lightly dressed her wounds. She opened her eyes and tried to move her limbs. Chains rattled as the strong iron cuffs held her ankles and wrists in place. She panicked, pulling harder, yet nothing she did to escape released her.

"You'll only make it worse. You're already weak from hunger and your wounds," Sarah said as she pulled the bloody cloth away from Kathleen's nose. Kathleen turned to face her captor's younger sister and jerked again.

"Let me out," she snarled at the younger woman.

"I can't. Isaac won't allow it and why should I?" she huffed, throwing the cloth on the floor.

"Sarah, please. I didn't do anything to deserve this. Please," Kathleen pleaded.

Sarah shook her head. "Isaac said I should feed you and tend to your wounds." She turned to the tray of food and poured a glass of water from the pitcher. "Your servant murdered my mother."

"I had nothing to do with that."

"So it was your sister who ordered my mother's death."

"I...I...I don't know. She's so busy with Tomas she rarely speaks to me. But I doubt that Calico would have ever ordered such a thing to be done."

"Then Isaac and I can only conclude it was under Tomas' orders."

"No."

Sarah lifted Kathleen's head with the palm of her hand and started to feed her prisoner. Kathleen glared at Sarah as she continued to feed her. "Where's your brother?" Kathleen asked between bites.

"He went with a unit of men to search Tomas' house and has yet to return."

Kathleen swallowed hard. Search Tomas' house? Her heart sank at the thought of Isaac discovering Bailey and her parents. There was certainly no way her parents could receive warning of Isaac's arrival with the soldiers. If Isaac had issued an order to search the house then he would also search the entire estate. How long would it take before Isaac either discovered the truth of Tomas' betrayal or her own family? Perhaps even both. She moaned with disappointment and closed her eyes.

"You must eat more. Isaac wants you alive and strong," Sarah ordered.

"I have a headache. Leave me alone."

Sarah grabbed the back of Kathleen's head and pulled her hair. Kathleen screamed as she opened her eyes. "You will do what I say or else," Sarah bellowed as the door to the bedroom opened.

"Leave her alone, Sarah. I have executed the murderers," Isaac ordered.

Sarah released her grip. Kathleen lowered her eyes with disappointment. As much as she wanted to hear her beloved's voice, those were not the words she had wanted to hear. Mary. Her poor, sweet older sister. How could she live another day without her beloved sister? She turned her head towards the wall as tears flowed down her cheek. Kathleen ignored the conversation between brother and sister. Sarah had claimed Isaac had gone to Tomas' house with a unit of men. There could have only been disaster when he reached the home that hid her family. Bailey wouldn't have been able to run, walk fast enough, or fight the unit that threatened their family. What about her parents? Sure, she had seen her father fight and he could hold his own, but her mother? Her mother didn't know how to defend herself. And what about Tomas and Calico? Just how long had she laid chained to this bed and what had happened while she was unconscious? Her wrists and ankles were sore from the tight cuffs that clung to her skin. Had Isaac done anything to her while she slept? She had so many questions that needed to be answered. Her heart skipped a beat as the door slammed shut.

"Look at me," Isaac ordered at the foot of his bed. Kathleen slowly opened her eyes and turned her face to the front. The powerful and arrogant Earl Isaac Turner studied her closely with his hands behind his back. His sister was nowhere in the room. She must have left before the door slammed closed. Kathleen swallowed hard, shifting her weight. God, how she hated the way he stared at her. "I went to your home," he said coldly. She couldn't flinch. She couldn't let him see the pain in her eyes and the hole in her heart caused by this words. She was Lady Kathleen Gregory, not Kathleen McGillpatrick, daughter of Alexander McGillpatrick. No, she couldn't be her. Isaac would kill that woman in a heartbeat. "Do you not wonder what I found?" he asked, clearly holding something behind his back.

"Nothing," she pushed out a grin.

Isaac grinned back with a huff. "Tell me again what happened the night you brought Sherlock's body to me."

"I don't recall much. I had a head injury."

"Tell me," he bellowed.

Kathleen heaved. What had it been that she told him? If she knew anything about Isaac she knew he would verify her story with Tomas and Calico. Yet, that could prove deadly considering she hadn't had time to consult them much about that night. She took a deep breath, trying to remember everything she had told him. "Tomas, Calico, and I were eating dinner when we noticed the barn was on fire."

"How could you? The dining hall faces the front of the house and not the rear."

"Tomas' father told us. He's Tomas' personal servant."

"Of course, he did."

Kathleen glared at him, wondering what he meant by those words.

"Go on, Lady Kathleen. I want all of it."

"Tomas, Calico, and I went to investigate. We found the barn on fire and ordered the servants to help us put it out. The next thing we knew rebels were all around us. They captured us and put us in Tomas' room."

"And then?"

Kathleen shook her head, hoping to God Tomas and Calico would have sense enough to come up with the same story.

"And then!"

"I don't remember."

Isaac pulled a bloody bag from behind his back and poured the contents between her legs. She screamed as the severed heads of Alexander and Padric laid between her legs. "You had already told me Padric told you about the fire. I suspected he was involved somehow when he disappeared yesterday after I placed the guards at his son's door. The other head, though. Is this the man who captured you?"

Kathleen screamed louder the more he spoke. She fidgeted as she wanted to escape from this horrible nightmare. Anger, fear, anxiety. Oh, God, that was her father's head! Her father's head!

"Lady Kathleen," Isaac yelled as he grabbed her father's head by the hair and held it close to her face. "Is this or is this not the man who helped Sherlock capture you?"

What should she say? How can she reply when Isaac had her father's head in his hand? Oh, God! This man murdered her father! Every ounce of her wanted to kill this man for what he had done but she couldn't let him know the truth. She only wondered how Calico had responded to Isaac's offense. Kathleen heaved between her screams.

"I will not ask again," he bellowed, moving the head closer to her. "Calm down and tell me the truth!"

"It is! He…he…he told Tomas, Calico, and me if we didn't help him he would murder all of Tomas' family. Padric and his sons were upset with Tomas because he refused to hand the estate over to them, so they asked the rebels to help them take back the estate. I came to you because I needed your help. When you arrived at Tomas' house unannounced I feared they would kill you as well and regain Kilmore. I wanted to appease them. That's why I asked you to bury Sherlock's body in ancient grounds. I thought if they saw that gesture they would leave Tomas alone."

"I believe you," he replied softly, lowering the head to her lap. "What about your servant?"

"Calico and I did not know she was Sherlock's wife until you revealed it to us. If she murdered your mother then she only did so because she saw the opportunity to aide the rebels. I swear to you my sister, Tomas, and I are innocent of this. What do you plan to do with her?"

"She must pay for her crimes."

"She's with child! You would kill the child when the mother dies. At least have mercy on the child and then kill her. If you execute her then the rebels will attack you for not only her death but the death of the child as well."

"What would you suggest?"

"Let her live long enough to give birth, execute her, and we will raise the child as our own."

"I shall consider the matter. Please forgive me for the way I have treated you."

Kathleen glanced at her father's head with the deepest of hate towards this man. Forgive him? Hadn't this man just murdered her older brother and father only to condemn her sister to death for a murder she knew Mary would have never committed? As much as she wanted to lash out at him for those atrocities, she couldn't. "You beat me and then held me captive in your bed!"

"I had to make certain you are who you claim to be. Ireland is a very dangerous place. Surely you of all people must understand this after everything you have been through."

Kathleen watched Isaac pick up the heads and put them back in his bloody sack. He lowered them to the floor, pulled out a key from inside his coat, and unlocked her cuffs. "Tomas and Calico?" she asked, sitting on the edge of the bed, rubbing her hands.

"I have removed the guards and Tomas is recuperating." He knelt before her, placing his hands on her legs.

She shivered from his touch. How can he be a monster one moment then the sweetest of gentlemen the next? She wondered if he treated Sarah like he had treated her? Was that the reason his sister was so scared of him? He grabbed the side of her face and kissed her. The smell of the blood all over his clothes sickened her. That was her father's blood on him. As much as she wanted to dismiss his attentions she had to play along. Her father was dead but she still needed Isaac to kill her brother. She opened her mouth and wrapped her arms around his broad chest. Isaac lowered her to the bed and began to work his way under her skirt. *Don't let him bed you. Seduce him and bed him only after your wedding,* Bailey's words entered her mind as his lips found their way down her breast. She pushed Isaac off of her and stood.

"You beat me, hold me captive, and now want to seduce me? What kind of woman do you think I am?" she yelled, gathering herself.

"I'm sorry, Kathleen. It's just. Well I have needs after I kill someone. Usually I…," he paused then closed his mouth.

"Usually you what?" she asked, arching her eyebrow.

"Nothing." Isaac rose from the bed. "I hope word does not find its way to Tomas that I held you captive in my bed and I tried to have my way with you. I would most appreciate it if this matter stays between us. I want to marry you, Kathleen. Will you consent to that?"

Consent to marrying the monster who murdered her family, beat her, and held her captive? She couldn't even form the words "I love you," between her lips anymore. Not after everything he had done to her. She had a mission for the rebellion. The two men she had always leaned on the most were dead at this man's hand. Yet none of this would have come to pass had it not been for Bailey. Isaac was only reacting in defense of Bailey's revenge. If she was going to stop Bailey she would need this man.

"Ask Tomas. If he consents then I will marry you. Good day, sir, and thank you for saving my family," she declared then stormed out of his bedroom. Kathleen ran down the hall, holding back her tears until she reached Tomas and Calico's chambers. She ran into the room and paused as Bailey's priest, dressed as a physician, prayed over Tomas' body. What was Bailey's priest doing here and why was Tomas unconscious?

"Close the door, Kathleen," Margaret's voice lifted from the shadows.

Kathleen complied with Tomas' mother's command. Tomas groaned, fidgeting as she closed the door. Calico sobbed, pacing behind him.

"No, stop, Tomas. Don't move. You will only make matters worse," the priest ordered, lowering Tomas' leg. Kathleen turned and gasped at the sight of Tomas' broken body. He had been recuperating the last time she had seen him, but now he was barely recognizable. There was only one way he could have become like this. He looked just like Bailey did when he had been captured.

"Isaac," she muttered, lifting her eyes to Calico.

Calico nodded from behind the priest.

"He told me Tomas was recuperating in his room."

Calico sniffed her nose and wiped away her tears. "Isaac beat him for information before he went to our home. When he returned he showed Tomas and me our fathers' severed heads and beat him again." Calico shook her head. "I asked that our personal doctor be sent for. Isaac agreed. I sent a coded message with Padric to Bailey and a few hours later, they arrived."

"Why you and not his physician?" Kathleen asked the priest.

The priest turned towards her. "Bailey never received her message. Padric had come to the estate to warn your parents as soon as he heard the news and then returned to Kilmore. That's when your sister found him. She sent him with the message for Bailey but he was captured before the message could reach your brother."

"How?"

"Everyone except Alexander, Jane, Bailey, and Margaret had evacuated the estate by the time Isaac arrived. When we saw Padric return to the estate we had hoped he would join his wife. Jane left with Bailey. Just as they left in the wagon Isaac appeared with ten soldiers. Alexander tried to cause a diversion, which worked long enough for Padric to give us his message. Padric told Margaret and me to escape then aided Alexander."

"This is all my fault. I...I...I never thought....," Calico muttered.

"You...!" Kathleen gasped with realization. She ran to her sister. "You murdered his mother then blamed Mary!"

"Girls, not so loud," Margaret corrected, standing by the door.

Calico nodded, "Bailey ordered Tomas and me to make certain Isaac arrested Mary for being Sherlock's wife. Tomas gave Isaac the rosary his mother showed us that day. He had told him he didn't know Mary was a rebel."

Kathleen threw a punch towards Calico. The priest grabbed her wrist in time as Calico flinched. She fought against the priest's tight grip.

"Stop it, Kathleen," the priest ordered.

Kathleen spit at Calico as the priest held her arms firmly. "She's our sister!"

"She's nothing but a problem," Calico yelled back. "Look what has happened to us all because of Mary."

"Ha, Mary didn't do that to your husband. You did!"

Calico began to punch her sister. The priest turned Kathleen just as her blow hit the side of his face. Calico gasped, "I hit a priest."

"Sit down, Calico," the priest ordered. Calico nodded then sat on the side of the bed. The priest released Kathleen then stood between the two sisters with his hands extended towards them. "Kathleen, Calico has admitted her sins to me and I have forgiven them. We will not speak of this any longer."

"But she…," Kathleen began.

"He's right," Margaret stated, tending to her son. "Calico did not have Tomas' permission to do so. Quite the contrary, Tomas would have never allowed her actions. She realizes this now and is already suffering the consequences of her actions."

"I don't see how. It should be her in Isaac's prison, not Mary," Kathleen claimed, crossing her arms over her chest.

"Child, the man she loves was beaten senseless and her father's been murdered. I think she is suffering a fate far worse in her mind than she could ever have in Isaac's cell."

Kathleen turned her eyes to Calico. Calico sobbed in her lap uncontrollably as the priest comforted her. He pulled a locket from inside his tunic and motioned for Kathleen to join them. Kathleen complied. "Hold out your hand," he ordered them. The girls looked at each other and then complied. He placed Calico's hand underneath Kathleen's and then laid the locket in Kathleen's hand. "My name is," the priest took a deep breath, smiled at them, then continued. "My name was Bailey O'Brian and this once belonged to my daughter."

"You share our brother's name," Kathleen replied.

"Alexander named his sons in the traditional Irish way."

"What is this and why are you giving it to me?" Kathleen asked.

"Open it."

Kathleen opened the locket. She took a deep breath at the image of another Kathleen on the left and her father on the right. She smiled at the beautiful woman holding a newborn son in her arms and toddler beside her. "Sherlock and Bailey," she whispered, looking up at the priest. "You said this once belonged to your daughter and our father named his sons in the traditional Irish way?"

"Was…," Calico began then swallowed hard.

"Kathleen was my daughter. Alexander and Kathleen named Bailey after me because he was their second son."

"I'm named after Sherlock and Bailey's mother?" Kathleen asked.

The priest nodded, "Indeed. And I know your stepmother would be proud of the both of you. My wife and I were there when she gave birth to Bailey then died. Her death...," he exhaled a deep breath and shook his head.

Calico interrupted. "I don't understand. The first born daughter is always named after the mother's mother and the second born daughter is named after the father's mother. Why wouldn't our father follow the traditional naming pattern as he had done with our brothers?"

"When Jane gave birth to you two, Alexander wasn't ready to be a father again. In fact, the day of your arrival had scared him so much he refused to be anywhere near Jane's bedside. I was there because your father feared the worst."

"Because his last wife had died in childbirth?"

"That and Kathleen's birth had been very hard on Jane."

"Why?" Kathleen asked.

The priest shook his head. "It had been years since Jane had carried children. The entire pregnancy had been hard on her. When the time for your birth came she endured a great pain she hadn't experienced in over twenty years. Her labor was long and difficult."

"Did she almost die giving birth to Kathleen?" Calico interrupted.

"No, but your father thought she had. Jane was so exhausted after she delivered Kathleen that she barely moved. Your father panicked and ran out of the room with Kathleen in his arms. He handed Kathleen to me and told me her name was Kathleen."

Kathleen asked, "So I was named Kathleen because in his mind the woman who gave birth to me was your daughter?"

"At first yes. I and everyone else around you, except your parents, had called you Jane until your christening. Alexander and Jane wanted to keep your name Kathleen."

"Why?"

"Your father had realized his mistake a few days after you were born. When I approached him at the christening about it he said he had spoken to Jane concerning the matter. Jane had agreed to allow the name to remain in honor of my daughter and because you had given your father hope. The man he was before he married your mother was a man of great sorrow and pain. Much like Bailey is today. When he met Jane something changed in him. Both he and Jane believed themselves too old to bear children and then you came along, Kathleen. You gave him something he thought he would never have again."

"A chance to raise a family with the woman he loves," Kathleen answered.

"Yes, and that is why you are named after my daughter."

"Bailey doesn't like me because I remind him of his mother's death daily due to my name."

"Yes."

"What about me?" Calico asked.

The priest smiled. "Ah yes, your birth. Kathleen was there."

"I was?" Kathleen asked.

"Your father held you as your mother gave birth. Jane barely had any warning before Calico decided to enter the world. Your mother had been walking with Alexander, holding you in her arms in the garden when her water broke. Calico wouldn't wait to come into the world. Alexander took Kathleen and helped Jane into their bedroom. It was soon after that Calico was born."

"Why was I named Calico?" Calico asked.

"You are named Calico to remind you of the poverty our people face at the hands of the English. Never forget that you are of Irish noble blood and never forget your people. You two girls are the future of this family and our people. Your father was not a fool. He understood that as women you have an easier chance of changing our fates through the next generations. Bear your men their children yet never allow them to corrupt your faith, heritage, and morals. Pass those onto to your children and teach them to do the same. Your father wanted Kathleen to have this."

The priest cupped his hands around theirs. "Your father wanted me to relay a message to both of you. You must work in harmony together despite your many differences. Save this family and our ways. Never let Isaac steal them from you. Raise your children Irish."

"We will," Kathleen and Calico said together.

Tomas groaned, "Calico. Ugh, Calico."

Calico turned to her husband. Tomas arched his head, moving his hand around her side of the bed. "I'm right here, Tom."

"Does he know?" Kathleen asked.

Calico lifted her head and shook it. "He drifts in and out of consciousness."

"His wounds?"

The priest answered, "Severe but there isn't any internal bleeding that I can tell. It will take him months to heal. We have to keep him safe. Isaac will kill him if he learns the truth of Tomas' deception. He'll kill the both of you as well. It's not wise to tell Tomas everything, yet."

Kathleen nodded as Calico lowered her gaze back to her husband. "Shh, go to sleep, my love. I'm right here." Tomas turned his head, closed his eyes, and fell back to sleep. "What do we do next?" she asked the priest and Margaret.

"We find Sherlock's documents and help Mary to escape," Margaret said. "Jane and Bailey are waiting in Dublin for them."

Kathleen glared at Calico and shook her head. "I don't see how Isaac will gain Tomas' consent to marry me if he is in this state.

"Marry you?" Calico asked.

Kathleen exhaled a deep breath. "He beat me, Calico, then cuffed me to his bed. When I awoke he demanded information from me. When I couldn't think of anything else to say he dropped father and Padric's severed heads on me. I screamed. It took everything I had not to react as if that was our father's head on my lap."

"But he believed you?" the priest asked.

She turned to him and nodded. "Yes," She turned back to Calico. "He uncuffed me and then tried to bed me."

"He didn't, did he?"

"No! I remember what Bailey said about him. But here's the interesting part. He told me when he kills he has to be relieved by a woman. I asked him further about it, thinking it had to do with something Bailey had told me once with the voices in the dungeon, but he wouldn't go any further."

"So you believe the accusations are true then?" Margaret asked.

"I do. I told him he couldn't have his way with me until we marry. He wants me. I told him if Tomas consents then I will marry him."

"Good," the priest answered.

Kathleen turned to him. "Good?"

"If you're his wife then you can aide the rebellion just as Bailey wants you too."

"But Isaac will know."

"Not if we keep him preoccupied."

Chapter 31

October 4, 1738

Kathleen sat in the bath tub with her head back and wiped her face with her hands, exhaling a deep breath. She was an emotional mess. For days she had pretended to love Isaac without mourning the death of her father. The hardest part of her day was accepting the constant attentions he gave her. While deep inside she loathed what this man had done to her family, there was still a part of her that was attracted to him. Yet that part wasn't as strong as it used to be. No, it had been replaced with the deepest of hate. Isaac hadn't left her alone for much of the day or the night. Her only sanctuary was when she was allowed to visit Tomas and Calico. Thankfully, Isaac had accepted the ruse that Bailey's priest was Tomas' new physician. Tomas' mother had disappeared from the estate before Isaac ever knew she had been there. Kathleen and Calico had sent word of their wellbeing to their mother with Margaret. Kathleen only hoped her mother would understand why she had been unable to send Mary with Tomas' mother.

Kathleen slid further into the tub, closed her eyes, and slipped under the water. Maybe she could just drown herself and find peace. But there was no eternal peace with suicide. Your soul was damned for an eternity in hell if you ever killed yourself. Besides, how was she going to save her sister and help Isaac destroy Bailey if she died? Bailey's priest had claimed her father wanted her to work with Calico, not against her. She and Calico were in the perfect positions to aide the rebellion, yet how could she ever trust to be alone enough to help the rebels? Isaac never left her alone, not even at night. She was so exhausted, insecure, and paranoid, it was hard to think. She couldn't even rest at night without him by her side. She would cry herself to sleep on his chest, only to wake up in the middle of the night screaming. Isaac believed her night terrors were due to all the atrocities she faced at the hands of the rebels. He vowed to her that he would do everything in his power to ensure not only her safety but that of Calico and Tomas as well. Seemed to her the more he ensured the safety the more they had become his prisoners in their own personal hell.

"Kathleen," Isaac's voice demanded. She paid no attention to his cries, allowing the water to continue to cover her face. "Kathleen," he cried louder, lifting her body out of the water. She gasped, placing her arms around his neck and opening her eyes.

"Thank God," he muttered.

"What are you doing?"

"Forgive me, my dear. I thought you had drowned," he apologized, lowering her back into the bath tub.

Kathleen glared at him as he knelt beside her. Isaac tenderly placed his hand on her cheek and kissed her gently on the lips. She reluctantly opened her mouth and allowed him to kiss her deeper. "I love you," he whispered, laying his forehead on hers. "I could not bear this life without you, Lady Kathleen. Please do not scare me like that again." He lifted his head while still clinging to her small neck. Just one wrong move and he could snap her head.

Kathleen nodded. "I wasn't trying to kill myself, Isaac. I love the water. I miss swimming in Tomas' lake and thought I could perhaps be alone with my thoughts in the bathtub. I truly think the best when I am under the water."

Isaac peered at the bath, released his hand, then looked back up at her. "Oh. I did not realize. Forgive me."

"Apology accepted."

Kathleen slid deeper into the tub with her legs hanging over the edges. She carefully kept an eye on Isaac as she bathed. His intense glare never left her body. She hated the way he always looked at her, especially now. It was improper to have relations or socialize while mourning. Why was he still pursuing her when he should be mourning the death of his mother?

Isaac kissed her deeply. He grinned, pulling away from her and glancing at her beautiful body. She watched him carefully as he lowered his hand to her flat stomach. How dare this man touch her! Let alone see her naked. "I look forward to the day when you carry my child, Lady Kathleen," he stated, rubbing her stomach. She swallowed hard as his fingers made their way between her legs. He kissed her inner thigh. Kathleen swallowed hard, determined not to react. But it was so hard when the warm water tickled between her legs, his finger massaged her clit, and he was sucking on the inside of her thigh. She lowered her legs into the water and sat upright, exposing her breasts. Isaac removed his hand from the water. "I am not your wife, sir. You have no right to seduce me or see me without my garments. This is most inappropriate behavior. You once called me a peasant yet here you are acting like one yourself."

"You're wrong, Lady Kathleen."

Kathleen cocked her head. "Wrong?"

He reached into his coat pocket and pulled out a thick tri-folded document with a long ribbon. "Tomas signed it this morning with his blessing," he said, handing the document to her.

"How?"

"How?"

"Isaac, you broke his wrists with the cuffs you used on him, his face is so swollen he can't see, and he has so many broken bones his physician claims it will take him months to heal. How could he sign those documents or understand your words when he drifts in and out of consciousness?"

"He was conscious enough to understand the document he was signing. As for his hand, his physician aided him."

Kathleen reached for the document, "I want to see his signature."

"Best if it doesn't get wet," he said, putting it back in his coat.

He rose from beside her and walked to her bed. Kathleen turned on her side and glared at the new yellow dress on her bed.

"So soon?" she asked. She wasn't certain if she was ready to bed this monster or not. But what choice did she have in the matter? She needed to become his wife. Isaac picked up a large diamond necklace and showed it to her.

"I cannot wait any longer, Lady Kathleen. You stir something in me no other woman has before," he claimed, kneeling before her with the necklace. "This belonged to my mother."

"You should allow Sarah to have it."

"No, it is yours. My estate is your estate, my lady. After we marry this morning you'll hold guardianship over Sarah. She needs a woman to guide her and with our mother gone she has become inconsolable once more. I would have waited to marry you in London during the Christmas season, but truth be told I need you now more than ever." He rose, walked to the bed, and lowered the necklace as someone knocked on the door. "Ah, good, he's arrived."

"Who?" Kathleen asked, lowering in the bath tub so no one could see her body.

"My physician," he answered as he walked to her door.

"I'm not ill, Isaac."

Isaac laughed, opening the door. "Kathleen, you misunderstand me," he said as the physician entered the room and Isaac closed the door. She stared at the older man then back to Isaac. Isaac walked towards her. "He's here to examine you."

"Examine me for what?"

"Fertility. I have to be certain you are healthy enough to bear my heirs. The woman whom I marry must continue the Turner line. I need an heir and a spare. Now get out of the bath and stand before us."

Kathleen swallowed hard, glaring at the slender, grey-haired physician. She reluctantly complied with Isaac's directive with more distaste and distrust towards the English Earl. The physician lowered his bag on her bed and stared at her slender frame. "She's a very fine specimen of a woman, Earl Turner," the physician claimed as he walked around her. He paused, took her face in his hands, turned her face, and examined both sides of her cheeks. "Smallpox?" he asked her, examining her scars.

"I suffered from it when I was a child," Kathleen answered.

"You are most fortunate to have survived. These scars speak of a severe case."

"My parents feared I wouldn't survive it."

"I have seen your sister's face. How is it she doesn't have the same scars?" Isaac asked.

Kathleen lifted her eyes to him. "I was worse than she was."

"Is that possible, doctor?" Isaac asked.

"It is," he answered then moved his hands down to Kathleen's breasts. "Her breasts are large enough to feed several babies. Any other previous ailments or conditions, Lady Kathleen?"

"No," she growled in Isaac's direction as the physician examined the inside of Kathleen's mouth.

Isaac crossed his arms over his chest as the physician examined her entire body. "Get on the bed, Lady Kathleen, and spread your legs," the physician ordered.

Kathleen walked to the bed and complied with the physician's order. She closed her eyes and leaned her head back. How dare Isaac have this done to her? It was bad enough he saw her naked but now this man? Sure, he was a physician, but she couldn't trust an Anglican physician. She gasped at the feeling of his fingers entering inside her. The physician placed his other hand on her stomach and peered up at her. "Relax, Lady Kathleen. This will be over soon."

"Well?" Isaac asked impatiently.

"She doesn't seem to have been violated, but the only way to confirm that will be at your bedding ceremony. I don't feel anything to concern me about her womb." He removed his finger then massaged her breasts. "The breasts feel healthy and her body is in superb condition. I do not find any concerns as to her health," he stated then rose from over her.

"Thank you, doctor. You're dismissed," Isaac said with a smile.

Kathleen watched the doctor leave the room then turned her eyes on Isaac.

"Get dressed quickly, Lady Kathleen. We marry within the hour. The priest has already arrived from Wexford to conduct the ceremony in our home. I have informed your sister of our union and she has agreed to stand as witness," he said then exited from her room.

She stared at the gown, jewels, and ribbons for her hair, wondering if the items had all belonged to his mother. How could she replace his mother's position at Kilmore Castle? Yet wasn't this what she needed all along? To be the countess? Yet even though she was to marry him today, she still couldn't officially become the Countess of Kilmore without King George coronating her as such. That would require a trip to London. She had never travelled outside Wexford County before, let alone out of Ireland. She wondered what that experience would be like and what King George would do if he ever learned the truth of her identity. Isaac claimed he had planned to marry her in London during the Christmas season. Did that mean he still planned to present her to the nobles in a few months? He would have to do it sometime in order for her to be coroneted as the Countess of Kilmore.

Kathleen peered down at her body and swallowed hard. He had touched where no man should ever touch an unmarried woman and then allowed another man to do so as well. This man knew no boundaries in his own home. She wondered how he behaved in public with the other nobles. Would he behave as a gentleman or as the monster he truly was?

Chapter 32

Music, laughter, and varied conversations filled the crowded grand hall as Kathleen sat beside Isaac at the wedding feast. Their wedding had lasted an hour in another hall. Afterwards, the couple had led their guests to one of the largest halls in the house, where they had enjoyed a wedding feast with their guests. Isaac's family had poured into the countryside from England in order to attend his wedding. She wondered how long he had planned their lavish wedding and when he was going to inform the family they were also here for a funeral. Aunts, uncles, cousins, friends from Dublin, friends from the English court, all attended their wedding festivities today. There were so many people it was hard for Kathleen to keep track of who everyone was. While she had enjoyed the company of family, friends, and other nobles, Kathleen was exhausted.

Kathleen looked to her left where Calico sat next to her. Her mind returned to the last wedding that had been held in this place. It seemed like only yesterday when Tomas had married Calico at Kilmore Cathedral then had their wedding feast here. Just as she had served as Calico's maid of honor, Calico had served as her matron of honor in the cathedral this morning. Yet this wasn't a dream. This was her wedding day. She had given her vows before God and their guests at the cathedral. She and Isaac had led the wedding processional from the cathedral to this room where everyone danced, got drunk, and had a good time.

Kathleen poked at the steak before her with her fork. It was so hard to be merry when all she could think about was how she had married the man who killed her father and brother. She glanced over her shoulder to Isaac. Isaac laughed hard then turned to face her. She grinned towards him, lowering her fork, and watched the jester in the center of the hall perform his tricks. Isaac leaned closer to her, took her hand, and whispered, "Are you well, my love?"

"Of course, Isaac. I'm a bit tired, that's all. We have been feasting since noon and it's well past dinner. The food has been wonderful. I've enjoyed dancing with you, meeting your friends, and being by your side. It's just…"

He gently cupped her face in his hands. "Shh, I know. The last few weeks have been hard on you, Lady Kathleen. I promise you I will never allow the rebels to harm you or your family again. You are my wife and for that you only deserve the best in life." He leaned close to her and kissed her deeply. Lost in their own little world they never noticed the music had ended.

"I think the couple is ready," an Englishman yelled from the back of the room.

The crowd laughed but Kathleen didn't care. She placed her hand around the back of his head, moved closer, and kissed with more passion. Isaac smiled, returned her kiss, and then pulled away from her. Her heart beat so hard in her chest she feared it would jump right out. "I love you, Lady Turner" Isaac whispered in ear.

"Well, well. May I have your attention please," the physician shouted from the floor. "It seems our newly married couple is more than ready for the bedding ceremony."

Bedding ceremony?

Cheers lifted from the crowd. Kathleen swallowed as her husband pulled his lips away from her. He gently stroked her cheekbone and stared deep into her emerald eyes. "Kathleen?" he questioned her in concern.

Ten men she had barely met made their way up to the platform towards the couple with jovial taunts and snickers. Kathleen gripped the side of her chair. Panic set in. What were these men doing so close to her with those lustful looks on their faces? She jumped as Calico placed her hand on top of hers.

"Calm down, Kathleen."

"Calm down," she snarled, leaning towards her. "You didn't have the bedding ceremony."

"Only because we left our wedding feast to care for you. You're not going to be that fortunate, Kathleen. The bedding ceremony is an old tradition that ensures the lord and lady consummate their union. You have to comply with it to ensure any child conceived on your wedding night is a legitimate heir. You have no choice in this matter."

Kathleen leaned back in her chair and stared out at the crowd. The mixed group of middle aged and younger men quickly descended upon them. Isaac rose from his chair and extended his hand to Kathleen. She slowly turned her eyes in his direction, loathing the fact he was about to give her over to complete strangers so they could systematically remove her clothes and fondle her. "Gentlemen," he grinned towards her. "Take care of preparing my wife. For this will be the one and only time you will ever touch her so."

Kathleen nervously placed her hand in Isaac's and rose from her chair. He quietly handed her to a large, middle-aged man who lifted her on his shoulder. Kathleen gasped as his large hand found the inside of her thigh. The group of ten men quickly turned into a large mob that surrounded them. Their hands groped her all over. She heard laughter from somewhere below. Her eye caught Calico and several aides overtaking her husband.

"Drop the gown," a younger man beckoned from behind her while the man holding her stepped down the stairs.

Kathleen inhaled a deep breath. It was bound to happen sooner or later. She had just hoped she wouldn't have lost her gown in front of so many. "Isaac," her captor yelled and stood her on a chair.

Isaac rose from beneath the ladies and turned to face the group of men with his coat disheveled and his white wig missing. "We want everyone to see what you get tonight," the man laughed. Someone's hands unbuttoned her gown from the back. They pulled her gown off and threw it to the side.

"Damn, Isaac, I want a piece of that," a young man teased from the back of the group.

"You can't have her," Isaac yelled. He grinned, casting his eyes up and down her body. Kathleen pressed her hands across her stay and stared deep into his eyes. How could he parade her around like she was just a piece of meat? How could Calico join those women and touch her man as if Isaac was her husband? She swallowed hard as the women removed his coat and threw it to the side. Their hands groped his entire body. Suddenly he was gone in the mad group of women and she was being hoisted back in the air, passed around the men. She never noticed they were moving her out of the room. Men passed her around as if she was their personal toy. Between groping her they removed her petticoat, shoes, stay, and stockings, throwing them all over the hallway. A part of her liked the way some of the men made her feel but another part wanted to reserve those carnal pleasures for her husband.

A blond-haired man opened Isaac's bedroom door. "That's enough," Isaac laughed inside with only his shirt on and with a crowd of women around him. He turned to face the door. His robust friend lowered Kathleen to the ground. She stood in the middle of the room, staring at the twenty people circled around them. Isaac took her hand. Her heart jumped as the door of their bedroom closed behind them. She turned to face the men who had accosted her only to find they had disappeared with the women who had brought Isaac into their bedroom.

"Lady Kathleen," Sarah beckoned her from behind Isaac.

Kathleen slowly turned her attention to her new sister.

"Sarah," Kathleen greeted her. Her face fell at the sight of Calico standing beside her. She slapped Calico on the cheek.

"What was that for?" Calico protested, rubbing her check.

"I saw you grope Isaac. You couldn't move fast enough to be part of the group of women who escorted him here. Your husband lies in his bed severally injured and you come to my wedding only to touch my husband in a way women should only touch their husbands!"

Calico sighed, "I never touched him."

"Liar."

"I'm telling the truth, Kathleen. Other women pulled his pants off and gave him a rise. I only took his shoes and stockings."

"Ladies I don't think this is the time to argue about this. What happened tonight at the start of the bedding ceremony does not leave the estate," an older woman interrupted.

Kathleen glared at the grey-haired, dignified woman. Sarah interrupted, "Lady sister." Kathleen turned to face her. "Lady Collins requests that I might stand witness on your behalf for the bedding ceremony. I gladly offer my services. I know you have no family other than your sister. I asked Lady Collins if some of our relations could join us. My mother would...," she swallowed hard, peered at the women beside her, then back at Kathleen.

Kathleen looked at the timid woman and smiled. "Of course with your mother so drastically ill that she must remain in seclusion it is hard for you to mention or think of her at such a joyous occasion as this."

"Of course, Lady Turner," Sarah answered with a curtsey. She turned to a middle-aged brunette woman beside her "My aunt, Lady Sophia Fitzsimmons. She is my father's sister."

"Lady Turner," she greeted with a curtsey. "My daughters Isabella and Madge," the woman said, presenting her twelve- and fourteen-year-old daughters.

"It is a pleasure to meet you," Kathleen returned the greeting. She turned to an order woman to her left.

"My grandmother, the Dowager Countess Sarah Turner, whom I am named after," Sarah said, indicating the short, elderly, slender woman. The countess stepped to Kathleen and tapped her hand. She looked up to her grandson. "Isaac, I must speak to your wife alone."

"She's a Turner. Whatever you have to say to her you can say to me, grandmother," Isaac objected.

"Oh, my boy, there are some things a woman must only say out of the presence of a man. Go speak to the men. Leave me with your precious wife."

Isaac looked to Kathleen. She nodded to him with an approving look. He reluctantly left the women and conversed with his colleagues.

The older woman motioned for Kathleen to lean closer. "There are secrets to being married to a Turner man. Secrets only I can give you. Secrets you should know," the woman whispered then grinned with a nod. The woman's odd words sent shivers down Kathleen's spine. What was so different being married to a Turner man that she should be afraid of? Wasn't a man just a man in God's eyes? The women made a tight circle around her. "Turner men can't be trusted," the older woman said softly in front of her.

"What do you mean, Countess?"

"She means what she says," Lady Sophia answered. "My mother speaks the truth. There is a reason Sarah asked us to join you tonight instead of members of her mother's family."

"More dangerous to be married to a Turner man than naught," Sophia's mother replied. She turned to the two women.

"I don't understand. Isaac is a wonderful man."

"Ha, you lie. I can see it in your face, child," the older woman responded

"He's already hurt her, mother. You can see it in her eyes," Sophia answered.

"Hmm, yes. I see it and yet you still desire to marry my grandson?"

Kathleen huffed, "I love him and he loves me."

"Bah, love has nothing to do with this marriage. Turner men only love themselves, child. You are only a means to an end."

"How so, Countess?"

Sophia laughed. "You can't be that naïve, Kathleen. Weren't you given a fertility test this morning?" Kathleen swallowed hard and sat on the edge of the bed. "He has to reproduce many sons. It's the law."

"Law?" Kathleen asked.

"You mean you honestly do not know about the contract?"

"What contract?" Calico asked, sitting beside her sister.

Sophia opened her mouth to speak but closed it as her mother gave her the look only a mother could give. "He has to reveal it to her after they wed. There's no choice in that matter. It's the law," the elderly woman answered.

"But Isaac should have…"

"It doesn't matter what Isaac should or should not have done, Sophia. She has to sign after their bedding ceremony. He knows that her name must be inscribed in the book by her hand, declaring she entered the relationship of her own free will. If not, the marriage is invalid and her heir illegitimate."

Kathleen shook her head, "I don't understand."

"You will, child. Turner men expect perfection out of their women. Be it wife, daughter, mother, or sister. Stand up and let us prepare you for bed" She turned her gaze to Sarah then back to Kathleen. Kathleen complied, standing straight and thinking about their words. Calico held her hand, reassuring her sister while Sarah and her cousins combed Kathleen's waist-long red hair. How she dreaded this union with Isaac even more. Sophia, Calico, and the countess all spoke to her about how to please Isaac sexually, yet only a few of their words remained in her mind. All she could think about was how much danger she had placed her life in. To what was the cost if she ever disobeyed her husband, or worse yet, if he learned of her true heritage? She had always been more concerned about her family's wellbeing than her own.

"She's ready, grandmother," Sarah chimed as the girls stepped away from her. Kathleen wiped the tears from her eyes and turned to face the Turner women.

"Child, don't let him see your weakness. Don't cry. You must be strong," the countess guided as she fixed Kathleen's face.

"Would...," she swallowed hard. "Would he ever kill me?"

"He can't. He's bound by contract to keep you alive. Your only duty is to please him and keep giving him heirs," Sophia answered.

"Even if that means I betray him?" she asked the countess.

The countess tapped her hand on the side of Kathleen's face. "You are bound to his punishment just as much as he is bound to protect you."

"Punishment for what?"

"That is not our place to say. He must inform you of this, yet if you refuse to sign the marital contract issued by the king after you consummate the marriage, you will place his life in jeopardy."

"Wha...?" she turned to Calico. "He showed a contract to me and said your husband had given his consent to marry me."

"It never happened, Kathleen," Calico said.

Kathleen tried to reply but couldn't form the words. She knew there was something suspicious about that contract. "The king handed you over to be his bride," Sophia answered.

"How and when? He never left Ireland after I met him."

The countess answered, "He didn't have to. His majesty had been pressuring my grandson to choose a mate for quite some time. Yet Isaac always delayed in his selection. That is until he met you. The day he met you he wrote a letter to King George proclaiming he had met the woman he wanted as his mate. The king could not verify the story of your heritage and deemed that you must be a commoner whose sister had tricked Tomas into marrying him."

"That's a lie," Calico retorted, rising from the bed.

Kathleen put her arm in front of Calico. "So Isaac has always known our story is based on lies."

"Yes, but it matters not to Isaac because he is fixated on you."

"And yet the king did nothing to stop my marriage to Lord Collins," Calico proclaimed with her fists clenched.

"Why should he?" Sophia said. "Lord Collins is of Irish descent and is a lower level noble. He's of no threat to the crown. Isaac was sent to Kilmore to ensure English law dominates in Ireland. Tomas has supported the English for years but should you or your husband prove to be a problem to England then my nephew has every right to remedy that situation. Do you understand what I mean by this, Lady Collins?"

"We understand he chose Kathleen in order to control my husband and me."

"That plus I honestly believe Isaac loves her."

Calico looked at Kathleen. "So the question is, who are you really, ladies?" the countess asked, crossing her arms against her chest.

Kathleen's heart skipped a beat as she clutched her sister's hand. "If I tell you the…," she began.

"We are of noble blood," Calico finished, glaring at Sophia.

Sophia and her mother glanced at the younger woman. "Sarah?" Sophia called to her niece.

"Aunt Sophia," Sarah answered.

"Tell your brother Kathleen will be ready for him shortly. He is to leave us alone. He must remain on the far side of the bedroom with the other men until we have finished our discussion."

"Yes, ma'am," Sarah answered, curtseyed, then walked the length of the large bedroom with her younger cousins. Sophia and her mother turned back to Kathleen and Calico.

"Your true identities, ladies," the countess asked with her arms crossed and her glare boring straight into their eyes.

"We are Ladies Kathleen and Calico McGillpatrick," Kathleen admitted.

The older woman laughed heartily.

"Mother, don't you know…," Sophia objected.

The elderly woman waved her hand at her daughter then calmly said, "This is priceless, daughter. Let him marry the daughter of his enemy. It's about time a Turner man be fooled at his own game and I believe she can do just that. Aren't you tired of being dictated to by your nephew? We are just pawns in their games. Finally, we have a woman who will play against him and not have the faint of heart to accept everything he says and does without a conscience of her own."

"You're not upset?" Calico asked.

The elderly woman turned to Kathleen's sister. "On the contrary, Lady Collins. Yet do tell me, does your husband know of your true identity?"

"Yes, he grew up with our brothers. He has known my sister and me since our mother birthed us. We left our Catholic faiths and joined his household shortly after he approached our father concerning my union. We never expected your nephew to spot Kathleen that day. We had been trying to keep her hidden so she could remain safe at our estate. Although my sister is older than I she can be a fool at times. It is out of her foolishness that Isaac met her and it is out of her foolishness that we are in the position we find ourselves today. For she has fallen in love with him just as much as he has with her."

Kathleen pushed Calico, "Not true! I hate him. He killed our father and Sherlock. Bailey almost died because of him and your own husband was beaten within inches of his life."

Sophia waved her hand in front of Kathleen. "Lady Kathleen, please. The walls of this house have ears and although the room is large it is not so large that Isaac can't hear us. If you must speak so loudly then do not do so within Kilmore. Trust me. There are plenty of people who serve my nephew. They would gladly turn you over to him. He may not be able to touch you but he can inflict great harm upon your sister. My mother and I want to help you, not hinder you."

"Can he hurt you?" she asked the women.

"No, a Turner man can never kill a Turner woman, but he can use her to aide in his missions," the countess answered. "We can no longer speak on this matter. The longer we wait to present you to Isaac the more he will grow suspicious. You must please him. And have no fear. Your secrets are safe with us."

"Thank you," Kathleen answered.

The elderly woman placed her hands on Kathleen's face. "Oh, how I wish I had been more like you, my dear. Now tell me the truth. Is Isaac's mother alive or dead?"

Kathleen shook her head.

"I see. How did she die?"

"I cannot speak of it. I am sworn to secrecy."

"Child there are no secrets among us. You are safe. What happened to the Dowager Countess?"

"I killed her," Calico admitted.

Kathleen turned to her sister and stood before her, blocking her from the woman. "Please understand, my sister…"

"Did her a favor."

Calico and Kathleen looked at each other then turned to the woman. "I don't understand. You're not upset?"

Sophia answered, "It is a far better fate for a Turner wife to die before her husband and not afterwards. There is a reason my mother lives with my husband and me. When a Turner man dies his wife is at the mercy of her children. She is useless and only inherits the title, not the wealth. Isaac did well by providing for his mother, but he was growing tired of her constantly bickering about one thing or another. She belittled him and that made her a threat. But he couldn't do anything to her and she knew it. Kathleen, if you are going to succeed where his mother failed then you need not only to be strong but also intoxicating to him. A Turner man loses interest quickly. Do whatever it takes to maintain that connection with him where he fully and foolishly trusts you wholeheartedly. It is truly the only way to protect all the women in this family and the children you give him."

Chapter 33

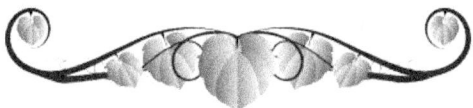

Kathleen sat on the bed thinking about the words Isaac's grandmother and aunt had spoken to her. It seemed quite odd yet somewhat refreshing to know the women in his family were on her side. Finally she had someone she could trust in other than her sister. The only problem was these ladies lived in England and they had firmly instructed her never to write down her true feelings on paper in fear Isaac might intercept her letters and learn the truth. Fortunately, they had agreed to stay at Kilmore for a few months to help her settle into her new position, then they would return to England with Isaac and her at Christmas for her coronation as Countess of Kilmore.

Kathleen paused as she stared at the group of forty witnesses in the room. When had the group of witnesses grown so large? She never heard the door open. Isaac stood in the center and turned towards her. He smiled, extending his hand. Kathleen looked to her sister, rose, embraced her, and whispered, "I don't think I can do this."

"You must. All of the Irish nobles attended your wedding and have been here throughout the festivities. The nobles who know of our true identities swore they would never reveal the truth. You can't back out of this, Kathleen. You're married under man's law and you must prove to marry under God's law."

"You never did."

"I had an excuse. You. Besides, the Anglicans who are loyal to Tomas swore before the Lords they witnessed our union under God. You don't have that luxury here tonight. The priest, the physician, and nobles must be here to see your union."

"Not in that bed. Not in the bed where he held me captive and threw father's head on my lap."

"Kathleen, you have no choice. It must be in his chambers, not yours."

Kathleen exchanged glances with her entourage while Sophia closed the door. She walked to the center of the room and stood before Isaac, holding his hands.

"Hello," Isaac addressed her softly.

"Hi," she replied.

"Did you have a wonderful chat with my family?"

"Yes, Isaac. They told me many secrets."

"Good," he smiled and glanced down at her shift with a large grin.

His long shirt tried to hide his well-formed body. Oh, why did this monster have to look like a god? Kathleen peered at the bed. How odd it seemed that she would have been bound to her father's bed and her father's head be thrown on her lap. This had been his room. The room where he and his first wife had conceived Sherlock and Bailey. The room where she was to lose her virginity. How much she hated and yet adored this room. She only hoped her father would understand her intentions while he was in purgatory.

"Kathleen," Isaac called to her. She turned her attention back to her husband. When had he removed his shirt? She stared down at his already erect, large penis and swallowed hard. Was he already filled with passion for her body or was that an effect of the many women who had groped him? Kathleen eyed the crowd around them. He gently placed his fingers on her jawline and turned her attention back to him. "They will be with us all night to ensure we consummate this union."

"All night?" she whispered.

"Yes. Remove your shift, my dear."

Kathleen shook her head.

"Remove it. It's alright, my love. They have to witness this union and ensure that you are pure."

"I am. Can't they just accept that?"

"I'm afraid not," he answered, removing the shift from her body and handing it to his grandmother. Isaac took her hand, led her to the four poster bed, and laid her on the mattress. He crawled into the bed with her and pulled down the covers. The crowd drew closer to the bed as a priest stood at the foot of the bed. He sprinkled oil on their bodies and prayed over them a fertility prayer. Kathleen hated all the attention the crowd gave them. Why did they have to appear naked before all these people? She clutched Isaac's hands, fighting the tears of embarrassment and remorse. Everyone was depending on her to save them but who was going to save her from her own personal hell?

"Amen," the priest said in unison with the crowd then pulled the curtains closed.

"Now what?" Kathleen questioned Isaac.

Isaac crawled on top of her with a devilish grin. "Now, we make an heir," he whispered in her ear and kissed her entire body. She groaned, opening her legs wider as his lips found their way to her clit. Why did he have to be so good to her when all she wanted to do was hate him? She clutched the sheets and arched her back with a long, drawn-out moan as his tongue flicked inside her.

Isaac grinned and kissed the inside of her thigh. "Oh, you're so beautiful," he whispered, kissing her beneath her jaw. Kathleen closed her eyes, taking in his warm kisses. She arched her head back, trying to forget the last time she was in this bed. She moaned as his tongue once again found its way between her legs.

"Shit, Isaac," she swore, widening the berth between her legs. His fingers drew closer to her clit as his mouth found its way to the inside of her thigh. The wetter she became, the more she forgot about her troubles.

"Isaac," she screamed out his name, lifting her bottom as their passions grew.

"There it is," he grinned then pushed his erect penis inside her. Kathleen gasped. Never before had she felt such wonderful sensations. She closed her eyes, taking in the increasing rolling waves he caused inside her. Perhaps this man wasn't as bad as she thought he was. Isaac pulled on one of her nipples. She opened her eyes and arched her neck, screaming as she clawed his back. He pushed deeper and harder than before. So he liked it rough. Well two could play at that game.

Kathleen pushed him underneath her and sat upright. Thankfully, Calico had taught her a thing or two about what a man likes in bed. She sat on top of his crotch and rocked her body. Isaac inhaled a deep breath through his teeth. "Fuck," he swore, placing a thumb on her clit. Kathleen rocked even harder while his other fingers found their way to her mouth. She sucked on his fingers then leaned on his legs. Over and over again the waves inside her grew with intensity. She loved the way his hands felt on her body as the waves increased. Her skin became flush and her tits grew hard. She didn't know if she could endure this any longer, but she wanted it more than anything. The couple rolled several times with greater passion, fondling and kissing each other. Isaac pushed her underneath him and thrust his penis hard with a loud grunt. The faster he pushed the more she wanted him. She let go of her inhibitions and clawed his back. Her thighs grew tight and she could hardly stand each thrust. She screamed things she never thought would ever leave her mouth. She listened to his deep groans. Isaac arched his back, closed his eyes, and grunted loudly. She felt something sticky inside her, yet he pushed deeper inside her. She gasped as her body couldn't take any more.

Isaac collapsed on top of her with a large grin as the crowd cheered. Her lower stomach ached. He withdrew his penis and rolled onto his back. Blood flowed between her legs. She spread her legs wider, letting it pour onto the bed. Why was she bleeding? He had been rough with her yet she liked it.

"We have finished and are ready for the confirmation," he declared loudly. Kathleen squinted as the curtains drew open around the bed.

"Well done," the priest congratulated them. Isaac rose from the bed with Kathleen.

They stood beside the witnesses with their hands joined, watching as a physician stepped away from the crowd and examined the sheet. He pointed to the small pool of blood on Kathleen's side of the bed. Kathleen glared at Isaac with terror.

"What did you do to me," she panicked, rubbing her aching lower stomach.

"I made you my wife under God. It's what we had to do."

"The blood, Isaac," she snarled.

Isaac chuckled. "Virgins," he muttered, turning his attention back to the bed. Kathleen stared at him with disgust. "When a man plucks a virgin she will bleed onto the sheet. The witnesses are here for two purposes. One to ensure we consummate our marriage, and the other to ensure that my bride is a virgin. I cannot trade a virgin for my wife, nor can I fake the blood spilled between your legs if I have witnesses present. I am a noble and my line of succession must be legitimate."

The physician motioned for Kathleen to approach him. Isaac guided Kathleen back to the bed. "Lie down with your legs apart," the physician ordered. Kathleen glanced at Isaac then complied with the directive. The middle-aged doctor spread Kathleen's legs wider and placed his finger in her vagina. She gasped as he moved his finger upward then withdrew his bloody finger.

"Well?" Isaac asked.

The doctor sniffed his fingers then peered at the stain on the bed. He nodded, wiping his fingers on a towel. "The blood came from Countess Kathleen. I concur she was a virgin before Earl Turner took her to his bed. He has broken his virgin wife before God and any heirs she produces for him shall be legitimate," the physician declared.

"May God bless this union with a son," the priest added.

Chapter 34

October 13, 1738

Kathleen ran down the hallway, clutching her lower stomach, sobbing profusely. "Kathleen, stop," Isaac yelled from behind her.

She turned quickly, shaking her head, heaving as he drew closer to her. She stepped backwards, tripped, and fell to the floor. The sudden jolt of her body increased the aches and pains all over her body. Rich, red, blood poured onto the floor from between her legs. "I can help you," Isaac said, crouching before her. He stretched out his hand. "I'll call the physician to help you. Just return to our bed, Kathleen. Please, my love."

"No, you did this to me," she yelled as she rolled to her hands and knees then rose to her feet. Isaac stared at the pool of blood on the floor and sighed deeply. He watched her stumble down the long hallway in her shift. The days since their wedding night had been the most wonderful time he had ever had with any woman. He had spent more time in bed with his new wife than in his study. Kathleen had seemed to enjoy his company as well until a few hours ago. Everything had seemed to be normal until Kathleen had complained of nauseating pain in her lower stomach. She had rolled over, sobbing, and grew even more panicked when they noticed a thick stream of blood between her legs and a large stain of blood on her side of the bed. He had tried to help her but with every word from his lips she had grown more agitated. Kathleen had burst from their room and ran towards the only older woman she could trust. His Aunt Sophia.

"What in the world is going on?" Sophia asked, emerging from her parlor on the other end of the hallway.

Isaac rose from the hallway and walked to his aunt. She held the sobbing Kathleen to her chest. Isaac placed his hand on Kathleen's back. She shivered and buried her head deeper into Sophia's chest. Isaac exhaled a deep breath, removing his hand. "I don't know, Aunt Sophia. She woke up in pain, agitated…"

"He broke my insides," Kathleen cried.

Sophia stared at her nephew in confusion. "I did no such thing. We have had sexual encounters many times since our wedding night. Never once has she denied me and she has thoroughly enjoyed every encounter. This morning I went to seduce her and found her in this state. There was blood on her sheets. She complains of pain and that I broke something inside her."

"Blood? Does it flow steady between her legs?"

"Yes."

"I know what is wrong with your wife and you did not break her insides." She peered down at Isaac's wife. "Come with me, Kathleen." Kathleen nodded. "Isaac," she said, lifting her head. "This may take a while. Return to your duties and she will join you when she is ready."

"I must return to my affairs in Dublin this afternoon. I had hoped she would receive my attentions before I must leave."

"That will not happen. I highly suggest you attend to whatever business King George desires from you. You do not want to displease him."

"No, no, you're right. Thank you, Aunt Sophia. Please treat her with the utmost respect and grant her anything she requires. She is the Lady Turner," he said then kissed her on the cheek.

"That is a fact you do not need to remind me of. I know what her duties entail and I assure you she will not dismiss them. Now go," she said then watched Isaac disappear down the hallway. Sophia pushed away from Kathleen, took her niece's face in her hands, and lifted Kathleen's head. "How old are you, Lady Turner?"

"Nineteen."

Sophia nodded. "Go inside and sit on the floor in front of the fireplace. I will be behind you."

"Yes, ma'am," Kathleen replied then entered Sophia's parlor. She clutched her lower stomach and leaned over her lap, crying from the pain. Her bright, long red hair clung to the sides of her face. How could she let Isaac do this to her? How could she produce an heir for him if he damaged her insides so severely she couldn't produce any children in her womb? The more she thought of his atrocities against her and her family, the more she hated him. Yet there was nothing she could do against him. Not yet, anyway. She hadn't yet been declared by King George as the Countess of Kilmore. As long as King George didn't recognize her marriage she had no true power over Kilmore even though Isaac insisted she be granted the respect and power due to her as his wife. She jumped at the touch of Sophia's hand on her back. Kathleen wiped the tears from her eyes and stared at the leather belt with a strap connected on each of its sides. Kathleen lifted her eyes from the belt to Sophia. Sophia placed it on the floor and handed her a cup.

"Drink it. It'll help with the cramping."

"You said Isaac didn't break me but I know he did, Sophia. I know he did! I can feel it," Kathleen declared, taking the cup from her.

"Kathleen, my nephew is blinded so much with the love he has for you he has yet to figure out your true identity. Now, Isaac isn't the type of man who lets anyone make a fool of him and yet he makes a fool of himself the more he is with you. If my nephew is so blinded by that, what makes you think he would ever want to hurt you?"

"He's a monster! He murdered my father and brother. He beat Bailey and Tomas close to death. Why wouldn't he hurt me?"

"Because he loves you and he cannot hurt his wife. It goes against the contract you will sign before the king in December."

"I have yet to sign it and have not been declared Lady Turner yet! He can still hurt me!"

Sophia gently placed her hand on Kathleen's elbow and looked sternly into her eyes. "Kathleen, you're not thinking with a clear head. Drink and then we will talk."

Kathleen glared at Sophia and then peered at the dark mixture. She sniffed the thick, brown liquid and squinted at the horrible smell. "What is this?"

"Laudanum mixed with alcohol and honey. It'll help with the cramping. My husband is a physician and I travel with the mixture in case my course starts. I had been sick for a long time and my course has become unpredictable. I keep praying to God that either my course ends or I become with child again."

"Course?" Kathleen asked, looking at Sophia.

"Drink and I will speak to you about it." Kathleen drank the foul mixture, swallowed, and handed the cup back to Sophia. "You will experience elation, depression, and exhaustion in a few moments, yet you will feel no pain. I doubt you will understand anything I say to you afterwards, so please listen closely to my words."

"Courses?"

"Yes, well sometimes a woman bleeds between her legs. It will not occur when you are with child, breastfeeding, ill, or under a great deal of stress. Sometimes the blood is strong and sometimes weak. The intensity and occurrence of your course can change over time, especially if you are living with another woman. For some reason, your course will change to match the timing of the other woman's course. I cannot explain it but I have seen it happen."

"So, he didn't break me and this is normal?"

"Oh, yes, my dear. A woman's course usually begins in her mid- to late teens. I take it your sister has never begun her course?"

"No. Our mother never spoke about it to us, either. Nor did Sherlock and Bailey's wives. Why is this happening to me?"

"It's something that every woman must go through and the hardest part of it all is when our men smell the blood we spill. They are intoxicated by it and want to have relations with us."

Kathleen nodded with a sniff of her nose. "Isaac did that. I thought he broke me and I denied his advances even though I know it is my obligation to grant his request every time he desires my body."

"Oh, Kathleen, he will not break your body by having sex with you while you bleed."

"He won't?"

"No, and you may find that you enjoy him inside you even more while you are bleeding. Some women do and others don't. It's just a matter of personal preference."

Kathleen's body grew numb. She smiled as a deep sense of happiness consumed her. Slowly, her body felt weightless and she slumped over, closing her eyes. Sophia gently lowered Kathleen to the floor and tapped her cheek. "Kathleen," she called to the younger woman. Kathleen groaned, turned her head to the side, and fell silent.

"Sophia," an elderly woman said, opening the parlor door from the hallway. Sophia lifted her head as her mother entered the parlor. "Good lord," the countess cried, walking swiftly to the younger women.

"I gave her some of my medicine," Sophia answered, lifting Kathleen into her arms.

The countess glanced at the blood on the back of Kathleen's shift and followed her daughter to the guest room. "Mother will you pick up the menstrual belt and tell my daughter to prepare it for Lady Kathleen?"

"Of course," the countess answered, turned back to the fireplace, and picked up the belt. "How is it she doesn't have one of these on?"

"This is her first and her mother never informed her of the transformation from girl to woman. Help me, mother, and then ask Isabella to attach a rag to the belt. I'll place it on Kathleen while she sleeps."

"The poor child, and I supposed being who she is her family could never afford one of these."

"Never, mother. I'll give her mine."

"But you need this. You still bleed."

"I sent Madge to acquire a new one for me. I have gained weight since I last wore it," she answered then entered the spare bedroom. Sophia lowered Kathleen's unconscious body onto the bed as her mother closed the door behind them. The countess went to the bed and pulled back the blankets. "Sophia, you saw her body. She has large breasts. Usually, a new woman's breasts form two years before she begins her course, yet Kathleen's body…"

"I thought she was older than nineteen, mother. Yet it seems the new Lady Turner is quite young and naïve. She is never going to survive under the responsibilities that are demanded of her without our guidance," Sophia said, placing Kathleen's unconscious body on the bed.

Chapter 35

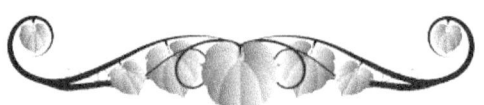

October 14, 1738

Kathleen walked down the hallway, periodically studying the English portraits on the walls, grateful Sophia and the countess had taken care of her yesterday. She had awoken from her deep sleep early this morning to breakfast in bed. Sophia and her mother had spared no expense in celebrating her entry into womanhood. They had explained the menstrual belt on her hip and how to clean the old household linens fashioned as a pad on a strap between her legs. At first the bulky fabric had felt strange between her legs, but eventually she grew accustomed to it. The three women had spent most of the day talking about womanhood until Kathleen told them of her plan to find and save Mary.

Kathleen paused next to a portrait with her hand on her lower stomach. She turned to view the bloody path she had created down the hallway. The cloth between her legs had tried to capture all of her blood but because her flow was heavy it often failed at its task. Thankfully, Sophia had ordered one of the servants to follow behind her and clean up the blood.

Kathleen turned to her right and stared down at the long unfamiliar hallway. Why did this house have to be so large? She pulled out a folded piece of paper from between her breasts and opened it. Kathleen peered at the map Isaac's grandmother had drawn for her. "Three hallways to the right from Isaac's chamber. Two hallways to the left and then five to the right," she muttered as she traced the map with her finger. Kathleen lowered the map and peered down the long hallway. She had walked down the endless hallways for an hour and followed the map precisely, yet where was the large tapestry with the door hidden behind it? Perhaps the map was wrong. But how could it be? Hadn't her father placed the door to the dungeon behind the tapestry when he finished updating that portion of the old castle? She exhaled a deep breath and placed the map back in her bodice. She had to find her sister. There was no turning back.

Kathleen walked slowly down the long hallway, taking note of every fine detail. She paused in her step at the sound of a crash coming from behind the wall on her left. Kathleen pulled the map out and peered at it again. There wasn't supposed to be a room here on the other side of the wall and it wasn't storming outside. Where could that crash have come from? A sound of a body slammed against the wall again. Her heart jumped. She put the map away and walked to the wall. Kathleen gently placed her ear next to the wall and leaned close. Thump. Crash.

"Bring her to me," Isaac's voice bellowed.

Kathleen swallowed hard, recognizing her husband's voice behind the wall. Wasn't he supposed to be in Dublin? She closed her eyes with disappointment and a hint of anger. Another lie. It's always another lie with her husband. How was she supposed to find her sister while he was still at the estate? Kathleen removed the saint's medallion from around her neck and clutched it. She had hoped Saint Anne would help guide her to Mary, yet she couldn't risk Isaac seeing her with a saint's medallion on. She kissed her medallion then whispered, "Blessed Saint Anne, protect me with all your wisdom and strength. Forgive me for denouncing you in this journey. Amen." Kathleen hid her medallion inside her gown's pocket then listened closely to the wall.

Isaac's voice came from the near distance behind the wall, "She's too ugly. Put her with the others. If she continues to resist beat her into submission."

"Yes, sir," a man responded.

Kathleen gasped, pulling away from the wall as she clung to her stomach. Bailey's rumors had been based in truth. But just how much of the rumors were true? If she could just get the information from Isaac then perhaps she could set her brother up in a trap and Isaac could kill Bailey. She walked down the hallway trailing her hand down the wall. There had to be a secret passage somewhere. She only hoped Isaac wouldn't kill her once he spotted her. Her heart skipped a beat as she found a passage behind something. Kathleen lowered her hand with the realization that a piece of fabric hung beside her. She walked around the tapestry and smiled. There before her was the large 15th century tapestry of Castle Kilmore and the surrounding countryside that had once hung in her father's bedroom. She stood amazed at the beautiful workmanship that had been presented to her royal ancestors at the completion of this side of the castle. She could stand here for hours just gazing at the colors and fine details. Another thump from behind the wall and then a scream. Kathleen lowered her hand and peered behind the tapestry at the hidden door to the dungeon. Whatever was going on down there she had to stop for Mary's sake. She wondered if Isaac had hurt her sister and how she might be able to rescue Mary without Isaac suspecting her true identity. If she was going to rescue Mary then she had to be careful.

Kathleen removed her saint's medallion from her pocket and the map from her bodice. She glanced at her surroundings then focused on the pair of armored knight statues across from her. "Thank you, Saint Anne," she whispered, kissed the medallion, then hid her items inside the helmet of one of the knights. She paused, seeing a name engraved on the inside of the helmet. "Sir Sherlock McGillpatrick. Earl of Kilmore 1457." Kathleen grinned. Who else would better suit to protect her identity than the ancestor her brother had been named after? She grabbed the helmet with both hands then whispered to it, bearing her eyes at the eyeholes. "Protect me well, grandfather." Kathleen kissed the top of the helmet then went to the hidden door. She swallowed hard at the sound of a woman's scream. Kathleen pushed the door to the side, stepped onto the landing, then closed the door behind her.

She stared at the long, steep staircase before her. Lit torches alternated on the walls every four steps. The screams grew louder with crashes, thumps, and the sound of beatings as she descended deeper into the darkness. Her fear grew not only for her own safety but also for the safety of those who were under such drastic conditions at the hands of her husband. She dared not to think what would happen if he turned against her. Was this the place where he had beaten Bailey and Sherlock? Was this where Mary was being kept?

Kathleen stood at the base of the steps, peered upward, then turned her attention to the room before her. There was no going back. She had come this far and if she were ever to gain the answers she sought she would have to confront this horrible place. She turned at the sound of crying. Kathleen stepped into the room and looked at the three cells against the wall of the small room. Dirty Irish children and women sat cramped in their cells. She swallowed hard at the inhumane conditions. Their eyes pleaded for her assistance. Yet she could do nothing. Something sticky clung to the base of her shoes. She lowered her eyes to the floor. Large puddles of blood mixed with brain matter and insides cascaded all over the floor. She moaned to herself, heaving her chest, backing away. She couldn't scream. No, she had to endure this torture chamber for her people. Kathleen bumped into something hard. She turned to see a wooden table in the middle of the room with the remains of a dissected Irish man strapped to the table. His severed head faced the cells. Kathleen turned her gaze to the woman and children it stared at. The small family sobbed together and backed away from the front of the cell at the sight of her long stare. Kathleen closed her eyes. So it was all true. Isaac wasn't selling the men. He was brutally torturing and then killing them in front of their wives and children so they would submit to his authority over them. But what was he doing with the boys?

"Lady Kathleen," Isaac bellowed from the other side of the room.

Kathleen opened her eyes and turned her attention to her blood-soaked husband. She swallowed hard as he approached her with a blood stained hand-held sickle and a look of rage in his eyes. Kathleen stumbled backwards. "Don't…I'm so sorry, Isaac. So sorry," she turned to run up the stairs but he was too quick for her. Isaac grabbed her by the wrist and turned, pulling her down the stairs.

He pushed her against the wall with his body against her and sneered in her face, "What are you doing down here?"

"I was lost."

"In the old part of the estate? The part I told you never to enter?" he demanded, grabbing her jaw.

"I am as interested in the heritage of this castle as you are. Why would it surprise you I might wander? You said this estate is mine as well, did you not?"

Isaac glared at her with the fiercest of looks. "You claimed you are on your cycle."

"I am. Did you not see the blood on our bed?"

"Hmm, then why are you here?"

"Sometimes walking helps to relieve my cramps. Why are you down here when you should be in Dublin?"

She couldn't keep her eyes off his for fear he might think she was playing him. Yet how could she deny the sickle he gripped in his hand? There truly was only one thing she could do to detract any suspicions he might hold against her.

"I am conducting matters of estate," he answered.

"Your prisoners look to be Irish. If you are conducting yourself on behalf of King George then perhaps you might consider some help?"

"Help?"

"Isaac, you have plenty of women and children down here. I could...oh, I don't know...help you with the prisoners? They are down here because you are commissioned to sell them to the colonies as punishment for being rebels, are you not?"

"That and more."

"More?"

Isaac glared at her with a deep look of suspicion then slowly lowered the sickle on his belt. He grabbed her hand. "Come with me. It is time you know the truth. You are correct, my love. I need your help."

"I'll do anything for you, Isaac."

Isaac nodded then slowly led her through the room to a larger chamber. Cells full of men, women, boys, and girls all separated from one another crowded the walls. A wooden platform with ankle chains stood in the middle of the room. "I am preparing for an auction tonight. These are for the slaves who are to be sold for the colonies. There are eleven chambers full of slaves to sell. The chambers are organized by ethnicity, gender, and purpose. I have a large shipment of African slaves and I recently acquired around 100 Irish rebels that I am processing for the auction tonight."

"How large is the African shipment?"

"Two hundred."

"African slaves are more expensive than Irish?"

"Yes, but I make more money the more Irish I have."

"How so?"

"Supply and demand, Kathleen. More people are attracted to good stock at a lower price."

"And the Irish you have?"

"Eh, they are good but I have another way to make even more money with some of them."

"How so?"

"You'll see," he said as they walked past the platform to another chamber.

Kathleen stared at the wooden bed in the middle of the room. A young woman lay on a wooden table with her arms and legs chained on the side. Cells of women and girls lined the room. Isaac led Kathleen to the woman on the table. He turned the woman's head and examined her face. "She's very beautiful and will bring us a fortunate, Kathleen. I know just the noble who loves to bed blonde, blue-eyed girls." He sighed then turned to face her. "I break all of them in so they know who owns them. If they resist me I beat them. If they have children, I kill them as soon as they are born. If they become useless to me then I kill them. The problem is these Irish women are so defiant I end up killing so many of them because they are so useless to me after I sell them to their first man. I need a woman to convince them to work with me and not against me. I need an Irish woman."

Kathleen clenched her jaw then looked at her husband. "So you want me to control your Irish whores?"

"Yes, Kathleen, I want to share all of my life with you. Especially, the service I provide to King George. My wife needs to aide me in my delicate matters of state, as will our children. I'm as much of a victim to the king as they are."

"How so?" she bellowed "You are selling the Irish women as whores and killing their men! You're as much of a monster as the McGillpatrick men are!"

"I knew this was wrong." He grabbed her by the arm and pulled her towards him. "You don't understand," he snarled. "I have to supplement our income with these women or we won't survive."

"King George loves you. He gave you Kilmore after you defeated the McGillpatrick family. Why wouldn't you have money?"

"We are broke, Kathleen. We have been broke since Queen Elizabeth ruled England and have been at the mercy of the monarchy ever since for our survival. Everything you see is just a façade. The money, lands, wealth, none of it actually belongs to my family. I am afforded this lifestyle as long as I please the royal family. But should I lose their favor, I and my entire family will suffer a fate much worse than these slaves."

"I don't understand," Kathleen muttered, wincing from his tight grip on her arm.

"My father's ancestor was one of the most ruthless pirates during the queen's reign. He gave his fidelity to her when she was recruiting pirates to defend England against Spain. All of the pirates who served her were rewarded with lands and titles. She was afraid of my ancestor so she demanded a contract be drawn between him and the crown before she granted him title and lands. The contract is valid as long as a monarch rules over England."

"Any monarch?"

"Yes. I am bound to the contract."

"And what are you and the heirs I am to produce for you bound to?"

"I am bound to serve the monarchy in any way a noble deems necessary as long as I do not betray the royal family."

"Any way?"

"I murder, steal, kidnap, provide whores, trade information, and anything else King George and his nobles require of me."

"But you were part of his privy council."

"I was only part of that council so he could keep a closer eye on me. I had the upbringing any nobleman's son is entitled to but when I began to excel at my studies and wanted to pursue a career of my own King George demanded my attentions at court."

"You knew the commitment your father expected from you and yet you still wanted to denounce it?"

"I was the youngest son, Kathleen. I did not believe the contract covered all the Turner men but just the heir. But I was sadly mistaken. When disease took the lives of my siblings the king took an even greater interest in me." He shook his head with a long breath. "You see, Kathleen, I can't escape from my life nor can my wife and children."

"You demand an heir from me because you are obligated to reproduce."

"I cannot marry an English noble and the union must be approved by the king. He consented to the union once I wrote of my intentions after meeting with you. The physician the night of our wedding was the king's personal physician. He could have stopped the union if he found fault with your health. Thankfully, he did not."

"And what would have happened to me if he did?"

Isaac shook his head. "You don't want to know, my love," he muttered.

Kathleen walked around the bed and stared at the woman. She lifted her gaze to him from across the table. She studied the young woman closely. Her heart sank as the Irish woman stared at her. How could she aide Isaac in his crimes against her people? Yet she didn't have a choice. Sherlock had once told her that sometimes you have to do something you truly despise in order to benefit the entire group. Oh, how much she despised what she was about to tell her husband. But there was no choice. Isaac's grandmother and aunt told her the king had informed Isaac he couldn't verify her identity. As far as Isaac was concerned she could just be a commoner pretending to be a noble so she could spy against him. She couldn't allow Isaac to jump to the conclusion that she was a rebel. Hadn't he formed that opinion of her when they first met? Thankfully, Tomas had been able to dispel Isaac's accusations against her. Yet she knew that although Isaac loved her he was still intrigued as to her identity and why Tomas would be protecting her and Calico if they were just commoners. Isaac's wandering mind was a dangerous thing.

"I'll help you with our Irish whores but I want control over all the females. Their clothes, surroundings, food, everything," she proclaimed, raising her gaze to Isaac.

"Agreed."

"As for their children. Let them conceive and don't kill their young."

"Kathleen?"

She leaned across the table and looked him squarely in the eyes. "Doesn't the law state any child an Irish woman bears is born into captivity?"

"Yes, but?"

"Isaac, you can use that against them."

"I don't understand."

Kathleen exhaled a deep breath and walked around the table. "A woman is very protective of her family, especially the children. You could….," she paused, placed her hand on his chest, peered at the woman, then looked back at her husband. "You could offer the mother freedom but insist you will not release her children. She will do anything to protect her child, even to the point that she will refuse your offer. If she doesn't please you then you could separate her from her children. She will be bitter against you for it but if you promise to reward her with reunifying her with her children her attitude should change."

Isaac put his hands on top of hers. "I like that idea."

"You can use the Irish whores for breeding stock as well. Charge a fee to anyone who wants to use them. That will give us even more money to work with, especially from the women who produce strong children. You would have to prove they have given strong children."

"We sell the children and inform the merchants who the mother is."

"Yes."

"I like the way you think, Kathleen. I have to get back to work, my love. I need to separate them for our new breeding program." He lowered his hands.

"I think you should breed with this blonde. I've heard of slaves breeding with their masters to produce a strong slave."

"It has happened."

"Well, we need strong babies to prove our breeding program is the best in all of Ireland. Is she married?"

"No. But I have other whores whose husbands I have yet to kill."

"Don't kill the husbands."

Isaac turned sharply to her. "What? The men are dangerous. I have better luck controlling the African men than the Irish."

"Isaac, let the men have relations with their wives to increase our slave population. That way we don't have to depend upon acquiring new rebels for our stock."

"Agreed but I will still have to hunt down the rebels and arrest them."

"Do so but don't let it be our only source of slaves."

Isaac nodded, lowered his pants, and climbed onto the table. The girl fidgeted as he pulled up her skirt.

"Not yet," Kathleen said, grabbing him by the upper arm. He turned to face her. "You want her compliance, so you need to seduce the girls into giving their complete obedience to you."

"Seduce them?"

"Let me, husband."

Isaac nodded then crawled off the table. He pulled up his pants and watched his wife slap the girl in the face. She gasped, opened her eyes, and screamed. "You see my husband," Kathleen whispered in the woman's ear. The woman nodded with a sniff of her nose. "Good. Do not scream or fight him. I want to help you."

"How?" the terrified young woman asked.

"Well, my dear, you help us and we'll help you. Aren't you tired of living in poverty?"

The woman nodded. "I can change all that for you. I can give you food, clothes, and the nicest place to live. I can save your family as long as you obey my husband and me."

The woman glanced towards Isaac. She opened her mouth to speak. Kathleen placed her finger on the woman's mouth and whispered into her ear so Isaac couldn't hear her. "Please my husband and I will please you in the name of the McGillpatrick clan." The woman turned her attention to Kathleen. Kathleen shook her head. "He doesn't know. I will save you and all women of Ireland. I promise. Keep my identity a secret and I will tell my brother about you. Tell him my secret and well you know what Bailey will do in order to protect Calico and me," Kathleen whispered so her husband couldn't hear. "Uncuff her," Kathleen ordered a soldier.

The soldier looked at Isaac.

"She's my wife. Do what she orders you to do," Isaac answered. The soldier complied.

"I promise to serve you well, Earl Turner," the young Irish woman declared.

Kathleen backed away as Isaac pinned the woman underneath him. He grabbed the woman's jaw and snarled. "Never forget that I own you. Understood?"

Kathleen turned away as her husband forced his authority over the woman and walked to the entrance of another chamber. She peered inside the smaller room. Several more cages lined the darker room. Kathleen's heart sank. She hated what she had done but she had no choice in the matter. Isaac was as much of a victim of the crown as her people were. Only problem was they were fighting against each other instead of joining forces. Perhaps she had misjudged the entire situation. He was fighting for his freedom as much as her people were fighting for theirs. She closed her eyes, ignoring the sounds of Isaac's domination. A tear fell from her eye. She wiped it away, took a deep breath, opened her eyes, and entered the room.

"Kitty Kat," Mary's voice lifted from a cage on the far left corner.

Kathleen turned her attention to the sound of Mary's voice. Mary stretched her arm out and smiled. Kathleen glanced back to the room with her husband then ran to her sister's side. She knelt before Mary and grabbed her hand. Finally! Finally she had found her older sister yet there was nothing she could do to free her.

Chapter 36

Mary leaned against the wall and smiled as she held her sister's hand. "What are you doing down here?" she whispered.

"I came to rescue you."

Mary lowered her hand and shook her head. She crawled to the back of the cell and vomited into a bucket. Kathleen's heart sank at the sight of her older sister's deplorable living conditions. Isaac hadn't shown Sherlock's wife any mercy despite her being with child. The stink of urine, feces, and rotten food lingered in the air.

"What does my husband plan to do with you?" Kathleen asked.

"Husband?" Mary questioned, turning sharply toward her.

"We married last week and he knows Calico and I aren't nobles."

Mary wiped her face and returned to Kathleen's side. "How?"

"He presented King George with the idea of our courtship soon after he met me. King George investigated Calico's and my story but couldn't find proof of our supposed lineage."

"Does he know the truth?"

"I don't believe so. His mother figured it out and had spoken to Isaac concerning her suspicions but he never believed her. Well, not until after Calico murdered his mother."

"Calico's dangerous, Kathleen. You can't believe a word she says to you. She's as much of a threat to your life as Bailey is to your father." Kathleen sighed and peered towards the other chamber. Isaac groaned loudly while the table scraped against the floor. She closed her eyes and sniffed her nose. She returned her gaze to her sister. Mary grabbed

Kathleen's hand. Kathleen opened her eyes. "What is it? Did he hurt you?" Mary asked.

"Only my heart."

"Kathleen?"

"Father's dead, as is Tomas' father."

Mary clutched her sister's hand tighter. "Mother?"

"She's in Dublin with Bailey."

"What happened?"

Kathleen sniffed her nose then wiped it with the sleeve of her gown. "After you were arrested Isaac suspected his mother's accusations against Calico and me were based in truth. He had his physician sedate me. I don't know much other than what I was told and saw."

"Tell me what you do know and we will figure out the rest together."

Kathleen nodded. "I woke up from my sleep early and walked to Isaac's room. I found him sobbing in his parlor with a lot of papers on the floor. When I confronted him he hit me in the face and I fell unconscious. I woke up to find myself shackled to his bed and his sister tending to my wounds."

"Did he violate you?"

"No. I don't know how long I was unconscious. When I woke up I asked his sister where her brother was. She told me that he went to investigate Tomas' estate. A few moments later Isaac returned to the bedroom, told his sister to leave, then threw father and Padric's heads on my lap. He asked me to verify the story I had given him about the attack on our home."

"And did you?"

"The best I could. He released me and I ran to Tomas' room. Bailey's priest was there along with Tomas' mother. Mary, did you know Bailey's priest is Sherlock and Bailey's grandfather?"

Mary looked at her with a confused look. "Are you certain?"

Kathleen peered at the door to the other chamber. Isaac's grunts grew louder. She turned back to Mary. "Isaac's almost finished with the slave. I can't speak for much longer. He is Sherlock and Bailey's grandfather and I was named after Sherlock's mother."

"That I have always known."

"You did?"

"Yes. It's one of the reason's Sherlock always protected you more than Calico. What else do you know?"

"Before Isaac confined me to his bed he interrogated Tomas."

"Is he still alive?"

"Barely."

"Calico?"

"She's locked herself in Tomas' room and won't leave his side. She feels horrible about what she did and the consequences of her actions. She blames herself for our father's death, the death of Tomas' father, and her husband's condition."

"As she should."

Isaac yelled. Kathleen turned her eyes to the chamber with a tear running down her cheek. "Kitty Kat," Mary called to her. Kathleen turned her attention back to Mary. "You still love him after everything he has done against you and our family."

Kathleen smiled, sniffed her nose and wiped away her tear. "I do and I hate myself for it. I promised to help him enslave and use our people. I am no worse than Bailey. How can I ever live with that?"

"You use it against him."

Kathleen turned towards the entrance then turned back to Mary. She gathered herself. "I haven't located Sherlock's papers yet. I felt them on Isaac the morning Calico killed his mother. I will find them for you and help you to escape. When I do you must run to Dublin. Bailey and your mother will meet you at the Emerald Cove."

"What name is he using?"

"I don't know. His priest is tending to Tomas' wounds disguised as his physician. He told me he would find you and let him know of your location. He plans to free you and return you to Bailey."

"Kathleen, you can't return me to my husband. You know what Bailey will do to me. He loathes that I am with Sherlock's child. Please, dear sister, you don't know the horrors my sister faced under his household. It's better that she is dead."

"Don't worry. I have a plan. He won't live for long, Mary. I can promise you that."

"Ah, there you are," Isaac said from behind her.

"How dare you touch me?" Kathleen yelled, pushing her sister's hand away and rising.

Mary lowered her head and returned to the shadows. Isaac walked beside his wife and kissed her on the cheek. "Everything alright?" he asked, walking to the cell.

"Isaac, I no longer require her services and you desire to punish her for the crime she committed. What are your plans for her?" Kathleen asked.

Isaac glared at Mary then turned to her. "Execution." Kathleen's heart skipped a beat. She gathered her emotions before she reacted and glared at her older sister. "When?" she muttered.

"Tonight. I plan to hang her before the auction. Why do you ask?"

"Well I have a better idea."

"She murdered my mother! The bitch deserves death! Besides, she's the wife of a rebel leader."

"Another reason not to execute her. If you execute her then..." Kathleen paused. It was all perfect. If word spread to Bailey that Isaac planned to execute Mary then Bailey would lead a group of rebels to rescue her. Bailey had always been infatuated with Mary and everyone knew it. She needed Isaac to kill her brother yet she didn't need to be in a position where he questioned her every move.

"Kathleen," Isaac tenderly called to her as he rubbed his hands on her arms.

"What?" she asked softly, shaking her head.

"My love, you do not look well." He gently stroked her cheekbone. "Perhaps you should return to your cham…"

"No, Isaac. I have an idea."

"What sort of an idea?"

"Delay the execution and make it public."

"Why would I do that?"

"Because the child she carries belongs to Bailey not Sherlock."

"Are you certain?"

"Mary told me she had an affair with his brother. When Sherlock died Mary was free to marry the man she truly loved."

Isaac grinned and stepped closer to the cage. "Is this true?" he demanded, grabbing her by the wrist and pulling her to the front. Mary spit in his face. He slapped her hard. "Answer me!"

"Yes, I'm Bailey's wife," Mary declared.

Isaac shoved her backwards with a huge grin. "Well, this changes everything," he said to his wife. "And you did not know the truth?"

"No, I believed her story as did my sister."

"The attack on Tomas' house makes sense now."

"Oh, how so?"

"Rumors are that although the McGillpatrick brothers worked well together on the battlefield they were bitter rivals in their personal lives. If Mary had an affair with Bailey and her husband learned of it she would want to hide so Sherlock wouldn't beat her for it."

"But she wasn't with child when she came to serve Calico and me. How would he know?"

"That only means she was still in communication with Bailey when she came to the estate. Could it be that she infiltrated Tomas' estate for Bailey and not Sherlock?" He looked at Mary and crouched before her. "How much does Bailey know?"

Mary shook her head. "Nothing. I went to serve at Tomas' house to escape the brothers. Nothing more."

"Liar! You will tell me the truth. What was your mission at Tomas' house?"

Mary shook her head and glared at Kathleen. Kathleen swallowed hard. She knew that look. It was the look of pure anger and disappointment. "Guards," Isaac yelled, rising from the floor. Two guards rushed to their side from the other room. "Open this door and shackle her to the wall."

"Yes, sir," the guards replied.

Kathleen clenched her jaw as the guards opened the door, grabbed Mary, and thrust her to the back wall. Mary whimpered as they forced her arms upward and placed her wrists and ankles in the metal cuffs. She fidgeted against the tight grip. "It's best not to resist," Isaac said, entering the small enclosure.

Mary heaved and tugged on the short length of the metal chains. She screamed in frustration. Isaac grabbed her by the jaw and pushed her head back. "You will tell me the truth or you'll soon find yourself praying to that idol saint of yours for mercy. I can torture you for the information or you can give it to me freely."

"I'm with child," she snarled.

"I don't care. Your child won't live long enough to see the light of day when I'm done with you. Now, what was your mission at Tomas' house?"

"Nothing. I was running away from the brothers."

"Liar," he punched her hard in the jaw. Mary glared up at Kathleen. Isaac grabbed her jaw and pushed her head back. "You will not look at my wife!" He leaned her head back, pushing her neck back as far as it would go. "Now, let's try this again. What were your intentions when you offered your services to the sisters?"

"Nothing. I wanted a life away from the brothers and thought since Tomas used to be friends with them he would understand my plight. He recognized me as soon as I entered his household. I told him everything and he granted my request to serve his wife and sister."

"Did he contact the brothers?"

"No, sir. He loathes them because they have promised his brothers they would return the estate to the control of the Irish Catholics. Tomas is Anglican. Tomas told me in order to serve his household I had to convert to Anglican and denounce the rebellion."

"And yet you did not. You're with child," Kathleen accused.

"I tried. Honest, mistress, I tried," she pleaded towards Kathleen.

Kathleen answered, "Then how is it you carry Bailey's child?"

Mary heaved and lowered her eyes. Isaac pushed the back of her head against the wall. "Answer her," he demanded.

Mary turned her attention to Isaac. "I thought I was free when you caught Bailey and Sherlock. But then I overheard some of Tomas' brothers talk about how Sherlock and Bailey had escaped. My heart felt for the brothers. I learned of the place where they were hiding and went to their side. Tomas' brothers helped me hide the truth from Lady Kathleen, Countess Calico, and Earl Tomas. When Bailey was well enough we had relations and when he learned I was with child he informed his father. Alexander had ordered that I inform Sherlock of the affair but I refused. He told Sherlock I was with child but not that that child belongs to Bailey. When Sherlock learned I was with child he came to Tomas' estate and demanded I return with him. Tomas refused. He told Sherlock that I had sought sanctuary with him. Sherlock told Tomas if that be so then how was it I was with child. Sherlock demanded Tomas release my service in three days or he would forcibly remove me from the property."

"The attack on the estate?"

Mary nodded, "I feared for my life and pleaded with Tomas to protect me. He tried but we all know the consequences of that decision." She turned to Kathleen. "I am so sorry, Lady Kathleen. I never meant to endanger the lives of your sister, Earl Tomas, or you."

"And yet how do you explain the murder of Earl Turner's mother? Neither my sister nor I ordered you to do so," Kathleen asked.

"She was a threat to you, Countess Calico, and Earl Tomas. I felt after everything that had happened I needed to prove my loyalty to the three of you."

"By murdering my mother?" Isaac asked. He snarled in her face, "Are you claiming that my wife, her sister, and Earl Tomas have something to do with the rebellion?"

"No sir."

"You just said my mother was claiming facts that would have endangered them. If that be true then you are claiming they are involved with the rebellion and perhaps Earl Tomas not only protected you but was somehow involved."

"No, sir. Please, no. I like the sisters and Earl Tomas. They have always treated me with respect. I would never say or do anything to harm them. You must believe me."

Isaac studied her face for a long time. Kathleen swallowed hard. She hoped Isaac would be foolish enough to believe Mary's story but deep in her heart she knew Mary's words had stirred distrust in him. "Husband," Kathleen called out to him, entering the cell. Isaac grunted, pushed Mary's head back, then turned to his wife. "Perhaps, we should announce her execution," she redirected his attention back to their previous conversation.

"I agree. If she tried so hard to leave Bailey only to have caused a rebellion, perhaps if Bailey sees her dead body he will leave you, Lady Calico, and Lord Tomas alone." Isaac walked out of the cell as he proclaimed. "She dies in five days. Tell Tomas to inform his brothers of her execution as I prepare for the announcement!"

Kathleen looked at Mary then ran after her husband. "Wait, Isaac," she yelled as she grabbed his arm. He turned to face her. "Tomas has no contact with his brothers. His family refuses to talk to him because of his betrayal to the Catholic faith."

"They share a mother, do they not?"

"Well yes, but…"

"Lady Kathleen, a mother's love is not biased. Surely, being a woman you know this."

"Well, I…hum…I guess so. But how will he inform her? He's bed-bound and you refuse to release him."

"Tell your sister everything that has transpired down here and that I grant her request to return to her home." He gently took her elbows in his hands as she stood dumbfounded. "I must prepare for the sale tonight. Will you join me tonight at the auction or are you unwell?"

"I'm fine. I just need rest. So much has happened today and I find myself speechless."

"Go inform your sister of what I told you then rest. I will come for you tonight when it is time for the auction. Lord and Lady Turner should stand together in all their ventures."

"I am not Lady Turner as of yet."

"Officially no. In my heart, you already are."

"But how am I to stand beside you when I have not been coroneted as Countess of Kilmore?"

"Don't worry about that, Kathleen. The king has assured me he will grant you your title, wealth, and honors when we visit his court during Christmas."

"It's just…"

"Do you not agree that we should stand by one another in all our transactions?"

"I…I…I do, Isaac. I want to be by your side in everything that you do."

"We do."

"Yes, we do. Sorry. I'm—"

"It's alright, Kathleen. I love you. Go, do what I asked of you, please," he said then kissed her on the lips. Kathleen returned his deep kiss then left the dungeon. She closed the hallway door behind her and leaned her back against it as she stared at the statue of her ancestor that held her

belongings. That was too close. Way too close for her comfort. She grabbed her belongings then ran down the hallway towards her sister's chambers.

Chapter 37

October 17, 1738
Collins Great House, Wexford County, Ireland

The wind blew hard against the large rock great house. Kathleen peered out of Tomas' window at his estate towards the long road that led north to Dublin, thinking about the events of the past few days. She had run to Tomas' chambers after she left her husband and told Calico everything. Kathleen had immediately wanted to rescue Mary but Calico convinced her otherwise. Afterwards, Calico, the priest, and Margaret carefully transported Tomas back to his estate while she remained behind to stand by Isaac's side at the auction. Hundreds of merchants had descended upon Kilmore's dungeon later that night.

The merchants had been allowed to preview the slaves as if they were cattle or sheep. The only slaves spared from the humility were the women and men Isaac had held back for their new breeding program. Isaac had made certain all of the available slaves were chained to the wall naked so the merchants could inspect them before the auction. The merchants' hands knew no boundaries as they prodded and groped the slaves they were most interested in. Once the auction began the merchants never stopped bidding, especially when Isaac periodically brought out a select few beautiful young women they had agreed to sell separately. The worst part of the auction was when no one wanted to buy a certain slave. If a slave, Irish or African, didn't sell, Isaac immediately deemed the slave unfit and shot him or her in the head. The first time he had done so had shocked Kathleen. He had tried to sell a thin, middle-aged Irish woman, claiming she was fit as a household slave. Yet his merchants were no fools. They could see the years of poverty had taken their toll on her body. When no one bought her Isaac pulled out his Irish Flintlock Pistol and shot the woman in the back of the head. Kathleen had almost gone to defend her by standing in front of Isaac's gun, yet just as the thought had crept into her head she denounced it. Despite how much she wanted to save her people Isaac had to know she would stand beside him in whatever decision he made. She watched fifteen slaves die that night.

After the auction, the guards removed the bodies as she joined her husband and the merchants in a secluded larger chamber. Pillows, beds, and sofas laid all around the room with naked women on them. This time Isaac wasn't selling slaves. He was hosting an orgy. She stayed by his side as one by one the men paid him to participate, then he closed the door when the last man paid them, locking everyone inside. Everyone undressed, including her and Isaac. She had wanted to run away from the event but she couldn't. She had to prove to Isaac she could be trusted. She participated in the large orgy with her husband, and despite her morals she had liked it. Sophia had been right. All the sexual encounters she had while she was bleeding had been more intense and more enjoyable than when she wasn't bleeding. Yet now she felt guilty for her sins and knew she needed a priest for her confession. But there was something she had to do before she sought absolution from a priest. Besides, what would the priests think of her after she admitted all that she had done against God?

"Hmm," Tomas moaned. Kathleen lowered the curtain and sat on the side of his bed.

"Tom," she whispered.

Tomas turned his head and tried to open his swollen eyes. "Calico," he whispered.

"She went with your mother to Dublin a few nights ago."

"Priest?"

"Father O'Brian stayed behind to care for you. We've been taking shifts. He cares for you throughout the night while I take care of you during the day. Your priest has given him shelter."

Tomas nodded his head and grimaced. "Why are you here and not with Isaac?"

"Isaac sent me here to deliver a message to your mother."

"What message?"

"A message for Bailey. The time has come for a change in leadership and you, Tomas, are going to help me." Tomas opened his mouth then closed it with a hard swallow. "I have a plan and if my plan works everything will change. Isaac believes the lies I tell him and so does Bailey. In the end there is only one person who controls this situation and protects our people."

Tomas turned his head to face her with a serious look on his face. "What happened to you?"

Kathleen froze at his question. What hadn't happened to her? How could she tell Tomas everything that had transpired? It was one thing to tell Calico everything she had done but Tomas? He had known her and Calico since the day they were born. Kathleen shook her head. "I…uhm…Tomas do you know about the Turner contract?" she asked, sitting next to him on his bed.

"Not much. Only that it exists and even that is questionable as I only heard of it through rumors. Isaac isn't very forthcoming about his private affairs."

"And what do you know about his transactions?"

"He has many. I know he sells African and Irish slaves. Why?"

Kathleen swallowed hard and diverted her eyes. Despite the close friendship Tomas shared with her husband, even he had been played. Was there no end to her husband's deceits? She wondered who Isaac confided in the most, other than her. Or was he deceiving her as well?

"Kathleen," Tomas called to her. Kathleen turned her attention back to the brutally beaten man. "What is on your mind?"

"Do you remember when Bailey told us he heard unnatural sounds coming from somewhere in the dungeon?"

"Yes."

"I know what he heard. I participated in it and to be honest I must say I quite enjoyed it."

"What is it?"

"Isaac hosts sex parties in a secluded area of the dungeon that is only accessible by a secret entrance. He charges the men a fee, grants them entrance, locks the door behind them, and then everyone unleashes their urges throughout the night. He leaves no boundaries and when I say no boundaries I mean…"

"He whored you out."

Kathleen bit her lower lip and shook her head. "He never left my side. I didn't know he was charging an extra fee for men to share me with him. There were so many last night. I only thought he was charging them for the experience. When I awoke in his arms the next day he told me we had made more money than he had ever made before with this experience by charging the men to seduce me."

Tomas groaned and took his head in his hands. "Your father…"

"My father is dead because of my husband and my own foolishness!"

"Your father wouldn't approve of what happened to you. You committed a sin with your actions. Have you sought a priest for absolution?"

"No."

"Kathleen, for the safety of your soul leave me and do so. There are two priests in my home. Find one and confess your sins."

"That is not a matter of concern for me at this moment."

"What the hell happened to you!?"

"To me?"

"Yes, you! Where is the innocent Kathleen who left my estate to marry Isaac? She would never deal with matters of her soul in this manner."

"She's gone, Tomas."

"No, she's inside you somewhere. I know it."

Kathleen shook her head with a tear streaming down her cheek. "I've changed, Tomas. I'm no longer the sweet, innocent child who lived here. So much has happened to me, Tomas. Sherlock died. Mary was arrested for a murder she didn't commit. You were beaten twice. I was beaten and held captive. Bailey injured my head and caused the accident that broke some of my bones. I was humiliated on my wedding night. I aided my husband in the enslavement of my people and participated in not only selling them but also allowed him to murder ten of them. I participated in his perverse sexual encounters and even encouraged him to start a breeding program with our own people! Tomas, there is no hope for my soul. I have already become something I never thought I would."

Tomas put his hand on top of hers. "Kathleen, God knows you are doing all of this in his name."

"Am I? Because to be honest I enjoyed my encounters with Isaac and the men he sold me to that night. I had never felt such great pleasure before, not even on my wedding night. I want to participate more in his orgies and he has guaranteed me there will be plenty."

"And what happens if you ever conceive a child during those encounters?"

"Isaac and I are working on a nursery for all the children the whores produce. Should I birth a child out of wedlock it will never know I am its mother."

"Kathleen, this isn't you."

"No, Kathleen McGillpatrick died the night she married Earl Tuner. I'm Lady Turner. I must stand beside my husband in everything he does in the name of England."

"Do you understand what that means? You were sent to marry Isaac in order to serve the rebellion, not turn into the English whoring witch he desires of you."

Kathleen rose from the bed and returned to her place beside the window. "I can be both, Tomas. I can control the monster Isaac creates in me."

"You can't expect to balance the life you want and the life you have all by yourself."

"His grandmother and Aunt Sophia know the truth about Calico and me."

"Kathleen!"

She turned sharply towards him with a large grin. "Don't fret, Tomas. They quite enjoy the thought of our marriage and the deceits I have told him. They have promised to aide me in all of my endeavors."

"All of YOUR endeavors?"

Kathleen walked to Tomas' footboard. "Yes, all of my endeavors. The time has come for the leadership of the rebellion to change."

"Change?"

"Yes, Tomas. Change. It came to me that I could control the English more effectively in my position than you can with yours." She leaned over the footboard. "Don't you see? The merchants were willing to pay a lot of money to share my body with Isaac. How much more effective would it be for our cause if I continued to offer them my affections in exchange for a few favors?"

"The power would be in your hands and not Isaac's," Tomas said as he sat upright.

Kathleen grinned. "Yes. But if I allow this knowledge to pass to Bailey he will—"

"—ruin everything."

"I didn't think you would come to that conclusion. You are his best friend, after all."

Tomas huffed with a smile and shook his head. "He was my best friend. He lost that favor with me long ago, Kat."

Kathleen shook her head and sat on the side of his bed. "I don't understand. Sherlock and Mary told me I couldn't trust you because of your close relationship with my brother. You have always sided with Bailey. I've seen you have private conversations with him."

"Those conversations were not about the rebellion but about Calico."

"Calico?"

"Yes. Bailey has been using my wife to spy against me. I am only protected by your father and mine."

Kathleen swallowed hard. So he didn't know the truth yet. Of course Tomas didn't know. Calico, the priest, and Margaret had wanted Tomas' mind at ease so he could recuperate from his injuries without the emotional upheaval of the news of their fathers' deaths. "Have you heard from them?" she asked softly.

"No. My mother said they went with Bailey to Dublin. I can only assume my father reached them in time to evacuate them and led them to refuge at my home in Dublin. I truly wish my father would send word to me."

"I'm certain he will," she lightly tapped his leg. "Tomas, why doesn't Bailey trust you anymore?"

"He thinks I betrayed him because I never came to his defense when the Turners reacquired Kilmore."

"But that was years ago. Do you mean to tell me he has been holding a grudge against you that long?"

"Kathleen, Bailey holds grudges a very long time and once you misplace his trust you rarely ever acquire it again. He seeks revenge on anyone who ever crosses him. I think in a way he beat me harder than he should have to prove a point."

"Which is?"

"I'm expendable in his eyes."

"Even more so if he learns I have Isaac's complete trust."

"Yes. He doesn't care if Calico becomes a widow or not. He'll use her just as much as he uses you."

"Not if I do something to counter that. I can defeat him, Tomas."

"I don't see how, Kathleen. I honestly don't."

"I have a plan but I need your help. I can lead the rebellion from within the very establishment that seeks to destroy us."

"It would be more dangerous for you to do so without Bailey's aide."

"The war with the Turners is not about the survival of our people so much as it is about Bailey's revenge. Bailey wants Isaac to suffer for his father. Yet Isaac is suffering already."

"I do not understand how you think Isaac is suffering when it is our people who feel his wrath!"

"It is not Isaac who controls the Irish. He's being controlled by the English king. If we want to end our sufferings then we need to strike the English crown. The only way we can do that is from the inside. King George knows Calico and I aren't English nobles."

"Then you and my wife are in danger."

"No, I don't believe so."

"How can you say that?"

"King George doesn't care about Calico. You're a lessor noble and it doesn't matter who your wife is, as long as she is loyal to the crown. As for Isaac, he's not allowed to marry an English noble. So as long as Calico and I aren't of English noble blood the king won't care where Isaac found me. I just need to prove my loyalty to him, which I believe I have already done. The problem with trusting Bailey is that he will take that trust and destroy you from within."

"This is true but there is nothing we can do to stop him."

"I can stop him, Tomas, but you must tell Bailey everything I am about to tell you."

"I can do that, Kathleen. I swear upon the cross of Jesus my loyalty only belongs to you. As for Calico, I cannot say that. Her loyalty to Bailey is very strong. It's one of the reasons I have had those conversations with Bailey. I tried to convince Bailey that Calico is my wife and not one of his pawns. But Bailey would never hear my words. He threatened to kill my parents if I ever disobeyed him."

"Really?"

"Yes. I can't betray him."

"What if I told you that he murdered not only my father but yours?"

Tomas heaved, clenching his fists. "No," he exclaimed, shaking his head.

"Isaac showed Calico and me their heads."

"Then it was Isaac who murdered them!"

"On the contrary, Tomas. The heads were delivered to Kilmore with a handwritten note from Bailey. Bailey claimed Isaac had been secretly working with my father to kill my brothers. He also claimed your father was spying against you. He executed them for their disobedience and sent a warning to Isaac that if he didn't leave the rebellion alone he would murder you, Calico, and me."

"He wouldn't."

"He already did."

"Where's the note?"

"Isaac burned it." Kathleen rose from the bed and tapped it. "Tomas, rest assured that when my plan comes to fruition Bailey will no longer be a problem for any of us."

"Speak the words you want me to deliver!"

Kathleen grinned. She had Tomas exactly where she wanted him.

Chapter 38

October 19, 1738

"Isaac. Isaac, wake up," Kathleen's voice entered his mind. Isaac stirred at the sound of his young wife's voice. He moved his fingers and wondered why he was in their bed. He had been suffering from a cold yesterday but it wasn't so bad that she needed to fret about him. A cold was just a cold, wasn't it?

"Isaac, open your eyes and speak to me," Kathleen urged him.

"Hmm," he moaned then coughed as he turned to his side. His tight chest ached with each cough. He was so tired. Why couldn't she just let him sleep? His stomach turned and he felt the burning of stomach acid in his throat. Isaac opened his eyes, leaned over the side of the bed, and vomited into the chamber pot. He coughed between spilling the contents of his stomach.

"Check his temperature and heart rate like I showed you, Kathleen," his aunt's voice lifted in the air.

Isaac closed his eyes and fell forward with extreme weakness. It took every bit of strength he had to vomit. He felt Kathleen's arms around his waist as she gently guided him back to the bed. "Ugh, Kathleen," Isaac moaned, clutching for the sheet. "So cold," he muttered with his teeth shaking. She moved her hands to his face.

"He's burning with fever," she called to Sophia. Her fingers moved to the side of his neck. "His heart's beating fast and his breathing is quick."

"Pneumonia," Sophia sighed. "He can't meet with the king's messenger today. If he appears weak the king will not be pleased."

"Isaac said after Queen Caroline died last year the king's meanness gave way to a tender heart. Surely, he would understand my husband's failing health."

"Not in this matter, Kathleen. King George never liked the Turner contract, but because he is so cruel he won't release my family from it. He never appreciated the fact that his father used my brother to spy on him. So when King George I died and George II was crowned, George II started making Isaac's life a living hell."

"Then it would seem to me he would want Isaac to die."

"Kathleen, you don't understand. The contract states if Earl Turner dies without an heir the entire family must be eliminated so that no one fights for control of the estate. Everything Isaac owns belongs to the crown."

"He told me we are poor."

"You are. The wealth he is allowed to display is greatly governed by Parliament. He is given a yearly allowance that is determined by how successful and obedient he is to the king's demands. His majesty keeps close account of all the Turner family transactions and every four months Isaac must give account before either the king or his messenger of all business transactions."

Isaac moaned, turning his head. The king! How could today be that day? Sophia was right. He couldn't appear weak to King George. He arched his head back and coughed. His lungs burned with each breath he took. Oh, why was it so hard to breathe? The door opened.

"Where's his physician?" Sophia demanded, placing a wet cloth on Isaac's forehead.

"I am told he returned to London," his butler replied.

"Then go and fetch Tomas' physician. Hurry," Kathleen ordered.

"Yes, mi lady." The sound of the door closing vibrated the pain in his head. He cringed at the sensation of cold pin pricks against his warm forehead.

"Shh, it's just water to lower your fever, Isaac. Open your eyes and speak to us." Kathleen's voice entered his ear softly. Didn't she understand how miserable he was? Isaac slowly opened his eyes and stared at the blurry image of his aunt.

"Aunt Sophia," he whispered then coughed.

"Shh, try not to speak too much, Isaac," she ordered, handing a dry cloth to Kathleen. Kathleen replaced it with a soaked wet cloth.

"So tired," Isaac whispered, closing his eyes, and turned his head as Sophia placed the cloth on his forehead.

"No, no, no, Isaac! Isaac, wake up," Sophia pleaded. She turned to Kathleen with her hand extended. Kathleen handed her another one. Sophia wiped his face. He cringed at the pin-prick feeling of the cold water against his warm skin. "Isaac, Sir Robert Walpole is the messenger."

Isaac opened his eyes and turned to face his aunt with a dumbfounded look on his face. Sophia leaned back. "Who is Sir Robert Walpole and why does that name surprise him?" Kathleen asked.

"I have to...," Isaac muttered, trying to sit upright. He leaned over his lap and coughed uncontrollably, trying desperately to breathe.

"What you need to do is lie down," Sophia said, grabbing his bare arms.

Isaac's shoulder-length brown hair fell around his angular face as he shook his head. "I know why he would come here and it's not for the king."

"You cannot help him. If you do King George will think you betrayed him."

"I know but I can't dismiss him. What if he...?" he gasped for breath, choking. He bulged his eyes, grabbed his aunt's bodice, and pleaded with his eyes, desperate for air.

"Take the pillows away from him," she ordered Kathleen.

Kathleen grabbed the pillows as Sophia lowered her nephew to the bed. Isaac gasped from the fresh air entering his lungs as he laid flat on his back. He closed his eyes. Kathleen's hands gently caressed his bare chest as the sound of a woman's heel echoed off his floor. He moaned, turning his head to the side. He wanted to know what his wife and aunt were doing but couldn't muster the strength to investigate. His foggy mind wondered what would happen if the First Lord of the Treasury was refused an audience with him due to his ailment. Sir Walpole controlled his finances. If he ever upset the older man he could run the risk of having less money awarded to him. He just couldn't think anymore.

"Shh, Isaac," Kathleen pleaded with him.

"Wake him up and have him drink this," Sophia said from beside them.

Isaac moaned and opened his eyes. He turned his head to the left and stared at the cup in his aunt's hand. "It'll help with the coughing," she said, handing the cup to Kathleen. Kathleen moved closer to her husband and leaned his back against her chest as she took the cup from his aunt. Isaac lifted his eyes to her as she placed the cup to his lips.

"Drink slowly," she whispered.

He lowered his eyes and complied. The warm liquid turned his stomach. He pushed her aside, leaned over the bed, and vomited. Sophia sighed. "Try not to drink so much all at once, Isaac. Small, slow sips. We have to keep something in your stomach or you'll die of starvation."

Isaac nodded and returned to his wife's chest. Kathleen wrapped her arm around his waist and held him tight as he sipped. "That's better," Sophia directed, walking around the bed to the window. She opened the dark curtains, allowing the sunlight to filter into his room. "Your doctor would say it is best for you to be in the dark and with the windows closed. My husband would tell you nonsense. You need the fresh air," she said, opening the window.

"Ugh, I wish your husband was here instead of in London," Isaac complained.

She turned to face him. "As do I but alas he is not and I am here. I will help you as much as I can until Tomas' physician arrives. Finish my tea then return to your slumber."

"Can't."

"You must."

Kathleen added, "I'll stay by your side."

"No," Isaac said, shaking his head.

"Dear husband, allow me to conduct myself in the manner a wife should when her husband is frail in health," Kathleen protested.

"You can aide me more in my transactions than be by my bedside."

"You would trust me with something I have no right to do."

"I told you, Kathleen. You are my wife. This estate and all that comes with it belong to you. I don't care if you haven't been granted your title yet. We're in Ireland, not England. We are one flesh and one mind. I speak for you and I am giving you permission to speak on my behalf while I suffer from this ailment." He groaned, turned to the side, and coughed into the chamber pot. How he wished this agony was over. Thankfully, Kathleen was here to grant him comfort. He could feel her hand gently rub his bare chest. Tears ran down his cheeks. He didn't want to die. Not like this. He heaved, grabbed her right hand, and pulled it against his chest. "Shh, I'm right here," she whispered in his ear. Isaac nodded and clutched her hand tighter as he vomited.

"Isaac, Sir Walpole won't listen to her. She's not recognized by the king, yet."

Isaac spit into the pot then said, "He will. Robert's a good man with a caring heart. He's done well in the service of the king but he has been falling out of favor with the king and other nobles due to the conflict between England and Spain over trade in the West Indies. He's desperate. Desperate men do desperate things," he said in Kathleen's direction.

"I'll have the cook make him some more broth," Sophia said, rising from the bed and walking to the door.

"Thank you," Kathleen answered.

"You're welcome. Take care of my nephew, Kathleen. I'll return to relieve you within the hour."

Kathleen nodded and returned her view to him as the door closed. "Ugh," Isaac moaned, rolling onto his stomach and releasing her hand. Kathleen straddled him and massaged his back. He cringed at her touch and groaned.

"It will help to break up the phlegm in your lungs," she whispered in his ear.

"Ugh, it hurts."

"Shh, close your eyes and think of something wonderful."

"Having sex with you while you bleed?"

Kathleen chuckled. "Well there's that."

"Are you still bleeding?"

Kathleen slapped him hard on the back. "Ouch," he cried.

"No and you are too frail to think about that. But it's good to see you still have your wits about you. Isaac?"

"Hmm," he answered, closing his eyes and coughing.

"I did everything you asked of me and yet our tenants have not spoken of any rebel movement."

"You can't trust our tenants."

"Oh?"

"They're Catholic and are loyal to the McGillpatricks." He chuckled, "One of them even tried to tell me how fortunate I am to be married to Kathleen McGillpatrick."

Kathleen paused.

"Kathleen?"

"I'm sorry. I thought I heard someone at the door. How preposterous of them to think I am her."

"I don't know. I've seen a portrait of Alexander, Jane, and their young daughters. You do sort of resemble her but who knows what the girl looks like now, and besides, you can't trust Catholics. They are horrible savages with a tendency towards thievery, deceit, and bloodshed."

"Where did you find the portrait?"

"It's in the Great Hall."

"How is it I've never seen it?"

"Hmm, you've never been in that side of the castle until you married me. My father moved the Great Hall to this side of Kilmore so he could entertain his visitors without anyone disturbing him. I was going to reveal it to you but...," he coughed.

"But there hasn't been the time to do so since our wedding night."

"Yes, it's one of my favorite rooms in the entire estate. When I became Earl of Kilmore I explored the estate, located as many artifacts as I could from the old part of the castle, and moved them to that room to honor the family who had built the estate."

"You honor the McGillpatricks when all your family wants to do is kill them?"

"Kathleen, the feud between the McGillpatricks and Turners began before I was born. I want an end to this conflict. There can be no peace in our lands if there is so much bloodshed. All those rebels do is cause chaos and bloodshed. You have to go forward with the execution today. I want Bailey to know I will not stand for his tactics against you, Tomas' household, or my own."

"I will, but if Bailey knows I am to execute his wife today I very much believe he will attack us."

"The soldiers are prepared to protect us at that time."

Kathleen nodded as she rubbed the sides of her husband's body. Isaac grabbed his pillows and arched his neck. "Ugh, get off me," he ordered, heaving.

Kathleen complied. He rolled to his side, vomited, and began to fall off the bed face forward. Kathleen grabbed him by the waist and pulled his back against her chest. "Shh, lean on my body, Isaac. I'll support you," she told him, wiping his mouth with a cloth. He leaned his head against her shoulder and closed his eyes.

"So cold," he shivered.

Kathleen put her hand on his forehead. "Your fever's rising. Lie down," she said, guiding him downward. Isaac clutched his stomach and cringed as she placed a soaking wet cloth on his forehead. He lifted his knee and arched the back of his head with a deep groan. She wiped his face, neck, and chest with another soaked cloth. "When Sir Walpole arrives, will your butler bring him to the Great Hall?"

"Hmm, yes. If he doesn't Sir Walpole will know something is wrong with me. I have to meet with him."

"You can't. What you have to do is rest so your body can heal. Now how do I get to the Great Hall from here?"

"Do you remember how to get to the hallway that separates my chambers from my mother's?"

"Yes."

"Good. The Great Hall lies between them. It is the largest room in the estate and was once the receiving area for the McGillpatricks. Father enlarged it but you would miss the room if you don't know what to look for. Walk out of the hallway and into the main parlor. Along the wall on your left will be a door that looks like a servant's entrance. Open that door and walk inside. That is the Great Hall."

"Your father never changed the private entrance?"

"No, my mother told me he had kept it so in order to evade any curious eyes should someone find their way to this side of the estate."

"And what of the quarters I asked you to procure for me? I need them for our whores."

"Ugh, the whores are still in the dungeon. I haven't had a chance to work on converting the wing I wanted you to use. Why do you ask?"

"I have a plan."

"Kathleen, you must be careful with Sir Walpole."

"He can be manipulated."

"No, he…"

"He's a man, Isaac. A mere mortal man and I'm Lady Turner. Your grandmother told me once that the Lady Turner can seduce any man to do her husband's bidding. Is that true?" Isaac opened his eyes and lifted them to hers. "Rest and everything will be alright between us and King George. I'll guarantee it with my life."

"I love you, Kathleen," he muttered then fell still with his eyes closed.

"Isaac," she yelled, tapping his cheek. Yet he never moved. "No, Isaac." She grabbed his face and leaned her ear close to his nose. Kathleen breathed a sigh of relief. He was still breathing. It was slow and shallow but he was breathing. He had only fallen asleep due to the fever. "Thank God," she whispered, laying her forehead on his. "Don't you dare die on me, Lord Isaac Turner," she ordered, kissed him on the lips, then swiped her hands down his chest as she rose.

The door opened. Kathleen stood beside the bed and looked toward the door. Sophia entered the room with a bowl of broth and set it on the dresser beside the bed. "Is he...?" she asked.

"No, he's asleep. I must change," Kathleen said, walking to her large armoire on the right hand side of the room as Sophia sat on the side of the bed. Kathleen removed her gown and pulled out her favorite yellow gown. They talked as she dressed. "Have you been to the Great Hall?"

"Never, why do you ask?"

"My husband claims he has McGillpatrick artifacts in there, even a portrait of the entire family when the daughters were children."

Sophia turned sharply towards her with a grave look on her face. Kathleen placed her finger to her lips then lowered it. "Isaac told me he entertains his visitors in that room and then fell into a deep sleep. I tried to call to him for more information when he fell unconscious. I think he can hear us. He may be ill but he has his moments when he is very conscious of what goes on around him."

"He's fighting for his life, Kathleen."

"Yes," she said glancing up at her husband. She then walked over to Sophia. She whispered in her aunt's ear, "So am I." Kathleen leaned away from her with a knowing look on her face. Isaac's aunt nodded with understanding. "I have matters of estate to attend to in my husband's absence. Will you be so kind as to care for him while I am away?"

"Of course. Do what you must, dear niece."

Kathleen walked around the bed and then stood at the door. She turned to the room. "Sophia?"

"Yes."

"Isaac said one of the tenants claimed I was Kathleen McGillpatrick. Would you know which tenant that was?"

"Oh there's an Irish family on the south side close to the barn that has been causing him much commotion. I believe Isaac took their eldest daughter."

"Blonde with blue eyes?"

"Yes, that's her. Why do you ask?"

"No reason. Thank you."

"You're welcome. Be careful, Kathleen. Don't place yourself in a position where neither I nor my mother can help you."

"I quite assure you that won't be a problem," Kathleen said then walked out of the room with a new plan brewing in the back of her mind. A plan that would eliminate not only Bailey but also anyone else who stood in her way.

Chapter 39

Kathleen ran quickly down the hallway that separated Isaac's chambers from his mother's. She swallowed hard, sensing her ghost all around her. She hated the feeling of dread that always followed the late countess. The closer she drew to the late countess' quarters the darker the energy became. She reached for her Saint Anne's medallion only to realize that she had hidden her rosary and medallion. Her heart sank. Saint Anne had always protected her from the spirits ever since she had become sensitive to them after smallpox had claimed her life. Her parents told her she had died in the middle of the night. They prayed for a miracle while she was dying. After she died her father had dug her grave, placed her body in the ground, and when he threw the first shovel full of dirt on her body she had returned to life, crying for him. The only explanation the priest gave them was that God had heard the prayers of his faithful servants.

Kathleen pivoted and faced the gloom that followed her. "In the name of Jesus Christ I command you to…," she paused at seeing the dark being replaced by the images of Sherlock and her father. Tears cascaded down her cheeks as she fell to her knees before them. Her father knelt before her. She heaved, trying to touch his face, but felt only air.

"I'm so sorry. I'm so sorry. It was my fault. Everything," she sobbed.

Alexander looked to Sherlock then back to her. "No, Kathleen. I saw the truth of everything too late. I knew I was going to die and offered my life so that Bailey, Jane, and Mary would live."

"We know of your plans, Kathleen," Sherlock said.

Kathleen swallowed hard and looked up at her brother. "I...I don't think I can go through with it. I've done things I shouldn't have ever done, but to take a life..."

"You can't make the mistake father and I did. We lived in fear of Bailey and he grew more powerful because of it. I once thought to shield you from Bailey but I was wrong. My efforts to protect you from him placed Mary and my unborn child in even greater danger."

"Mary told me you wanted to bring me with you to New Orleans."

"Yes, but I should have taken Mary to New Orleans when I first conceived the idea to do so instead of protecting you. Perhaps had I done so I wouldn't have abandoned my wife and child with my passing. I cannot change the path I chose, nor can I rest when I know Mary's life is in danger. You must defeat my brother and give Mary the documents I died with."

"I cannot leave my husband."

"You mean you won't leave his side," Alexander added. She turned to face her father. "I know you still love him."

"I try so hard not to. He's a monster and I've done things with him that I..." She swallowed hard and buried her head in her lap. Kathleen cried, thinking of all the atrocities she had committed against God and the things she had yet to do that went against her faith. A cold draft traveled up her spine with the gentle sensation of her father's touch on her back. He sat beside her and leaned close to her ear.

"Kathleen, I know the feelings you face. Sherlock and I have been there so many times when we have had to confront our sins. There is absolution if you seek to confess your sins to a priest."

"How can I, father? I'm Anglican."

Sherlock huffed, "You're as much of an Anglican as I'm a horse." Kathleen lifted her face as Sherlock knelt before her. "We all have had to do things we never wanted to do before."

"You don't understand, Sherlock. I've done things that are unforgivable."

"Nothing is unforgivable unless you have blasphemed against God. Have you?"

"No, never. But I...I...," she swallowed hard. "Sherlock, remember the voices you and Bailey heard when my husband held you captive?"

"Yes."

"Those were unnatural, were they not?"

"Most unnatural."

Kathleen shook her head and bit her lower lip. She rose, declaring, "I have to go." Kathleen turned and walked a few paces towards the parlor. Alexander and Sherlock suddenly appeared before her with their arms crossed over their chests. Startled, she stepped back.

"What did you do?" Alexander demanded.

"Nothing," she lied, trying to evade them. It didn't matter which way she turned, Alexander and Sherlock were right there, boring their gazes into her eyes. She exhaled a deep breath. "Alright, alright! Isaac collects young Irish women and then prostitutes them out for profit. The noise you heard in the dungeon was one of his planned orgies. He has them quite frequently so he can turn a greater profit from them. I stumbled upon one of his gatherings and participated."

Alexander bellowed, "You what!" The energy threw her backwards. She landed hard on her right side, cried out, and clutched her knee. Sherlock stepped in front of his father.

"Perhaps she had no choice in the matter," he countered.

"The only man who is to touch her is her husband," Alexander growled, pushing Sherlock aside. He stood over his daughter.

Kathleen gazed up at her father with tears in her eyes. "He's right. I have no choice in how I conduct myself in this house. Father if you knew what it meant to be his wife you would have never allowed Tomas to consent to this marriage. It is a most dishonorable, deplorable thing to be his wife! On the outside I am a nobleman's wife, Countess of Kilmore. But in the English courts I am just a pawn the king uses for his own pleasure."

"What do you think being a noble is, Kathleen? The nobles serve the king. They are entrusted with his land and money so they may govern over the peasants in his absence."

"No, father, it is much more than that and I am…I am…"

"Countess," the butler's voice lifted from down the hallway. Kathleen turned her gaze to the end of the hall. Bailey's priest ran to her side with a medical bag as the butler followed behind him. She turned to face where her father and Sherlock had stood. They had disappeared.

"Let me help you," the priest said.

Kathleen shook her head. "No, my husband is very ill. He requires your attention more than I," she said, trying to stand then fell into the butler's arms. "Thank you," she said to the butler as she gathered her strength and stood up.

"Are you certain you are well enough to walk on your own, Countess Turner?" the butler asked as the priest stood.

"The countess has always been quite clumsy. Her sister asked me to give her this," the priest said, pulling out a dark brown bottle and handing it to Kathleen. Kathleen took it from him with a suspicious look in her eyes. "Your pain medicine, should you require it in your current disposition."

"Of course," she grinned, catching on to his meaning. She turned to the butler and ordered, "Take him to my husband."

The butler bowed then walked behind the priest. The priest placed his hand on her forearm and handed her a small rolled-up note. "Burn this after you have read it. Bailey sends you word," he whispered, turned, and then followed the butler, who had already walked to the end of the hall.

Kathleen turned, walked to the end of the hallway, and opened the door to the parlor. She leaned against the door, opened the rolled up note, and began to read.

"Who is that from?" Sherlock's voice entered the room. She exhaled a long breath and stared into the room.

Alexander and Sherlock stood before her. "Are you two ever going to leave me alone?" she asked.

Father and son looked at each other and then glared at her, saying in unison, "Not until our wives are safe from Bailey."

Kathleen rolled her eyes, turned to the left, walked to a red couch, and sat down. "I will save them. I promise. But the manner in which I do so may not be fitting for my father and eldest brother to watch." She read the note. "Perfect. Bailey, Calico, and Tomas are doing what I want from them."

Alexander huffed. "Tell me your plan and then we will discuss your course of action."

"Father, please. I do not have time to sit here and tell you of my plans. I have matters to attend to. Now if you will excuse me. I have something to do," she said, placing the vial and note into her bodice. She rose from the couch and tried to pass them.

Alexander shook his head. "I may be dead, Kathleen, but I'm not stupid. You may think Bailey is doing whatever you plotted for him to do, but he's smarter than you."

Kathleen couldn't believe her father would insult her like that. She opened her mouth to speak but the words never left her lips.

"Don't take it like that," Sherlock defended Alexander.

She turned to face him, clenching her jaw.

"Bailey is much older than you and has more experience in these matters. You are only nineteen, Kathleen. You can't outwit wisdom. Tell us your plans and we'll help you. Just like the old days."

"Alright, my plan is to restore order to the rebellion. That's it. Nothing more," she declared then walked to the other side of the room.

Alexander and Sherlock appeared before her, barring her from entrance into the Great Hall. "The rebels follow Bailey because he is loyal to our people and their ways. What makes you think when he's gone they won't turn to Tomas?" Sherlock asked.

"Because his brothers are moving against him. They blame him for their father's death."

"Alright," Alexander answered. "Say it is so, then how will you gain their support if you are married to the man who desires their destruction?"

"I'll seduce the king after he grants me my title and honors. Then I'll convince him to demolish the penal codes and free our people."

Alexander and Sherlock laughed heartily at her suggestion. "That will never work," Alexander said. He and Sherlock disappeared at the sound of someone entering the room.

Kathleen turned towards the sound. A tall, heavyset man with a long white wig and dressed in the finest of clothes stood beside one of the servants. She swallowed hard, recalling all the proper protocol lessons she had learned from Calico. Kathleen watched the servant bow in her direction.

"Countess Kathleen Turner, may I introduce you to the Right Honorable Sir Robert Walpole, Knight of the Garter, Privy Counsellor, Order of the Bath, Knight Companion. He has requested an audience with Earl Turner."

"My husband is too ill to receive visitors at this time."

"Yes, ma'am. I have informed him of such but he stated you would grant his request after you viewed this letter," the servant said as he handed Kathleen a royal order. She took the three-page, sealed papers and kept her eyes on the regal-looking man beside the servant. Walpole slightly nodded his head with a grin. There was something about this man she couldn't quite trust.

Kathleen opened the letter and read the contents. Her heart sank at the words. Isaac had claimed Walpole was losing favor with the king but by what she read she couldn't verify that claim. She lowered the papers and looked at her unwelcomed visitor. "Sir," she called to him as she folded the letter. "Do you agree with the king's findings against my sister and me?"

"Lady Kathleen, I am only a messenger," Walpole answered.

"That is Countess to you, sir."

Sir Walpole stepped in her direction with his keen eyes on her. Her hands slightly trembled at this powerful man. He had so many titles she knew he had to be the most important man she had ever met. But what was he doing at Kilmore? Why would the king send him here instead of a lessor noble?

"Lady Tuner, if you are even that," he demanded her attention.

She gasped, clutching the papers. How much she wanted to strike this man for insulting her. "I am the wife of Earl Isaac Turner and you will treat me as such, sir!"

"You are not the Countess of Kilmore, yet. The king believes you are a simple commoner without any titles. I am being kind in calling you a Lady, Lady Kathleen. Do not make the mistake in thinking I will always be so kind to you. Earl Turner is the property of the king and what he does with his life is a matter of state affairs. The king will not allow you to meddle in his affairs. Now, Lady Kathleen, where is your husband?"

"I'm afraid he is quite ill. His physician has declared no one is allowed in our bedchambers."

"I require proof of life. You will take me to him."

Kathleen turned to the servant then back to the Earl.

"Now, Lady Turner. Or shall I inform the king of his untimely death?" he declared, opening an ancient, large book he held under his arm. Kathleen peered at the Turner Family Crest on the cover. He pulled a feather pen from his pocket, walked to a desk, put the book down, and began to ink the feather. Kathleen couldn't think. Bailey was close to the estate and claimed in his letter he would attack Kilmore within the hour. She had to do something to stop this man from declaring her husband dead. She couldn't lose Kilmore to the crown. Wasn't she trying to preserve it by handing it back to her people?

"Wait," she declared, running to the front of the desk. She traced her fingers on the book as she walked around the desk seductively. Kathleen kissed the man's earlobe. He swallowed hard and lifted his head as her hand found its way to his crotch.

"Your husband, Lady Turner," he ordered, fighting the urge to be with her.

If she could just keep him busy enough for Calico to lead Bailey into the dungeon. Kathleen moved her hand into his pants. He grabbed her wrist and turned his head towards her. "Where is your husband?"

"I told you, he's very ill and cannot be disturbed."

"You will take me to him."

"Wouldn't you like a taste of what he has?" she whispered in his ear.

"It is against the law for me to bed you. The contract clearly states no Turner woman may have sexual relationship with the king, princes, members of the privy council, or whomever the king appoints over finances in order to protect the monarchy. Now you will remove yourself from me and take me to your husband!"

Kathleen grunted and stepped away from the man. "Very well, follow me," she snarled, walking to the door. She opened the hallway door at the sound of the righteous man behind her. How was she ever going to make her way to the dungeon if she was busy entertaining her husband's unwelcomed guest? She reluctantly made her way down the long hall to her husband's parlor and opened the door. "Stay here and I will let him know you want an audience."

"No, I will join you," he ordered, closing the door behind him.

"Sir, this is my home, not yours," Kathleen bellowed disrespectfully.

"On the contrary, the king owns the entire estate, belongings, and your family. I am here to take account of everything. Now you will take me to your husband or I shall send word to the king of your refusal. If he does not find you loyal he will have no choice but to dissolve this marriage and imprison you as a rebel."

"I'm not an Irish rebel."

"That has yet to be determined, Lady Turner. Take me to your husband. I shall not ask again."

Kathleen hissed between her teeth and turned towards her bedchambers. This man was becoming more annoying every moment she was with him. She opened the door to her bedchamber and stared at her husband while the king's messenger stepped into the room. Isaac fidgeted as Bailey's priest applied wet clothes to his forehead. "Earl Turner, you must remain still." He turned to the servant who was pouring water in a wooden bathtub. "Fill it faster," he ordered loudly then turned back to Sophia, who sat on the other side of the bed. Isaac groaned, rolled to his side, and vomited in the chamber pot his aunt held.

Sir Walpole stared at Isaac then turned his gaze upon Kathleen. "What did you poison him with?" he asked.

"Nothing. He has pneumonia," she countered, exchanging places with Sophia and handing her the royal order.

Sophia turned in her direction then curtseyed before the English premier. "Sir Walpole," she said, rising from her curtsey.

He nodded silently at her, lowered the book and feather pen to a desk, and walked to the side of the bed. He lifted his gaze to the priest who was pretending to be a doctor. "Do you, physician, conclude it is pneumonia or has he been poisoned?"

"It is pneumonia, sir."

"You are not the physician the king assigned to him. Where have you come from?"

"I am Earl Tomas Collins' physician, sir."

"Is he not bedbound with severe wounds?"

"He is."

"And yet why are you here and not by his side?"

"Countess Kath…"

"That's Lady not Countess."

The priest looked to Kathleen then back to his interrogator. "I attended Lady Kathleen and her sister while she remained at Collins Great House. She asked that I would attend to her husband while his physician travelled to London."

"Kathleen," Isaac muttered in a delirious state.

Kathleen grabbed his hand and touched the side of his cheek. "I'm here, Isaac."

He groaned and turned to face her.

"It is ready, sir," the servant announced from beside the filled bath with an empty bucket in his hand.

"Good," the priest said, pulling down Isaac's covers. He carried his naked patient to the bath and gently put him in the cold water. Isaac grasped the side of the bath, leaned his head back, and inhaled a deep breath as he opened his eyes. He fidgeted, coughing.

"Stay in the water," Kathleen urged, running to his side and kneeling beside him. She took his hand as he turned his head, took the servant's bucket, and vomited.

"Don't hold anything back, Earl Turner. The foulness in your body must be removed," the priest directed.

Isaac wiped his mouth, lowered the bucket, and descended into the water. He arched his head back and stared at the figure behind his wife. "Sir Walpole," he exclaimed, rising from the water.

"No," Kathleen, Sophia, and the priest yelled.

Isaac turned to his wife. "Your fever's too high. Lower yourself back into the water."

"Too cold," he retorted.

"Isaac, you feel cold but you are not. Do what we require of you," Sophia directed while reading the royal order.

Isaac glared at his aunt, complied with her direction, and gazed at Sir Walpole. "Sir Walpole, what brings you to Kilmore?" he acknowledged his superior.

"His majesty requires verification of your bonding with a loyal woman," Walpole proclaimed.

"I provided that. My physician is on his way to London to give testimony to His Majesty of my bedding ceremony."

"Ah, yes, well that is not all that he requires from you. After your wife conducted herself so rudely to me and lest I forget tried to seduce me, I can see why His Majesty would have some concerns regarding your union."

Isaac turned his face to Kathleen with a look of horror. "I warned you!"

"Isaac, don't be upset with me, please."

He grabbed her by the bodice and pulled her towards him. Isaac stared at the vial and the note between her large breasts. He reached into her bodice with his other hand. Kathleen tried to pull away from his grip yet the more she fought him the more he tugged her. "No, don't," she cried as he pulled her into the bathtub. Water splashed everywhere.

"Isaac?" Sophia asked, stepping towards them.

"Give it to me," Isaac snarled, pulling Kathleen closer.

"No," she said as his hand dug deeper into her bodice. She cried as he pulled the vial and the note out from between her breasts. "Don't. Just don't," she pleaded, reaching for the note. He turned his back on her and pushed her away with his shoulder as he learned over the bathtub and tried to read the note. "Isaac, please," she cried.

Isaac squinted his eyes, desperate to read the note, but his fever was making it hard to do so. It had taken every bit of his strength to fight with his wife. He glared up at his aunt. The blurry form of a three-page letter with a ribbon on the back caught his attention. "What is that?" he asked.

Sophia turned her eyes on Walpole then to her nephew with a dire look upon her face. "It seems word of your mother's murder has reached his majesty."

"How, is that possible?" he snarled to Walpole.

Sophia continued. "He believes you murdered your mother and concocted a story to hide the truth. He also claims that you have conspired against the crown with the help of your wife," she gasped, lowered the paper, and glared at Walpole. "That is ridiculous! He has done nothing but faithfully serve the king for years."

"His mother was murdered and he has yet to bring the murderer to justice."

"I'm still investigating," Isaac yelled. He heaved then looked at Sophia, unable to breath.

"Kathleen," she ordered.

Kathleen reached across the bath, grabbed her husband, and pulled him against her chest. She lowered their bodies further into the tub. Fresh air entered his lungs. He struggled against the fever and tightness of his chest. "Shh, shh, Isaac," she coaxed, pouring water on his head with her hand. Isaac closed his eyes for a long moment, relaxing under her gentle touch.

"You have taken too long with your investigation, Lord Turner. His majesty demands you hand over the person responsible or admit that you had done the deed yourself," Sir Walpole demanded, stepping closer to the bath.

"Don't you have any sympathy?" Kathleen snarled.

"I do, Lady Kathleen, but in this case I cannot afford him any."

"He's the king's messenger," Isaac pushed out of his mouth. "Am I being summoned?"

"That is up to you. Who murdered your mother?"

Isaac shivered and shook his head. "Don't know."

"Didn't the murder happen before you married Lady Kathleen?"

Isaac nodded.

"Your personal matters do not take preference over matters of state. You should have delayed the wedding until you had arrested the murderer."

"I arrested someone I suspected to have murdered my mother."

"Who?"

"Mary McGillpatrick."

"And where is she?"

"In my dungeon awaiting her execution. She's to hang today. My wife is to carry out the order."

"I see. You do understand that you have no right to execute someone for the murder of a noble without the express permission of the king."

"Yes, sir. But I thought in this case it would be warranted."

"If you felt that way, why didn't..." he paused as Isaac fell unconscious. The letter and vial dropped to the floor beside Sir Walpole.

Kathleen tapped Isaac on the cheek. "Isaac," she called to him. Isaac moaned. "Isaac, wake up." Still he did not move. Kathleen turned to the priest. "He's not responding."

"Shock," Sophia and the priest said together.

"Get him out of there," Sophia ordered. The priest ran to the bath and helped Kathleen lift Isaac to the bed. Sophia pushed Walpole aside, gathered the blankets on the floor, and placed them on the bed. Kathleen, the priest, and Sophia worked together to revive him. Isaac gasped, rolled over, and vomited into a chamber pot his wife held.

"Kathleen McGillpatrick, is this the poison you used on your husband?" Kathleen and Isaac stared into each others eyes at the sound of Walpole's question. Her heart beat fast. She couldn't tell if Isaac believed the man's accusation or not. Isaac was a skilled interrogator. He wouldn't reveal his true feelings nor let them get in the way of finding out the truth. But would he be so willing to share his life with her if he learned the truth? Hadn't this been the man who said he wanted to end the feud between her family and his?

"I am not her nor have I poisoned you," she whispered to her husband. He swallowed hard and rolled onto his back. "Isaac," she said, tapping his cheek. "You believe me, don't you?"

He turned his head and kissed the palm of her hand. "You owe him an answer," he said with a serious look.

"My name is Lady Kathleen Turner. Wife of Earl Isaac Turner, who has and always will entrust his heart to me alone! I will and have never betrayed him. My husband has pneumonia. The vial you have in your possession is my pain medicine given to me by my physician, who is attending to my husband."

Isaac smiled at her. God, he loved how strong and independent she was. He hadn't met any woman with that fiery spirit, caring nature, and genuine wisdom. He wanted to protect her from the crown but in his capacity he didn't know how long he would be able to remain conscious enough to defend her.

"The letter claims you are Bailey's sister. Explain this," Sir Walpole said.

"My father...," Kathleen started. She glanced up at Sophia.

"Her parents are dead and the woman in the cell is his wife. Kathleen and her servant were once very close. Bailey may believe she is his ally when in reality she is his enemy. You know these Irish. They're all related in one way or another," Sophia answered.

"And are you an ally, Lady Kathleen?" Walpole asked.

"I'm Irish but I am no ally of any rebellion," she answered defiantly.

"Robert," Isaac muttered, motioning for the interrogator to approach his bedside. Kathleen moved to the side, covered her husband's legs with a blanket, then watched as the men conversed. Walpole sat in a chair next to the bed and took his friend's hand. "I...," Isaac began then lifted his head with a low moan as the priest placed a wet cloth on his head. Walpole lifted his eyes to the man.

"His fever lowered so suddenly while he was immersed that it threw his body into shock. It would have done his body well to remain in the water for sometime but it cannot endure the treatment. His fever has begun to rise yet again. He is very weak, Sir Walpole, and requires much rest."

"Very well, rest he will have," Walpole said, rising from the bed. "We will continue the interrogation in London. Guards," he yelled towards the door.

"Sir Walpole, please," Sophia pleaded as a unit of ten soldiers burst into the room. "He's too weak to be moved. I beg of you have mercy upon him."

"There is no mercy for Lord Turner."

Chapter 40

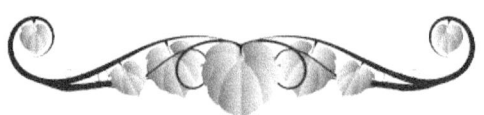

November 19, 1738

Kathleen paced inside her large chamber within the tower where nobles were detained by the king. She had feared the king would demand she be placed in isolation at the bottom of the prison where the peasants lived in deplorable conditions, chained to a wall. Her father had been an Irish nobleman turned rebel leader in the eyes of the English. When he was deposed from his estate and position at Parliament, the king had taken not only his wealth but his title and honors as well. She was a peasant but the king had shown mercy to her due to her marriage to Isaac and ordered that she be placed with her husband in the top of the tower.

"Kathleen," Isaac called to her from their bed.

She turned to face her husband. Isaac sat upright in the bed as the king's physician listened to his heart. She glanced at Sir Robert Walpole as he stood beside their bed then turned back to her husband. "What's wrong?" he asked.

Kathleen shook her head as the parliament leader turned his gaze upon her. "You've been sick for a month and we almost lost you on our journey to London. I'm worried."

"Don't…," he coughed several times.

"Doctor?" Walpole asked the rising physician.

"He is on the mend but it would not be wise for him to leave his bed. I have left some medicine for his wife to give him to ease the coughing. If his fever should return, send for me."

"He has not had a fever in a week and he is more coherent than when we first arrived," Kathleen protested.

"I understand, Lady Kathleen, yet until he has fully recuperated he is in danger of a relapse." He turned back to Walpole. "I will inform His Majesty of Earl Turner's condition."

"There is no need to do so," Walpole countered.

"His Majesty has charged me with the Earl's health and desires daily updates on his condition. I will inform the king of my findings and return tomorrow for the Earl's daily examination as I have done for almost a month."

"Good day, Doctor," Earl Walpole dismissed the lanky, older gentleman, annoyed that the man had countered him.

The physician bowed, gathered his belongings, and left the room.

Kathleen sat on the side of the bed, took Isaac's hand, and looked up at the overweight English Earl. He scoffed at them, turned on his heel, and headed to the door. "Why are you doing this, Robert?" Isaac asked to his back.

Walpole paused with his hand on the doorknob.

"You're a good man, Rob, and we've been friends for a long time."

Walpole turned to face him with a long face. "Things have changed at court."

"The king has never liked me and it's not like you to play into his hands. "You've always defended my family."

"Your family is an asset to the crown that cannot be tainted. Good day, Lord Turner and Lady Turner," Walpole said, before he opened the door and left the room. He stepped back as guards shoved Calico and Tomas inside then exited the door behind them.

"Tom," Isaac called to his friend.

Tomas glanced at his friend as the sisters embraced. "You want to tell me what the hell I'm doing here?" he demanded, storming to his friend's side.

"What happened?" Isaac asked then coughed.

"As if you don't know," Tomas challenged. He put his knee on the bed and grabbed Isaac by the collar of his shirt. "I have been your friend for years and you have my estate confiscated?"

"He didn't do it. Kilmore has been confiscated as well," Kathleen challenged, walking to the other side of the bed. Tomas glanced at her then back to his friend. "His sister sent word to the king their mother had been murdered and that he had married one of the daughters of Alexander McGillpatrick. Sarah told him Calico was my sister and that we had duped Isaac into believing all our lies so that he would do Bailey's will."

"Dear God," Tomas gasped, lowering his hand.

"We're under investigation for treason," Kathleen stated.

"All of us?" Tomas asked.

"No, I'm the victim." Isaac answered. "If I am found to be a liability the king will eliminate not only me but our entire family as well. My dear sweet sister had no idea she had placed her fate in the king's hand when she sent the letter to him."

"Where is Sarah?"

"In another cell with my Aunt Sophia, her family, and our grandmother. How could you, Tom?!"

Tomas lifted his hands and stepped back. "I tried to convince you not to have interest in Kathleen. Remember?"

"You should have told me the truth!" Isaac coughed uncontrollably, clinging to Kathleen's hand as she rubbed his back.

"Doesn't look like you're too upset with her," Tomas stated.

Isaac swallowed then glanced over at his friend. "She's innocent. Kathleen told me everything a few nights ago, including her distrust of you and her sister."

"Which sister?" Calico asked.

Isaac turned in her direction, "Which sister?"

"Mary is our sister, too."

"By marriage."

"By blood. We have the same mother, different fathers. Which sister did Kathleen have a trust issue with?"

"You," Kathleen yelled, pointing to Calico from beside the table.

"Wait, Mary's your sister and Bailey's your brother. But aren't they married?" Isaac asked in a confused state.

Kathleen turned to him. "She married Sherlock and her sister, Anne, married Bailey before our father married their mother. After Sherlock died Bailey made her his wife but she doesn't love him."

"But she's with child."

"The child belongs to Sherlock. I wasn't too honest with you in his demise. He had recuperated long enough for them to bond several times and then he died." She turned back to Calico. "You are so blinded by your need to please Bailey that you're blinded to the truth, Calico! Now we're going to die all because of your need to be the perfect sister."

"Die?"

"Treason is a death sentence," Isaac finished then coughed.

"But after they had Bailey's priest heal Tomas they brought us here when all his wounds had healed. Why would they do that?" Calico asked, walking to the footboard.

Isaac chuckled, periodically coughing, "They won't execute anyone who isn't in perfect health. Our trial has been delayed until I have fully recuperated from the pneumonia."

"Ours has not. We are to appear before the king in two days," Tomas said. He sat on a wooden chair and stared at Kathleen.

"Bailey?" she asked him.

Tomas shook his head. "The dungeon was empty by the time he led the rebels there. He knows the situation and is plotting for our release. Mary?" he asked her.

"In the lower parts of the dungeon as far as I know. They refuse to answer my questions as to her status."

Tomas groaned, lowering his head to his lap. "This is all Bailey's fault."

Calico huffed, grabbing the footboard and pointing to Isaac. "No, this is his fault. His family started this war."

"Bailey murdered our fathers," Tomas countered, rising from the chair.

"He what?" Isaac asked, turning his gaze to his wife.

"That's a lie, Tomas. He would never take our fathers' lives. I don't know...," Calico argued.

Tomas grabbed his wife by her arms and snarled in her face, "Stop it. You would believe the sky is green if he told you so. You're being naïve and stupid! Bailey has us right where he wants us. As long as no one is at Kilmore and Collins, he can lead the rebels and take both estates under his control! Don't you see, Calico? This game of chess was never played by Isaac. No, quite the contrary, we are still pawns being moved around the board by your brother!"

"I murdered both your fathers, not Bailey," Isaac interrupted.

Tomas lowered his grip, turned sharply to Kathleen, and clutched the footboard. "You told me your brother killed them!"

"I didn't want you to act against my husband and me."

"Act....huh...," he pushed the footboard and walked swiftly in her direction. "You have some nerve, Kathleen McGillpatrick Turner!"

"How could I trust you? You and Calico have always sided with Bailey. He's your best friend. That's why you don't see the monster Bailey truly is."

"I told you I am not loyal to Bailey! She...," he pointed to Calico, "on the other hand is so stupid she'd believe anything Bailey told her."

"I'm not stupid," Calico cried. "None of this would have been a problem in our lives had Isaac not—"

"Oh, no. Don't you start blaming this on me," Isaac defended then coughed uncontrollably.

Kathleen sat on the side of the bed and leaned him on her chest. "Tom, there's a vial on the side of the bed."

Tomas huffed, lowered his arm, and passed the medicine to Kathleen. Kathleen gently placed the vial under her husband's lips. "Sip," she coaxed him between coughs. Isaac complied then almost spilled the contents of his mouth with a deep cough. She wiped the medicine onto his lips. Isaac sucked the medicine back into his mouth with his head back. He closed his eyes.

"Ugh, my head hurts."

"I can't believe you love him," Calico huffed with her arms crossed.

Kathleen lifted her eyes to her sister. "He's not as evil as you think he is."

"You only say that because you love him, Kat. Tomas told me what you said in his bedchamber while I was in Dublin. How could you do such horrible things?"

"I did what needed to be done in order to survive."

"No, you did what needed to be done to make him believe you weren't Kathleen McGillpatrick so he would return your affections."

Isaac huffed, opening his eyes. "She never had to prove anything to win my affection." He turned his gaze to Tomas. "I am sorry I killed your father, Tomas. He betrayed you."

Tomas snarled, "I could have controlled him!"

"Your brothers sided with Bailey because of your conversion and yet if you claim you could control your father then I can only deduce your conversion was a façade."

Tomas stood still and swallowed hard. He lifted his eyes to the door then turned them to his wife. Calico shook her head. "I see," Isaac said. Tomas turned back to his friend. "And was our friendship a lie?"

"Never, Isaac," Tomas admitted as he sat on the side of the bed. "I will always be your friend just as I will always be...," he pulled out his rosary from inside his vest pocket and placed it in Isaac's hand.

"Catholic...," Isaac finished.

Tomas took the rosary and hid it back in his vest. "I have led the rebellion alongside Bailey and Sherlock for years. We were best friends in childhood and as adults. I've hidden a priest in my home, allowed him to conduct mass there, and have educated my Catholic tenants. It never mattered how much I gave to my people, my brothers have always sided against me and have secretly been working to eliminate me so the rebellion could claim the estate through my wife."

Isaac lifted his eyes to Calico. "Did you know about his brothers?"

"No. I didn't know Tomas was plotting against Bailey with Kathleen, either," she snarled in her husband's direction.

Tomas waved his hand in her direction with his eyes firmly fixated on his friend. "I love her, Isaac, just as much as you love her sister. We're kin, now. Brothers, and we have a common enemy. An enemy that will—"

Isaac turned sharply to Tomas, "Who killed my mother?"

Tomas lowered his hand with a drawn out sigh. "Mary McGillpatrick."

"You would testify to that?"

"You tortured me for that information and I told you the same answer."

"I didn't know back then what I know now, Tomas. How many times have you betrayed me?"

"Isaac," Tomas snarled, leaning closer to him. "We are not in a situation where we should be fighting amongst ourselves."

"The vial I found on Kathleen?"

"What vial?"

"Don't play me for a fool, Tomas! I can protect my wife but I don't have to protect you or her sister."

"Kathleen came to me with a plan. I don't know what it was only that she told me to send a message to Bailey and ask his priest to aide her."

"Priest?"

"The physician is a priest and Bailey's grandfather," Calico answered.

Isaac turned to Kathleen. "Did you know?"

"I didn't know who he was until after you beat Tomas. No one knows his true identity, not even Bailey. He was a physician before he became a priest."

"And what was your plan?"

Kathleen gently stroked the side of his face. "It doesn't matter now. It—"

He grabbed her wrist and looked sternly into her eyes. "What was your plan?" he snarled.

"I was going to give Mary a sleeping potion so she would appear dead before I hung her. I would claim she took her own life. The label on the bottle was of a toxin known to kill within seconds, but—"

"The physician changed the contents," Calico said. Isaac turned to his friend's wife, still holding Kathleen's wrist. "When Bailey learned of her plan he ordered his priest not to change the contents. Bailey didn't care about Mary. He had ordered me to persuade you to eliminate his problem. So when he learned of Kathleen's plan and that Mary was still alive he decided he was going to storm the estate to make it seem to Kathleen that he was going to rescue Mary, but he intended to kill both of them."

"What?" Kathleen gasped.

"The vial you were given was intended to stop Mary's heart."

"How dare he! I thought the priest was on our side."

"Ha! And Tomas calls me the naïve one? That priest is loyal to Bailey because he's his grandson! We don't matter in the equation, Kathleen, because we are Jane's daughters not Kathleen's!"

"I told the priest the plan, not Bailey. Bailey was never supposed to know the truth. Bailey—"

"—played you for a fool," Isaac calmly stated, lowering his hand. "Mary too. She killed my mother and then used her charms to make you think she didn't do so. But what doesn't make sense is why Bailey would want to kill the woman he loves unless Mary…"

"Bailey manipulated her in the same manner she had done to my sister and me. I am truly sorry that she killed your mother, Isaac," Calico interjected quickly.

"Humpf," Kathleen huffed with a deep glare at her sister. How had Calico learned to lie so well that anyone would want to believe her? She wondered if Isaac was foolish enough to believe her sister's lies. Certainly a man who tortured others knew when someone was lying or not.

"Isaac," Tomas said from beside the small I-shaped window. All eyes turned in his direction. He nodded to the window, "We can argue about what occurred all we want to but it's not going to save our lives. I can hear them build the scaffold, can't you? Seems to me, Sir Walpole doesn't think the king will side with Calico and me. I don't want my wife and me to hang. And if we are found guilty what makes you think that won't add to the case against you with the king? Your best friend and your wife's sister, traitors to the crown?"

"You have a point," Isaac snarled. "But I will not forget that you betrayed me, Tomas."

"Betrayed you," Tomas huffed. He walked to the bed. "How the hell did I betray you? I never acted against you."

"How did Bailey and Sherlock escape? You knew where I was keeping them."

Tomas nodded, "I told Alexander where his sons were being kept and helped him rescue them. I told them when you were leaving for London and helped them plan the rescue."

"You knew I would find Kathleen attractive and placed her at the lake so I would happen upon her?"

"Oh, no. That was a mistake. I didn't know Kathleen had left the estate that day. I only learned she was missing because Calico was looking for her."

Isaac turned to Calico. "Is this true?"

"Yes. My sister and I have always been close. I knew she was upset about what you had done to our brothers and when she's upset she likes to be alone. I thought she had wandered to talk to the priest Tomas had been hiding. Kathleen is a very devout Catholic. Her spiritual life is important to her. When I couldn't find her with the priest I could only think of one other place she could be—"

"The lake?"

"She loves the water."

Isaac turned to face his wife. "I would have killed you for what you did to Bailey and Sherlock had Tomas not interceded," Kathleen admitted.

"So you went to the lake to set up a trap for me? You knew I liked young women?"

"I went to the lake to clean my clothes and relax. I never thought I'd see let alone meet you," Kathleen explained. "When Bailey learned of our encounter and that you had feelings for me he wanted to use me to gain Kilmore through our marriage."

"Is that why you seduced me?" he growled as he grabbed her jaw.

"No, Isaac. I pushed you away because I didn't want your attention. You were a monster in my eyes. I didn't want to end up like Bailey and Sherlock."

"Then how is it you came to me when you were injured. Those injuries were real and you had your brother's body in the back of the wagon."

"Bailey hurt me so you would have compassion on me. Sherlock died from the head wound you caused. Bailey shot him in the head to make it look like Tomas' estate was attacked. He beat Tomas to make it look like it happened."

"Except what Kathleen doesn't know, Isaac," Tomas interjected and Isaac turned to his friend, "is that Bailey wants me dead and Alexander knew nothing of it."

"It's true," Calico sighed. "But my brother doesn't want my husband dead. He only wants to teach him a lesson."

"Calico! You saw my injuries. You saw what he did to your sister, and yet you still defend him," Tomas yelled at her.

"He's my brother."

"He's the monster, not Isaac," Kathleen defended.

Isaac pushed off Kathleen and sat upright. He stared Calico down with a look of authority. "You know," he said pointing to the three of them. "I should have all three of you arrested for being rebels."

"Can't. We're already arrested," Tomas proclaimed as Isaac coughed.

"Eh," Isaac replied, lowered his hand, and laid his head against his upright pillows. He closed his eyes. "There are so many lies it's hard to tell where lies the truth."

"What does your heart tell you?" Kathleen asked.

Isaac turned his head to her and lifted his eyes to face her. "I can't trust any of you," he mumbled.

"You can trust me, Isaac. I love you," she pleaded.

"I know you do but you lied to me, Kathleen. You lied so many times I don't know what to believe about you. I see you have a good heart but are you loyal to me?"

"Yes."

"Who murdered my mother?"

Kathleen swallowed hard.

"If you were loyal to me you would have told me the truth right away."

"I..."

"I did," Calico answered.

Isaac turned to face the raven-haired beauty. "I know you did but I wanted to hear it out of Kathleen's mouth."

"What?" Kathleen objected.

He turned back to her. "The dress I found in Mary's room was the same one Calico wore to lunch that day."

"I told you," Tomas yelled at her.

Isaac turned his attention to Tomas, "But I didn't know you were involved I figured Kathleen knew but not you."

"She didn't know and Calico did not have my permission to murder your mother. On the contrary, I scolded her for her actions. She was stupid enough to try to pin the evidence on Mary because Bailey had made it clear to her that we were supposed to devise some way for you to arrest Mary. Calico and I were supposed to kill Mary before you sold her but Calico for some reason thought it would be best if you executed her. Like I said, my wife is stupid and naïve. I pray to God she grows some wisdom in that head of hers as she ages. You are quite fortunate that Kathleen is smarter than her age. I only married Calico because she is young, Irish, and Catholic. I need an heir but I was stupid enough to fall in love with her. I should have known better than to trust a woman who has yet to see her twentieth birthday."

"I...but..."Calico objected.

"They are but children, Isaac."

"You knew about Mary and you were going to execute her," Kathleen objected.

Isaac turned to face her. "No, I only told you that so you would believe that I thought she was the one who murdered my mother. I had a buyer who wanted both her and the baby. I was going to make her disappear. But you ruined that when you wanted a public execution. I had no choice but to comply with your desires and I thought you would have freed her. If you had it would have given me just cause to prove my suspicion that you were aiding your sister. I had hoped it wasn't true but I needed to know."

"You set me up!"

"Indeed. Hadn't anyone ever told you not to trust me, Kathleen?"

"I did," Tomas replied. "Isaac, we have a problem."

"Hmm, sisters. Young, inexperienced sisters who think they know better than their husbands."

Kathleen huffed, rose from the bed, and walked to Calico. Calico took Kathleen's hand. "They are going to get us killed," Tomas said as he took Kathleen's place.

"And how am I supposed to trust you, Tom? You knew Calico killed my mother yet aided her?"

"Oh, I didn't aide her. I was quite livid about what she had done."

"Not livid enough to tell me the truth. I didn't have to beat you so hard, you know? All you had to do was tell me the truth and I would—"

"You would have killed my wife."

"True. She is the daughter of my enemy."

"So is your wife. Would you kill Kathleen?"

"No."

"I have the same problem you do, Isaac."

"Oh, what's that?"

"I'm hopelessly in love with one of the daughters of Alexander McGillpatrick."

The men stared at their wives for a long time with their arms crossed over their chests. "Good in bed?" Isaac asked.

"Hmm, couldn't get enough of her. I think that's about the only benefit of their youthfulness," Tomas answered.

"Oh, I agree," Isaac grinned.

"Best friend?"

"I can tell her anything. Loyal?"

"To the heart."

"She's all I think about."

"Me too."

"We have it bad, Tom."

"I know and there ain't no cure for what ails us. You just have to face the truth, Isaac. They are Bailey's sisters and there's nothing we can do about that. They love us so deeply that they would do anything to be by our side. Kathleen might have started your relationship with the goal in mind to use you against her brother, but I don't believe that's the only reason she sought your attention out. She loves you, Isaac, just as I know Calico loves me."

"It doesn't matter if we die. What's more important is their happiness. If we all die we won't be together. I know where my soul belongs and it isn't in heaven. I also know if I die and Kathleen lives she will never be happy."

"Calico too."

"There really is only one thing we have to do."

"Lie so hard it'll save all of our lives."

Chapter 41

November 21, 1738

Kathleen frantically paced with endless, terrifying thoughts running through her mind. She had awoken early that morning to the sound of their cell door opening. She had been asleep in Isaac's arms with only her shift on while Tomas and Calico had been asleep on the floor like common servants. Isaac had instinctively covered her body with their blanket and demanded why they were being interrupted when the sun hadn't even risen for the day. Walpole's only reply was that the king wanted Tomas and Calico's hearing to be early in the morning so they could be executed in the afternoon, should the need to do so be warranted. He had demanded Calico and Tomas dress quickly. Twenty minutes later her sister and brother-in-law were escorted away in chains.

"Kathleen," Isaac called to her from the bed. Kathleen turned in his direction. "I can't sleep with you pacing the floor."

"Did you ever learn how to tell time just by looking at the sun?" she asked, walking to the window.

"No, why?"

"I wonder what time it is. It feels like they have been gone forever. What….," she turned to face him. "What if we never know the fate that befell them? I…"

"The more you worry the more frantic you will appear to the guards. The more frantic you are the more they will report you appear guilty to the warden. You need to keep your strength."

"That's not your sis— ," she started, pointing to the door.

"My sister's life is in danger as well!"

Kathleen slowly lowered her hand. She turned her attention to the window. At least there was no sign of Calico and Tomas being led to their slaughter. Isaac had told her that after Tomas and Calico testified to the king the story they had all concocted they wouldn't face execution. Only the king's compassion for the death of Tomas' father and for the damage they had incurred at the hands of the Irish rebels would save themr. But Kathleen wasn't too convinced it would happen the way Isaac had told her. She and Calico had been the best of friends throughout their lives but something about their current situation didn't feel right to her. Mary and Sherlock had told her plenty of times not to trust Calico or Tomas but she had never heeded their warnings. Calico would never betray her and Tomas had proclaimed his loyalty to her. Surely, if their lives were on the line they would protect her as well. Wouldn't they? Isaac seemed confident that their plan would work but how could she trust her husband? The hard part was she loved him so much the more she denied a relationship with him the more her heart hurt. Yet how could she reconcile with the man who had betrayed her? She leaned against the wall and peered towards the main entry of their prison with a long, drawn out sigh. How many times had she looked forward to a trip to England? Now all she wanted to do was return to Kilmore. Bailey didn't seem that bad when compared with the English.

"Kat," Isaac said then coughed to the side.

"You have no right to call me that. Only those who are close to me call me that and right now I don't want anything to do with you. The only reason I share that bed with you is because I'm your wife but I would much rather sleep on the floor with Tomas and Calico than with you."

"It's been hours since Tomas and Calico left. All you do is pace the floor. How am I supposed to rest when I know your heart is heavy?"

"Find a way," she snarled in his direction. Kathleen exhaled a deep breath and picked at the wall. She couldn't keep the pain locked up for to long. She felt a tear escape down her cheek. Kathleen inhaled a deep breath, sniffed her nose, and buried her tears once again. Why did it matter how she felt? Isaac could only delay the inevitable for a month and then they would be found guilty. Then… She felt a hand on her back and jumped. Isaac stood before her with a gentle look in his eyes. "Don't be a fool, Isaac. Go back to bed."

"Not until you join me. You rose early and have barely had anything to eat. I'm worried about you. Come to bed and talk to me, Kathleen. I miss you."

Kathleen groaned with a sniff of her nose. How could this man she hated so much make her want to spill all of her emotions. She hated the way his tender eyes peered deep within her soul. She gently took his hand and followed him back to their bed. Kathleen removed her robe and dropped it on the floor next to her clothes. She was a mess, emotionally and physically. Her body craved sleep but her mind just wouldn't stop running. She lay next to Isaac and buried her head on his strong chest as he pulled the blankets over them. "Did you see anything out the window?" he asked.

"No," she whined, playing with a string on his shirt.

"That's good news, Kat," he coaxed, rubbing her back.

She glared deep into his eyes with a frown.

"You can't hate me forever and I like that name for you. You're as unpredictable, independent, and fiery as any cat I've ever seen." Kathleen smiled. "There it is. That warm, beautiful smile," he said then kissed her gently on the lips.

His touch warmed her heart and lowered her guard. How dare this man make her feel vulnerable? She turned her head and sobbed, releasing all her built-up sorrows. "I don't want to die, Isaac. I don't want Calico to die."

"Shh, they'll find fault with Mary and not us. I promise."

"I don't want Mary to die, either. Mary's innocent. The only reason she was at the estate was to look for documents that Sherlock had on his body when he died."

"The contract and money?"

Kathleen lifted her eyes to face him. "I knew you had stolen it."

"I didn't steal them. My mother had them. I didn't find out about them until she accused you one day of betraying me."

"How did she get them?"

"The servants told her about your accident and she came to me. She must have lifted the documents before she showed me his body."

"But why? I knew she was shrewd but to steal from the dead?"

"Kathleen, she was Lady Turner for a long time and she served my father well in all their dealings. She was only trying to protect me."

"When did she start questioning my identity?"

"The moment I send word to the king about you."

"But you said you did that after we first met."

"Yes, and my mother was concerned it was all a trap. I didn't listen. I told her there was no way you could be Catholic. But seems my mother was right concerning who you and your sister truly are."

"Are you upset with me?"

"Hmphf," he coughed uncontrollably. Kathleen rubbed his chest until his cough subsided.

"Are you?" she asked, raising her eyebrow.

He turned his head to face her. "I'm more upset that I allowed myself to be fooled by you. There is not a man or woman alive who has ever manipulated me. Yet you somehow hold that power over me. My mother saw it and in my own arrogance I rejected her aide. Now she's dead."

"So are my father and Padric."

"Hmm," he nodded, playing with her hair. A long moment of silence fell between them. Kathleen studied her husband's face, not quite certain what Isaac was thinking or how he felt about her. He obviously felt something for her. Hadn't he admitted to Tomas he was madly in love with her? Isaac chuckled.

"What is it?" she asked out of curiosity. Isaac lowered his hand, placed the back of his head on his pillow, and continued to laugh. "What?" she pleaded with her hand on his chest. He lifted his eyes to hers.

"There I was explaining the history of Kilmore Castle and the land to the one person who knew it all along."

Kathleen smiled. "Well you did sound quite foolish in some of your arguments about my family's history."

Isaac turned on his right side and supported his head with his hand underneath the pillow. "Tell me what I don't know, will you?"

Kathleen leaned closer to him. "You should ask Toma…" Tears ran down her cheeks.

"Shh," he coaxed, wiping away her tears. "He'll return. I promise."

"How do you know? I don't even think I would believe the story we all plan to tell. Calico…she…hates Mary as much as Bailey does."

"Why's that?"

"Mary never sided with Bailey." Kathleen smiled, recalling her youth with Sherlock and Mary. "Sherlock and Mary were like second parents to me."

"Is that why you were so adamant that I would give Sherlock a proper burial with your ancestors?"

Kathleen nodded. "I knew about the ancient graveyard because that's where our parents took Calico and me to play when we were younger. Father told us all the stories. He knew each and every one of our ancestors buried there and made certain we knew our heritage through their lives."

Isaac ran his hand through her long, loosely-worn red hair. "Kathleen?" he asked.

"Hmm."

"Sherlock and Bailey never had red hair nor did your father. Calico and Mary do not have it, either. Where did it come from?"

Kathleen shrugged her shoulders. "I don't know. I was always the odd one in the family. Sherlock used to say the day I was born was a shock to everyone because I had a lot of red hair and no one in the family knew where it came from. They said I was destined to be someone special. Nothing much happened to me until the day I died from smallpox."

"Died?" he asked tracing the scars on the side of her face.

"Your physician was correct when he examined me. I had a very severe case of smallpox as a child. My younger brother and I died on the same day. Sherlock had already buried most of his children by then and helped our father to dig the graves. They buried my brother and then went to me. Father placed me in the grave and when he threw the first shovel full of dirt over my body I gasped for air. Sherlock stopped father, jumped in the grave, and pulled me out. He ran to get the priest as my father rushed me into the house."

"What did the priest say?"

"He said God brought me back to life like Lazarus because he had something special in mind for me to do with my life. After that...," she sighed, lowering her eyes.

"After that?" he asked, lifting her face. The image of Sherlock's ghost next to the door caught her attention. Sherlock crossed his arms over his chest and glared at her with a look only a father could give. Kathleen slowly rose from the bed with her head cast down in disappointment.

"Kathleen," Isaac called to her as she walked around the bed.

"I'm sorry," Kathleen replied to her brother.

"Sorry! You're sorry," Sherlock bellowed. Isaac's bed shook as if an earthquake had just occurred. Sherlock stepped towards her while the bed died down and a frightened, confused Isaac called to his wife. "You assured me you were going to save my wife, Kathleen."

"I am."

"Then how is it that Tomas and Calico are telling the king that Mary not only killed Isaac's mother but also duped the two of you into marrying so she could use you and Calico against the crown? Your plan is going to not only kill Mary but also my unborn child!"

"Sherlock, please. It's not my plan."

"Kat, I warned you to be careful with Tomas and Calico."

"I know but…"

"There are no buts in this matter, my dear sister. Calico and Tomas have you right where they want you and Mary. The foolish thing is by doing so they not only endanger my family's lives but their own and yours as well."

"Isaac says the plan will work."

Sherlock glanced at Isaac. Isaac coughed uncontrollably, leaned over, and vomited into a chamber pot. "You should have let him die." He turned back to Kathleen.

"Do you say that because you want revenge?"

"I say that because I'm trying to protect you! Your husband is as dangerous as Bailey."

"My husband is a good man."

"Then why don't you trust him?"

Kathleen opened her mouth to speak then closed it. "How do you know that?" she whispered.

"It doesn't matter. Kathleen, I know you love him but please heed my warnings. You must be careful with your words. The English king only cares about himself."

"I promise, Sherlock, I'll save Mary. Isaac told me his mother stole your documents."

"Where are they?"

"I don't know. But if our plans work Mary will be on a ship to New Orleans with mother."

"And you?"

Kathleen shook her head.

"Kathleen, there is enough money for three tickets. One for you. One for Mary, and there was one for me."

"Mary can use the funds for my ticket for supplies. I want to stay with my husband."

Sherlock exhaled a long sigh with a shake of his head. He walked over to the bed and stared at Isaac from across the footboard. Isaac lay on the bed with his eyes closed, mumbling for Kathleen. She walked to the bed, sat beside him, and took his hand.

"Shh, I'm right here, Isaac," she coaxed him.

He opened his eyes and turned to face her. "Kathleen?" he asked.

She smiled at him then turned back to Sherlock. "He'll help."

"You can't trust him nor can I," Sherlock guided.

"Sherlock, I know he will help me. Tomas—"

"Don't trust him, either, Kathleen. Tomas sides with Bailey."

"Not anymore. He's loyal to me. It's your grandfather I can't trust."

"What grandfather?"

Suddenly Alexander appeared beside Sherlock. Sherlock and Kathleen turned to face their father's ghost. "The trial is over. We must go."

"What happened, father?" Kathleen asked.

He turned to face her then turned back to Sherlock. The two men disappeared. "No," Kathleen shouted, crawling to the footboard. "Don't do that to me! No! No! Father! Sherlock," she screamed louder. Isaac placed his hand on her back. She jumped from his touch with tears strolling down her cheeks. The trial was over but her father wouldn't tell her what the verdict was. Maybe…perhaps... "No," she muttered then rose and ran to the window. Her heart beat hard with anticipation and fear as she studied the courtyard. Empty. How could it be empty? Maybe it was empty but Tomas and Calico were being led to the scaffold. Maybe the king wanted to execute Mary with them. Maybe…her heart jumped at hearing the door open. She turned swiftly and exhaled a deep breath at the sight of Calico and Tomas calmly entering their chamber, bathed and nicely dressed in fresh clothes.

Calico paused in the middle of the room and stared at her sister. "Who was it?" she asked, stepping towards her.

Kathleen shook her head with a tight jaw.

"Who was it?" Isaac asked.

Calico and Tomas exchanged glances. "You never told him?" Tomas asked Kathleen.

"Tell me what?" Isaac asked, annoyed, then coughed several times.

"He's Anglican. He wouldn't understand," Kathleen whispered.

"The Catholics don't understand and it's only because your father was a noble that they didn't persist in the allegations that you were either mentally ill or possessed by a demon," Tomas explained. "We said we were all going to be honest with each other from now on. Does he know you died?"

"That I do know, Tomas. What don't I know——," Isaac said, sitting upright.

Calico grabbed Kathleen by the arm and led her to the footboard. "Tell him," she urged, pushing her sister forward.

Kathleen huffed. She shook her head and tried to walk away but Tomas barred her from doing so. "Tell him," Tomas urged.

Kathleen slowly turned to face Isaac. "You promise not to declare me a lunatic?"

"Depends," he answered.

Kathleen shook her head. "I can't do this. He said not to trust him," Kathleen objected to Tomas, pointing to Isaac. "Why are you so nicely dressed? Are they going to execute you all dressed up?"

Tomas grabbed her by the arms and bore his gaze at her eyes. "Kathleen, don't worry about why my wife and I are here in our good clothes."

"Can you see them?" she yelled at Isaac. "Can you hear their words?!"

"We're not dead," Calico objected.

"Why would she think you're dead?" Isaac asked.

"Because your wife can see and speak to the dead as clearly as we see and speak to you," Tomas explained.

Isaac lifted his gaze to Kathleen and straightened his posture. "You..." he swallowed hard then shook his head. "Are you telling me that you practice witchcraft? I thought you were Catholic."

"I am," she snarled. "I've seen and spoken to the dead since I survived the smallpox. At first, it was overwhelming but I learned how to control it."

"Who came to you?" Tomas asked.

Kathleen turned back to him. "Sherlock's upset with me because he heard your words against Mary. He claims you are working with Bailey and I shouldn't trust you."

"Of course he did," Tomas growled then removed his grip on her arms. He stepped away from her and looked out the window.

"Tomas, why did the king grant you new clothes and your wife has jewels?" Isaac asked.

"His majesty believed our story and has sent us to bring Kathleen to him. We have fifteen minutes before the guards come."

Kathleen stepped back in a panic state. "No, no. Sherlock said I had to watch my words. He said Tomas' plan will get Mary, Calico, and me killed. He said—"

"He's dead and should remain so," Tomas yelled at her.

"You betrayed Isaac and me," Kathleen accused, pointing to Calico and her husband. "That's why Sherlock came to warn me. You two never left Bailey's side. You want Isaac, Mary, and me dead so you can control Kilmore. The king gave you Kilmore, didn't he?"

"It's not like that," Calico objected, stepping towards her.

"Get away from me," Kathleen shoved her sister and yelled. She ran to the bed and clung to Isaac's side. Isaac embraced her and glared at the couple.

Tomas pulled a tri-folded letter from his pocket and handed it silently to Isaac. Isaac clenched his jaw and pulled the order from Tomas's hand. "I did it to save us. Your plan would have never worked," Tomas explained.

"Huh, I bet you did," Isaac snarled, opening the king's order. Kathleen turned her head on his chest as he read it. She wrapped her arm around his waist. The suspense was killing her. Every time she tried to read a sentence, Isaac would pull the order away from her. He coughed, lowered the order, and turned his head to the side. Kathleen rubbed his chest. "Sherlock was right," Isaac said.

"About what?" she asked.

Isaac wiped his mouth with his sleeve then turned to face her. "Not to trust Tomas and Calico. He played you for a fool, Kathleen. He manipulated the king into granting him guardianship over Kilmore and my line," he snarled in Tomas' direction at the last sentence.

Tomas beamed, rocking on his heel. "I'll take the order, please, Lord Turner. All your affairs have already been turned over into my custody. I have your first contract. His majesty requires proof of loyalty from your wife. If she cannot provide this then I'm most afraid I will no longer be able to protect her."

"Protect me!" Kathleen yelled, pushing her hand on Isaac's chest. Isaac grabbed her wrist and pulled her back.

"Kathleen, I love you and Calico dearly. I have been friends with Bailey and Sherlock since childhood. I never agreed with Bailey when he wanted to eliminate you and Mary. He knew you needed to be severely injured when you arrived with Sherlock's body but his order to eliminate Mary also included you."

"I never told Tomas of it because I couldn't lose you," Calico explained.

"Then how did he know?" Kathleen asked.

"I showed him the second order after you two were arrested. He knew I was hiding something from him and I could no longer keep my secret."

"Were you two arrested or is this a ploy to acquire Kilmore?" Isaac asked, handing the order to Tomas.

"A ploy. It wasn't Sarah who had contacted the king. I did," Tomas grinned. "Sir Walpole came to my estate. Calico told him everything and then he went to your home. I had already convinced him it was in the crown's best interest that you keep your title but the lands and business transaction would be better managed by an impartial, loyal Anglican."

"But you're not impartial. My sister is your wife," Kathleen objected.

"Yes, but dear sister, you have been so traumatized that you require our assistance to deal with your mental illness. You are most unstable. When the king learned of your condition he wanted to send you to a nunnery but I convinced him it would be in your best interest if I was granted guardianship over you," Calico explained in a sweet voice.

"Traumatized, huh," she gasped. "I'll show you traumatized," she snarled and rose to leap across the bed. Isaac pulled her back with a sharp look of disapproval.

"That's a real order, Kathleen. It has the Turner mark. You can't hit them," he instructed then turned to face them, "No matter how much they deserve it."

"This entire time I trusted you," she cried to Calico. "You're my sister."

"Well so is Mary. I told you several times not to trust her, Kathleen. But you never listened. If you had anyone to blame then it lies with Sherlock and Mary not Tomas and me. We're only trying to protect you."

"Protect me! You're more interested in reclaiming Kilmore than protecting me. I was the one who was going to acquire Kilmore for our family, not you."

"Yes, well, that may have been the plan when you first went to Kilmore but Bailey, Tomas, and I recognized that wasn't going to happen because you love Isaac. You would rather stand beside this English monster than destroy him."

"Monster," Isaac objected. "Seems to me the only monsters in this room are you and Tomas."

"Lord Turner, I would watch what you say to us unless you would will for me to report to the king that you are unwilling to appreciate your new circumstances," Tomas warned.

Isaac clenched his jaw. "I am the king's servant. What's the order?" Isaac asked extending his hand.

"That's a good man. I'm certain we can all be friends. It would be better for everyone if we could come to some mutual appreciation of one another." Tomas pulled a tri-folded letter with a long ribbon descending from the royal seal from his coat and handed it to Isaac. "The king requires proof of the elimination."

"I understand," Isaac sighed, taking the order. "Means of delivery?"

"None; we are to accompany you when you do so. Mary's fate lies in Kathleen's hands."

"How so?"

"Kathleen is to denounce the Pope and convert to the Anglican faith publically."

"No," Kathleen yelled.

Isaac grabbed her hand and pulled her closer to his body as he read the order. "When?" he asked.

"Today. She must swear fealty to the English king and denounce her Irish heritage."

"She'll do it."

"No," Kathleen protested.

"If she refuses she'll hang for treason next to Mary and me." Calico leaned across the footboard. "I did what they required of me because I was offered the same fate you are. I don't want to die nor do I desire my sisters' deaths."

Kathleen spit in her sister's face. "You only accepted because you don't want to die. You care nothing for Mary and me!"

"Not true. I hate Mary but I love you, unconditionally. Take the deal, Kathleen," she snarled.

"Will Mary be offered the same deal?"

"No, she's a rebel leader's widow. The king is merciful, though, and has agreed to allow her to travel to New Orleans with our mother."

"How do you know about that?"

"I found the documents," she grinned.

"Do you have them?" Isaac asked.

"I placed them somewhere where only I can find them." She turned back to Kathleen. "Kat, take the deal or die with Mary and me."

Kathleen turned to her husband. She loved both her sisters but hated the position she was being forced into. Give up her faith? How could she betray God like that? What kind of good Catholic men and women force others to abandon their faith? Calico and Tomas had claimed several times they were only acting on behalf of God's holy church. Sometimes you have to sacrifice for your faith. She could sacrifice her own life. That didn't scare her much. Yet it wasn't just her life she was sacrificing. It was Mary's and Calico's lives as well. Who was she to condemn them to death?

"The needs of the many outweigh the needs of one person," Tomas instructed.

"May I have a private moment with my wife?" Isaac asked, lowering the order.

"Of course," Tomas said as Calico started to object.

Isaac pulled the blanket over their heads and rolled closer to Kathleen. He stroked the side of her cheek with the crook of his finger. "I am sorry," he whispered to her.

"He's asking me to betray God."

"Shh, I know what he is asking of you, Kathleen, but I don't see that you have much of a choice in this matter. You could do what Tomas did."

"Publically denounce my faith but keep it privately?"

"Yes."

"And you won't turn me in?"

"I love you too much to ever do that. I'll help you out as much as I can, Kathleen. I promise."

Kathleen lowered her eyes and stroked his chest. Her life had been turned upside down so much she didn't know who to believe or even if she could trust Isaac. Hadn't he already betrayed her once?

"Time's up," Tomas' voice lifted loudly in the small room.

Kathleen lifted her eyes to meet Isaac's with a stern look on her face. She grabbed his head and kissed him deeply. "I love you, Isaac," she whispered as the blanket was lifted away from them.

Kathleen rose from the bed, grabbed her clothes from the floor, and dressed.

Chapter 42

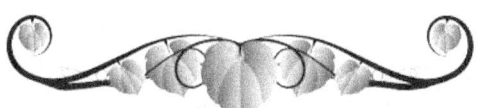

December 5, 1738
Dublin, Ireland

Kathleen silently stared out the window at the rows of houses and construction. The carriage that carried her, Mary, and Isaac passed by the busy city. She had never been to Dublin before but had heard stories about the capital from her parents. Dublin was the oldest city in Ireland and its history could be traced back to when the Celts roamed Ireland. This was her people's city. Truly Irish no matter how much the English wanted to change it. Her ancestors' blood, sweat, and tears had built the capital and its surrounding area. Although new to her, Dublin had always held a special place in her heart.

Like London, she had dreamed of visiting the city, yet not like this. In her own idealistic world the Irish would once again sit at Parliament, rule over the lands, and drive the English out of Ireland. She smiled as she thought of Saint Patrick driving the English away just as he had done with all the snakes that had inhabited Ireland. Her plan would have worked had not Tomas and Calico interfered. She was supposed to be an English duchess with a nice home in Dublin and her husband a respectable man of Parliament. Isaac's lands and possessions had been confiscated by the crown and handed over to Tomas and Calico. Most people would have never known just how poor she and Isaac truly were. Although everything they owned had been confiscated they were still able to live the life Isaac had been accustomed to. On the outside they were nobles with land, a large house, and plenty of wealth. But in reality they could do nothing without strict permission from Tomas and Calico. She had given up everything just to be enslaved by her own sister. What true and loyal Irish enslaves another Irish?

"Kat," Mary called to her from the other side of the cabin. She turned to face her older sister. Mary sat on a bench with her hand on top of her protruding stomach and tapped the bench with her other hand. Kathleen turned to Isaac. He nodded approval then stared out the window with a disappointed look. Kathleen carefully navigated her way across the cabin to Mary's bench. She sat next to her sister as Mary wrapped her arm around her back.

"Sherlock refuses to speak to me but I know he's around you. I can feel him," Kathleen whispered.

"Has he spoken to you since you left the tower?"

"No. I hate it, Mary. I feel like he's being silent to me because he disapproves of my actions. You know how he used to be when he disciplined me?"

"I don't think he's upset with you, Kathleen, just the circumstances we are faced with. He loves me and our child, dearly."

Kathleen placed her hand on Mary's stomach. "So do I. Can you feel the child yet?"

Mary smiled. "Yes." She turned to face her younger sister. "Kathleen, be honest with me. Do you trust your husband?"

Kathleen glanced at Isaac. Trust him? A few weeks ago she might have told Mary absolutely not, but ever since they had returned to Kilmore Isaac had changed. The first week was horrible. Isaac was so weak he had remained in his bed for four days and denied her entrance into his bedchambers. She had feared he blamed her for everything that had occurred to him. She was, after all, Bailey's sister. Her strong husband had become deeply depressed and his doctor had feared he would never recover. She couldn't blame Isaac. His world had been turned upside down and inside out. Everyday she pleaded with Isaac to grant her entrance and on the fifth day he rose from his bed, fully recovered, and opened the door.

They spent days in his room talking and eventually rekindling their passionate marriage. It was the most intimate time they had ever had.

Isaac turned his gaze to her. "Kathleen?" he asked.

She smiled back at him and turned her attention back to her older sister. "He's a good man placed in a terrible position. The king is holding his family in the tower until he proves his loyalty to the crown. If Tomas reports Isaac is guilty of treason then we will all be executed. Isaac's worried Tomas will report his failure even if he succeeds, and he's worried that his family would suffer because of Tomas' actions."

"You could come with me."

"I can't. I want to but I won't leave, Isaac. I love him."

"Mary," Isaac said loudly. The women lifted their heads to face him. "Stop trying to convince my wife to act against the crown."

"I was not doing so."

He turned to face her with a serious look on his face. Isaac leaned over his lap and glared deep into her eyes.

Mary ignored him and turned back to Kathleen. "Can you trust Calico to deliver the documents and funds I require?"

"She will," Isaac flatly responded. "Kathleen did what was required and I must prove my loyalty to the king. We aren't far from the docks. I suspect it will happen sometime soon," he said.

Annoyed, Mary confronted Isaac. "Bailey's not stupid. He'll know something is wrong when Tomas meets him, and not many people in the rebellion trust Tomas because of his conversion."

"I know, that's why I asked Kathleen to leak it to our tenants that we were released because the king found fault with Sir Walpole's accusations. I had arrested you for murdering my mother and had hidden you away from the house because I didn't trust my wife. We are escorting you to the slave handler who paid a very high price for you. Bailey doesn't want you or my wife to survive. That means he will plan to intercept this carriage at some point. Tomas plans to lead the attack at the docks."

"And you would allow him to do so?"

"I hate this as much as you do, Mary McGillpatrick, but I have no choice in the matter."

She leaned as far as she could to meet his gaze. "What is there to hate, Lord—"

"That's Earl to you. Your father-in-law was disposed of his rank."

"Very well, Earl Turner. I know you hate Bailey and are grateful you have been given a chance to eliminate him, but what of this situation do you actually hate? The part that says the Irish rebel controls Kilmore, or that your wife has been placed in such a perilous situation?"

"I understand why you Irish believe Kilmore would be in better hands under the McGillpatricks, but the reality of the situation is this. The Penal Laws are in place for a reason."

"For the English to do what they do best. Steal and destroy."

Isaac leaned back and huffed. He crossed his arms, looked at Kathleen, then to Mary. "I am not an evil man, Mary. I want to help you."

"Help me! Ha. You threw me into your dungeon, barely fed me, and left me to rot in deplorable conditions while I am with child!"

"I was going to spare your life. If you should be angry at anyone then perhaps it should be my wife. After all, I did not plan to execute you until she insisted upon it."

Mary turned sharply to Kathleen. Kathleen shook her head. "I...I...I was trying to save your life."

"Trying to save my life? How is that trying to save my life?"

Kathleen shrugged her shoulders. "I didn't know Isaac's plans. I thought if I could somehow delay your execution then I would be able to save you."

Mary exhaled a deep breath and nodded. "I understand."

"My plan didn't quite work out the way I wanted. I'm sorry."

"I hate to admit it but Isaac is right about one thing."

"Oh?" Isaac asked with peaked interest.

She turned to face him. "She's young and naïve. If you are going to be her husband then teach her how to survive in your world. The decisions she makes are often idealistic and bare no wisdom behind them."

Isaac lifted his eyes to Kathleen's. The couple exchanged a long look as if they were reading each other's minds. She could see the pain hidden deep in his eyes where only she had been granted access. Despite the rumors among her people Isaac never enjoyed taking a life. He would rather sell slaves than murder them but there was also a harder aspect of him that everyone saw. The monster had the heart of an innocent child that wasn't well known about.

The fast carriage suddenly came to a halt and shook the cabin. Isaac grabbed hold of the window and braced himself while Mary mirrored his actions with her own window. Kathleen flew to the other side of the cabin, hit the wall behind Isaac, tumbled off the bench onto the floor, rolled several times, and came to a halt with her upper arm on the side of Isaac's bench. She gasped as the pain radiated all over her body. The carriage jerked several times then fell still. She lay on her stomach, not wanting to move. Blood tricked down from her forehead. She wiped the blood from her eyes and tried to move her right arm but couldn't.

"Kathleen?" Mary asked. She turned her head to the sound of her pregnant sister's voice. Mary knelt beside her with her hand on the side of Kathleen's face.

"Isaac," Kathleen whispered.

"He's trying to find out what happened."

Kathleen nodded. "Are you and the baby okay?"

"We're fine. I'm more worried about you. That was a hard fall."

"I'm...," she started as she tried to rise.

"Don't get up," Isaac instructed, pulling away from the window beside her.

"What?" Kathleen asked.

He crouched in front of them and shook his head with a finger next to his mouth. "Tomas set us up. We're not where we are supposed to encounter Bailey and there's another carriage in front of ours."

"Where are we?"

"It looks like one of the older streets. The street is narrow and we are blocked on both sides by two large buildings. I can't say for certain. Is anything broken?" he whispered.

"I don't know."

"You said you wanted me to kill Bailey, right?"

Kathleen nodded. "That was my plan but...," she struggled to feet and extended her left hand as she babied her right arm. "I'll do it. Give me a gun."

Isaac peered up and down her body then started to hand her one of his Irish Flintlock pistols. He pulled it away from her just as she had touched it. Kathleen gave him a look that could kill. How dare he tease her! "Have you ever used a gun before?"

"No, but how hard can it be. You just point and shoot."

Isaac chuckled. "It doesn't work that way. You said your plan was to have me kill your brother, right?"

"I changed my mind."

"Kathleen, you are in no condition to fight. You can't even stand still. You keep swaying and you're being very tender with your other arm."

"Give me the gun! He's my brother—"

"Isaac's right," Mary said, stepping between them.

Kathleen lowered her hand with shock. Mary was taking Isaac's side? How was that even possible? The entire journey this morning from Kilmore to Dublin had been full of bitter silence between them, now Mary was taking his side? Mary placed her hand on Kathleen's upper arms. "You need to let Isaac kill Bailey. You're in no condition to fight anyone and whatever happens out there will be a fight. It's better that we remain in here."

Kathleen reluctantly nodded her head and sat on the bench behind her. She closed her eyes, giving way to the pain and blurry vision. She smiled, feeling Isaac's hands on her legs, and slowly opened her eyes. The blurry vision of her husband slowly came into focus.

He gently touched the side of her face and rubbed her cheekbone with his thumb. "Kathleen?" he asked.

"I'm fine, really."

"Stop trying to convince me of that. Mary will help you and I promise when this is over my doctor will—"

"Stop treating me like a child, Isaac. I'm fine."

"I would rather have our doctor tell me that. You hit the wall and bounced off of the bench. Please, Kat, have more concern for your health than my mission to kill your brother."

Suddenly the door to the cabin started to open. Isaac grabbed his pistol from the floor, rose, and stepped in front of the women, ready to defend them. He aimed his gun just as the door cracked open, ready to kill, and then froze at the image of Tomas entering the cabin with women with hooded cloaks hiding their faces. Tomas closed the door behind them.

"Lower the gun," Tomas ordered.

Isaac reluctantly complied. "What's the meaning of this? You said we were on our way to the docks."

"We are but I had to make certain my plan would work. I did and we are here. Calico," he said, turning to the shorter woman.

Calico lowered her cloak, "Change clothes with me, Mary."

"What?" Mary objected from behind Isaac.

"Do what she says," Jane ordered, lowering her cloak.

"Mother," Kathleen and Mary greeted her enthusiastically as Jane approached Isaac. She slapped him hard on the left cheek, "Get away from my daughters!"

"Isaac," Kathleen shouted as her husband stumbled to the opposite side, rubbing his cheek, and hunched over. He spit blood on the floor and lifted his eyes in his mother-in-law's direction.

"Do you know what I could do to you for that?" he growled, standing upright and lunging at her.

Jane punched him in the eye. Isaac once again fell. He wasn't about to let this woman beat him. The monster inside him roared for revenge. He grabbed his gun, spun, and lifted his pistol to her head. "Strike me again, mother. I dare you," he snarled at her with a deadly look.

"Isaac, stop it. She's my mother," Kathleen pleaded.

"That's the only reason she's not dead yet!"

Jane stepped backwards, extended her arms out, and shielded Kathleen from Isaac's view. "Go ahead, Earl Turner. Show my daughter the monster you really are. You killed her father and her brother. Show her how merciless you truly are."

Isaac moved his head side to side to catch a glimpse of his wife, but with every move he made Jane would counter him. Why did this woman have to be so God damn annoying?! He didn't have to see Kathleen to know she was upset. And she had every right to be. He had killed her father and now threatened to kill her mother. He knew the sting of losing your parents so well. Hadn't her sister killed his mother? When was this feud ever going to end? He lowered his pistol and turned his back on Jane.

"Isaac," Kathleen called to him.

He waved his hand at her while he faced the opposite wall. Kathleen knew that look. It was the man trying to control the monster the English had created inside him. She leaned her head back and allowed Isaac his space. After a moment of silence Isaac turned to face a hooded woman. "And you are?" he asked the mysterious woman.

The woman lowered her hood with a deadly look. "Another woman you made a widow, sir. I be Tomas' mother! You will help mi son or so I swear by all the saints you'll pay dearly for all the treachery you've caused. We have a common enemy and once he's been eliminated don't be thinking either of our families will ever be kind to you again," Margaret proclaimed then spat in his face.

Isaac wiped her spit from his face and looked up at Tomas. "I understand. Tomas, my wife has sustained injuries."

"I'll take care of my daughter," Jane answered, removed her cloak, and sat beside Kathleen.

Isaac turned back to Tomas. "The plan?"

"Bailey is expecting you at the docks with Mary and Kathleen. He believes everything I have told him and is overjoyed that the rebellion has control of Kilmore. He plans to intercept your carriage on the way to the docks with a few of my brothers. I changed our drivers so Bailey will believe my carriage is yours."

"I thought you said your brothers were against you."

"They are," Margaret said. "Bailey plans to kill Tomas and Calico once he has eliminated you, Mary, and Kathleen. I told mi son of Bailey's plans as soon as I heard them. My sons believe I do not side with Tomas. The truth is they are all my boys and I hate the bickering between them. Bailey will destroy my family if nothing is done about it."

Tomas handed Mary a stack of documents and a bag of money. "These belonged to Sherlock. My wife and I were going to hold on to them until Bailey was dead but I am not certain as to what will happen today and I don't want Bailey to have Sherlock's items."

Mary scanned the documents and examined the money. She closed the bag with a nod. "Thank you, Tomas."

"You're welcome. I added to your funds."

"Thank you, but I don't need the extra funds. Kathleen's not going with me."

"You will buy three tickets."

"Three?"

"Jane, my mother, and you. Get them out of Ireland, Mary. Promise me that."

Mary exchanged glances with Margaret and Jane then nodded at Tomas. "I promise. Why am I in Calico's clothes?"

"Calico will accompany Isaac and me in our carriage. She's going to pretend to be you. In the meantime, I want you, Kathleen, Jane, and my mother to go to the docks. Buy the tickets and board that ship. Jane has given the captain all of your belongings as well as her own and my mother's. The ship leaves at dawn tomorrow. Kathleen will wait at the ship until her husband returns to her side. If Isaac doesn't show up by the time the ship is to set sail then she will board the vessel with you. Use the extra funds to buy her ticket. If Isaac returns, then she will remain in Ireland and you can use the funds for whatever supplies you require."

"How can we trust you?" Kathleen asked while her mother tended to her wounds.

Tomas turned to her. "I am only trying to help you."

"Help us? You stole from us and enslaved Isaac and me! If Isaac is dead and I'm in New Orleans then all you have to do is declare the Turner line terminated. You would own Kilmore without lording over another family."

"I don't want that, Kathleen. I promise you. Calico and I are trying to help you."

"Humpf." She grimaced then turned her attention to Isaac.

Isaac smiled in her direction and addressed his master. "How long must we wait? I want to enjoy our Dublin home tonight with my wife."

"We should leave," Tomas replied.

Tomas walked to his mother, embraced her, then silently walked out of the cabin while Calico bid farewell to her mother. Calico lifted her hood and followed her husband. Isaac pretended to follow his sister-in-law then swiftly turned around and knelt before his wife. He grabbed the back of Kathleen's head and kissed her deeply. Kathleen opened her mouth wider, grabbed his back and kissed him passionately. She smiled as he slowly pulled his tongue out of her mouth. "I love you. Come back to me, Isaac."

"I will. I love you, too." The couple laid their foreheads together and breathed hard for a long moment. "I don't want to leave you, Kathleen."

"I know but you must. Kill Bailey and don't allow Tomas to kill you."

Isaac silently rose, pulled down his vest, nodded at the women, and exited the cabin.

Chapter 43

Kathleen stood on the deck of the large shipping vessel and stared out at the docks with her arm in a sling. It had been hours since they had arrived at the dock. The captain had been very kind to her family, especially since he had known Sherlock and had always supported her family. As soon they had arrived he had escorted her, Jane, and Margaret to his cabin then sent one of his sailors to fetch a physician. Kathleen had objected, fearing the doctor would recognize her as Duchess Turner. She didn't need the aristocrats of Dublin to know she was on a ship that was heading to New Orleans. What if Isaac died in the battle? How would the English king respond if she had run away to New France with her mother and sister? When the time came the physician had no idea who she was, only that he was aiding an Irish noble. Her clothes and mannerism had given way to her position, as did Mary's attire. Kathleen explained to the man she had been travelling in Dublin with her sister when rebels attacked her carriage. The captain and his wife had graciously offered their support. He had believed every word she spilled. He informed her that her body was still in shock from the accident and it would take days for her true condition to appear. Kathleen had thanked him after he set her broken arm and informed him she would seek her physician's care once she returned to her estate.

"Any word?" Mary asked behind her.

Kathleen shook her head and peered at the long row of ships in front of them. Mary gently placed a blanket around her and pinned it together with an Irish brooch. Kathleen stared at the ancient symbol then turned to face Mary to object.

"You can't hold the blanket on your own and it's starting to get cold," Mary responded before Kathleen could get a single word out.

"Where did you get this?"

"Mother had it. She said it belonged to the McGillpatrick family and she wanted you to wear it. It's very old, Kathleen. I never knew your father had any of the McGillpatrick heirlooms. I assumed they had all been confiscated, but mother said Alexander had always kept it close to his heart on the inside of his vest to remind him of his heritage. She said you deserve to have it because you are a McGillpatrick and have taken your rightful place at Kilmore."

"Huh, rightful place. Calico rules over Kilmore, not me."

"She may lord over you but you're the one who lives in the castle and hold the title as Duchess of Kilmore. Your ancestors would be proud of you. You did well, my little sister. Look at all that you have accomplished."

Kathleen stared down at the ancient Irish brooch and memorized every detail. For hundreds of years, the chiefs of the McGillpatrick line had worn the brooch as a symbol of their leadership and heritage. She smiled, thinking of the great honor it was for her to wear the circular metal pin. "Thank you," she whispered.

"You're welcome," Mary said. She placed her hand on Kathleen's lower back then walked away. Kathleen followed her sister. The two women silently walked to the front of the ship and watched the sailors on the docks in a long moment of silence.

"I can't take this," Kathleen cried, turned around, and leaned her back on the railing. "What if he's injured?"

"Kathleen?"

"What if Tomas killed him?"

"Kathleen?"

"What if…"

"Kathleen, look," Mary exclaimed and grabbed her sister's arm. She turned to face the direction in which Mary was pointing. Isaac slipped through the busy crowd with his hand over his stomach and blood all over his body. His white wig was gone. His clothes were tattered and torn. He stood in front of a tavern and stared up at her with a smile on his face.

"My dear, sweet lady. Permission to escort you home," he called to her then bowed.

Kathleen grinned ear to ear and leaned over the railing as he rose. "Is it finished? We've won?"

Isaac walked slowly to the ship with a limp. "It is finished. Bailey will no longer bother you or your family."

"And Tomas?" Mary asked.

"Well that is a different matter. He's alive, as is Calico. I'm sorry it has taken me so long to return to you," he said, turning his gaze to Kathleen. "After the battle I had to accompany Tomas and Calico to an English vessel, where I presented Bailey's body to Sir Walpole. He inquired of you, and Tomas informed him you had sustained injuries. You were being treated at our home in Dublin."

"And your wounds?"

"Ah, well," he said then looked down at his side then back up at her. "I believe I may have broken a couple of ribs, not too certain. Kathleen," he called to her as he approached the plank.

Kathleen smiled, forgetting time and place. All she wanted was to be with him. She started down the plank and met him halfway. Kathleen embraced him and kissed him passionately. Isaac wrapped his arms around her and returned her kiss. It was over. It was all finally over. Bailey was dead and Isaac held her in his arms. She stroked the side of his face and pulled back her lips. "Let's go home. You promised to show me our house in Dublin," she whispered close to his lips.

"That I did," he said then picked her up in his arms. She laughed as he carried her down the plank.

"Write to her often, Mary," he called to Kathleen's sister.

"We will. Thank you, Isaac," Mary replied loudly.

"You're welcome. Stay safe and have a better life in New France than you would ever have in Ireland. Rebuild the McGillpatrick family."

"We will."

Isaac lowered Kathleen and held her hand as they walked in the direction from which he had come. "There's a physician waiting for us at our home. Tomas has assured me we will have plenty of time to rest and recover from our wounds," Isaac assured her after they walked a few moments in silence.

"I look forward to that," she grinned. "My sister?"

"She's alive. Kathleen, remind me never to cross Calico when she's angry. That woman is dangerous."

𝔇ark 𝔚inter

ℭhapter 1

December 29, 1739
Kilmore, Ireland

The sharp, strong wind blew hard against the walls of the large castle. Isaac ran down the long hallway, pushing aside anyone who stood in the way. He had had about enough of Tomas' interference. It was one thing for Tomas to oversee all of Kilmore's business transactions. He could handle that. But this! This was outrageous.

He turned down the hallway, clutching the order in his right hand and turned to his right. Isaac thrust the door open and barged into Tomas' office. "Are you out of your...?," he yelled then paused as Sir Robert Walpole stood behind Tomas' desk.

"Earl Turner," Walpole addressed the distraught British man.

Silence filled the room with the exception of the howling wind beating on the glass of the large window behind the wooden shutters. Tomas sat behind the desk with several maps and open books in front of him. He lifted his gaze from the book to Isaac. "What do you want?" Tomas asked with a long sigh.

Isaac exchanged glances with the men then slowly walked up to the desk. His heart pounded in fear with each step he took. He had known better than to approach Tomas with such disrespect but he couldn't help it. He was livid. Tomas couldn't be trusted and as long as the king made Tomas regent over the entire Kilmore estate he could do nothing against the traitor. If he dared to present a case against him to the king then the king might find all of them at fault. He wasn't about to endanger either Kathleen or his family.

Isaac placed the order in front of Tomas. Tomas looked at the order with a slight grin and handed it to Sir Walpole. "Something amuse you, Tomas?" Isaac snarled. "That order is uncalled for. If you want to punish me then do so but don't punish my wife!"

"Oh, I have no plans to endanger Kathleen's life. Your child on the other hand…"

Isaac swiped his hand across the desk in a fit of rage, knocking all the papers and books off. He grabbed Tomas by the vest and pulled the older man towards him. "I am bound by the Turner contract to provide an heir and a spare to my line. Kathleen is with child. You can't deny her rations because you need her to give me a son!"

"Plenty of Irish women have given birth to children even though they have had little to eat. Kathleen will be fine. She's used to poverty."

"So is your wife but I doubt you took food away from her."

"Of course not. Calico's carrying my child. I would never deny her the extra nourishment she and the child require."

"Release him, Earl Turner." Sir Walpole ordered.

Isaac reluctantly released his grip with a huff. He pulled down his vest and gathered his senses. Every ounce of him wanted to beat Tomas until he retracted the order. It wasn't the first time Tomas had done something against them. The past year had been a difficult one for Isaac and Kathleen. After defeating Bailey, he and Kathleen had enjoyed the rest of the winter in Dublin without incident. But when they returned to Kilmore that Spring Tomas had completely taken over the estate. All in the name of King George. Even though Kilmore belonged to Isaac and Kathleen, Tomas had relocated the couple to the medium-sized wing

where Kathleen and Calico had grown up and had taken Isaac's accommodations. Kathleen hadn't seemed to have any problems with it. In fact, she had preferred it, claiming it was too hard to sleep in her father's bed because it was there where Isaac had thrown his head onto her lap. But Isaac couldn't agree. It was a stab in the back. This man who had pretended to be his best friend had only wanted one thing—Kilmore in the hands of the Catholic Irish. Tomas had fooled the English king and there was nothing he could do about it.

"Good. Now that we have your attention there are pressing matters we need to address with you," Walpole said.

"The order?" Isaac asked with an arch of his eyebrow.

"Ah, yes. The order. Well, if you do what we ask of you then I will see to it your wife has everything she needs, but if you fail, well the king might not look so favorably upon your family. Especially if the child she delivers is a stillborn," Tomas said with a grin.

About the Author

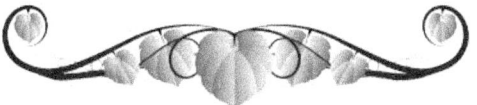

Bestselling author Allison Bruning has always had a passion for the literary arts. She originally hails from Marion, Ohio but lives in Indianapolis, Indiana with her husband and their Australian Cattle Dog, Lakota Sioux. Her husband hails from Marfa, Texas.

Allison is the author of six historical fiction series: Children of the Shawnee, The Secret Heritage, Irish Twist of Fate, New Hope, Lost Identity and Cherokee Tears. The first books of Cherokee Tears, New Hope, Lost Identity and Irish Twist of Fate are set to be released in 2014.

Allison's Irish roots run deep from County Down, Ireland to the Appalachian Mountains. She is a member of the McCann, McCarlde and Hill families.

Allison's educational background includes a BA in Theatre Arts with a minor in Anthropology and a Texas Elementary Teaching certificate, both acquired at Sul Ross State University in Alpine, Texas. Allison received National Honor Society memberships in both Theatre Arts and Communication. She was also honored her sophomore year with admission into the All American Scholars register. She holds graduate hours in Cultural Anthropology and Education. In 2007, Allison was named Who's Who Among America's Educators. She is also the recipient of the Girl Scout Silver and Gold Awards. Allison received her Masters of Fine Arts in Creative Writing at Full Sail University on June 28, 2013. She is an educator, writer, speaker, screenwriter, film director, and publisher.

Allison's interests include Ohio Valley history.

www.ingramcontent.com/pod-product-compliance
Lightning Source LLC
Chambersburg PA
CBHW070837246626
47170CB00007B/2409